Black Raven's Lady

By Kathleen Harrington

Black Raven's Lady
Lachlan's Bride
The MacLean Groom

Black Raven's Lady

HIGHLAND LAIRDS TRILOGY

KATHLEEN HARRINGTON

AVONIMPULSE

An Imprint of HarperCollinsPublishers

BLACK RAVEN'S LADY. Copyright © 2014 by Kathleen Harrington. All rights reserved under International and Pan-American Copyright Conventions. By payment of the required fees, you have been granted the nonexclusive, nontransferable right to access and read the text of this e-book on screen. No part of this text may be reproduced, transmitted, downloaded, decompiled, reverse-engineered, or stored in or introduced into any information storage and retrieval system, in any form or by any means, whether electronic or mechanical, now known or hereafter invented, without the express written permission of HarperCollins e-books.

EPub Edition OCTOBER 2014 ISBN: 9780062226358

Print Edition ISBN: 9780062226365

10 9 8 7 6 5 4 3

Prologue

June 1504
Archnacarry Manor
Western Highlands

"COME AWAY WITH ME tomorrow, Nina," the dark-haired man implored. "Meet me here at daybreak, and we'll flee together. If you love me, dearest, come with me."

His deep brown eyes filled with tenderness, he drew the beautiful lass close and kissed her tenderly on the forehead, then used the edge of the yellow-and-black tartan pinned to his shoulder to wipe away her tears.

"My father has received an offer of marriage for me from Laird Cameron," Nina replied, her voice shaking with fright. "Should I run away with you, Torcall, my parents might never forgive me. Perhaps, if we pleaded with them together, they would understand how much in love we are."

"I can't wait any longer, dearest," Torcall said. "The king has pronounced my father a traitor and with him all our clan. I must go and help defend our home and our lands."

Nina clutched his strong hand in both of hers and brought his fingers to her lips. Her hair, a stunning red-gold, gleamed in the forest's dappled sunlight. "Oh, Torcall, I do love you so."

"Don't be afraid, darling lass," he told her, his voice ringing with the optimism of youth. "We'll go to Steòrnabhagh. My father's castle on the Isle of Lewis is impregnable. We'll be married there. One day I'll be chief of Clan MacMurchaidh, Nina, and I will give you all the things I so long to give."

She smiled, her blue eyes filling once more with tears. "Your love is all I need, my dear, and all I want."

Torcall hugged her close, then bent his head to place a gentle kiss on her lips. "You'll meet me here tomorrow, then?" he asked. "You'll run away with me?"

Nina nodded, a smile curving her lips. "Aye, I'll flee with you, Torcall. I'll meet you here, right by this tall pine tree, when the sun rises tomorrow."

In the faint light of the following morning, the glen where the couple had stood seemed to wait in hushed anticipation of the coming dawn . . .

HER HEART POUNDING, Raine awoke with a start and stared at the bed's canopy above her head. She'd first had the dream when she was fourteen years old. The year after her father, Gideon Cameron, had been murdered. Raine knew it wasn't an ordinary dream. 'Twas a vision of her mother and Raine's natural father.

Chapter 1

"THEN YOU'VE MADE up your mind," Aunt Isabel said.

Raine looked up from her packing to see her aunt enter the bedchamber and quickly close the door behind her.

Isabel's eyes twinkled mischievously. "I don't suppose there's anything I can do to prevent this foolhardy escapade?"

Raine returned to the task of shoving her journal, containing remedies for everything from gout to the relief of painful menses, into the leather satchel that held her herbal concoctions. "You won't say anything until I'm gone?"

Isabel lifted her plump shoulders, but the smile curving her lips assured Raine of her intent to keep her own counsel. At least for the moment. "What exactly do you have planned, my dear?"

It was Raine's turn to shrug. "All I know for certain is that I'm going to find my father."

"Your father is buried in the kirk cemetery," Isabel chided softly. "He was a brave and honest man."

"Gideon Cameron was brave and honest and noble," Raine agreed. "No one could have asked for a better father. But you and I both know, Aunt Isabel, that your older brother was not the man who sired me." Raine knelt and reached under her bed to pull out a canvas bag.

"Have you tried asking your mother again?" Aunt Isabel suggested.

Raine gave a soft snort. Every time she'd touched on the subject, Lady Nina had reacted with swift admonishments, scolding Raine for even hinting that Gideon wasn't her father. Though they loved each other dearly, the matter had caused a feeling of estrangement between mother and daughter.

"What should I say?" Raine asked. "Oh, by the by, Mama, I'm quite certain that you deceived the honorable man you married, and I was the by-blow of that traitorous liaison?"

"Don't be too harsh in judging your mother, dearest," Isabel admonished. "We mortals cannot choose with whom we fall in love. Why, even the faery folk show very limited willpower when it comes to their romantic proclivities."

"Perhaps not. But we can resolve to act with honor and dignity. We're not chained by our baser inclinations."

Isabel sank down on the feather mattress, picked up a velvet gown, and started to fold it. Traces of oatmeal rested on her shoulders, sprinkled there to ward off the faeries. Bits and pieces fell on the smooth red velvet. "Where will you begin to look, Raine? Have you had another vision?"

Raine sat back on her heels and closed her eyes. "Not a

vision, really. Well, sort of." Bowing her head, she buried her face in her hands. "I'm not sure what I saw." She looked up and met her aunt's worried gaze. "But of one thing, I'm certain. If I don't go now, 'twill be too late. I'll never meet my father."

Isabel nodded in understanding. "You could be heading into danger, child," she cautioned. "Seeing what's going to happen in a vision doesn't mean you can prevent it. Quite the contrary."

"I'll be traveling with a group of Poor Clares who leave this morning from St. Margaret's Nunnery. They're to set up a hospital in Inverness dedicated to Saint Columba. They'll carry the saint's finger bone with them for protection."

Relief washed over Isabel's round features. "Still," she said, "perhaps you should take a strong servant to guard you."

"The nuns will have a retinue of servants with them," Raine reassured her. "Should it become necessary, I can hire a bodyguard at Moray Firth, until I can board the ship. But where I'm going, there's only one man who can protect me."

Isabel nodded, her hazel eyes filled with compassion. "You speak of Keir MacNeil, of course."

Raine swallowed painfully. The thought of having to ask the chief of Clan MacNeil for help nearly choked her. "Of course."

"Well, darling of my heart, if you were a voluptuous female of questionable repute, MacNeil would most likely hasten to your assistance. At the very least, you'd have his complete attention for the space of an evening. But as it is . . ."

There was no need for Lady Isabel to point out the fact that Raine's figure lacked the curves so admired by the opposite sex. Her aunt raised her brows in calm speculation. "Since the two of you have never gotten along, I have to wonder why you think he'll agree to help you find the man who sired you."

"Pooh," Raine countered. She pursed her lips and scowled. "Who *could* get along with The MacNeil? He's loud and rough and a a braggart. He's totally unlike his half brothers, Rory and Lachlan. Besides, the stubborn dolt has no belief whatsoever in magic."

Isabel chuckled. "Well, Keir's certainly no beauty, I grant you that. He doesn't come close to matching Lachlan MacRath's astonishing good looks and courtly manners. Nor Rory MacLean's regal attractiveness."

Raine looked away in an attempt to hide her feelings from her astute aunt. Since the summer she'd turned seventeen, Raine had fought an inexplicable attraction to Keir MacNeil. 'Twas a purely physical attraction. One she was determined to squelch, for the notorious womanizer seduced and discarded mistresses the way other men tossed out their stained shirts.

She rose to her feet and tossed the canvas bag on the bed beside her aunt. "Don't bother folding that fancy gown, Auntie," she said with a rueful smile. She bit her lower lip and blinked back the sudden tears that pooled in her eyes. "There won't be dancing where I'm going. A few plain dresses will have to do."

"Still," her aunt said with a loving smile, "a lady should

always take a few pretty gowns with her whenever she travels."

Raine nodded and stuffed the red velvet along with several others into her bag.

"Pray, don't be afraid, sweetie," Isabel said in a hushed tone. "I believe 'tis your destiny to discover the identity of your natural father and learn why he left your mother while she carried his bairn. Be brave, niece, and do not falter."

Raine sat down beside Lady Isabel, who immediately put an arm around her shoulders. "Sometimes," Raine said," I think I'm foolish searching for him, when he's never made any attempt to find me. Perhaps he doesn't even know I exist. He may deny that I'm his daughter."

"You will never know the truth," Isabel said, "unless you're brave enough to search for the answer."

It was barely dawn. The faint morning light peeked through the partially drawn curtains. Raine intended to leave the manor grounds before sunrise on the pretense of an early-morning ride. A sinking feeling churned in the pit of her stomach. 'Twas a ride from which she might never return.

She'd be traveling into the center of a storm.

War had come to the Highlands.

Six months before, Donald Dubh, the illegitimate son of Alexander Macdonald, the last high chief of the Isles, had been rescued from imprisonment in the island fortress of Innischonaill. A band of Macdonald clansmen had made their way unobserved through the heart of Campbell country, rowed silently across Loch Awe, rushed the castle, and freed its nineteen-year-old prisoner. He was immediately proclaimed lord of the Isles. The whole of the Hebrides rallied to his cause. Nearly every Macdonald in the Highlands and Isles, and their allies with them, rose up in rebellion against James Stewart.

The king of Scotland had designated Laird Keir Mac-Neil master and commander of a squadron in the royal fleet. The king had commissioned him to help put down the rebellion. Keir's stated goal was to capture the traitors and bring them to Edinburgh for trial and hanging. One of those traitors was the man Raine believed to be her natural father, Torcall MacMurchaidh.

She had to reach him before Keir.

"I have something to give you," Aunt Isabel said with an encouraging smile. She placed a smooth stone which had been chiseled into the shape of a heart in Raine's palm. Uncounted years before, the stone had been engraved in an ancient language, incomprehensible today to most people. Only those familiar with the riddles and enchantments of the Tuatha De Danann—the faery race—could discern its meaning.

Raine brushed her thumb across the strange symbols. "What does it say?"

" 'Tis a rune for your safety, my dear. Keep it with you at all times." Isabel reached down and lifted a richly embroidered purse, filled with coins, off the bedcovers. She pulled the cords loose and dropped a handful more into the bag. "Here's a few more gold unicorns to take with you, dear heart."

Raine nodded as she placed the rune carefully inside her purse and fastened it on her girdle. Drawing a deep, steadying breath, she rose from the bed and held out her hands. Her aunt took them in her firm grasp and moved to stand beside Raine.

"When you reach the Isle of Lewis," her aunt said, "you must go to the stones of wonder at Calanais. I've told you much about them, but you should visit the temple to the Mother of the Universe yourself." Isabel clasped Raine by the shoulders and kissed her forehead. "I, too, have had a vision, my dear. I believe you will remain safe as long as you stay with Keir. 'Twill be very important that you are not separated from him during your journey."

Raine slowly shook her head. "I don't think the chief of Clan MacNeil will be agreeable to my hanging on to him like a bawling halflin."

The picture that came to mind made them both laugh.

Laird Keir MacNeil was the most formidable warrior in the whole of Scotland. And beyond.

Chapter 2

June, 1504
Inverness
Scottish Highlands

"THE LADY RAINE to see you, laird," announced Macraith.

At his uncle's words, Keir looked up from the map table in astonishment to see Raine Cameron stride into the room. She carried a leather satchel in one hand and a canvas bag in the other, both of which she dropped on the floor with an unceremonious plop. She then folded her gloved hands and gazed at him with an air of unruffled composure.

Standing stock-still, Macraith MacNeil continued to hold the door wide, clearly unwilling to retreat from such a fascinating spectacle as an uninvited female visitor in the chief of Clan MacNeil's private quarters. The quizzical look on Macraith's craggy, sea-weathered features mirrored Keir's own bewilderment.

Tossing his ruler and compass down, Keir abandoned his mathematical calculations and stared at the black-eyed lassie. He then gazed over the top of her head, fully expecting either Lady Nina or Laird Alex—or both—to come through the doorway behind her.

Not giving Keir a chance to say a word, Raine hurried to stand directly in front of him, as though she feared he'd bolt from the room before she had an opportunity to speak. When neither her mother nor uncle appeared, a prickly sensation crept up the back of Keir's neck.

"What the hell are you doing here, Raine?"

She wrinkled her nose at his coarse language, then sighed as though vulgarity was no more than she'd expected of him.

"I'm here to see you," she answered in her maddeningly determined way. She lifted her arched black brows and her gaze swept the small room, lighting briefly on the unmade bed in the corner and the near-empty decanter of wine from the evening before still on the bed stand. The remains of breakfast cluttered the room's small dining table. When she met his eyes again, a tiny smile flickered across her lips. "I do hope I'm not interrupting anything," she added.

Fortunately, the night's tart had already left the inn with her fistful of silver groats a good half hour earlier.

"You're not."

"Hmph." Macraith released an audible puff of air—whether in admiration of Raine's perspicacity or in reproach of Keir's gruff manners wasn't clear.

Keir jerked his head, signaling his uncle to leave. Macraith grinned good-naturedly at the curt dismissal, but his boots remained planted on the floor.

"Charming as ever, Laird MacNeil," Raine responded. "May I sit down?"

"You may n—"

Before Keir could finish, a shrill scraping drowned out his words, as his uncle shoved a three-legged stool across the bare floorboards from its place by the table. "My lady," Macraith said in his deep gravelly voice.

"Thank you, sir. You're very kind."

Raine gave a brief nod and sat. She lifted the hood of her lightweight traveling cape and let its blue folds drape over her shoulders. A thick black braid sat like a crown on the top of her head. Perched on the stool with the straight-backed posture of a princess, she calmly waited, wrapped in that damn aura of blithe self-assurance that always seemed to surround her. She appeared unaware of the inappropriateness of her sudden appearance in their inn, alone and unprotected.

Raine grew more beautiful each time Keir saw her. He'd been struck, once again, by her grace and charm when he'd spied her at the royal wedding last summer. She'd been surrounded by a group of boisterous young gentlemen, all vying for her attention. Keir had himself well in check, however, and immediately removed himself from her presence, lest he scatter the fawning jackanapes across the polished floor like lawn bowls.

"Where is Lady Nina?" Keir demanded bluntly. An uncomfortable suspicion tightened his jaw, and his words had come more harshly than he'd intended. After all Raine was only a lass, albeit a headstrong one. Far too headstrong for a female. But even a headstrong female would know better than to travel across the northern Highlands without an escort. If that was, in fact, what she'd done.

"My mother remains at Archnacarry Manor, as does Uncle Alex and Aunt Isabel," she answered, confirming his initial conjecture.

"You didn't come here alone?" he asked warily.

She had the decency to blush, but she didn't look away. "If you're asking did I come to Inverness alone, Laird MacNeil, the answer would be no. I traveled from Archnacarry with a contingent of Poor Clares. If you're inquiring whether I am presently on my own, I would have to say yes."

"Jesus," Keir muttered. "The nuns agreed to take you, unescorted by a servant or guard?"

"The good sisters believed that I intended to become a postulant in the Franciscan order. I daresay I can't explain how they reached that conclusion."

He gave a snort of disbelief. "I'm sure you could, if you cared to."

Keir looked over to meet his uncle's startled brown eyes and read the discomfiture they both felt at the news. On hearing Raine's explanation, Macraith had quietly closed the door behind him and stood with his legs braced and his arms folded.

Raine's chin jutted out. "I came here to the Red Boar's Inn directly from the nuns' hostelry. I was never in any danger."

Keir peered at her through narrowed eyes. "Your mother doesn't know you're here, does she?"

"Oh, she most certainly does," Raine protested, meeting his accusatory gaze straight on.

He frowned and propped his hands on his hips. "I don't believe Lady Nina would allow you to travel all the way from Archnacarry to Inverness without a family member. Or at the very least, an armed escort to protect you. Everyone knows there's a rebellion sweeping through the Hebrides."

"Well, this is not the Hebrides," she pointed out.

Lady Raine Cameron rose from the wooden stool and carefully skirted the large man glowering at her with such ferocity. She moved to the diamond-paned window and looked out upon the three magnificent warships riding at anchor in the harbor.

Tenders loaded with supplies plied back and forth through the lapping waves from the dock to the *Sea Dragon*, the *Black Raven*, and the *Sea Hawk*. She could see the crewmen scurrying about on the decks, unloading the crates and barrels and stowing them in the holds.

Keir had followed her to the window. He now stood directly behind her, cutting off any escape she might attempt, should she falter and panic. She didn't need to see the glowering colossus to know he was scowling. She was quite familiar with the chief of Clan MacNeil.

Known to the Scots people as the Black Raven—after his ship—his enemies called him the Black Beast's Spawn—after his notorious father. The aggravating male stood well over six feet. He had a massive chest, and the muscles of his shoulders and upper arms bulged beneath his linen shirt. Today he wore the breeches and knee-high boots of a pirate. But she'd seen him many times in the green-and-black MacNeil tartan, his pleated kilt swinging above his strong calves.

His next words came as a low, threatening growl in her ear. "You're telling me that your mother agreed to this?"

Raine didn't make the mistake of turning to face him eye to chest. Keir MacNeil was the most ferocious man she'd ever known. And she'd known him ever since she could remember. He was the youngest of three half brothers. The "Hellhounds of Scotland" just happened to be close friends of her family. Raine knew better than to show a hint of timidity in front of Keir MacNeil. She'd sparred verbally with him in the past. He could deliver a tongue-lashing that stung worse than a whipping.

Not that anyone had *ever* lifted a hand to her.

"Mama knew I'd be traveling safely with the Poor Clares," she explained. "I told her that I'd meet up with you here in Inverness and place myself under your protection."

"You told her *what*?" His voice shook the rafters, his words echoing around the small inn room.

Raine dared a peek back over her shoulder. A vein bulged on the side of his forehead. His swarthy features were flooded with crimson in his rage. He grasped her elbow and spun her around.

"Jesus, Raine! What the hell were you thinking? In a few days, I'll be sailing into battle. I can't take responsibility for you."

"I'll be responsible for myself," she promised, steeling herself to meet his piercing green eyes. He could skewer her with a look, but she wouldn't allow him to demoralize her. "I need to be on the *Black Raven* when you leave the Moray Firth. I must reach Steòrnabhagh as soon as possible."

"What the devil is in Steòrnabhagh except a nest of traitors?"

Raine bit her lower lip as she frantically recited the answer she'd rehearsed all the way there. "I have a cousin who lives in the nearby village of Tolm on the Isle of Lewis. Lavinia MacAlistair is with child and due to deliver in a few weeks. She wrote imploring Aunt Isabel to attend her during the birth. But we decided the journey would be too taxing for my aunt and that I should come instead."

Keir studied the lass's wide-set ebony eyes, searching for some sign she was lying. She had to be lying. 'Twas impossible to believe that her mother or uncle would have agreed to such an outrageous plan. And if they had, they'd have written him, requesting his assistance.

He wouldn't put such lunacy beyond Lady Isabel, however. Everyone knew the woman was half daft, with her potions and magic spells. She'd infected Raine Cameron with her foolish beliefs in faeries and elves when the lassie was still a wee halflin. He believed Isabel's influence to be the reason for Raine's estrangement from her loving mother. Lady Nina was much too sensible to set any store in her good-sister's self-proclaimed magical powers.

The second sight.

Hell. What goddamned nonsense.

Shaking his head, Keir strode across the room. He braced a booted foot against a carved sea chest in front of the rumpled bed and stared at the far wall. One thing was certain. He was now responsible for Raine. The Camerons had been close family friends since before he was born. Gideon Cameron, the maid's dead father, had fostered Keir's oldest brother, Rory. There was no way Keir could abandon Raine to her fate. He glanced over to meet the exasperating lass's self-satisfied gaze. Damn. She knew it too. In fact, she'd planned on it.

"Just for the sake of plain speaking, Raine," he said, "I don't believe your preposterous story. Not a word of it. But I'm obviously now responsible for your safety, whether I want to be or not."

Keir turned to Macraith. "Have two horses brought to the front of the inn. I'll see to my young charge here while you finish charting our course out of the firth and into the North Sea. I'll meet you on board the *Raven* in four hours. We sail at high tide."

"Aye, aye, captain." His uncle flashed his wide grin and hurried out the door.

"Where are we going now?" Raine asked with a frown.

"You'll need a heavier cloak," Keir told her. "And sturdy boots suitable for a sea voyage."

Her jet eyes sparkling, she smiled in triumph. "What a fine idea! There were some things I couldn't purchase at home."

"No doubt."

Keir would have laughed at her naiveté, if he hadn't been so damn irritated by her arrival. Just how gullible did she think him?

She couldn't have secured those things in Archnacarry

because someone would have asked if she were planning on going to sea.

SEATED ON A sturdy bay mare, Raine gazed up at the square stone fortress that rose high on a cliff overlooking the Firth of Moray. True to his word, Keir MacNeil had escorted her to the market center of Inverness, where they visited several of the shops that lined the winding cobbled streets. She'd purchased a heavy cherry-red mantle with sable trim around the hood, sturdy boots, and a pair of fur-lined leather gloves. She'd placed them carefully in the canvas bag tied across from the leather satchel on the back of her horse.

Mounted once again, Keir had led Raine out of the harbor town, ringed by hills and anchored on the sea at the eastern end of Glen Mór. The cozy burgh straddled the River Ness and stood poised on the edge of the great Loch Ness.

They cantered side by side up a road that followed the precipitous edge of a rocky bluff. Heather bloomed along the hillside. The scent of Scots pine filled the crisp air. Farther up, a forest of spruce and larch rose against the blue sky.

"Where are we going?" Raine asked, though she'd already surmised their goal was the soaring tower house ahead. Her fingers clenched the reins as a feeling of unease tightened the muscles of her shoulders and neck. She forced a smile. "You told me we'd be sailing on the evening tide."

"That's Inverloch Castle," Keir replied in his usual brusque manner. "I need to speak with Laird MacSween before boarding ship. He's promised to stable my horses while I'm gone."

When they arrived at the fortress, Keir motioned to the sentries guarding the main gate. One of the men recognized the chief of Clan MacNeil and immediately waved them through. At the sudden clatter of hooves on the cobblestoned courtyard, a young groom came hustling from the stables to take their horses.

Keir dismounted and moved to stand beside Raine. He clasped her booted ankle in his strong grip and squeezed a warning. "Now be a good lass and mind your manners while we're here. And for God's sake, don't tell Lady Mac-Sween that you traveled to Inverness from Archnacarry without a decent escort."

"I had an escort of nuns," she protested. "You can't get more decent than that!"

He grinned mirthlessly as he lifted her down from the saddle. "Leaving your home without permission can hardly be considered decent, Raine. Not by anyone's standards. Not even your fool-headed aunt's."

"Aunt Isabel is far cleverer than you know, Laird Mac-Neil," she retorted. "And when you address me, please use my title. I'm no longer a child."

He shrugged. "When you start behaving like an adult, Raine, I'll address you as a lady."

Keir led her across the courtyard and guided her into the windowless ground floor filled with provisions. He spoke quietly to an elderly servant, who stood scooping grain from a barrel into a large crock. At the white-haired man's invitation, they followed him up the steps to the second story and into the great hall.

Raine looked around the cavernous room. The tower house appeared well prepared for a siege. Lochaber axes, pikes, and claymores decorated the stone walls, along with swaths of blue-and-white tartan. In the past the Macdonald lords of the Isles had sacked and burned the city of Inverness, putting its inhabitants to the sword.

Raine and her gruff escort waited in the hall only a few minutes before the castle's laird and lady hurried in to greet them. Laird MacSween had a thick brown beard and a bald pate. Though he lacked Keir MacNeil's sheer muscular bulk, the middle-aged man appeared to be as battle ready as his castle. His wife had a large, square frame and a face splashed with freckles. Wisps of graying red hair poked out from under the edges of her unfashionable double-horned headdress. But her wide smile conveyed a sunny disposition.

The two men clasped hands, then turned to their feminine companions.

"Keir!" Lady MacSween exclaimed. "What a surprise to see you! We thought you'd have set sail by now." Her blue eyes alight with curiosity, she looked questioningly at Raine and then back to Keir.

Keir honored his hosts with the briefest of smiles. "May I introduce my young charge, Lady Raine Cameron?"

Finn MacSween smiled broadly in welcome. "I greatly admired your father, Lady Raine," he said, taking her hand to kiss. "I felt sore distressed at the news of Gideon's untimely death. How is your dear mother?"

"I left Lady Nina well," Raine murmured, surprised that her host was acquainted with both her parents. Until that moment, she had never met Laird MacSween.

Keir bowed to the castle's amiable chatelaine. "Perhaps you ladies might enjoy each other's company, while I speak privately with your husband on the king's business."

"Certainly, certainly," the portly man immediately agreed. He brushed a knuckle back and forth under his bearded chin as he glanced over to his wife with a dismissive tilt of his head.

"What a delightful idea," Lady Dorothea agreed. With an encouraging smile, she clasped Raine's hand and pulled her gently along. "Come, dear, we can sit in the garden. We'll partake of refreshments while the men talk."

Though Raine hated to let Keir MacNeil out of her sight for even a moment, she could scarcely refuse her hostess's gracious invitation. As she and Lady MacSween withdrew, Raine glanced over her shoulder to find the tall warrior watching her departure with smug complacence. She'd rarely seen Keir MacNeil look so self-satisfied. Which meant, of course, that she dare not trust him. He was, no doubt, hatching some clever scheme to be rid of her.

KEIR WATCHED THE two females leave, then turned to Finn MacSween. "Lady Raine traveled to Inverness with a group of Poor Clares, who've come to set up a new hospital," he clarified. "She surprised me with her arrival." Keir hooked both thumbs in his sword belt and scowled. "I have a favor to ask of you, laird."

Finn nodded with a knowing wink. "Aye, and I've a notion I ken what it is. Come, my friend, let's have a draft of ale while you explain how the young maid of Archnacarry came to be in your custody just as you're about to sail into battle."

They sat down at a long table before an enormous fireplace and waited while a servant brought two tankards of ale and set them on the bare board.

Keir quickly described how Raine had shown up unexpectedly at the Red Boar's Inn that morning with no family or guards to protect her. He admitted to Finn that it seemed probable she had, in fact, traveled to Inverness with a group of nuns, just as she claimed. But though she denied it, he suspected she'd left her home without permission.

"I'm hoping," Keir told his host with an apologetic smile, "that you and your kind wife will offer her the safety of Inverloch Castle until her uncle can come to fetch her home. I'll send Laird Cameron a message informing him of her whereabouts before I board the *Raven*."

Laird MacSween smoothed his pudgy fingers over his bare head and lifted his thick brows in astonishment. "Of course, of course. I'll gladly offer Lady Raine our protection. But what in God's name was the lass thinking to attempt such a dangerous journey with only the company of a few religious women?"

Keir shook his head. "Damned if I can explain such willful behavior, except to say that her Aunt Isabel must have had something to do with it. That secretive female dabbles in spells and magical concoctions. Her foolishness seems to have spilled over to the lass. Raine claims to have the second sight."

Finn pursed his lips and gave a low whistle. "Perhaps she does," he said with a speculative lift of his shoulders. "I've a distant kinsman known to see things before they happen. Willem saw his father on his deathbed a month before the old man died."

Keir gave a snort of disbelief. "Old men are known to die quite regularly. And sooner rather than later. I wouldn't wager two farthings on Raine having any special powers. She's nay more than a halflin herself."

"What reason does the maiden give for this astonishing escapade?"

"She claims that she wants to reach the Isle of Lewis, where a cousin is nearing childbirth," Keir replied. "Since Lady Isabel couldn't respond to the summons for help because of her advanced age, Raine elected to go in her aunt's stead. Though what an unmarried lass would know about birthing an infant remains to be explained."

Finn nodded thoughtfully. "Aye, but who can decipher the workings of the female mind? Especially when it's anything to do with the mystery of childbirth." He lifted the pewter tankard and drank deeply. Setting it down with a thunk, he wiped his bearded chin with the back of his hand. "Now tell me about the rebellion, lad. What plans do ye have to quell the unrest sweeping the Isles?"

"I'm to sail the *Raven* with my brothers' two ships under my command to the Isle of Lewis. I've been commissioned by the king to lay siege to the castle at Steòrnabhagh, where we believe Torcall MacMurchaidh is harboring Donald Dubh Macdonald. I'll take both traitors into custody for transport to Edinburgh."

Laird MacSween rested his forearms on the tabletop. "You've your work cut out for you there, lad. Castle Murchaidh is nigh impregnable. The bulwarks are ten feet thick with cannon emplacements all along the sea walls."

"We've cannon enough ourselves," Keir said, "with swivel mounts and master gunners to man them. The fortress will fall in less than a week After that we'll rendezvous with the royal fleet at Calgarraidh Bay."

MacSween clucked his tongue in somber reflection. " 'Tis a bad business," he said with a rueful shake of his head. "Bad, indeed. Too many lives will be lost in a needless cause that's doomed before it's begun. Surely some compromise could be reached with the other rebellious clan chiefs, once Donald Dubh and MacMurchaidh are captured."

"I'd like to think so, but I doubt it." Keir tipped his tankard up and drained it. Then he stood and braced one foot on the wooden bench. "I lay the entire fault at the earl of Argyll's feet. If he hadn't imprisoned his own grandson for years, some agreement might have been reached by now. Donald Dubh has to be seething with bitterness and hatred. As the heir to the lord of the Isles, the lad's ripe for leading a rebellion of the entire Macdonald clan and their allies."

Finn nodded his agreement. "Meanwhile, Argyll seems to be obsessed with turning all this turmoil, all the bleeding and dying, to his own advantage. I believe the greedy bastard hopes to gain control of the trade route to Ireland in the end, whether it takes him one year or twenty."

Keir had to agree. "King James made a grave mistake in appointing Argyll the Master of the Royal Household. He and the other councilors quickly abandoned the king's attempts at reconciliation with the chiefs of the Isles. Instead, they embarked on a policy of coercion guaranteed to stir up old hatreds."

Laird MacSween rose to his feet and laid a hand on Keir's shoulder. "You'll be wanting to take your leave of Lady Raine, before you go."

"Nay, you're wrong there, laird," Keir said with a shake of his head. "I'm not telling Raine Cameron that I'm leaving her here with you and Lady Dorothea. And I'd appreciate it if you'd wait awhile before you inform Raine of my departure."

Finn MacSween burst into loud guffaws. "Oh, aye," he said between chortles of laughter, "I ken what it is you're about, lad. 'Tis far easier to face the boom of a cannonade than the screeches of an outraged female."

Keir didn't disabuse his friend of the belief that Raine would attempt to get her way with a shrieking tirade. However, Keir knew better. Rather, the problem centered on the fact that Raine had been given her own way by every member of her doting family for her entire life.

Keir intended to be on board the *Raven* and sailing up the Firth of Moray before Lady Raine Cameron realized she'd been tricked. Hell, she'd known him most of her life. She should have realized he had no intention of taking her with him. But once she acknowledged the certain fact that he'd sailed without her, she'd come to her senses and agree to wait for her Uncle Alex to arrive at Inverloch Castle and collect her.

Keir and Raine had butted heads before, when she'd tried to convince others that she had the second sight. But he knew that, as stubborn and single-minded as Raine might be, his will would always prove stronger.

After all he was deceiving her for her own damn good.

Chapter 3

THE THREE SHIPS sailed in close formation into the North Sea, leaving behind the calmer waters of the Firth of Moray. Keir stood on the starboard side of the quarterdeck and watched the *Black Raven*'s sister ships, the *Sea Dragon*, captained by Fearchar MacLean, and the *Sea Hawk,* under the command of Colin MacRath, cut through the churning waves like white-winged birds of prey.

A feeling of elation took hold. Keir smiled to himself, savoring the moment. Heading out to open water always brought a thrill.

A sudden niggling of guilt spoiled the moment. He scowled at the thought of Raine's abject disappointment, when she realized he'd abandoned her. Hell, he hadn't exactly *abandoned* her. He'd left her in the care of two kindhearted people, who'd watch over her until her family arrived.

In the end she'd given him no other choice. For he could

never have taken Raine on board the *Raven*. 'Twould have been unthinkable. Having her so near and not succumbing to his desires might prove more difficult than anything he'd ever done. He sure as hell didn't intend to find out.

Keir's gaze swept the horizon. 'Twas perfect sailing weather, with the air so clear small details could be seen a great way off. From the corner of his eye, a glimpse of bright red cloth, snapping and blowing in the brisk sea breeze, caught his attention. He squinted against the sunlight and peered at the deck of the *Hawk*.

The memory of Raine trying on a red cloak flashed before him. She'd lifted the sable-trimmed hood over the satin sheen of her dark hair, and her eyes had sparkled like polished jets in her pleasure.

"Macraith!" he roared.

His uncle hastened to his side but failed to realize that Keir was glaring at the nearby *Sea Hawk*. Macraith stared out over the waves to the far-off horizon, expecting, no doubt, to see the sails of an enemy vessel approaching. "Captain?" he asked, clearly befuddled.

"Signal the *Hawk* to heave to and prepare to be boarded," Keir ordered. "Then lower a boat and send Barrows over to transfer Lady Raine to the *Raven*."

Macraith's head swiveled as he turned to look at the trim galleon running alongside them. "Lady Raine?" He all but choked out the words. "Why—why, I thought you'd left the maid at Inverloch Castle."

"So did I, dammit," Keir gritted through clenched teeth. "So the hell did I."

Twenty minutes later Barrows returned and timidly

approached his glowering captain. "Beggin' pardon, sir," the grizzled seaman said, his weather-beaten face flushed with mortification. He snatched off his cap and clutched it in bent, calloused fingers. "The Lady Raine sends her regards to the ship's captain, sir, and says she'd rather remain on board the *Sea Hawk*."

"What?" Keir snapped.

Barrows leaned closer and, with an air of confidentiality, spoke just above a whisper. "The lassie says she's nay comin' aboard the *Raven*, but she thanks ye for the invite."

"I'll fetch her," Macraith offered before Keir could bellow in outrage.

"Do it," Keir grated. "And tell that—tell Lady Raine if I have to come and get her, she won't sit down for a—"

"I'll bring her," Macraith interrupted with a wave of his large hand. "There's nay need to threaten the wee lassie with a punishment you'd never administer."

"I don't make threats I won't carry out, and you damn well know it. Now get going. And when you return, take her to my cabin immediately," Keir ordered. "We don't need to discuss her reluctant arrival in front of the entire crew."

RAINE GAZED AROUND Keir's private quarters and waited in trepidation. She'd seen him watching from the quarterdeck above them, as his uncle had helped her clamber up the ladder. 'Twas an embarrassingly clumsy process, with Macraith lifting her up from the swaying boat below, while another seaman pulled her up over the gunwale and onto the main deck. Had she weighed ten pounds more or were the men any less strong, Raine was certain they'd never have gotten her aboard.

Macraith had led her to the captain's cabin where he dropped Raine's bag and satchel on its ornate Turkistan rug and left her in ominous silence. The apprehension in Macraith's solemn brown eyes told her the coming interview with his volatile nephew wasn't going to be pleasant.

She didn't have long to wait. Nor near enough time to gather her wits and fabricate a suitably heart-wrenching story.

Keir MacNeil stormed in and kicked the cabin door shut with the heel of his boot. He moved swiftly across the floor to stand in front of her, planted his hands on his hips and leaned down, bringing his face closer to hers. The battle scar that ran through his right eyebrow and across the broken bridge of his nose heightened the sinister cast of his blunt features.

"Are you happy now?" he demanded before she had a chance to say a word. "Are you completely satisfied, Raine Cameron, now that you've gotten your way? Now that you've put yourself in jeopardy and burdened me with your safety in one fell swoop? And all to help some woman who'll probably deliver her baby before you even arrive."

Raine retreated two small steps, halting when the back of her knees bumped against the edge of his large bed. She attempted to swallow, but her mouth had gone dry. When she tried to speak, her upper lip stuck to her front teeth and she was forced to run her tongue across them. "You were the one who insisted I transfer to the *Raven*," she pointed out. Suddenly breathless, she forged ahead between gasps for air. "I would have . . . much preferred . . . to stay . . . under the protection . . . of Colin MacRath."

Keir straightened and folded his powerful arms across his chest. His words came drenched in scorn. "Oh, aye! You'd have enjoyed that, wouldn't you? To stay on board the *Hawk,* where you could twist that impressionable lad around your wee finger."

Refusing to back down, Raine looked her tormenter straight in the eye. "Colin's a grown man and captain of his ship. He can make his own decisions."

"Not when I'm bloody commander of the squadron, he can't," Keir gritted.

They were interrupted by a polite tap on the door.

"Come in, Macraith," Keir called over his shoulder. "You can see for yourself I haven't strangled her—yet."

Macraith entered, his worried gaze moving from one to the other, as though to assure himself that the young lady was holding her own. But he waited in cautious silence, clearly used to riding out his nephew's intermittent bouts of temper.

"Well, go on," Keir told his uncle, with a wave of his hand. "Say what you've come to say on Lady Raine's behalf. I can see it in your eyes. You're about to defend the indefensible."

"Err . . . I was about to suggest that the lass can have my cabin. I'll bunk with the ship's quartermaster, sir. 'Twill be no trouble. No trouble, at all."

Keir looked up at the ceiling and shook his head in apparent exasperation. "An excellent suggestion, Macraith.

Because I sure as hell am not giving up my quarters."
He grinned malevolently as his gaze ensnared Raine's.
"Unless, of course, you'd like to share them with me."

"You're an ogre," she said quietly. "You always have
been. And you always will be."

"At last, we are in complete agreement, Lady Raine."

THAT EVENING KEIR and Macraith sat at the intricately
carved oak table used for dining in the captain's quarters,
waiting for the arrival of their tardy guest.

"I was afraid this would happen," Keir said, gesturing
with impatience for the towheaded midshipman to stand
back and refrain from serving the meal. "By now Lady
Raine will be too ill to keep anything in her stomach,
and she'll only get worse through the night. We'll have
to make for the first safe harbor in the morning and pray
to God we can find a reputable family to leave her with."

"Och" Macraith remonstrated with the tranquility of
age and experience, "almost all passengers suffer from a
bout of nausea their first time out. Don't predict the worst
for the lassie, till the worst actually happens."

Keir scowled at his uncle's calm demeanor. "Dammit
to hell, a spare-built female like Raine can die of seasick-
ness, and we both know it."

Keir felt half nauseous himself, as though someone had
administered a punishing kick to his gut. God knew, he'd
tried at Inverness to avoid this very thing. The thought of
Raine lying helpless in her bunk, unable to keep anything
in her stomach as she grew increasingly weaker, brought

him to his feet. He'd go look in on her now and not wait for things to get any worse.

Just as Keir slid out of his chair, Raine appeared in the open doorway, attired in a lavender gown. Her lustrous ebony hair, plaited in one thick braid and wound into a figure eight, had been fastened at the nape of her neck with a blue satin ribbon. Her dark eyes sparkled, their luminous depths framed by long, curved lashes.

A picture of glowing health, she smiled sedately, apparently unaware of the misery she'd just put him through. "I'm so sorry to keep you both waiting." She looked from one man to the other without an iota of contrition. "I was standing at the railing, watching the dolphins frolic in the waves. I simply lost track of the time."

"Then you feel up to eating?" Keir asked, unable to keep the relief from his voice. He stood in front of the table, too astonished and grateful to move.

Macraith jumped to his feet and indicated for Raine to be seated.

She nodded to Keir's uncle as she slipped onto her chair. "Ah, indeed I do. I haven't eaten since this morning when I—" She stopped abruptly, no doubt remembering that 'twas Lady MacSween who'd last offered her refreshments at Inverloch Castle.

Keir signaled the seventeen-year-old midshipman to begin serving the meal. Hector MacFarlane stepped forward to ladle the thick broth filled with chunks of lamb and vegetables into Raine's bowl. She picked up a warm loaf of bread from the wooden tray on the table, broke off a piece and inhaled the aroma wafting up from her trencher.

"Mm, it does smell wonderful," she said, with another appreciative sniff.

Keir watched in surprise as Raine dipped her bread in the stew and began eating with relish. When she noticed him staring, she lifted her brow.

"Is there something wrong?" she asked.

Keir shook his head as he sat back down. "Not at all. We were just saying that we hoped you weren't suffering from the pitch and roll of the ship. These northern currents can be treacherous, even in the summertime. We'll experience some choppy seas until we reach the calmer waters of the Minch."

"Oh, I came prepared for that," she said with a soft laugh. "Aunt Isabel packed some ground root known for preventing illness at sea in my satchel, along with my other remedies."

"Known by whom?" Macraith asked, his craggy face alight with a lively interest. The kindness of his smile showed the warm affection he felt for the young lady. "I've nay heard of such a cure."

"Well, my aunt, for one, knows the beneficial properties of ginger," she told him. "And I as well. I've studied healing recipes under Aunt Isabel's tutelage since I was eight."

Macraith grinned at Keir. "Now here's a lass o' parts," he said with a chuckle, waving his spoon in the air.

"Oh, aye," Keir agreed. "I've always known that Raine had wits enough for two females. 'Tis plain commonsense she's lacking."

Macraith leaned closer to her and spoke softly in her

ear. "Pay no attention to yon blathersnipe, my dear. You'll make some lucky fellow a fine wife one day."

"Oh, I don't plan to ever marry," Raine replied with unruffled composure.

"And why not?" Macraith asked, making no attempt to hide his astonishment. "A sonsy lass like you will have to fight the lads off with a belaying pin."

Keir took a piece of bread and dipped it in his stew. "Lady Raine quite possibly believes she'll never find any gentleman worthy enough to garner her affections," he offered sardonically.

Raine met his gaze, seemingly mystified at his derisive tone. "Oh, it isn't that at all," she protested. " 'Tis simply that I intend to devote myself to the healing arts, like my aunt. And like her, I shall remain a maid."

"A hell of a waste that would be," Macraith declared. He turned to his nephew. "Don't you agree?"

Keir sat back in his chair and twirled the stem of his glass of port between his thumb and forefinger. "If Raine believes she should spend her life grinding up roots and casting bones like her spinster aunt, she's even more foolish than I thought."

Raine looked at him quizzically, as though trying to understand if there was a deeper meaning to his caustic remark. She tipped her head to one side and studied him. Her perceptive eyes seemed to read his carnal thoughts. "You don't seem to be in any hurry to wed, yourself, Laird MacNeil," she pointed out.

"Now there, you're wrong," Keir told her, immensely pleased to find that she couldn't read his thoughts at all—

carnal or otherwise. "As a matter of fact, I am presently in negotiations for a bride. Before leaving on this campaign, I instructed my uncle, the earl of Appin, to approach the lady's father with my offer."

Macraith stared openmouthed. "The devil, ye say! That's the first I've heard of it."

Ignoring his uncle's incredulity, Keir watched Raine's reaction through narrowed eyes. Just as he expected, she smiled in tranquil detachment, completely unaffected by the thought that he was going to wed. Hell, that came as no surprise.

"May I offer my congratulations?" she inquired sweetly. "Or is it too soon? Perhaps we should wait to find out if the lady accepts your proposal."

"You mean to imply that 'tis likely no lady would ever accept me for a husband?" he baited, pushing her to admit that's exactly what she did believe. "You think the negotiations are bound to fail when the maiden declines my offer?"

"Nay, lad," Macraith interrupted. "No one is so foolish as to believe that! Why, you're the legitimate heir to a personal fortune. You've widespread lands and a castle on Barra. What woman in her right mind would refuse the chief of Clan MacNeil?"

Raine lifted her delicate brows, her jet eyes sparkling with laughter. "Well, then," she said, "let's hope the laird of Clan MacNeil has offered his affections to a young lady in her right mind."

"I didn't say my affections were in any way engaged," he replied with an indifferent shrug. "I offered for her hand in marriage. Nothing more." He stopped short, realizing she'd been teasing him in their old familiar way.

Keir was all too aware Raine had been hopelessly infatuated with his handsome brother, Lachlan. *Hopeless* being the key word, for as fate would have it, Lachlan was now a married man, deeply in love with his exquisite wife and devoted to their children. It must have been quite a shock to Raine when he returned to Scotland with his pregnant Sassenach mistress.

No doubt, Raine's unrequited passion was the real reason she fancied she'd never marry. For what female would be satisfied to spend her life casting spells and claiming to see visions?

When the meal was over, Lady Raine excused herself to return to her cabin. Keir and Macraith moved to the chart table to plot the ship's course through the North Sea.

" 'Tis strange you never mentioned Duncan Stewart is presently negotiating your marriage," Macraith commented in a low, offhand tone.

Keir kept his head bent over the map, refusing to meet his uncle's inquisitive gaze. "You may be second in command of the *Raven*, but I'm not obliged to keep you informed of my personal matters."

"Och, man," Macraith replied with a chuckle, "I never meant to say you were. But indulge my prying nature, laddie. Who's the fair lady that's so beguiled you?"

Keir laid his quill pen down on his sheets of calculations. "I thought we covered that subject at supper."

He was deeply attached to his uncle. Macraith was the younger brother of Keir's deceased father. Ruaidh

Athaeuch MacNeil, otherwise known as the Black Beast of Barra, had been slain on the battlefield when Keir was only seven. In the years that followed, it had been noted by many that Keir was the very spirit and image of his ruthless sire. Early on, he'd been labeled the Black Beast's Spawn.

Lady Emma MacNeil, after the death of her third husband, immediately moved her household from Kisimuth Castle on the Isle of Barra to her brother's home at Stalcaire in the Highlands.

Macraith had visited Keir often in those early years, strengthening the bond of love between uncle and nephew that had begun at his birth. At ten years old, Keir had been fostered to the king's admiral, Sir Anthony Wood, who took him to sea. Macraith had sailed with them, teaching Keir the lore and love of sailing. When Keir launched his own ship, the *Black Raven*, Macraith sailed with him as his second in command. They'd protected each other in battle and rejoiced in their mutual successes as the king's privateers.

"Nay, not completely," Macraith remarked with a grin. "You never did mention the name of that comely lass who's stolen your heart."

"Stolen my heart!" Keir repeated with an ironic laugh. "Don't be a fool. Negotiating a marriage contract doesn't mean my affections are engaged, and you damn well know it. When two wealthy families merge, the primary issue is the assets each party brings to the alliance."

Macraith shook his head, setting his narrow side-braids swinging gently. "Don't sell yourself short, lad. You deserve a wife who fancies you. One who'll dote upon the children you'll give her."

"A dutiful wife will respect my authority," Keir responded, keeping his irritation in check. "It'll be her goddamn duty to respect me."

"Ah, I see," his uncle replied. "And what about you? Are you fond of the lass in question? Whoever the hell this mysterious lassie may be?"

"There's nothing mysterious about her. If you must know, I've instructed Duncan to enter into negotiations with Laird Fillan MacNab for the hand of his daughter, Mariota."

"The maid of Strathfillan? Jesus, lad! You can't be serious!"

"And why not?" Keir retorted. "She's young and healthy and bonny enough. There's nothing to indicate she won't be a fruitful wife and a devoted mother."

Macraith sat back on the high stool beside the map table. He scrubbed his large hand over his beard plaited with beads and eyed his nephew with a look of dubious speculation. "And have you ever spoken more than two words to the lass, I ask you?"

"Oh, aye," Keir said, unable to conceal a grin at his uncle's astute remark. "I'll admit Mariota is as timid and quiet as a wee mouse. She'll have no trouble living up to the lines in her wedding vows when she pledges to be meek and mild in bed and at board."

"And that's what you want?" Macraith asked in disbelief. "A wife who's afraid to speak up and tell you what's on her mind? A female so docile she'll marry whichever man her father chooses without so much as a whimper of protest?"

"Am I such a bad bargain then?" Keir demanded, finally losing his patience. "Must a maid be forced to marry—"

They were interrupted when Barrows appeared in the cabin's open doorway.

"Beg pardon, sir," he said, stopping just outside the threshold.

Keir and Macraith looked over to see the able seaman's weathered face blanched with fear.

"What is it?" Keir asked.

"Best come up on deck at once, if it please ye, sir," Barrows answered. He pointed his crooked index finger toward the cabin's low ceiling. "The lassie's up in the riggin' with the ship's boys. We just looked up and saw her there. One minute she was standin' by the larboard rail, the next she'd disappeared. Nobody even seen her climbin'. We don't ken what to do. We're afeared to go up there to fetch her, lest we startle her into fallin'."

Throwing down his compass, Keir dashed past the worried bosun's mate and hurried up the companionway. Macraith followed close at his heels.

On deck the morning watch stood bunched together, staring upward in mutual horror at the mainmast.

Following their line of sight, Keir spotted Raine perched on an upper crosstree, one arm wrapped about the mast. Dressed in a sailor's loose shirt and breeches, she appeared to be engrossed in the view of the ocean, unaware of her terrified audience below.

Ethan and Robbie Gibson sat on a yardarm close by, their young faces creased with worry. She must have followed them into the rigging. Frightened for her sake, they sat absolutely still, praying, no doubt, that they wouldn't be blamed should she fall.

Keir held his hand up, signaling the crew to stay silent. "Keep the men absolutely quiet," he told Macraith.

His heart smashing against his ribs, Keir started the climb. He prayed to God Raine wouldn't look down and suddenly realize the incredible danger she was in.

Keir made his way up the rigging as soundlessly as possible, then pulled himself onto the crosstree where she was perched. Without a word, he signaled the lads to descend. Smiling in relief, Ethan and Robbie slid quickly down the ropes to join the other sailors on the main deck.

Raine gave Keir a welcoming smile. "Oh, you've come to join me." The sea breeze had pulled soft tendrils from her braided hair, framing her face in an ebony cloud.

"I have," he replied in a calm tone. He longed to throttle her for putting herself in such terrible danger. Even as a youngster, she'd been fearless.

"You seem a little out of breath," she said on a note of surprise.

Seated on the other side of the mast, he forced a smile. His heartbeat had slowed till it was almost back to normal, but she wasn't out of danger yet. He'd get her safely down before he ripped into her.

"What are you doing up here?" he asked conversationally. He fought the urge to catch hold of her wrist. Any sudden move could mean disaster.

She peeked around the mainmast, her eyes dancing with happiness at her latest exploit. "I'd been watching the lads scamper up and down the ropes. I became curious to discover what could be seen from such a great height." She looked around and released a long, slow breath of wonderment. " 'Tis truly beautiful. This ship. The ocean. The *Hawk* and *Dragon* sailing so close by. I could stay up here all morning."

"It's time to get down now," Keir said, still keeping his voice steady and even. "On board a privateer, you need always ask permission before going aloft. Otherwise there'd be too much confusion."

She turned her questioning gaze on him, skepticism in her eyes. "I didn't notice anyone else asking permission. Not even Ethan and Robbie."

Ignoring her dissent, Keir continued with ruthless determination. "It's a nautical law, Raine. You can ask any man on board. They'll verify the truth of what I say. The ship's boys had their orders this morning."

She burst out laughing, the sound reminding him of how he'd reacted to her provocative nature that past summer in Edinburgh. A reaction he'd suppressed with ruthless intention in the months since. Christ Almighty, he'd known her presence on the *Raven* would be untenable.

"I'm quite certain," she said, "that every man will swear to anything you say. But may we have just a few more minutes before we start down? I'd like to admire the extraordinary beauty of it all." Her gaze implored him to agree.

Keir gave a quick jerk of his chin. "Aye, 'tis quite lovely, isn't it?"

He glanced out at the ocean and the two warships that sailed alongside the *Raven* in close formation. The sight had always stirred his blood.

But not today.

Rather than admiring the weatherly galleons, he fought the tension that tightened every muscle in his body. The possibility of Raine slipping off her perch kept him ready to grab her instantly.

"We'd best get down now," he said shortly. "I'll go first and help you place your feet." He paused. "By the way, where the devil did you find those clothes? Or did you bring them from Archnacarry?"

"Oh, no, I hadn't thought of it then," she replied, patting the knees of her woolen breeches. "I borrowed these from a cabin boy on the *Sea Hawk*. Colin gave me permission to take them."

"I should have guessed," he said with a wry grin. "How else could you have found clothes to fit you?"

Keir swung down from the crossbeam, the mass of rigging under his feet going taut beneath his weight. "Once I'm positioned beneath you," he told her in a stern tone, "hang on to the crosstree with both arms and let your feet dangle loose. I'll set them on the ropes for you."

For once Raine didn't argue with him. She must have sensed from his voice that he'd brook no disobedience on her part. She followed his directions, allowing him to clasp her ankles and position her shoes on the rigging beneath her.

"Don't look down," he cautioned. "Keep your gaze straight ahead."

Astonished by Keir's gentle touch, Raine allowed him to guide her descent by placing her feet carefully on the ratlines below. She had never imagined that the fierce, sharp-tongued privateer she'd known from her youth could be so gentle. She felt the reassuring presence of his large, muscular body, ready to catch her should she slip and fall. And the nearness of this attentive stranger unnerved her far more than the dizzying height.

As they made their way to the deck below, the crew waited in complete silence, until Raine's feet were planted firmly on the boards. Then, to a man, they roared a hurrah at her safe return to the deck.

Smiling at their approbation, Raine turned to thank Keir for his help, only to find him glaring at her. His jaw was taut with anger.

"What's wrong?" she asked warily. She could scarce believe his sudden change in demeanor. But then again, this was Keir's usual self.

"What's wrong?" he thundered. "My God, you could have been killed. You could have slipped and fallen to your death!"

But I didn't," she said, dismayed at his complete reversal. For a few moments, sitting high on the crossbeam together, they'd seemed to be in neighborly accord as they gazed in quiet appreciation of the beauty around them. "I'm perfectly fine," she added.

"You're fine because I brought you safely down." He turned from her and addressed his uncle, who stood hovering nearby. "Get Barrows over here now."

"Barrows," Macraith shouted.

The little man hustled forward, his cap clutched in his blue-veined hands. "Cap'n, sir," he said.

Keir clasped Raine's shoulders and turned her to face the

wizened seaman. "Jasper Barrows is the *Raven's* sea-daddy. He's responsible for the safety of the young midshipmen on board. From now on," Keir instructed tersely, "Barrows is to stay right beside you whenever you're on deck. He'll be responsible to see that you never, ever climb up into the rigging alone again. Is that perfectly clear to you, Lady Raine?"

Raine looked into the older man's harried blue eyes and felt a rush of mortification. It was clear Barrows felt he'd been given the duty of watching over a recalcitrant child and was none too happy about it.

"I wasn't up there alone," Raine protested. "And I'm quite capable of taking care of myself. I don't need a sea-daddy."

"Nevertheless," Keir stated, "you have one now. We assign all new youngsters a veteran seaman to show them the ropes and keep them out of harm's way. And if you manage to slip away from Barrows and clamber up there by yourself, he'll be the one I toss overboard." Keir raised his voice just loud enough to drive the point home. "Do you understand?"

"Aye, aye, sir," Barrows replied, as though Keir had addressed him, rather than Raine.

"This is preposterous," Raine stated with a rebellious toss of her head.

Keir rounded on her. "No, it is not preposterous. It's an order. And on my ship, under my command, you will follow orders or suffer the consequences. If you go up there without me ever again, Raine Cameron, you'll get the thrashing you deserve."

Raine straightened her spine and threw back her

shoulders, refusing to show just how intimidated she felt. No one had ever threatened her before. Only someone as ill-tempered as Keir MacNeil would dare to do so in front of others.

"And do you intend to flog me before the crew?" she asked.

Something in her question brought an unholy light to his deep green eyes. His low voice reverberated with a sardonic humor. "Nay, lass. I'll administer your punishment in the privacy of my quarters."

Thankfully, not one of the sailors listening gave so much as a snicker.

"You're a vile, evil man, Keir MacNeil," she whispered. "I regret the day I came aboard your ship. And now with your permission, I'll retire to my cabin," she added, remembering too late that she couldn't turn and leave with a regal swish of her skirts. Not when she was clad in boy's clothes.

"An excellent idea," Keir retorted. "And Barrows here will escort you."

Raine didn't wait for the gray-haired bosun's mate. She drew her dignity around her like a protective cloak and walked quickly past the gaping crew, with the surprised Barrows hurrying to catch up.

Keir watched Raine retreat with all the composure she could muster, her slender figure, attired in the loose sailor's clothing, straight and taut as a pikestaff.

When had there ever been such an aggravating female? He had to admit, however, few women would've had the courage to stand up to a battle-hardened privateer—and a MacNeil clan chief, at that.

A picture of Mariota rose before him. The one and only time he'd spoken to the maid of Strathfillan, she'd hung her head, too ill at ease to speak above a whisper. In spite of her reticence, he'd been certain she'd fit his requirements in a wife. Namely, he'd never fall in love with her, nor she with him.

A burgeoning doubt regarding the wisdom of that decision appeared like an unmapped sandbar in an otherwise welcoming harbor. He shook his head, wiping the image away. He'd made his decision, and by God, he'd stick to it.

Chapter 4

FOUR DAYS OUT of Inverness the three warships reached the Pentland Firth, which ran between the northernmost tip of the Scottish mainland and the southern end of the Orkney Islands. They'd made acceptable, though not excellent, time. The weather had held, with a steady wind filling the sails and a few clouds scudding across the bluest of skies. Every afternoon the ships would take time for gunnery practice, shooting the eighteen-pounders at empty barrels, until the sky darkened with the soot of gunpowder and the air hung heavy with the stench of sulphur.

At their present latitude, the June days were long and filled with sunshine. The night sky grew blacker than Hades, the stars, brilliant lanterns in the heavens.

To Keir's pleasant surprise, Raine didn't hold on to her anger over their open confrontation in front of the crew. Unlike some gently bred members of the weaker sex, she didn't appear to nurse feelings of ill treatment while at the same time plotting to repay the offending male in kind. Nor did she descend into the cowardly tactic of aloof silence. She'd apologized for climbing up into the rigging without permission and promised never to do it again.

While on deck, Raine visited with the men on watch and happily shared her meals in the captain's cabin with whomever Keir invited to join them.

When he offered to take Raine up into the rigging that fourth morning, she accepted with an eager smile. He followed directly behind her, ready to catch her should she have a misstep. They sat on a crosstree on either side of the mainmast, enjoying the magnificent view.

"I've been wondering," Keir said, keeping his tone pleasant and even, "how you managed to leave Inverloch Castle. I'd asked Laird MacSween to watch over you until your family came to fetch you home."

Raine peeked around the mast to meet his gaze, then turned to look out across the waves. "To tell the truth, I left the castle before you did. I told Lady MacSween that I'd forgotten something in my satchel. When I entered the stable, I found the groom hadn't yet unsaddled my horse. 'Twas no trouble at all to simply ride back the way we came. Naturally, I cautioned the stablemen not to mention I'd left, indicating I wanted it to be a surprise."

"How clever of you," he said with grudging admiration.

She peeked around the mast once again, her dark eyes sparkling with merriment. She wrinkled her nose impishly. "I thought so."

Keir felt the rush of sensual longing he'd stomped on like a too-short fuse lit by mistake. A longing that kept flickering back to life despite his best efforts to smother it out completely.

"And so," Raine continued, clearly unaware of his lecherous urges, "I reached the *Sea Hawk* well before you boarded the *Black Raven*. And when Colin learned about the impending birth of my cousin's child, he graciously agreed to take me with him to the Isle of Lewis."

Keir gave a snort of disbelief. "Why is it I feel there's something you're not telling me, Raine?"

Her eyes widened at the accusation. "When have I ever lied to you, Keir?"

"I'm asking myself the same question."

She gave a nervous little laugh. "And have you determined the answer?"

"Not yet. But I will," he promised.

When it came time to descend, Keir went first, careful to touch her as little as possible.

That afternoon Keir stood on the quarterdeck, keeping an eye on the close-hauled sails above them, when he noticed Raine and Barrows coming up the companionway. Still dressed in sailor's attire, she'd plaited her hip-long hair in one thick braid, letting it fall down her back. She looked much younger than her nineteen years.

"Full and by the wind, Mr. Buchanan," Keir told the officer of the watch before moving across the deck to meet Raine and her gray-haired sea-daddy.

With a slight tilt of his head, Keir dismissed Barrows, who'd been shadowing the headstrong lassie exactly as he'd been instructed. The bosun's mate touched the knuckle of his forefinger to his brow in recognition of his captain's silent order and retreated to wait amidships. Still in view should he be needed, but well out of hearing range for ordinary conversation.

The relief on the able seaman's weathered face at handing over his responsibility, if only for a short while, didn't surprise Keir.

In fact, Keir had the distinct feeling that he, himself, was one of the few men in Scotland who could exert some measure of control over Raine Cameron.

Not that he'd ever lay a hand on her in anger.

Macraith had been right about that. But Keir couldn't think of another man whose force of will or sheer dominating presence could intimidate the plucky female. Or even slow her down, once she decided on a course of action. Including attending the birth of her cousin's baby.

"Will you show me how you measure the ship's position, Laird MacNeil?" Raine asked, her aura of self-sufficiency only slightly diminished by their conversation earlier when he'd all but accused her of lying.

Recognizing a request for a truce when he heard one, Keir smiled warmly. "I'll be delighted to show you how I use the astrolabe, Lady Raine. But first you need to be familiar with the major constellations."

"I began studying astronomy with my father when I was thirteen," she replied, "but Papa was killed before I'd had the chance to make any real progress."

The smothered pain in her voice was barely discernible, but Keir recognized her unspoken sorrow. Gideon had been defending his wife's honor when he'd been murdered—struck from behind by a coward.

Lady Nina Cameron had been the target of gossip about her daughter's parentage, for Raine had been born a black-haired, black-eyed child in a family of pale-eyed blonds.

In the Highlands and Isles, the Celtic belief remained strong that the Tuatha De Danann, motivated by love, would take someone exceptionally beautiful with them to the Otherworld. Superstitious people whispered that Raine had been sired by a black-haired elf prince. Some were ignorant enough to claim that the lassie was part faery and possessed magical powers. Others believed she had the second sight.

Keir and his two brothers had stood in the kitchen of Archnacarry Manor and pledged on Gideon Cameron's decapitated head to find the murderer and bring him to justice. At that same moment, the protection of Raine and her mother had become not only Alex Cameron's responsibility, but the three half brothers' as well. 'Twas a duty none of them had ever taken lightly.

Keir chucked Raine under her chin in a silent gesture of consolation. "Meet me this evening on the quarterdeck, and we'll begin your lessons."

"Thank you, Keir," she said, a heartfelt smile lighting up her face. "Thank you so much."

"You're welcome."

Darling lass.

THAT NIGHT KEIR stood directly behind Raine on the starboard side of the quarterdeck, teaching her to recognize the constellations. He'd been correct when he'd told Macraith she'd brains enough for two females. She was the brightest woman he'd ever known. And that included his wise and perceptive mother, Lady Emma.

"Now over there," he told Raine, "you can clearly make out Ursa Major." He put his hands on her shoulders, turning her slightly, and pointed to a group of stars almost directly above them.

Her face uplifted, she smiled in recognition. "Ah, yes," she said, scarcely above a whisper. "Papa taught me about the Great Bear stalking across the night sky."

" 'Tis also known as the Plough," Keir explained, "because of the shape made by its seven brightest stars. The two stars at the front of the Plough's blade are called the Pointers. Do you see them?"

"I do," she said, nodding happily.

Keir glanced down at Raine, her delicate features as close to perfection as any he'd ever seen. Her skin glowed flawless in the pale light of the crescent moon.

He resumed the lesson, determined to resist the effect of her tantalizing nearness upon him. "A line drawn through the Pointers leads directly to Polaris," he continued, tracing the imaginary marking above them with his index finger. "The Pole Star lies only one degree from the north celestial pole—a mariner's guidepost in the night sky, so to speak." He paused and looked down to meet her inquisitive gaze. "Am I boring you with too much information?"

"Oh, no," she declared. "I find it fascinating."

Keir shared her feeling of fascination, but that night it

wasn't with the stars. He fought the urge to trace the line of her smooth forehead down her dainty nose to her soft mouth. To brush his finger over her full bottom lip, across the edge of her teeth, and touch the tip of her pink tongue.

He knew, without a doubt, how shocked and repulsed she'd be by such familiarity—and her feeling of utter betrayal by someone who was supposed to be a trusted family friend. A friend she had known from childhood.

"Did you know that the constellations were named by the Greeks?" he asked, fighting his way through the fog of lust that enveloped him. "And each one has its own mythological tale."

During Raine's lesson with Keir, Abid al-Rahman, the ship's Moorish navigator, gave instructions in the use of the astrolabe on the forecastle deck. His two students, Ethan and Robbie Gibson, had been fostered to Keir the previous spring. The boys' father was a MacNeil kinsman who'd entrusted their training to Keir and his uncle to prepare them for a life on the sea.

Suddenly the two ship's boys were standing at Raine's elbow, looking up at the stars with them. "Ask the captain to tell you the story of the Great Bear," Robbie suggested. The ten-year-old had a thatch of bright red hair above a round face, liberally sprinkled with freckles.

"Pray tell me, Captain MacNeil," Raine said with a laugh of bell-like purity. "What is the story of the Great Bear?"

Al-Rahman had followed the Gibson brothers from the forecastle, ready to pull them back at a signal from Keir. The starboard side of the quarterdeck was the sole domain of the ship's captain.

"Forgive us for the interruption, sir," the Moor said. "I'd released the young gentlemen to their quarters. They must have been drawn by the presence of the lovely lady."

Keir was well aware of the audience scrutinizing his every move. 'Twas no accident the entire night watch had managed to creep within hearing distance. Two look-outs hung in the rigging above Keir and Raine, perilously close over their heads.

Stifling a grin, Keir resumed his lesson. "Ursa Major is associated with the huntress, Callisto, a favorite of Artemis, the goddess of hunting," he told Raine. "One day Zeus assumed the guise of Artemis and lay with Callisto."

"Zeus is the strongest of the gods," Ethan interjected in an attempt to be helpful. Two years older than his brother, he had dark auburn hair and a faint splash of freckles on his nose. "Zeus can tell all the others what to do."

"Like our captain," Robbie added proudly.

"Oh, I see," Raine said, nodding to show she understood. She glanced at Keir, her eyes sparkling with laughter.

Despite her hilarity, Keir returned to the lesson. "Callisto bore Zeus' son, Arcas. But Hera, the wife of Zeus, became jealous and turned Callisto into a bear."

"Two women fighting over Zeus," Robbie pointed out, "just like—"

"Shh," Ethan hissed, as he clamped his hand over his younger brother's mouth.

Keir frowned at the two and prayed the remark went over Raine's innocent head. "Then Zeus placed Callisto in the heavens as the Great Bear to prevent her from being accidentally killed by a hunter." He turned to his navigator.

"And now, Mr. al-Rahman, if you've finished the evening's lessons, you can release the midshipmen to their quarters."

The three immediately withdrew, retreating down the steps to the main deck and disappearing into a companionway.

Her dark eyes flashing in the moonlight, Raine met Keir's gaze. "Whenever did you learn about Greek mythology?" she asked. "Not in your days as a privateer, I should think."

Keir grinned at her open astonishment. "Contrary to court gossip, Lady Raine, I didn't spend all my time at the university in Paris drinking and gambling. Just a great deal of it."

"When will you teach me how to use the astrolabe?" she persisted.

Assuming the mien of a disapproving professor, he frowned at her. "You'll need to recognize more than one constellation, lass, before you can do that."

She laughed outright at his tone of condescension. "You doubt I could learn? Indulge my curiosity, if you please. I'd like to know how you chart our course across the unmarked ocean."

"Navigation requires a great deal of mathematical calculations," he hedged. "I'm afraid you'd find it all very boring."

"Still you could explain what you're doing the next time you plot the ship's course. I might not understand everything, but perhaps I could follow a bit of it." She wrinkled her nose mischievously. "After all, you agreed with Macraith that I am a lass o' parts," she reminded him.

"Aye, I did," Keir agreed. "But my uncle would make a better tutor than me. Macraith has far more patience with impetuous halflins." At her look of disappointment, he added impulsively, "We could try one morning and see how well you like it. You're free to tell me, if it becomes tedious."

Too late Keir realized he'd just made a serious misstep. In his attempt to please her, he had committed himself to spending time with Raine in the confined space of his cabin. Naturally, either Macraith or Barrows or both would be right at their side. He'd damn well see to it.

THE NEXT MORNING Raine stood at the bow of the ship, looking out over the waves. The crisp air fanned her cheeks and tickled her nose with the tangy scent of salt water. She closed her lids and lifted her face toward the cerulean sky, enjoying the sensation of moving across the living sea. A sea that teemed with fish and dolphins, while gannets and gulls soared overhead.

When she opened her eyes, Keir stood beside her.

" 'Tis bonny in the morning," he said with a grin of understanding.

She nodded. "It seems so peaceful with only the *Hawk* and the *Dragon* in sight. It's hard to believe that somewhere men are planning to wage war."

Keir turned his head and looked across the whitecaps at the two galleons racing along beside the *Raven*. Raine could hear the regret in his somber tone.

"Aye," he replied. "The more we Scots fight amongst

ourselves, clan against clan, the weaker we become as a nation."

"Do you think we'll ever know peace?"

"I hope so," he said. "Once this rebellion is put down, and the traitors are taken to Edinburgh to be tried and executed, there may be a chance for a lasting peace."

"Who is it you suspect of treason?"

Keir met her gaze, a scowl creasing his scarred forehead. "Not *suspect*, Lady Raine. Torcall MacMurchaidh has declared his support of Donald Dubh. That makes him guilty as sin."

"So you'll kill him without a qualm if he doesn't surrender his castle?"

Keir shrugged. " 'Tis the way of it, lass." He must have read the dismay on her features. A dismay she tried to hide. Or perhaps 'twas the way she'd stiffened at his words. "I'll nay kill a man if I don't have to," he said, his deep baritone revealing his stubborn pride. "I'm not a bloodthirsty monster, in spite of what you may have heard."

Remembering how she'd called him an ogre, Raine bit her lower lip in embarrassment. She peeked up beneath lowered lids to meet his solemn gaze. "I know that, Keir. Gideon held you and your brothers in the highest esteem. And my mother loves the three of you as though you were her own sons."

"And do you think of me as a brother, Raine?" he asked, his words so low she could barely hear him. He bent his head, as though intent on her reply. His side-braids fell forward and the gold hoop in his ear swayed.

She stared at Keir in shock at the preposterous suggestion. The memory of her vision of the two of them brought a flush to her cheeks. Her words came out in a plaintive croak. "Do you think of me as a younger sister?"

He paused for the space of a second, then seemed to choose his words with care. "I think of you as the beloved daughter of a close family friend."

Inexplicably, his polite, measured answer brought a feeling of acute disappointment, as though a marvelous prize had just slipped through her fingers.

Raine turned to look out at the wood-carved black raven, its wings spread wide above the long, pointed bowsprit. "What more do you know of Laird MacMurchaidh, other than his support of Macdonald as the lord of the Isles?"

"Torcall is kinsman to the earl of Argyll by way of marriage. And as you must already know, Donald Dubh is Argyll's grandson.

"Have you ever met MacMurchaidh?" she persisted, knowing she risked rousing his suspicion with too many questions.

"A few times," he said. "Why do you ask?"

"Simple curiosity," she lied.

They turned at the sound of the ship's bell ringing the hour. Raine had learned to tell the time by its pleasant *ding-ding-ding*, for it measured the day and night every thirty minutes. A continuously ringing bell would mean a man had fallen overboard, or worse—abandon ship.

"Time for the midday meal," Keir said, apparently distracted from their conversation by the thought of food.

She smiled in relief. "I wonder what Cook has prepared for us today."

RAINE FOUND LIFE on the three-masted galleon exhilarating. She quickly learned many of the seamen's names and their assigned tasks. The bosun, Adam Wyllie, was in charge of the deck crew and rigging. He was a tall, cheerful man with hands the size of melons and a mahogany braid so long he tucked it into the back of his belt. Iain Davidson, the ship's carpenter, stood no taller than Raine and had a perpetual squint, as though always looking straight into the sun. The quartermaster, Simon Ramsay, was a solemn-faced man with a lantern jaw who rarely smiled. He attended to the steering, the ship's compass, and the signals amongst the three ships. While the cook probably held the most important post of all—feeding a crew of two hundred and fifty hungry sailors three messes a day.

Fortune had favored Raine when Keir assigned Jasper Barrows to be her sea-daddy, for the little man had a garrulous nature and he regaled her with endless stories of the *Raven*'s sea battles and the individual heroism of each member of the crew. Two seamen, however, captured her special interest.

"Tell me about the Moor," she said, indicating the crewman on the forecastle deck. Standing well over six feet tall, he wore a lavishly embroidered caftan with loose-fitting trousers tucked into knee-high red leather boots. In his wide cloth sash, he carried a huge, curved scimitar. The Moor's hairless head, decorated with intricate inked swirls, glistened in the bright sunshine.

"That's Abid al-Rahman, the *Raven*'s chief navigator," Barrows told her with an amused chuckle. "As a young lad, he was trained as a scholar in Alexandria. He'd even written a paper on the many uses of the astrolabe. His owner, a rich pasha, sold him off as a galley slave in a fit of anger. The cap'n rescued al-Rahman from the wreckage of a sinkin' Ottoman galley."

"Oh, my," Raine said sympathetically. "What could have made the pasha so angry?"

Barrows looked out over the waves. "That I would nay ken, milady."

Raine had the distinct feeling that he did know, but wasn't about to tell her.

"And the seaman standing beside the Moor?" she asked, motioning to the man with a ferocious visage. His black beard and mustache were trimmed short and neat, leaving multiple scars still visible beneath. "Why does he address me so politely as *domina*?"

That's Apollonius the Greek," Barrows replied. "He was an orphan raised by Christian monks on Rhodes. They taught the laddie to be a scribe and how to copy manuscripts in Latin. When the monastery was overrun by pirates, he was taken captive."

"How did he end up on the *Raven*?"

"We boarded a pirate ship durin' a sea battle. Apollonius came forward, surrendered his sword to the cap'n, and begged to be rescued."

One afternoon Raine and her sea-daddy were joined on the aftercastle by the ship's youngest midshipmen, also called middies and midshipmites in jest. "Tell us more about Captain MacNeil," Robbie asked, sitting down cross-legged beside her.

Attired in the borrowed sailor's outfit, Raine sat on the edge of the poop deck, her legs swinging over the side. "Oh, aye," she agreed. "Tell us another story."

"Indeed, I shall, milady," Barrows said with a chuckle. "Ye should've seen the cap'n the day he earned that scarred-up busted nose of his. Himself scalin' up the side of an enemy galleon like a bloody baboon and runnin' smack into an evil-eyed whoremonger of a Dutchman with a cutlass as long as his arm."

"I've heard this story before," Robbie whispered, leaning in closer. " 'Tis a good one."

His shock of auburn hair ruffling in the sea breeze, Ethan nodded his agreement. "You'll like it, Lady Raine," he assured her. "No one's braver than our captain."

Barrows harrumphed, pretending annoyance at the interruptions.

"Oh, do go on," Mr. Barrows," Raine encouraged. "I'm anxious to hear the rest of the tale."

"Well 'twas a blessin' the clumsy bugger struck the cap'n with the weapon's handle and nay the blade," her sea-daddy continued. "The blow nearly knocked the cap'n back into the water. After the boardin' and fightin' was over and done, himself sat on an upturned barrel on the blood-soaked deck while Mr. MacNeil stitched up the cut as neat and tight as a wee, dainty maiden sewin' her weddin' clothes. 'Twasn't nothin' could be done for that crankled snout, howsoever."

"The captain has a broken nose," Robbie explained in earnest, pointing to his own pug one covered with bright orange spots.

"That's what he means by a snout," Ethan added.

"Oh, he does?" Raine asked, pretending amazement.

Barrows tipped back his grizzled head and hooted.

The two lads joined in with such infectious laughter that Raine started to giggle.

At that moment, Keir MacNeil came up from belowdecks to stand beside them. The sun glinted off the gold hoop in his ear, and with his scarred, battered face, he looked more like a pirate than the commander of a squadron in the king's fleet. He raised a jagged brow in speculation.

"Seems Barrows is keeping you well entertained," he said, looking from one to the other with obvious suspicion. "I hope he's teaching you something instructive about life on a ship and not just indulging in idle chatter."

"Oh, indeed," she replied with a solemn air. "We would never sit and gossip like fishwives. I'm truly learning a lot."

The two brothers leaped to their feet, gave their captain a quick salute, and hurried away.

Raine and her sea-daddy exchanged furtive glances, then looked out over the churning waves, each in an opposite direction. She bit her lip and held her breath, determined to stifle the giggles bubbling up from inside.

As LIFE ON board ship fell into a routine, Keir would accompany Raine up into the rigging every morning, where they'd sit on the same upper crosstree, one on each side of the mainmast, and look out upon the vast ocean just as the sun rose above the horizon. They were often content to sit in silence, simply appreciating the beauty around them.

'Twas here that Raine glimpsed a side of Keir she'd never suspected. She'd always thought him lacking in any genteel feelings. Unlike his gifted brother Lachlan, Keir had never written a ballad praising a lady's beauty and grace. Once, however, he'd entertained the Scottish court by changing the lyrics of an elegant love song Lachlan had composed into a bawdy ode to a lusty milkmaid. Everyone seemed highly entertained. Everyone except Laird Mac-Rath and his ladylove.

Raine had been too young at the time to be present at court when it happened. She'd overheard the grown-ups reminiscing with great hilarity about it later. By that time, Lachlan had joined in the laughter with his two half brothers.

She'd learned early on that the three Hellhounds of Scotland shared a wicked sense of humor. Yet where Rory and Lachlan believed that Raine had been blessed with the second sight and listened respectfully to her visions, Keir had always been quick to voice his skepticism about anything to do with magic charms or spells. Especially where she was concerned.

"You seem to be getting along well with your sea-daddy," Keir commented the morning after he'd found them laughing together.

"Oh, yes," Raine said. She peeked around the mast to meet his gaze. "He's been telling me about your exploits in battle," she explained. "According to Barrows, you're nigh invincible."

"I wish to God that were true," Keir replied soberly.

He looked out at the far horizon as though deep in thought, and when he spoke again, she could hear his concern for the men under his command. Men who would sail into hell with him, should he ask it.

"No one can predict how a sea battle will go," he continued quietly, as though speaking half to himself. "We can only prepare for combat as best we can. We can practice at blowing up barrels till we're choking in the smoke and soot. We can drill the crew in the setting and trimming of the sails over and over again. However in the heat and confusion of the fighting, anything can happen. A chance change in the wind can spell sudden disaster."

Raine sat in silence, not knowing what to say. 'Twas as though she'd just peeked into Keir's private world to discover an inner fear, not for himself, but for the lives of the seamen who viewed him as some sort of demi-god. Till that moment, she'd only known the brash, self-confident privateer. And what she'd just learned left her feeling bewildered. And a little guilty. She'd wormed her way on board the *Raven* by trickery and deceit. At the time, she'd only considered how best to outwit The MacNeil in order to reach her own goal. Not the burden she'd placed on his shoulders by her unwanted presence.

When it came time to descend, Keir helped her make her way down as he always did, carefully guiding her feet, staying as close to her as possible, ready to catch her should she slip. Never touching any part of her except her ankles, covered in the thick boys' socks.

Once safely back on deck, he accompanied Raine toward the forecastle, where Barrows stood on the larboard side like a conscientious nursemaid waiting for her charge's return from an outing with a parent.

"We're fast approaching Cape Wrath," Keir told her as they walked across the main deck. "We'll soon be sailing into the Minch. This afternoon, Macraith and I will meet with Fearchar and Colin, along with their seconds in command, to draw up the siege plans for the castle at Steòrnabhagh."

At the mention of her father's fortress, a cold hand seemed to clutch Raine's heart. She'd heard the rumors that Torcall MacMurchaidh had not only joined the rebellion, but he was also sheltering the self-acclaimed lord of the Isles.

"Perhaps you can persuade Donald Dubh to give himself up," Raine suggested, though she knew such an extraordinary thing would probably never happen. The enmity and distrust between the clans of the Hebrides and the kings of Scotland had festered for generations.

"As the high chief of Clan MacDonald, the lad's not likely to sue for peace before there's so much as a skirmish fought," Keir replied. He clasped Raine's elbow and brought her to a halt. "When we approach the Isle of Lewis," he continued, "I'll send a boat ashore with three strong men to guard you. That will be three days before our ships enter the harbor, so you'll be safe during the bombardment of the castle. My men will take you to your cousin's village of Tolm. Perhaps you'll be in time to help your kinswoman with the birth of her child after all."

"Oh, no!" Raine cried, appalled at the news. "I must go on to Steòrnabhagh with you."

Keir scowled. "Nay, lass, you can't be on board the *Raven* during the battle. 'Twould be far too dangerous.

We'll put you ashore well before we sail into Steòrnabhagh harbor. After Castle Murchaidh is taken, I'll send an escort for you."

"There's no reason for me to go to Tolm," she admitted reluctantly, looking out across the waves to avoid his eyes. "I've no Cousin Lavinia, and no one I know is giving birth to a child on the Isle of Lewis or anywhere else."

He stared at her, a growing awareness of how completely she'd tricked him darkening his gaze. "Then you lied to me from the beginning," he said in a low, cold tone. "Damn it to hell, Raine, you've been lying to me from the moment you arrived in Inverness. Why on God's earth would you put yourself in such danger for no good reason?"

"Well, you're wrong there," she replied, refusing to be cowed by his anger. "I have a very good reason. I simply can't share it with you."

"You'll tell me," he grated through clenched teeth. "You'll damn well tell me, Raine Cameron. Or you'll spend the rest of the voyage locked in your cabin."

Chapter 5

IN SPITE OF Keir's threat, Raine was allowed above decks to greet Fearchar MacLean and Colin MacRath when they came aboard the *Raven* that afternoon. With them were their seconds in command. Colin's father, Walter, had sailed with the *Sea Hawk*'s owner and captain, Lachlan MacRath, since the day the galleon had been launched at the shipyards of Dumbarton. Tam MacLean had started as ship's boy on the *Sea Dragon* when it first put out to sea. Both were experienced sailors as well as loyal kinsmen. Every man wore a sword at his side, a claymore on his back, and a dirk shoved into his belt.

Raine had changed for the occasion from her boy's garb to a primrose wool gown. She'd wound her long single braid into a coronet on the top of her head. The steady sea breeze tugged wisps loose in front of her ears and the unruly tendrils brushed across her cheeks and got caught in her eyelashes.

"L-lady R-raine," Colin said, sweeping off his plumed Scottish bonnet. He wore the red-and-black MacRath plaid, and his fiery hair blazed in the sunlight. The young man bowed and kissed her hand with quiet gravity. He leaned back a trace and searched her eyes, as if to reassure himself that he'd made the right decision in sending her over to the *Black Raven*. "You're l-looking w-well," he said, pausing to study her further. Waiting, no doubt, to hear her affirm that she had, indeed, not suffered from Keir MacNeil's well-known temper.

His father, Walter, stood beside him. He bowed to Raine, whom he had first met at Archnacarry Manor when she was a youngster. "Milady," he said in his deep, gravelly voice. " 'Tis a pleasure to see you again." His wide grin, with its chipped front tooth, revealed a good-natured acceptance of the follies of mankind.

Coming to join them, Fearchar flashed his infectious grin. His good eye, the color of a robin's egg, twinkled merrily. Placing his huge hands around her waist, he lifted Raine off her feet and twirled her in a circle. "My bonny lassie," he boomed, "you're brighter than a new-minted penny. Have you learned to chart the *Raven*'s course yet?"

He set Raine back down, bent and kissed her forehead with a noisy smack. He'd known her since she was a toddler, had bounced her on his knee. Each time he and his cousin, Laird Rory MacLean, had come to visit Gideon Cameron at Archnacarry Manor, Fearchar had brought a trinket for Raine from their wide-ranging travels aboard the *Sea Dragon*.

Surprised by her old friend's astute remark, Raine glanced at Keir, who stood glaring at Colin.

"Aye, nearly so," Macraith answered for her. "We're just about to begin Lady Raine's schooling at sea. The lassie's meant to be an admiral of the fleet."

Fearchar gave a crack of laughter. Nearly seven-foot tall, he was a giant of a man with a black patch over the eye he'd lost in battle.

He was the only person Raine had ever met who was larger—and possibly even more ferocious—than Keir MacNeil. Like Keir and Macraith, while at sea, Fearchar wore his long hair in a seaman's pigtail, along with two narrow side-braids fastened with exotic glass beads.

His kinsman, Tam, had the golden hair of the MacLean clan and their tall, athletic frame. "Lady Raine," Tam said with a warm, almost flirtatious smile. "What a pleasure to see you again. The sea air agrees with you, I see, for you are fairly blooming, with your rosy cheeks and lovely gown." Unexpectedly, he reached out and released a tendril of her hair that had snagged on her pearl earring.

The next instant, Keir stood beside her, his hand at her elbow. When she glanced up at him from the corner of her eye, she found him in a staring match with Tam. If she didn't know better, she'd think The MacNeil was jealous.

But in fact, she did know better.

She'd been present when Keir had declared in front of the entire Scottish court that one bonny lass was much the same as another. 'Twas last summer at the royal wedding in Edinburgh—right after he'd offered to marry Lachlan's pregnant mistress.

At the present moment, the group gathered around Raine looked more like cutthroat pirates than civilized Scotsmen loyal to one another and their king. But she knew they'd mutually pledged their lives and honor to capture and deliver for trial and subsequent hanging every traitor who'd risen up in rebellion against the Crown. And that included the dishonorable coward who'd deserted her pregnant mother—Raine's natural father, Torcall MacMurchaidh.

THE VISITORS TOOK over the starboard watch's mess for the midday meal. 'Twas the only room on the galleon that could accommodate their formidable bulk and give them some elbow room. Even then, the tallest among them couldn't stand up straight without banging their heads on the low ceiling's crossbeams.

Seated around the long rectangular table, the six men discussed their war plans while they ate. After the trenchers had been cleared away, Keir spread out a map of the Isle of Lewis.

"The entrance to the harbor is too narrow for us to sail abreast," he told them, running his fingertip along the waterway shown on the chart. "We'll have to enter in line formation till we've passed Arnish Point."

"There'll be guns in position to rake us as we come in," Fearchar warned. "There's a cannon emplacement on the point guarding the entrance to the harbor. Three twelve-pounders—iron breech-loaders—with a few men to guard and fire them, if need be. In happier days, Rory and I put in at the Steòrnabhagh shipyard, when the *Dragon* needed repairs."

"I'd rather not alert the castle of our coming," Keir replied. "We'll have to take them out."

"Aye," Macraith agreed with a jerk of his chin. He stroked

his beaded beard thoughtfully. "We can take a small landing party the night before and spike any guns on the point."

Fearchar nodded. "The harbor's deep. Once past the guns, there's plenty of room for three galleons to maneuver with ease."

"The *Raven* will go first," Keir said, tapping the map. "Followed by the *Hawk* and then the *Dragon*. We'll take up position for broadsides directly in front of the castle, but well out of their range until we can assess the size of their guns."

"No bigger than fourteen-pounders, I'm certain," Fearchar interjected. "And none with swivel mounts."

Keir returned the giant's smile of satisfaction. Like Fearchar, Keir loved the thrill of battle. "Amongst the three of us, we've the firepower of forty-eight long-range eighteen-pounders, plus the lighter pieces on our bows and sterns. Castle Murchaidh should fall in a matter of days."

"Who'll take charge of the prisoners?" Tam asked, a look of expectation on his comely face.

"We're only taking Macdonald and MacMurchaidh back to Edinburgh, plus any rebel chieftains we might find there. The rest we'll leave at the castle. We'll divide the felons among us." Keir turned to Fearchar. "We'll separate Donald Dubh from The MacMurchaidh. I'm going to entrust Macdonald to you."

Fearchar smoothed his fingers down his thick beard and grinned. He readjusted the band that held his eye patch and chortled with anticipation. "Forbye, 'twill be a pleasure to clap that pawky bastard usurper in chains and toss him in the *Dragon*'s hold."

"What about Lady Raine?" Colin blurted out as clear

and precise as a town crier proclaiming the news. The handsome redhead only stuttered and stammered around the beautiful ladies. That hadn't stopped him from gaining a reputation in the boudoir last summer. Thanks to his married Sassenach mistress, his prodigious stamina had been the talk of Edinburgh.

"Lady Raine's safety is *my* responsibility," Keir informed him in clear and precise words of his own.

Colin stiffened visibly, and Walter put a warning hand on his son's shoulder. "Aye, 'tis true enough," the elder MacRath agreed. "But as you know, we're all fond of the lassie. We would nay want to think of her caught in the midst of a siege bombardment."

"She won't be," Keir told them curtly. "Several days before we enter the harbor, I'll send Lady Raine ashore to the tiny village of Sanndabhaig with three able seamen to protect her. There's no chance she'll be caught in the fighting."

"What's at Sanndabhaig?" Tam asked with a baffled frown.

"Nothing but a few fishermen's huts," Keir replied. "She'll be perfectly safe. We can pick her up on the way back to the Minch."

"With your permission, sir," Colin persisted stubbornly, "Lady Raine has asked to return with me to the *Sea Hawk* this afternoon."

"Permission denied," Keir snapped.

Beneath his freckles, Colin's face grew white. He clearly struggled to control his redheaded temper. Like all Highlanders, he had a deep streak of independence and wouldn't tolerate being treated with contempt.

Fearchar met Keir's angry gaze, and the amusement lighting the giant's battle-scarred features brought Keir back from the brink. He glanced across the table at Walter, whose good-natured grin revealed the seasoned warrior's chipped front tooth. The humiliating awareness that every man at the table now suspected the secret that Keir had kept hidden for the last two years—even from himself— brought him to his feet.

"After the castle falls," he said, "we sail for Skye. Dismissed."

RAINE STOOD AT the larboard rail and watched the two longboats pull away from the *Raven*. She'd had only a short time to say good-bye to her friends before they disappeared over the side. And only a few brief minutes to speak with Colin alone. When he'd offered his apologies, she hadn't been the least surprised that Keir had refused permission for her to return to the *Sea Hawk*. She tried to hide her disappointment. She was fully aware that Keir stood on the quarterdeck above, watching them.

"Here," she said with a halfhearted smile as she handed Colin a faery arrow. "Take this with you. Long ago, tiny arrowheads such as this were used on mortals. The person struck was taken to the dwelling place of the faeries. But now the elf-bolt will shield you from misfortune."

Colin held the tiny piece of chipped flint on his large calloused palm for a moment, then closed his long fingers over it. He looked up from her offering to meet her gaze. His deep blue eyes shone with quiet understanding. "I—I appreciate y-your concern, L-lady Raine," he'd told her. Then he'd turned to make his way over the side of the *Raven*.

Now Raine clutched the railing, watching as the two longboats reached their respective ships.

"I think it's time for our interview now," Keir said, suddenly standing beside her. He clasped her elbow and led her down the companionway to her small cabin.

Once inside he folded his arms across his chest and glared at her. He didn't waste a minute getting to the point. "Why did you tell me that cock-and-bull story about a cousin needing your help during childbirth?" he demanded. "And this time, Lady Raine, I'd like to hear the truth. 'Twould be a welcome change, if nothing else."

Raine hung her head and bit her lip in an attempt to look penitent, while she ransacked her brain for a suitable—and believable—answer.

But Keir was evidently at the end of his patience. At her delaying tactic, he made a sudden move toward her, and for a split second Raine thought he was going to grab her and shake the daylights out of her. Instead he braced both hands on the wooden beam over her head, effectively trapping her without actually touching her. In the cramped space between his massive frame and her bunk, she was forced to tip her head back to meet his eyes, blazing now with what she could only assume was pure rage. Over twice her weight, with a body hewn of solid muscle, he hovered over her, and Raine had the unsettling sensation of being smothered by his overwhelming presence.

Her mouth suddenly dry, she tried to swallow and her throat constricted so painfully tears sprang to her eyes.

When she attempted to draw a deep, steadying breath, she made what sounded like a child's frightened whimper. She all but choked on her humiliation. She wasn't going to wail like a scared halflin in front of him.

Not Keir, of all people.

She blinked her lashes furiously, making a desperate attempt to stop the tears. She wasn't some insipid miss, who resorted to crying to get her own way.

Keir watched the crystal drops clinging to Raine's long black lashes and steeled himself against her utter femininity. He clutched the timber overhead with whitened knuckles, while he beat back the sexual desire coursing through his veins.

He realized too late, he should never have taken Raine into the privacy of her cabin. Not half-crazed with jealousy. Not pulsing with white-hot lust.

He'd reacted to Colin MacRath's attention to Raine like a possessive suitor. But dammit, the broad-shouldered redhead's prowess in bed had been the talk of the Scottish court that previous summer. Raine certainly must have heard the clattering tongues gossiping about Colin's exploits in Lady Diana Pembroke's bedroom.

"What did you give Colin just now?" Keir growled.

Raine stared at him as though he were mad.

"I saw you give him something before he left," Keir insisted. "What was it? A love token?"

"Why would you think that?" she said on a tiny hiccup of laughter. "I gave him a faery arrow to protect him. I gave one to Walter as well. In the past I've given them to Fearchar and Tam."

"But never to me."

"Why would I give one to you?" she asked in obvious bewilderment. Her brilliant eyes widened at the thought. "You don't believe in magic."

Bringing his hands down from the beam overhead, Keir stepped back and moved to the door. His gaze swept the room's Spartan furnishings before meeting her expressive eyes. "You'll remain here in your cabin, Lady Raine, until you're ready to tell the truth. I want to know why you're so intent on going to Steòrnabhagh that you'd stoop to lies and deceit."

Raine stared at the closed door, astounded and bewildered by Keir's behavior. Why would he care what she'd given to Colin? It didn't make sense.

What did make sense, however, was her pressing need to devise a believable reason for wanting to go to Steòrnabhagh. For she surely couldn't tell Keir the truth. If he knew she was trying to reach Torcall MacMurchaidh—the man he believed to be a traitor—Keir would do everything in his power to prevent it.

WITHIN THE SPACE of two days, Raine had had enough of being detained in her stuffy cabin. Thankfully she hadn't been condemned to solitary confinement. Her sea-daddy continued his lessons, teaching her the names of the *Black Raven*'s decks and various compartments.

They were joined by the ship's two young middies, who were expected to master mathematical calculations and the exact measurements of a galleon's sheets and yards. The computations were solved in their journals, which would be submitted to the captain at the end of each week for his perusal.

Barrows explained to Raine the importance of their skills at math. A small mistake in plotting navigation could result in arriving at the end of a voyage hundreds of leagues from their intended destination.

The sons of a wealthy Privy Councilor to the king, twelve-year-old Ethan Gibson and his ten-year-old brother, Robbie, would one day take their places as captains in the Scottish navy. They'd been fostered to Keir's supervision the previous spring in Edinburgh.

Using a worn book containing illustrations sketched for the purpose of instruction, Barrows would point to a drawing on a tattered, yellowed page. Sitting at the small table across from him, the three students would vie to be the first to identify the ship's section.

"Forecastle."

"Main deck."

"Amidships."

"Galley."

"Larboard quarters."

The youngsters' naturally sunny natures filled the cabin with chatter and boisterous competition. When Raine mistakenly identified a main staysail as a main topgallant, the two lads laughed uproariously. And when she called a mizzen sail a jib, they rolled on the floor in hysterics.

Whenever lessons were finished early, Raine would entertain the boys with Celtic wonder tales. "If the Tuatha De Danann become enamored of a comely lad or lassie," she told them, "they take the helpless mortal to the faery homeland of Avalon, somewhere in the western sea. Our legendary hero, Cúchulainn, was taken by a faery queen, who'd fallen in love with him. There was music and dancing and abundant food and drink at her palace. She kept him there for three years, before acceding to his many requests and allowing him to return to his home."

"I hope a faery never takes me," Robbie said, his blue eyes wide with concern.

"Don't worry," Ethan replied, punching his brother on the shoulder. "You're nay comely enough for a faery to fall in love with you."

Everyone broke into laughter, including the youngster himself.

Still, in spite of the boys' spirited companionship, being confined to her quarters started to take its toll.

GLANCING OUT THE small window of her cabin on the third morning after Keir delivered his ultimatum, Raine longed to climb up into the rigging with him to watch the sunrise. She admitted reluctantly to herself that she missed the way he'd explained the various sails and their purpose. She missed his teaching her how to recognize the constellations during the stillness of night watch. She missed sharing meals with him in his personal quarters. Keir had always invited one or two men to join them, and the dinner party always enjoyed a lively conversation. Now she ate a solitary meal in her cabin and hated the loneliness.

Restless and bored, Raine felt as though she'd been cut off from the life of the ship. 'Twasn't Keir, himself, she longed for but the camaraderie of the entire crew. They'd soon be approaching the Isle of Lewis, and Keir intended to set her on shore several days before sailing into the harbor of Steòrnabhagh.

That afternoon, she interrupted Barrows' lesson with a question of her own. "Would you be kind enough to set our schooling aside for the day? I've a request to make."

Barrows lifted his bushy gray brows and eyed her suspiciously. He'd been in enough trouble on account of her already. Clearly he had no intention of going from the boiling kettle into the flames. "And what would that request be, milady?"

"Please find Laird MacNeil and beg him to spare me a moment of his time."

Her sea-daddy grinned his approval. "Lesson's over, gentlemen," he told the two brothers, who immediately jumped up from their chairs and raced through the open doorway.

"Aye, Lady Raine," Barrows continued, "I'll be pleased to take your message to the cap'n. And I daresay, he'll be happy to receive it for he's done nothin' for the last two days but glare at the lot of us and bark orders like a cantankerous ol' seadog."

Less than five minutes later, Barrows returned. "The cap'n says he'll see ye now, milady. I'm to escort ye to him."

FROM HIS PLACE on the starboard side of the quarterdeck, Keir watched the bosun's mate bring Raine up through the companionway and lead her across the main deck.

Keir had no intention of meeting her in private. By God, that was one mistake he wouldn't make again. Three days ago he'd almost grabbed Raine and pulled her to him. Not in anger as she most likely believed. Nay, 'twasn't rage that nearly turned him into a slavering beast. 'Twas plain unguarded jealousy and lust. He cringed inwardly when he thought of the revulsion that would have crossed her perfect features had she suspected what was in his thoughts.

The Camerons had been loyal friends to Keir and his brothers for years. He wouldn't repay their past kindnesses by betraying their trust. For though they may not have sent Raine to him as she'd first claimed, they would expect him to protect her from evil. And that included his baser self.

Keir watched her approach, once more dressed in the borrowed clothes of a cabin boy, with Barrows by her side. Even in the male attire, she exuded an untouchable, inviolable purity. She was femininity in its most perfect form.

Nay, Lady Raine Cameron wasn't for the likes of the Black Beast's Spawn. Her mother and uncle would most likely be the first to point out that Raine deserved a young, unblemished gentleman, perhaps the son of an earl or a member of the king's Privy Council. Hell, his own family would probably be quick to agree, for Keir had a reputation as an inveterate womanizer.

But neither was Raine for the likes of Colin MacRath or Tam MacLean. No man of Keir's acquaintance was worthy of her. But somewhere in Scotland there had to be an estimable man deserving enough to be her husband.

"Lady Raine," he greeted with a curt nod when the pair reached him. Glancing to meet Barrows' eyes alight with rampant curiosity, he dismissed the bosun's mate with an almost imperceptible jerk of his head. Keir knew better than to say a word within hearing of any man-jack of the crew. In the close quarters of a warship, gossip spread like wildfire. He wasn't about to feed the flames.

As Barrows moved away, Keir turned his attention back to Raine. "You asked to see me?" he inquired sternly. "I take it you're ready to tell the truth at last."

She gazed up at him, her wide-set eyes somber. "Aye," she replied in a tone of quiet resignation.

"Well," he prodded impatiently. "I'm waiting."

"You asked me to tell you the reason I came on board the *Raven*. Well the truth is, I embarked on this voyage because I wanted to reach the Isle of Lewis, where I hoped to see the standing stones of Calanais."

Keir stared at her long and hard, testing to see if she'd blush or turn her gaze away, a sure indication she was lying. He found her explanation hard to fathom. "Why would you want to see that collection of old rocks?"

She released a long, drawn-out sigh, as though unable to believe the absurdity of his question. "Aunt Isabel told me about the ancient stone circles when I was only a child. I want to visit the site and see for myself if there is any truth to the tales told about them."

"What kind of tales?"

"Tales of wonder and magic."

Keir stepped closer and bent his head. "Raine," he said softly, "the clergy frowns upon visits to the standing stones."

"I don't care," she answered with a stubborn lift of her chin.

Her determination didn't surprise him. Isabel Cameron had imbued Raine with foolish superstitions, including an unshakeable belief in magic. Fully aware of the curious gazes fastened on them, Keir drew a deep calming breath before continuing in a low voice. "What you and your aunt do in the safety of Archnacarry Manor is one thing. Exploring a primitive spot linked to pagan idolatry is another. Do you know, lass, what happens to women who are accused of dabbling in magic?"

A rosy hue spread across her cheeks, indicating that she did, indeed, know that anyone suspected of practicing witchcraft could be burned at the stake. "That's why I kept my reason for traveling to Lewis a secret," she said barely above a whisper. " 'Tis why I made up the story about a cousin having a difficult pregnancy."

Christ.

As maddening as Raine's explanation was, he didn't doubt the truth of it. Thanks to her befuddled aunt's influence, Raine had departed the safety of her home and family to go on a dangerous quest to observe the forbidden stones at Calanais.

Keir didn't have time to argue with her now. At the moment his goal was to sack the castle at Steòrnabhagh and take Donald Dubh Macdonald and Torcall MacMurchaidh prisoners. Then he'd disabuse Raine of the possibility of her errand.

Chapter 6

UNDER COVER OF the dense morning fog, the three galleons slipped past the gun emplacement on Arnish Point in line-ahead formation and into the natural sheltered harbor of Steòrnabhagh. Keir had planned to wait for several more days, giving the shore party plenty of time to spike the cannons on the point and return safely to the ship. But with the fortuitous appearance of the fog, he'd moved his timetable for the siege ahead.

From the *Black Raven*'s forecastle, Keir gazed through the drifting mist to the ancient fortress that had been the stronghold of the chiefs of Clan MacMurchaidh for centuries. As the ships tacked into the calm harbor and luffed into position for broadsides just out of reach of the castle's outdated iron cannons, he recalled the departure of Lady Raine with her capable escorts in the longboat the previous evening.

Along with Barrows, Keir had sent two of his strongest

men to guard her. Will MacElvie stood six feet tall with broad shoulders and muscular limbs. Stocky and built like a bull, Davie Swinton had proven his courage in the midst of battle time and again.

Raine seemed to understand he was sending her away for her own good. Seated in the bow of the longboat, she held her blue cape tight about her, the satin-lined hood covering her hair and part of her face. She never once looked back at the *Raven*..

The tiny fishing village of Sanndabhaig boasted only a few small crofts. The fishermen there were little interested in the problems between the clan chiefs of the Hebrides and the king of Scotland. They fished the nearby waters of the Atlantic and raised their flocks of sheep and goats much as their ancestors had for centuries. The sturdy fisher wives would offer the wellborn visitor their warm hospitality and shelter her in a cozy stone hut. Even now Raine was probably waking to the welcome smell of porridge cooking on the open fire. Keir remained certain 'twas the best decision. He was happy knowing she was safe.

Now when the fog gradually lifted, the inhabitants of Castle Murchaidh would be waking to discover a trio of warships with gun-ports open and long-barreled brass cannons ready to commence firing, clearly out of range of the fortification's ancient breech-loading weapons.

On the *Black Raven*, Keir stood beside his uncle. He waited patiently, giving the castle gunners the time to fire, certain his own ships were safely beyond their reach. He had no wish to demolish the fortress unless absolutely necessary. Once it became obvious the castle was outgunned, the chief of Clan MacMurchaidh might well make the decision to surrender before any great loss of life or the total destruction of his home.

Aboard the *Sea Hawk* and the *Sea Dragon*, Fearchar and Colin watched for the *Raven*'s signal to begin the siege. Every seaman on board the three galleons stood at his post. Belowdecks the gun crews waited, ready to load and fire the long-range eighteen-pounders.

In the breathless anticipation of the impending battle, the unnatural silence seemed to stretch on endlessly as the last of the morning mist lifted. Into this frozen tableau sailed a bright yellow fishing boat, its single patched sail stretched taut in the cool morning breeze.

"What the devil!" Keir rasped. He raced to the gunwale and watched the boat move steadily across the harbor, sailing directly between the castle and the three privateers bristling with guns. His heart stalled in his chest at the sight. Aboard the small vessel a slender figure wrapped in a blue cape clutched the mast with one hand and held up a piece of white cloth with the other.

"Mother of God," Macraith choked out in a strangled voice.

Not taking his eyes off Raine, Keir rapped out his orders. "Tell Apollonius to fire a warning shot well ahead of the fishing boat's bow. And tell the Greek if that cannonball comes anywhere close to Lady Raine, I'll personally skin him alive. Then lower the cutter for me."

When the order reached the master gunner on the gun deck below, a single cannon boomed. The shot fell harmlessly into the water well in front of the yellow boat, and her owner immediately reefed his solitary sail and waited to be boarded.

Before the captain's cutter could be lowered, another vessel moved into the arena. Skimming across the flat water, the *Raven*'s longboat closed in on the becalmed fishing boat.

IN THE YELLOW sailboat, Raine watched in fright as Barrows, MacElvie, and Swinton, pumping their oars as fast as they could, pulled alongside the fishing craft. She would never have willingly put them in danger. She thought the castle's bombardment was still days away. Dear Lord above, the dense fog had hid their imminent peril until it was nearly too late. "Get in the longboat, milady," Barrows shouted. "Quick! Quick! Before they start bombarding the castle!"

"You, there," MacElvie hollered at the fisherman whose boat she'd hired. "Help the lady with her things. If you don't do as we say, you bloody bastard, our captain will seize your boat and use it for cannon practice."

That brought him to the side of the sailboat. The tall, sea-weathered man heaved Raine's canvas bag carrying her personal effects into the longboat. "Please, I beg you, my lady," he said, "I can't make a living without my wee boat. I'll gladly return the unicorns you paid me."

"Of course," she agreed, giving Barrows her hand and clambering into the longboat. She looked back at the fisherman. "Keep the coins," she told him. "You've earned them with your courage. Thank your wife for her kind hospitality."

STANDING WITH HIS uncle at the *Raven*'s gunwale, Keir had watched the brief, animated discussion amongst the seamen in the longboat and the fisherman on the yellow sailboat. Relief washed over him when Raine joined the *Raven*'s oarsmen.

Deprived of his valuable cargo, the fisherman immediately spread sail and scooted across the harbor toward the town's port and out of harm's way.

"Look," Macraith told Keir, pointing to the castle's battlements. "They've struck their colors." They watched as the MacMurchaidh clan banner came down the flagpole and dropped out of sight.

"Aye, and thank God for that," Keir said, as he hurried toward the main deck.

The crew on board the *Raven* waited in mute dismay as the three men in the longboat plied their oars and quickly came alongside the galleon. Lady Raine was handed up the ladder first and helped over the side, followed by Barrows, who started his explanation even before his feet hit the deck.

"The lassie gave us the slip last night whilst we be sleepin', Cap'n," he began, as MacElvie and Swinton clambered over the gunwale behind him.

Speechless with fury, Keir reached Barrows in an instant, grabbed him by the collar of his shirt and the seat of his pants and hurled him overboard. The other two seamen immediately jumped over the side, saving him the effort.

Raine gasped in horror. She raced to the railing and looked down. Several crewmen had already descended to the longboat and were fishing the drenched men out of the cold water with boat hooks.

She whirled to find Keir stalking toward her, his face dark with rage.

"You beast!" she called, not caring who heard her. "Those men could have drowned!"

Without saying a word, he grasped Raine by the waist and picked her up, lifting her entirely off her feet. For a moment, she panicked, certain he was about to fling her over the side as well.

"I can't swim!" she screamed in terror, clutching at his shirt.

Not a member of the crew moved to save her.

Raine had the sickening realization that, to a man, they would stand by and watch as their commander tossed her overboard to her death.

Grim-faced, Keir set her back down and released her. His eyes crackled with a cold, banked anger. "There was never any danger of them drowning," he said in a low, terrible voice. "Every man of my crew knows how to swim."

Keir turned to his uncle. "I'll leave you to escort the lady to her cabin before I do something we'll all regret."

Macraith took Raine's elbow and gently turned her toward the companionway.

"He's a savage brute," she said, making no attempt to lower her voice.

Macraith shook his head. "Nay, you're wrong there, milady. 'Twas either toss the three idiots overboard or have them flogged, which they richly deserved," he continued calmly as he led her down the steps to her cabin. "And my nephew would nay have a man flogged whilst you're on board. So the fools ken they got away lightly enough, seeing that your safety was in their hands and they failed in their duty.

"Well, I—" she began and then stopped, as a dawning awareness of her own culpability cut short her explanation. Every man on board ship realized the three men's dunking had been her fault. Had they been flogged, the crew would have blamed her for every stroke of the lash.

The previous evening she'd bribed the fisher wife and waited until her three guards were sleeping. Then along with the fisherman, Raine had slipped out of the village and onto his yellow sailboat, just as the sun came up. She'd planned to reach the town of Steòrnabhagh and from there ride the short distance to Castle Murchaidh long before the bombardment started.

THE CASTLE FELL without a shot being fired.

Torcall MacMurchaidh and his guest, Donald Dubh, had sailed out of Steòrnabhagh harbor with their men-at-arms two weeks before, leaving only a small band of men to secure the fortress.

A talkative captain of the guard, relieved to still be alive, told the disappointed invaders that no one had expected privateers coming from the north. They'd been assured by informers that the royal fleet was amassing at the Dumbarton shipyards and would sail from the south for the Outer Hebrides in the next few weeks. Hence, Mac-Murchaidh's own galleon was hurrying southward to meet up with his Macdonald allies in anticipation of a sea battle.

No one was more disappointed to hear the news than

Raine. She'd risked so much only to have her hopes dashed once again. She hadn't been allowed to set foot onshore at Steòrnabhagh, let alone visit her father's surrendered fortress.

She'd believed that if she could reach the castle, she would meet the man who'd abandoned her pregnant mother. She wanted to ask him why, during all the years that followed, he'd never made a single attempt to seek Lady Nina's forgiveness. Or learn anything about his illegitimate child.

Raine had learned from Aunt Isabel that Torcall Mac-Murchaidh had married and fathered three sons. His third wife had died in childbirth fifteen years ago, after giving birth to a daughter.

Heartsick and disillusioned, Raine stood at the *Raven*'s taffrail and watched the castle grow smaller in the distance, as the three men-of-war sailed in line formation out of the harbor and into the Minch.

Raine knew that Keir remained on the quarterdeck above her, watching the filling sails and the men scampering amongst the ratlines and out onto the yards with unconscious grace. He hadn't come near her since that awful moment when she thought he was about to toss her overboard. After that, she'd never caught him so much as looking in her direction.

Dear Lord above, there was no doubt about it now.

He hated her.

She'd known since she was seventeen that Keir disliked her. He'd all but avoided her since that summer he'd come to Archnacarry Manor with Lachlan for a visit. Until then, Keir had been friendly enough in his rough, outspoken way. He'd sometimes teased her when she was a child, tugging gently on her braids and quizzing her on the multiplication tables. Truth to tell, she'd always compared Keir to his handsome older brother and found him wanting. 'Twas Lachlan who entertained her family with his Spanish guitar and magnificent voice. 'Twas Lachlan who had the looks of an archangel and the manners of a knight-errant on a quest for the Holy Grail.

When Lachlan MacRath had left for England the previous spring to escort the Tudor princess to her wedding in Edinburgh, Raine had known he would come back with his pregnant English mistress. She'd seen it in a vision and had shared the secret with Aunt Isabel.

The summer before, when she'd just turned seventeen, Raine had also seen Keir in a vision, which she'd shared with no one.

No one at all.

For at the time, the dream seemed to evoke an erotic longing she'd never felt before. She'd refused to accept it then. And now, knowing that he hated her, she no longer needed to worry that the vision might come true. She had no intention of being added to Keir MacNeil's long list of discarded mistresses.

TWENTY MINUTES AFTER Keir had issued the invitation for Raine to join him at the evening meal, the stubborn lass appeared in the open doorway. He watched as she stopped short, her wary gaze flying around the otherwise empty cabin and then back to meet his eyes. She still wore the shirt and breeches of a cabin boy, but her ebony hair streamed over her shoulders, as though she'd been loosening her braid when his summons reached her.

"Don't worry, Lady Raine," Keir drawled, rising from his place at the table. "We won't be dining alone. Macraith will be joining us shortly."

She remained at the door, stiff and unsmiling, with her hands held sedately in front of her. When she spoke her voice sounded reedy and thin. "First I'd like to apologize for putting the lives of your three men in peril. If I'd known your ships would sail into the harbor that morning, I would never have risked our lives or the life of the innocent fisherman. I'd been told you wouldn't begin the siege for two more days."

Keir could read the sincere contrition in her worried eyes. He knew what a blow to her pride she'd suffered in humbly asking his forgiveness. "I changed our plans to take advantage of the fog," he explained, "and I accept your apology. I'd also like your promise never to leave the *Raven* without my permission."

Raine stared at him in obvious consternation. She lifted her chin and scowled. "I promise I will never put your men in jeopardy again."

"That's not what I asked."

"Since Mr. MacFarlane isn't here either," she parried, "I think it best that I return later."

"Nay, don't leave," he said, motioning for her to come farther inside. "There's something I need to ask you before Hector begins serving our supper." Keir gestured to the chair across from him. "Please, sit down."

"I'll stand," she replied in an icy tone. "What is it you wish to know?"

She could adopt the distant, imperial air of royalty when she chose to. 'Twasn't one of her more endearing traits.

"Sit down, Raine," he growled, his patience growing thin. He'd known this discussion would prove difficult, but he hadn't thought he'd have to wrestle her into her chair.

At his stern command, she dropped onto the cushioned seat, folded her hands in her lap, and lifted her brow expectantly.

Regaining his own place at the table, Keir leaned back and folded his arms. He wasted no time in coming to the point. "I want you to give me your purse of coins," he said bluntly.

She turned her face to the wall, presenting him with her flawless profile. "I don't know what you're talking about," she said, as she pretended to study the French tapestry he'd taken from a Flemish privateer three years ago.

"Aye, but you do," he countered, struggling to keep his tone easy and conversational. "I want the purse you brought with you from Archnacarry, Raine. The one holding the coins you used to bribe that damn fisherman at Sanndabhaig."

"Pooh," she replied scornfully. "What makes you think I gave him anything?"

"That poor soul may be an illiterate fisherman, but he's not an imbecile. Only a great deal of money would entice a rational man to give up a day's fishing to ferry a lady across the bay, leaving her guards behind."

"Perhaps he did it because I asked him politely to help me," she retorted, meeting his gaze at last. "Not everyone behaves like a . . ." She took a deep breath, as though suddenly afraid to go on.

Keir rose and braced his hands on the table, leaning closer. "Like what?" he prompted. "Like a beast? Don't cavil at the name-calling now, Lady Raine. We're quite alone. You've no one to shock here."

Her jet eyes flashing, she pressed her lips together as though struggling to keep a rein on her unruly tongue.

"Either you give me your purse," he continued quietly, "or I'll have your cabin searched. And if we don't find it there, I'll search your person myself."

"You'd go through my clothing and steal my money?" she asked, her words creaky with disbelief. "Why, you're no better than an Edinburgh pickpocket."

"You can consider me your banker," he said with a smile. She'd finally admitted she had the coins hidden somewhere. "I'll return the purse to your guardian the day I return you safely to your mother."

She blinked back tears. "Pray, don't do this, Keir. I beg you."

Her simple plea struck a weak spot somewhere in the vicinity of his carefully guarded heart.

Jesus.

Was she going to resort to weeping?

"Don't cry, Raine," he told her sternly. " 'Twill not work on me."

"I'm not trying to get your sympathy, you damn fool!" she said, dashing the back of her hands against the crystal drops clinging to her lashes. "These are tears of frustration because I'm a woman. For if I were a man, I'd—" She reached beneath the hem of her shirt, pulled out an embroidered moneybag from the waistband of her breeches, and threw it on the table. "There, Judas," she said. "There's your thirty pieces of silver."

Keir untied the cords and poured the gold unicorns and silver groats on the table. There wasn't a farthing nor a half-farthing nor a penny in the pile. "This is a king's ransom," he said in astonishment.

"My family has always been very generous to me," she replied. "And I knew better than to start out on a journey without some ready funds. 'Twould have been foolish."

" 'Twas damn foolish of you to begin this journey in the first place," he told her sharply.

Keir lifted a small heart-shaped stone, nearly hidden in the pile of coins. He turned it over in his hand, studying the strange writing carved into it. "What's this?"

She held out her hand. " 'Tis a token to bring good fortune," she said. "My aunt gave it to me for my protection just before I left Archnacarry."

"What does it say?"

"I'm not certain. 'Tis written in the age-old language of the Tuatha De Danann. Isabel promised it would keep me safe. May I have it now, please? 'Tis of no value to you."

At that moment, Macraith came through the open doorway. He bowed graciously to Raine as his gaze took in the scene. "My lady," he said with a warm smile, "what a pleasure to have you join us this evening."

Her face drained of color, Raine rose to her feet and

snatched up the stone Keir had replaced on the table. "I'm afraid I don't feel up to eating anything at the moment," she said with the briefest of curtsies. "So if you gentlemen will please excuse me, I think I shall retire."

Not waiting for an answer, she hurried out the door.

Macraith sank down on a chair across from Keir. "What's all this?" he asked, motioning to the coinage spilled across the dining table.

"I took Raine's purse from her for safekeeping," he told his uncle. "Just in case she takes it in her head to run off again."

"From the look on her face, I'd guess she was none too happy about surrendering her gold," Macraith replied. He smoothed his calloused fingers across the table, pushing the coins toward his nephew.

For a brief moment, Keir covered his eyes with one hand, then met his uncle's solicitous gaze. "What goddamn difference does it make if she's angry about it? I'm acting in her best interest." He shrugged. "She already detests me."

"Now, that's a wee bit strong," Macraith said. "Though at the moment, I'd hazard a guess that you're not high on her list of heroes."

"Oh, I'm not her hero, all right. You heard what she called me," Keir replied. "She thinks I'm exactly like my notorious father. A savage beast."

Folding his arms across his burly chest, Macraith shook his head. "Don't be an ass, man. At the time Lady Raine said it, she thought you'd just heaved her sea-daddy into his watery grave—and she'd be the next one tossed overboard. Of course, had that happened, there would have been two hundred and fifty seamen over the side in an instant, pulling her out of the water."

Keir recalled the fear that had propelled him to her that awful morning. He'd been so overjoyed that she was alive and unhurt, he'd almost pulled her into his arms. He'd almost showered her beautiful face with kisses and told her—what? That his heart had nearly stopped when he'd seen her aboard that goddamned fishing boat? That he wanted her more than he'd ever wanted any woman? Given her anger, she'd have spit in his face.

Keir glowered at his uncle. "How the devil could she believe I'd throw her into the sea to drown? What kind of monster would do that?"

"Perhaps you might consider showing the lassie your softer side," Macraith suggested. "I've never seen you treat a female so sternly before. You're usually busy coaxing the ladies into your bed."

Keir scowled at the idiotic advice. "Married ladies," he pointed out, "who were already cheating on their husbands before I ever came on the scene. Or trollops. I've never seduced a virginal maid—or a faithful wife—and you damn well know it."

"Christ, ye glaikit simpleton!" his uncle exclaimed. "I'm not telling you to seduce the lass! Just behave a wee bit kinder."

"Kinder!" Keir roared, losing all patience. "After seeing her almost killed through her own obstinate, willful behavior?" He began picking up the coins and slipping them back into the embroidered silk purse. "Do you realize how close Raine came to being killed?" he continued in a calmer tone. "If we hadn't waited for the castle's guns to deliver the first volley, or if MacMurchaidh hadn't already sailed, leaving a token contingent to guard the fortress, that goddamn fishing boat would have been blown clean out of the water. 'Tis only by a miracle Raine's alive today."

Macraith nodded solemnly. "Aye, you've the right of it there, lad. Where the devil did she think she was going anyway?"

"She refused to say. But I believe she wanted to reach the town, where she could pay someone to take her by horseback to Calanais."

"Why, in God's name?"

"To see the standing stones." Keir rose and rubbed the back of his neck. "Raine told me the whole reason for her journey was to visit the site of the ancient stones."

"Why ever would she want to visit such a desolate place?"

"God alone knows," Keir said. "But I'd lay the blame on her batty aunt. I warned Raine that the church discourages people from going to that pagan site."

"Aye, but we're going there anyway, aren't we?" Macraith said with a cheerful laugh. "That's why we broke formation this morning and are presently beating to windward, nor by nor-west."

Keir grinned. "I thought if I took Raine to Calanais, she wouldn't keep trying to sneak off. I don't have eyes in the back of my head, for Christ's sake. Short of chaining her to the bed in her cabin, I can't be certain she'll not try leaving again. And she's already proven she can outmaneuver three of my steadiest seamen and leave them swamped and floundering in her wake."

"Perhaps you should entrust her to Fearchar," his uncle suggested mildly. "She's fond of the old pirate. She might listen to him. Perhaps be less likely to run off."

"Raine is my responsibility and mine alone," Keir declared, unwilling to mention the fact that Tam MacLean was on board the *Sea Dragon*. "I will see that she gets home safely. I can do nothing less."

From the corner of his eye, Keir caught Hector peeking around the doorjamb. He carried a platter of beef pastries and stood waiting for the order to serve the meal.

With a wave of his hand, Keir signaled the lad to come in.

"Take a plate of food to Lady Raine's cabin," he told the midshipman quietly. He motioned to the bowl of oranges and apples in the center of the table. "Be sure she has the fresh fruit she likes and a glass of wine from my opened bottle on the sideboard there. And make certain there's clean linen and silver for her. Then you can come back and serve us."

Keir avoided his uncle's canny gaze. But he knew without looking, Macraith had a wide, speculative grin on his bearded face.

There was no privacy to be had on a galleon.

And keeping a secret was goddamn hard, if not impossible.

Chapter 7

KEIR PULLED ON the oars, sending the cutter shooting across the lapping waves and deeper into the sea's wide inlet on the western side of the Isle of Lewis. The setting sun behind him seemed to light their way across Loch Roag.

In the bow, Raine sat erect, holding on to the sides of the boat, her back straight and her gaze fastened on the destination ahead. He could sense the excitement coursing through her slim figure, an excitement so intense she seemed to vibrate with an unbounded energy.

The cool evening breeze pulled unruly tendrils from the long, thick braid that fell down her back. Beneath her heavy red cape, she wore her borrowed shirt and seaman's loose trousers.

"Are you certain this is the correct inlet?" Raine asked in a worried tone. She glanced at him over her shoulder. "Have you been to see the stones before?"

"Never," he said. "But aye, I'm quite certain. I've a detailed map of the loch and the area surrounding Calanais."

They had left the *Raven* anchored farther out in the wide sea inlet that emptied into the Atlantic Ocean. Keir wanted to be certain that members of the night watch couldn't see the two of them exploring the forbidden site. He had weighed the wisdom of bringing someone else along, for he'd been careful never to be alone with Raine since the evening he'd taken her purse. In the final analysis, however, the only person he could trust to keep their visit to the standing stones a secret was his uncle. And as second in command, Macraith needed to remain on board the *Raven*. 'Twas unlikely that an enemy ship would appear on the western side of the island, but it wasn't a chance Keir wanted to take without precaution.

Raine felt a thrill go through her as the stones appeared high on a ridge above them, outlined against the fading blue sky. There must have been at least fifty monoliths, rising up like sentinels from the distant past, gazing out to the far horizon and the uncharted ocean beyond.

During daylight the standing stones would have been visible from miles around on the windswept moor. Now the rays of the setting sun streaming through wisps of clouds bathed the stones in a soft pink glow.

"Oh, my," she said, tingling with exhilaration. " 'Tis just as I'd imagined from the wonder tales my aunt told me as a child."

"Isabel Cameron visited this site?" Keir asked, surprise apparent in his voice.

"Yes, several times in her youth," Raine replied. "Her

grandmother was born on the Isle of Lewis. She brought Aunt Isabel here to teach her about the age-old healing ways handed down by mouth from mother to daughter."

Keir steered the cutter up to the bank, stowed the oars, and jumped out. After he'd pulled the boat solidly onto the shore, he moved to help Raine. Her fascinated gaze remained locked on the standing stones above them.

Now that the sun had nearly disappeared beneath the western horizon, the monoliths rose up as dark shadows. To Keir's surprise, Raine calmly allowed him to scoop her up in his arms and carry her to dry ground. As he walked up the mossy bank, she placed one arm around his neck and looked up at him.

"Thank you for bringing me here," she said, her soprano voice soft and sweet in his ear.

"I was interested in seeing the place myself," Keir lied, "once you put me in mind of it."

Beneath her quiet scrutiny, his heart smashed against his ribs like the recoil of an eighteen-pounder. He assumed she was studying his disfigured face, now that she was up so close. 'Twasn't a pretty sight, but battle scars seldom were, and many a Highland warrior had suffered as bad or worse. His just happened to be across his broken nose, where none could miss it.

Glancing down, Keir met her inquisitive gaze, astonished when she offered a tentative smile. Well, hell, this was a definite improvement. She'd shown him nothing but scowls and a cold shoulder ever since he'd taken her wretched bag of coins. She'd succeeded in making him feel like the goddamned cutpurse she'd accused him of being.

"Tell me about these wondrous tales you heard as a child," he said, wanting to prolong the marvelous opportunity to hold her so close their faces were only inches apart. Her cool breath fanned across his cheek, sending a surge of desire spiraling through him.

"First let's go farther up on the ridge," she suggested. "And by the way, you can put me down now. I'm probably getting a little heavy, since we've been climbing steadily."

"You're not afraid I'll drop you?" Keir asked, and pretended to stumble.

Raine clung tighter, just as he'd hoped, and her smooth cheek brushed against his jaw.

"Ouch," she complained with a soft laugh. "Your whiskers are too rough. Now set me down, I insist."

Reluctantly, Keir complied, refusing to dwell on the thought of his bristly stubble brushing against her delicate skin. The heat of his need pulsed through his veins, as he inhaled the scent of roses.

God Almighty, she smelled like heaven.

They had come to an avenue outlined by a double row of standing stones, each taller than an average man and leading to the middle of the ancient site. He followed Raine as she hurried up the grassy pathway.

More standing stones formed a ring from which a line of smaller stones radiated in all four directions in an approximation of the Celtic cross. Keir watched Raine move into the ring, where she twirled in obvious pleasure.

Looking about with a radiant smile, she motioned for Keir to join her. As she caught his hand in hers, she pointed to four large stones that made up the innermost circle.

"Do you know why these stones are here?" she asked.

He shrugged noncommittally. "I've heard that the people on the Isle of Lewis call them *fir bhrèige*, false men," he said. "According to local tradition, these stones were once giants who lived on the island long ago. When they refused to be converted to Christianity by Saint Kieran, they were turned to stone as punishment."

Raine burst into laughter. "This place has nothing to do with Saint Kieran or any other saint. On this sacred ground is a temple dedicated to the Triple Goddess," she told him. She pointed toward the east. "Look at the hills just beyond. Some people say 'tis the shape of an old woman reclining."

Keir followed the direction of her finger, where the outline of the hilltops appeared against the darkening sky, "Aye, I can see that clear enough," he said. "But the old crone doesn't resemble a goddess to me."

Raine met his gaze, her flashing eyes still visible in the fading rays of sunlight. "Yet some people see a young woman with child whom they call the sleeping beauty. Not surprising, because this enduring landscape is dedicated to honoring the three phases of a woman's life."

She led Keir to one of the four stones that comprised the innermost circle. "This triangular stone represents the virginal maiden," she explained. "But of course, in order to become fertile, to become with child—which is necessary for the propagation of humankind—the female will need a male."

Keir looked down into Raine's heart-shaped face. In spite of her factual knowledge, her innocence shone from her luminous eyes. Her words left him struggling to breathe, as though the air had been sucked out of his lungs by a bilge pump.

"Aye," he agreed in a creaky voice, "that's usually the way of it."

Keir wondered if Raine had any inkling of the effect she was having upon him. He steeled himself against the allure of a temptation so overwhelming, no sane man could resist it. In spite of his high-minded intentions, his body reacted with traitorous urgency. His manhood thickened and pressed against the snug crotch of his breeches.

Purposefully and with an iron will, Keir pictured Raine in her early years, with her pair of long braids swinging about her. In her youthful exuberance, she had challenged him to an archery contest, undaunted by the fact that he was seven years older. At thirteen, she probably knew she had no chance to best him, but that hadn't stopped her from trying. Nothing and no one had ever intimidated Raine.

Clearly unaware of his licentious thoughts, Raine caught Keir's hand and led him to a smooth column that reached above his head. "Here," she said, patting the monolith. "This is the male stone. Can you not see it?"

With a jolt, Keir realized exactly what she was trying to show him. The sight of her graceful hand placed on the phallic symbol brought the image of her soft fingers caressing him in the most intimate way possible. Unfettered passion surged through him with the force of a tidal wave, threatening to submerge the carefully built barriers he'd erected against his rampaging desire for the last two years.

God help him, he was drowning in a sea of lust.

Serene as an angel reaching out to save a dying wretch, Raine tugged on his sleeve, leading him to the next standing stone. "And here," she explained in a matter-of-fact manner, "is the pregnant female, the mother of mankind."

In the last rays of the setting sun, the stone glowed blood red.

Looking up at him expectantly, she waited for his reply.

"You have a vivid imagination, lass," he said, hoping she wouldn't detect the carnal need in his raspy voice.

She chose to ignore his cynical remark. "And that rough stone over there," she said pointing to the fourth one of the inner circle, "represents the old crone in whom resides the wisdom of humanity's longing to reproduce itself." She lifted her arched brows and added as an afterthought, "Which, thankfully, we humans have accomplished since time immemorial."

Keir chose not to comment on the obvious truth of her statement. He had no intention of discussing mankind's unbridled concupiscence down through the ages with Raine. "We'd best be returning to the ship soon," he told her gruffly. "We shouldn't be absent too long."

"Of course," she replied. "But first, I'd like to view the stone circle from that vantage point over there."

"Aye," Keir agreed, reluctant to bring their visit to a close.

Together they climbed a small ridge and turned to look back at the standing stones outlined against the night sky. Gradually the full moon appeared through the dispersing clouds, so low on the eastern horizon it seemed to be hovering at the feet of the reclining beauty. As they watched, transfixed by the heavenly phenomenon, Keir slipped his arm around Raine's shoulders, drawing her close.

Above the four standing monoliths comprising the inner circle, the moon's brilliant orange glow approached the maiden stone, then slowly moved on, so low on the horizon that the lunar orb appeared to be penetrated by the tip of the phallic stone.

"Oh, look at that!" Raine exclaimed. "Did you see it?"

Keir nodded. "I did," he replied in astonishment. "Though I can hardly believe what I'm seeing."

The luminous tangerine sphere, closer to the earth than reasonably possible, seemed to dance along the top of the stones. Passing over the mother stone, the moon slowly moved along the hilltops to the reclining female's face and then finally approached the stone of the old woman.

Having studied the heavens, Keir realized that Raine's pagan temple must have once been used by the ancients for astronomical observations.

"I believe this site was designed for rituals connected with the movements of the sun, moon and stars," he told her in a hushed voice. "We've just witnessed a spectacular lunar event. I've never seen one quite like it before, where the moon appears so low on the eastern horizon as to touch the earth."

Raine smiled at her companion's scientific explanation, but shook her head in disagreement. "Perhaps the men of long ago used this place to study the stars," she conceded. "But for women it has always been a temple to the Mother of the Universe."

He grinned complacently and turned her toward the

east. "Follow that line of stones to where it leads into the sky," he insisted. "That group of bright stars is the rising Pleiades." He immediately added, " 'Tis also known as the Seven Sisters."

"And is there a story to help me remember that particular constellation?" she quizzed with a teasing laugh.

"There is," he replied with a soft chuckle. "The Greeks believed that the Pleiades were the seven daughters of Atlas and Pleione. The great hunter, Orion, saw the lassies one day and admired them. But the sisters became frightened and ran away."

"All too typical of some fainthearted females," she said, shaking her head in mock disgust. "But pray, continue."

"The hunter followed them, not wanting to lose sight of the lovely sisters."

"All too typical of some overzealous males," she interrupted again. When he lifted an eyebrow, indicating his exasperation, she waved her hand. "Do go on."

"When the timid lassies appealed to Jupiter for protection, he changed them into doves and they flew up into the sky. But amongst the stars, the hunter still seems to be running after the seven sisters. On cold winter evenings, Orion rises above the horizon soon after the Pleiades and strides across the heavens, followed by his dogs."

"I'll certainly remember that story," she said with a laugh. "You rival my aunt with your wondrous tales. Perhaps I *shall* master the constellations before our journey's end."

Keir felt a sharp jolt of unhappiness at the thought of her leaving his ship, of his continuing the voyage without her. Raine gazed up at him, her delicate features caressed by the moonlight. Her expressive eyes shining with happiness, she smiled at him shyly, and he knew, in that instant, she was the most desirable woman he'd ever known. Would ever know.

And with that realization came the sudden ache of irreparable loss. He would always and forever be his brutal father's brutal son. How many times had Keir heard it said that he was the living replica of the Black Beast of Barra? A man who'd been disliked and feared by everyone around him, including Keir's lovely mother.

When Keir spoke, his words came harsh and grating. "I shan't look forward to seeing you go, although I know you must."

At the tall warrior's words, Raine stopped short. She met Keir's gaze, and a sudden, unexplained yearning blossomed somewhere deep inside her. She stood absolutely still, just looking up at him, really seeing him for the first time without comparison to either of his older brothers. The world around them seemed to pause, as though waiting for something marvelous to happen.

Raine could feel the quiet of the night envelope them like a sheltering tartan. In her mind's eye, she took in the entire scene. The inner circle of four symbolic standing stones, the outer ring, the outlying avenues leading in the four directions, north, south, east, west. The two of them standing in a pool of moonlight. They might have been the only living beings on the face of the earth, and the whole world seemed to be holding its breath.

Raine gazed into his eyes, filled with an unexplained tenderness, and something stirred deep in her soul.

"Keir," she whispered, not knowing what it was she

wanted to tell him. "Keir . . . I . . ." She stepped closer and lifted her hand to his face. "I . . . want . . ." She traced her fingers along the square line of his jaw, prickly from a day-old beard. She inhaled the tangy smell of leather and Scots pine, as she followed the line of his upper lip with her index finger. He drew a deep, ragged breath at her exploring touch.

As Raine lifted her face to his, the fearsome warrior gently cupped her cheek in his hand and brushed the pad of his thumb across the closed seam of her lips. Keir gently slipped his thumb inside her mouth, moving across her teeth, to sweep along the sensitive edge of her tongue. The penetration was shockingly erotic. Raine tried desperately to hide the sexual excitement awakening inside her. With a deep sigh, she turned her face and pressed her lips against his calloused palm.

At the feel of her innocent kiss, Keir pulled Raine to him. No man could resist such incredible sweetness. In spite of all his resolutions, he lifted her up and covered her lips with his open mouth. He coaxed her closed lips open and touched the tip of her tongue with his, exploring the taste and feel of her. She responded by wrapping her arms around his neck and moving her tongue into his mouth. The unexpected intimacy threatened to bring him to his knees.

Her entire body quivering in delight, Raine brought her hands down to loosen the cords on the collar at the base of Keir's throat. She slipped her hands under his shirt in timid exploration. She could feel the muscles of his powerful shoulders tauten beneath her fingertips. She splayed her fingers along the base of his strong neck and felt his pulse throbbing beneath her thumbs.

Keir broke the kiss to follow the delicate line of Raine's jaw with his open mouth. He pressed light, lingering kisses along the pale column of her neck. He breathed in her intoxicating floral scent and groaned deep in his chest.

"Darling, darling lass," he murmured, before coming to his senses.

Keir abruptly set Raine down and stepped back, incensed at his own lack of control.

Dammit. Dammit. Dammit.

He'd brought her to this forbidden place with one intention and one only. And it sure as hell wasn't to seduce her.

After their visit to the standing stones of Calanais, she'd have no reason to run off. He could be assured that she would remain on board the *Raven*, until he reached a port where he could find a reputable family to protect her. When the rebellion had been quelled, he'd take Lady Raine Cameron home to Archnacarry Manor and her family. And goddammit, he would marry the maid of Strathfillan and make the best of it.

"We'd better go now," he said brusquely.

Before I lie with you in the soft grass.

Before I cover your body with mine.

Before I confess just how much I want you.

Averting her gaze, Raine gave a quick nod. "Yes," she whispered, "we should go now."

Together they quietly made their way back down the slope and returned to the cutter. Keir lifted Raine into the boat, shoved it into the water, jumped in, and retrieved his oars.

He looked back at the monoliths outlined by the

gleaming moon behind them, clearly the seat of an ancient power center. Keir was forced to admit to himself that Raine's aunt had been correct. The standing stones were wondrous, reaching back into mankind's collective memory. No one could visit them without becoming aware of the undying legacy left by Scotland's earliest peoples. 'Twas as though Keir and Raine had somehow communed with their remote ancestors.

They remained in awed, reverent silence as he rowed the cutter across the loch to the *Black Raven*.

Raine sat in shock at what had just occurred between her and The MacNeil. There could be only one explanation. They had blundered into a celebration of the Tuatha De Danann—the faeries. Lady Isabel Cameron believed in the faery faith, as did most of the people of Celtic descent, despite the conversion to Christianity by their forebears. In the Highlands and Isles, as well as all of Ireland, the two beliefs existed side by side, for the knowledge and acceptance of the faery world went too deep and was far too pervasive to be extinguished by the mere warnings of the religious clerics.

When Raine was young, Aunt Isabel had explained that the standing stones had been erected thousands of years ago as a temple to the Mother Goddess. But for the last millennium, it had also been a gathering place for the faeries. The belief in the coming of the Shining Ones by the local folk had been the real reason the clergy had forbidden visits to the sacred site.

Her aunt had taught Raine about the Tìr-na-nog—the Otherworld. The world inhabited by the faeries. At

Calanais, Raine and Keir hadn't just become enraptured by the power of the standing stones and the moon's mysterious standstill. Oh, no. At the entreaty of the faeries, the Mother of the Universe had coupled them together, as surely as if they'd said their marriage vows in the cathedral of Edinburgh. There was no human being on the face of this earth who could change it.

It had happened.

That was that.

'Twas imperative now that Raine leave the *Black Raven* before any intimacy occurred between her and Keir. If she kept her distance from him, if she remained vigilant, careful not to touch him or—God forbid—kiss him again, perhaps she could escape the ship before the irresistible attraction caused by the evening's magic took over their individual self will. Not that it would change anything in the end. All she could do was gain a little time. Time enough to find her father.

At last she understood the vision she'd seen during her seventeenth summer. The eroticism of the dream had been a foretelling of things to come. If she were ever to find her natural father, if she were ever to accost Torcall MacMurchaidh with his despicable behavior toward her mother, she had to leave the *Black Raven* as quickly as possible. And in order to leave, she had to retrieve her money.

Deep in his own thoughts, Keir plied the oars in a steady rhythm. Guilt and self-loathing at his failure to keep his distance from Raine sat across his shoulders with the weight of an anchor.

He should never have touched her.

He would never touch her again.

As they approached the galleon, with its stern lanterns winking across the still water, his lovely companion broke the quiet. "Now that you've taken me to see the standing stones, will you give me back my coins?"

Her abrupt question brought a sense of grave unease. Could that explain why she'd so willingly returned his kisses? She needed the coins to leave the *Raven*.

As Keir continued to row, he debated the answer to her question. It might be safe to return her stash of coins, but the way she averted her gaze and stared out across the sea loch raised an annoying suspicion. Had she lied to him once again about the reason she'd come on this voyage? She'd appeared sincerely thrilled to visit the standing stones. Yet there could have been a second reason for leaving the safety of her home. One she'd kept well hidden.

"Not yet," he said at last.

She glowered at him, clearly upset at his answer. "Well then, when?" she demanded. "When will you give me what's rightfully mine?"

"I told you before," he replied, certain now that he'd made the right decision, "I'll give the coins to your uncle when I return you safely to Lady Nina."

"They belong to me," she said, putting an emphasis on every word, as though he were the court fool.

"That's too much money for a wee lassie like you," he countered. "Everyone knows females have nay the practical commonsense to handle more than a few pennies at a time."

She gasped. "Why, you pompous, braying jackass!"

He lifted a scarred eyebrow in derision. "Back to name-calling, are we?"

Scowling at him, Raine folded her arms and refused to reply.

Keir brought the cutter alongside the *Raven*, where Macraith stood at the gunwale, waiting for them. Keir lifted Raine up the ladder, while his uncle helped over her the side.

"Where have you been?" Macraith asked in a worried tone. "I was beginning to wonder if I should send out a search party."

Keir frowned. "What the devil do you mean? We were only gone a short while."

"Dod, man," Macraith said, keeping his voice low. "You've been gone most of the night."

Keir shook his head in confusion. "I must have lost complete sense of time."

Stunned, he glanced toward Raine. During his hushed conversation with his uncle, she'd quickly moved to the companionway and was starting down the stairs to her cabin.

"I hooked the cutter to the chains," he told Macraith. "We can bring it on deck tomorrow before we make sail. There's no need to wake the morning watch unnecessarily."

Keir glanced up into the rigging, where the dark outlines of the lookouts hovered above them. He swore softly to himself. The entire crew would know by noon that he'd taken Lady Raine ashore and been gone for a suspiciously long time.

Chapter 8

SOMEWHERE BETWEEN SLEEP and awake, Keir heard the sound of the door opening. He reached for his broadsword lying on the floor beside his bed. As his fingers grasped the handle, he swung his legs over the edge of the mattress and moved to his feet.

Raine seemed to hover near the doorway, bathed in the moonlight that streamed through the cabin's windows behind him. She still wore the red cloak from earlier that evening. When she pushed down the sable-trimmed hood, her ebony hair cascaded over her shoulders.

'Twas the middle of the night.

And he stood bare-ass naked.

Sword in hand, Keir glanced at the door she'd closed behind her. "What's wrong?" he asked, ready to move past her and ward off any danger that threatened.

"Nothing's wrong," she answered softly. "I couldn't sleep after our disagreement this evening. I didn't kiss you because I wanted my money back, Keir. I know that's what you think, but it's not true."

"We can talk about this in the morning," he said curtly, replacing the weapon on the rug. "You should go back to bed now, Raine."

Keir took a deep breath, trying to regain some equilibrium and calm his immediate response to her presence. Every nerve in his body sang with desire. His staff grew rigid and heavy at the thought of Raine lying in the rumpled bed behind him. Any second, she'd realize the state of his engorged arousal and run for the safety of her own quarters.

Instead, Raine seemed to float across the room, her bare feet making no sound on the rug. "Not yet," she insisted in a dreamy, faraway voice. "I'm not going back to my cabin until I convince you what I say is true."

She released the cords at her throat. The red cloak drifted to the floor, where it pooled around her toes. She stood there nude, her female body exquisite perfection in the moonlight.

"Raine, you don't have to do this," he said, certain her goal was to recover her coins.

"I want you, Keir," she whispered. Her dark eyes grew moist and two teardrops spilled down her cheeks. "Don't you want me?"

With a groan, Keir reached out and pulled Raine to him. He cupped her round buttocks in his hands and lifted her up for his kiss. Covering her lips with his open mouth, he thrust his tongue inside, tasting her honeyed warmth. Her scent filled his nostrils as he lifted her higher still, until he could take one pink nipple into his mouth and then the other. He suckled her gently, making the twin globes sway.

"Maybe we should talk first," she suggested.

"Nay, lass," he replied. The feel of her cool, bare skin pressed against his fevered body assured Keir he was about to enter paradise. He wasn't going to risk heaven for some needless conversation. If she wanted him, he wouldn't refuse her.

His heart thundering, he carried Raine to the bed and sank down on the soft mattress beside her. Leaning over her, he gently brushed one whiskered cheek and then the other across her silken breasts. Tracing the tip of his tongue from the hollow of her collarbone to the tip of each perfect globe, he licked her soft, pliant nipples into hard wee buds.

Whispering hushed endearments, Keir kept a tight rein on his burgeoning passion. 'Twas her first time.

"I'll go slowly, darling," he soothed. "I'll teach you what it's like to lie with a Highland warrior."

Keir slipped his palm along her smooth thigh, and his heart skidded to a halt at the fragile beauty of her body. He lifted his large bulk over her slender figure, easing himself between her bent knees. The need for her threatened to overwhelm his control.

"Raine," he said hoarsely, "Tell me you want me to take you."

She gazed up at him with huge, dreamy eyes. "Take me now, Keir," she urged.

"After tonight," he warned, "you'll belong to me, Raine. And I'll never let you go."

He rose up on his hands, ready to bury himself deep in her welcoming warmth . . .

. . . and awoke from his dream.

WIDE AWAKE, KEIR threw the covers from his overheated body and went to stand at one of the cabin's tall windows. The full moon shone through wisps of clouds. Waiting for his heartbeat to slow and his sexual desire to ebb, he braced one hand against the window frame and gazed out at the lapping waves, phosphorescent in the silvery light. He'd had the same recurring dream, or one very much like it, off and on for the last two years.

Dammit to hell.

He could control his thoughts and his actions during the day, but his body took over at night.

He had tried to quench this fever racing through his veins. He'd seduced married women of the highest rank, who'd grown tired of their husbands and were seeking a few guilty pleasures. He'd paid expensive harlots and bedded them two and three at a time, certain that if he rutted long enough and often enough with enough voluptuous females, he'd wipe Lady Raine Cameron from his exhausted brain and his tortured body. And with the decision to choose a bride, he'd thought he had succeeded at last.

Until Raine had appeared at Inverness and blasted his hard-won success into a thousand pieces, with a heedless power equivalent to a long-range cannon. And the ensuing shrapnel had pierced the armor around his carefully guarded heart.

Goddamn that Colin MacRath.

If that idiot hadn't allowed Raine to trick him into taking her aboard the *Sea Hawk* with her outright lies about a cousin's childbirth, none of this would have happened.

Keir shook his head at the bitter realization that the same could be said for him. He'd been just as big a fool. Worse. He'd allowed Raine to dupe him more than once.

Macraith's suggestion that Keir transfer Raine to the *Sea Dragon*, entrusting her safety to Fearchar, would have been an excellent solution. Except for the fact that Tam MacLean served on the *Dragon* as second in command. And that tall, yellow-haired Highlander, with his too-ready smile and his over-quick hands, would prove even more of a threat than Colin. The afternoon Tam had dared to reach out and touch Raine's hair, Keir had been sorely tempted to send him overboard with a swift kick to his rear. Unfortunately, he couldn't do worse to the clever fellow—and everyone present knew it. Tam was Rory's kinsman.

Nay, there was nothing for it, but to keep Raine on board the *Black Raven*.

And hold her at arm's length.

THE FAINTEST GLIMPSE of dawn peeking through the small window of her cabin found Raine already dressed and pacing the floor. She'd been awake since returning to the ship, wrestling with her dismay and confusion. What she'd told Keir about the ancient monoliths had been quite true. But she'd held back something far more important. Something she knew he'd refuse to believe.

Over and over during the early morning hours, she'd revisited what had happened between her and Keir. She didn't need to ask why the stern and disapproving chief of Clan MacNeil would suddenly kiss her in such a sensual manner. Or why she'd returned those kisses as though drugged with a magic elixir.

Dear God above, she'd reacted to Keir's seductive overtures by touching her tongue to his. She'd untied the cords that fastened his collar and slid her fingers beneath his shirt to caress the solid muscles of his chest and shoulders.

Keir MacNeil.

The man she'd always considered rough and outspoken and lacking in any tender feelings whatsoever. In the past the only emotions he'd shown toward her ranged from mild irritation to outright rage.

Raine sank down on the edge of her mattress and clasped her hands as though in prayer. But she didn't pray. Her racing thoughts mirrored her racing heartbeat. If Keir hadn't stopped of his own accord, would she have had the strength to pull away? The unfamiliar stirrings of sexual desire had nearly overcome her natural reticence.

'Twasn't guilt that spurred her thoughts. 'Twas the certainty that what had happened at the standing stones had set in motion a chain of events that would tie her to Keir MacNeil forever.

The vision that had secretly haunted her for the last two years unfolded before her.

Surrounded by their families, Raine stood beside Keir, his arm placed protectively around her shoulders. He looked down at her swollen belly and beamed with unmistakable male pride.

Raine had often wondered if she understood the vivid dream of her seventeenth summer. Since that time she'd become ever more determined that the vision would never come true. Although she'd pretended to be unaware of the court gossip about Laird MacNeil's many beautiful mistresses, she'd have had to be deaf not to hear the prattling tongues.

Raine bent her head and covered her face with her hands. She was quite familiar with the Celtic legend of Tristram and Isolde.

Sir Tristram had been sent to Ireland to bring back Isolde the Fair, the promised bride of a Cornish monarch. But during the return voyage, the two unknowingly drank an enchanted potion from a goblet—a magical elixir that had been meant solely for the future groom, King Mark, and his bride. Tristram and Isolde had fallen irresistibly under the spell of an unending and tragic love.

The only possible reason Keir and Raine had responded to each other in such an inexplicable way at the site of the standing stones was that they'd become enchanted. A spell had been cast over them by the Tuatha De Danann, perhaps because the unsuspecting pair had interrupted the faeries' celebration of the mystical standstill of the moon.

Raine waited impatiently for the sun to rise above the eastern horizon. She'd go to Keir at once and explain what had happened. Together they would hold fast against the faeries' magic by the sheer dint of their combined willpower. She knew it would only bring a temporary reprieve at best. But hopefully one long enough for her to slip away from the *Black Raven*.

EARLY THAT MORNING, Keir stepped out of his bath and ran a piece of linen toweling over his wet body. A light knock sounded on the door behind him, just as he reached for his breeches.

"Come," he said, expecting MacFarlane to enter and begin emptying the large wine cask, which had been cut in half to serve as a tub. An audible intake of air told him Hector hadn't just entered the cabin.

"I'm so sorry," Raine said, her strangled voice betraying her embarrassment at his nudity. "Please forgive my intrusion."

But she didn't leave.

Keir pulled on his breeches and turned to face her. She still wore her seaman's garb from the previous evening. Long wisps of her braid had come loose and framed her face, giving her the tousled appearance of having just climbed out of bed. The languorous effect tightened every muscle in his body.

"If you came to join me for breakfast, my lady," he said, bracing his hands on his hips, "you're a wee bit early."

Raine gazed at the colossus before her, the magnificent sight leaving her speechless. Keir's wide shoulders and scarred chest bulged with muscles. A holy medal hung from a silver chain around his neck. Celtic bands encircled his massive upper arms. His soaked black hair fell loose to his shoulders, the side-braids still intact and tied with leather thongs. A moment before, she'd had an excellent view of his broad back and taut buttocks. An inked image of the *Black Raven*, all sails filled, covered his shoulder blades.

Holy Lord.

The MacNeil's physique was a paean to the fierce Highland warrior.

Raine's mouth went suddenly dry, and she ran the tip of her tongue over her lips. She had to fight the feelings the sight of him stirred within her. She mustn't be overwhelmed by his sheer masculine presence.

Raine drew a deep breath and continued, her voice reedy and high-pitched. "I . . . I came to explain what happened last night at the standing stones."

"I ken what happened," he told her with a scowl.

"Not . . . not really," she countered, stepping farther into the room. Raine was determined not to let her resolution falter, no matter how angry he became. "At least, you don't know *why* it happened."

His answer came clipped and surly. "I think I do. You wanted your purse of coins, so you kissed me."

"Oh, 'tis much more than that," Raine said. She looked down at her hands, fingers interlaced and clasped tightly at her waist, searching for an explanation he'd be willing to accept. Finally she looked up to meet his cynical gaze. "Do you know the story of Tristram and Isolde?" she blurted out.

Keir stared at her as though she'd lost her mind. "Of course," he said at last. "Every Gaelic-speaking child has listened to that fireside tale more than once. What the hell does it have to do with last night?"

Raine prayed she'd find the right words to convince him. Keir had to return her bag of coins and allow her to leave the *Raven* at once before the faeries' spell became too strong. If not, she'd never find her father—because she'd never willingly leave Keir's side. Even now she found it difficult to think or speak clearly.

"We . . . you and I . . . we are like Tristram and Isolde," she told him earnestly. The Tuatha De Danann were there last evening, Keir. We must have interrupted their singing and dancing in the moonlight, and they wrapped an enchantment around us so we couldn't see them. That's why we —"

"Stop." Keir held up his hand, apparently exasperated. "What happened between us had nothing to do with faeries, elves, witches, or wizards, Raine. I wanted to kiss you. You wanted your money. End of story. Don't make it into something it wasn't."

"But don't you see," she insisted, her words hoarse in her desperation. "We have to fight this together. We mustn't let it happen again."

His emerald eyes glittered as he jerked on his shirt. "I promise you, Raine, it will nay happen again."

They were interrupted by the sound of footsteps. Hector had stopped just outside the open doorway. "Excuse me, Captain," he said with a quick jerk of his chin. The towheaded lad held a bucket in one hand, with toweling folded over his other arm. He took a hesitant step back. "If it please you, sir, I'll return later."

"No need," Keir said, motioning for him to come in. "Lady Raine and I have finished our conversation."

Raine clamped her mouth shut, unwilling to speak further in front of the young man. Without another word she whirled and hurried out of the cabin.

Hunting lodge near the Scottish border
The duke of Northumberland's estate
North Yorkshire, England

ARCHIBALD CAMPBELL, EARL of Argyll, slowly rose to his feet when Northumberland came into the room. After his journey from Edinburgh in a jolting, uncomfortable carriage, Archibald's foot, tortured with gout, ached incessantly, and he'd propped it on a low stool.

"Ah, you've arrived," Henry Percy said, clearly in a jovial mood. He was attired in hunting garb, his face flushed with the exuberance of outdoor sport. Peeling off his gloves and tossing them on a nearby table, he appeared unaware of his older guest's discomfort. He was followed by a liveried servant, who went to a sideboard, which held a decanter of wine and several goblets.

"Only just," Archibald replied, eyeing the brash Englishman thoughtfully. He wondered if the impetuous young noble had gained any patience since they'd last met. "May I offer my felicitations on your appointment as Warden of the Eastern Marches? King Henry must think highly of you."

The duke of Northumberland smiled and strode across the room to shake Archibald's hand. "It was in the way of a reward for escorting Princess Margaret safely to Scotland and her marriage to your king. I trust you see the irony in the honor bestowed on me by my grateful sovereign."

"I hope your hunting was successful today," Archibald remarked politely, as the serving man poured the wine and presented the goblet on a silver tray. "I spied several deer as I came through your park this morning."

The earl of Argyll had no intention of discussing their failed plot in front of the servant. He hadn't reached his middle years by being careless. The wrong word in the wrong ear, and they could still lose their heads on the executioner's block for their attempt to sabotage the Treaty of Perpetual Peace between Scotland and England.

"Indeed," Northumberland replied, his eyes alight with satisfaction. "We'll have fresh venison for dinner this evening. And I'll have a magnificent rack of antlers to show for it." He looked up proudly at the trophies from previous hunts displayed on the lodge walls. "That will be all," he told his servant.

As the houseman silently exited the room, the two men sank into the lodge's comfortable chairs. They hadn't seen each other since the royal wedding at Holyroodhouse the previous summer, when their plans had been overset in such a disastrous manner. At the time they'd felt lucky to come away with their heads still on their shoulders.

But Argyll had kept up a secret correspondence with the English duke. And when rebellion broke out in the Hebrides, both noblemen saw their chance to gain from the confusion and turmoil, while at the same time even the score with the notorious Hellhounds of Scotland.

"All has gone according to plan, I take it?" Archibald asked.

"Three English-built carracks are on their way to the Hebrides," Northumberland replied with smug complacency. "Each privateer is under the command of an experienced captain, with a full complement of sailors. When joined by the rebellious clans, they will bring unmatched military power into the Scottish Isles."

"Ah, good news, good news," Archibald said. "I've sent word to the chief of Clan MacMurchaidh to meet the ships at Port nan Long on the western coast of North Uist with the sea charts to navigate the treacherous Sound of Harris. My brother-in-law, Torcall, will deliver a force of Macdonalds and their allies, including his own kinsmen from the Isle of Lewis. Nine hundred fighting men armed with longbows and crossbows will transfer from their unarmed galleys onto the English carracks with their cannons."

"And you've brought the second payment for the privateers?"

"In gold crowns," Archibald replied. He pressed his fingertips in a steeple beneath his chin, contemplating their scheme and all the possibilities of failure.

He knew the handsome, swaggering duke had only recently been awarded the title by a grateful King Henry VII. Being given to lavish displays of magnificence—Northumberland had produced a spectacle of enormous proportions for the Tudor princess on her journey to Edinburgh—the young nobleman was now saddled with crippling debt.

Although Scotland and England were ostensibly at peace, the alliance having been secured by the marriage of King James IV and Princess Margaret Tudor, the Macdonald rebellion offered an opportunity to weaken the royal grip on the Highlands and Isles. A boon to the clan chiefs and to any nobles quick enough and strong enough to take advantage of the shifting political landscape.

"And Donald Dubh?" Northumberland asked with a gesture of mild interest.

"My bastard grandson is presently in the custody of MacMurchaidh," Archibald said softly, as he studied the large ruby ring on his finger. "He will be safe enough."

The earl of Argyll didn't need to mention that unfortunate lad was a mere tool in the hands of the rebel forces. Archibald had imprisoned his daughter's bairn—Donald Dubh Macdonald, direct heir to Iain Macdonald, the last high chief and lord of the Isles—in the fortress of Innischonaill since he was a child. Only to be released by the perfidy of Clan MacIan of Glencoe, thereby unleashing the dogs of war and the golden chance to gain immeasurable wealth. And for Archibald Campbell, the coveted trade route to Ireland.

"Tell me, Argyll," Northumberland asked with curiosity, "why do you hate the three Hellhounds so intensely?"

Archibald rose to his feet, whipped into fury by the mere mention of their names. He limped back and forth across the room, clenching the stem of his wineglass. "The eldest brother, Rory MacLean, thwarted my plans to wed my son to the maid of Glencoe. Had I been able to accomplish that feat, the alliance between the Glencoe Macdonalds and the Campbells would have strengthened my hold on the entire western coast of Scotland."

"I can see why you despise MacLean," Northumberland said with an indifferent shrug. He leaned back in his chair and crossed a booted foot over the opposite knee.

"And of course, we both have reason to hate Lachlan Mac-Rath for ruining our plans to kill his mistress, Lady Francine, and her daughter on their journey to Edinburgh. Too bad my cousin, Lychester, was killed in the misfiring of the plot."

Archibald tossed off the rest of his wine and moved to the sideboard to pour another glass. "If not for that bastard Kinrath," he grated, "we'd have infuriated the English king and destroyed the treaty of peace between our countries. Both of us would have benefited from the resultant chaos."

"Nothing's more profitable than war," Northumberland agreed as he held out his glass. "It weakens and impoverishes the monarchy and makes the nobility stronger and thus richer." He smiled in apparent resignation. "It was a good plan, except for the interference of the earl of Kinrath. And so, why your hatred for the youngest brother?"

Archibald filled the duke's glass with the ruby liquid. "The chief of Clan MacNeil is merely a means to an end. If I can stop him from putting down the rebellion in the Hebrides, I can once again begin to gain control of the western coast of the Highlands. And," he added with a smile, raising his glass in salute, "nothing could exact such sweet revenge as killing the Hellhounds' youngest brother."

Chapter 9

THE *BLACK RAVEN* flew before the wind, running south along the western coast of the Isle of Lewis. On her long, pointed bowsprit, a carved black raven, its wings outspread, soared above the waves. The galleon was making a strong seven knots, the green sea slipping fast by her prow. Two days after leaving Loch Roag, the fair weather continued to hold, and Keir had ordered all sails the ship could bear.

Keir stood on the quarterdeck, looking up at the fore and main topsails and the lookouts high in the rigging above him. The sustained fine weather seemed to lift the crew's spirits. The previous evening the seamen had sung and danced on the forecastle to the beat of a drum and the shrill notes of a hornpipe.

The frivolity had lured Raine out of her self-imposed exile in her cabin, where she'd hidden since seeing him naked two days ago. She had laughed with delight at their antics as the crew performed the sailors' jig, the watches vying for top honor as the best dancers onboard. The mere presence of the exquisite lady enlivened everyone, even the officers, and the usually stoic al-Rahman chuckled, his deep baritone rumbling in his chest. The men were a trace more subdued this morning under the bright glare of the summer sun.

Keir understood his crew's attempts to please Lady Raine, for he'd waited impatiently for her to resume her frequent walks on the main deck. At every opportunity he'd sent special treats by way of the ship's two middies. He had been certain the lass wouldn't refuse any offerings brought by Ethan and Robbie Gibson. He'd been right on that score. She'd invited them to share in the plum pudding and berry cobbler. But Keir's best efforts to coax her into forgiving his surly behavior or his steadfast disbelief in faeries had gone unrequited.

From the corner of his eye, Keir caught a flash of blue. He turned his head, expecting to see Raine coming up the companionway. Instead, he spotted the ship's lantern-jawed quartermaster. The usually solemn Simon Ramsay had tied his dark brown pigtail with a brightly colored ribbon. Though not an unusual adornment for a sailor, this particular hairband matched the deep sky-blue of one Raine had worn on several occasions.

At that moment the officer of the watch came to report the log. "Seven knots, if you please, sir."

Keir nodded. "Very well, Mr. Buchanan. Tell the bosun he can pipe the men to breakfast now."

Just as the burly helmsman moved away, Macraith

joined Keir on the quarterdeck. "I've insisted on Lady Raine having breakfast with us this morning," his uncle informed him in a low tone. When Keir made no reply, he continued. " 'Tisn't right for the lassie to eat alone in her cabin. No matter what happened between the two of you in that hell-tarnished place, there's nay call for her to be treated like a prisoner."

Keir scowled at his uncle. "Raine has not been confined to her quarters, dammit. She's made the choice to take her meals in solitary. And nothing of any consequence happened at Calanais. The belief that the standing stones are somehow magical is mere superstition."

As the two men strode across the deck toward Keir's quarters, Macraith gave a cynical snort. "All the same, I've never kenned the lass to be unsociable before. You, howsoever, can be a downright pain in the arse when you've a mind to. So if there's a problem between the two of you, I'd wager the fault is yours."

"I don't recall asking for your opinion of my behavior or anyone else's," Keir replied sharply.

They entered his cabin to find the comely lassie under discussion already seated at the table and being served by an attentive Hector MacFarlane, who hovered over her like a self-appointed protector. Apparently, Macraith wasn't the only one aware of the problems between Keir and Raine. She looked up with a tentative smile, as though unsure of her reception in his quarters.

"My dear Lady Raine," Macraith said, his weather-seamed features creased in a welcoming grin. He sank down on the chair beside her. "Pleased to see you've joined us this morning. We've missed your uplifting conversation and your bonny smile."

It was the first time Keir had been within speaking distance of Raine since she'd entered his cabin unannounced two days ago. She wore a rose-colored gown with frilly lace trim adorning her bodice. Keir noticed immediately that she'd woven a red velvet ribbon into her thick braid. Against her ebony hair, the effect was stunning.

He reached out and lifted the end of the long braid with his index finger. "Quite a lovely ribbon," he said. "Have you, by any chance, mislaid your blue one?"

"Oh, not at all," she replied. "I know exactly where it is. Why do you ask?"

He shrugged his shoulders dismissively as he took his seat across from her. "No particular reason."

Macraith glanced from one to the other. When he met Keir's gaze, it was clear he, too, had spotted Ramsay's bright blue plumage.

Avoiding either man's gaze, Raine looked down at the eggs on her plate and felt the heat rising on her cheeks. She silently prayed that she wasn't flushing noticeably. Good Lord. She hadn't thought The MacNeil would notice such a trifling thing as a lady's hairband.

Since the day she'd been forced to surrender her coins into Keir's keeping, Raine had puzzled over how she could retrieve them. She'd come to the conclusion that attempting to pry them out of Keir's grasp would merely prove an aggravating waste of time. She'd have to find another way to gain the means to search for Torcall MacMurchaidh. God knew, there'd be no point in leaving the ship without money.

To add to her difficulty, Barrows took his responsibilities as her sea-daddy seriously, although sometimes he did leave Raine in her cabin to her own devices while he took Ethan and Robbie to the main deck to practice knotting and splicing. The previous afternoon she'd slipped out of her quarters and discovered a small group of seamen on the gun deck below, clustered between two cannons and betting on a game of dice. The answer had come to her in that second. She could win the coins she needed to make her escape.

Since she had no money to wager, Raine offered her hair ribbons, believing any winners would set them aside for their sweethearts back home. She'd certainly been wrong on that score.

But first she had to learn the rules of the game they were playing, which took a good while longer than she'd expected. In the end she did acquire thirty farthings—either by sheer luck or the grace of God, she wasn't sure which. But not before losing several hairbands.

"We're going to take our reckoning at noon," Keir said, interrupting her worried thoughts. "After which we'll calculate our present location and begin charting our course through the Sound of Harris. Perhaps you'd like to join us?"

"I'd enjoy that!" she answered, delighted he was willing to set their bad feelings aside.

"Fine," he replied, a ghost of a smile skipping about the corners of his lips. "We can meet on the quarterdeck at midday."

"Thank you, Keir," she said. She met his deep green eyes, filled with amusement, and the memory of his nude backside flashed before her. The thought of the well-defined muscles of his sculptured male body made her feel suddenly short of breath. Uncertain if he was remembering her intrusion on his bath as well, she turned to his uncle, searching frantically for a suitable topic. "You seem so completely at home onboard ship, Macraith. Did you go to sea at an early age?"

He awarded her with a broad, encouraging grin. "Aye, lass. I was born on the Isle of Barra. Salt water runs in my blood. Don't you ken that the MacNeils are descended from Celtic sea kings?"

Keir gave a derisive bark of laughter. "What my uncle means, Raine, is that we come from a long line of pirates. In earlier days Kisimuth Castle provided Clan MacNeil with an impregnable lair in which they could hide from punishment for their crimes of pillaging and rapine."

Unconcerned with the harsh indictment of their mutual ancestors, Macraith merely shrugged. "We're nay the only clan in the Isles to have indulged in a bit of piracy in the past."

Hesitant to ask any questions, Raine waited for further explanation. No one had ever spoken to her about Keir's father. Not even Isabel Cameron, who knew everything about everyone in the Highlands and Isles. Once Raine had asked her aunt about Keir's deceased sire.

"Never listen to foolish gossip," Lady Isabel had told Raine with a chiding wag of her finger. Her hazel eyes, usually flashing with a mysterious, otherworldly humor, grew serious. "Keir MacNeil's mother loves him dearly. Let that be the end of it."

Her answer had only deepened the mystery for Raine.

Good Lord above, why wouldn't a mother love her son? How could that even come into question?

"Did you enjoy your exploration of the standing stones?" Macraith asked, interrupting her reverie.

Startled, Raine met Keir's hooded gaze. He'd been taking advantage of the opportunity to study her closely, perhaps wondering about her thoughts and what she knew about the violent history of his clan. "Very much," she replied quietly. She glanced about to find that Hector had disappeared, most likely into the ship's galley for another platter of food. "I mean to say, the stones were fascinating. We witnessed a lunar event that can only be described as spectacular. Did Keir tell you about it?"

"Nay," Macraith answered with a hearty chuckle. "My nephew refused to say a word about your excursion ashore. Except that the time slipped by too fast. He claimed he hadn't realized how long you'd been absent from the ship."

"There was something strange about the passage of time," Raine agreed. She could have given more of an explanation, but the stern cast of Keir's jaw warned her against it. Perhaps Macraith would be more receptive to the presence of the Tuatha De Danann at the ancient site, but now was not the time to suggest it.

At that moment Hector reappeared with a plate of pears and figs especially for her, and the conversation moved on to less dangerous topics.

THE SUN WAS shining directly overhead when Lady Raine joined Keir and Hector MacFarlane on the forecastle with their two energetic pupils. Keir smiled in welcome at the sight of her, pleased she was willing to be in his company once again. After breakfasting together, her mortification at seeing him naked had apparently faded. As for himself, that memory had been seared into his brain. The mere thought of her curious gaze moving across his bare flesh sent a flood of sexual desire to his groin. A desire he was determined to repress.

She wore a pair of faded breeches and a striped Guernsey shirt that Hector had outgrown.

"I don't wish to interrupt your class," Raine said in an apologetic tone. "I'll just stand quietly and watch."

Keir motioned for her to move closer. "You're not interrupting, Lady Raine. Mr. MacFarlane is giving the instructions this afternoon. It's important the lads learn to use all the various mariner's instruments."

Ethan looked up from the instrument he held in both hands. "We've been practicing on the quadrant, Lady Raine." The twelve-year-old offered the nautical tool to her with a gracious smile. "We use it to measure the altitude of the sun at noon."

Raine took the brass instrument made in the shape of a quarter circle and studied it with open curiosity. "How does it work?"

"Here," Hector said, coming to stand beside her. His blue eyes gleamed with pride at the chance to teach the lovely lady. "Hold the quadrant so the plum bob falls straight down toward the deck at your feet," he explained, turning it to the correct position for her. "That establishes a vertical line of reference."

"See the markings on the quadrant," Robbie said excitedly, anxious to be a part of the lesson. His bright hair glistened like a copper helmet in the sunshine. Holding up his own quadrant, he pointed to the calibrations etched on the brass. "These lines are called degrees, my lady."

Hector nodded, smiling with pride for his enthusiastic students. "The quantitative measurement provided by the quadrant is used to determine the ship's present latitude," he told her. "We'll be pleased to demonstrate."

"Oh, I'd like that," she exclaimed. Her eyes lit up with the joy of learning something new and challenging.

'Twas a trait Keir had admired in Raine since she was a youngster quizzing him on his latest voyage. On each visit to Archnacarry Manor, he'd shown her on one of Gideon's maps the exact route he'd taken to the Mediterranean or to the coast of Africa. Her thirst for knowledge had always been insatiable.

Keir watched with pleasure as the two lads, under Hector's supervision, happily explained the use of the quadrant to the ship's newest recruit.

"Tonight," Hector said at the end of the lesson, "we'll work on using the cross-staff to determine the altitude of Polaris." He dismissed Robbie and Ethan to their sea-daddy's charge and bowed to Raine before leaving.

At that moment Keir took Raine's elbow and eased her away from the others on deck. "I wanted to ask you again, lass, whether you've misplaced any of your ribbons."

She looked up at him in wide-eyed surprise. "I haven't mislaid a thing," she assured him.

Baffled by her reply, Keir glanced around the busy

deck. Not only did Ramsay sport a blue ribbon suspiciously similar to one Keir had seen in Raine's hair, but Apollonius, the ship's master gunner, had tied his long black pigtail with a bright green hairband as well. From across the length of the main deck, Keir could see him talking with Abid al-Rahman. Deep in conversation, the *Raven*'s baldheaded Moorish navigator turned slightly. Even from this distance, a silver disk could be seen hanging at the end of a new lavender ribbon tied around his neck.

" 'Tis a serious crime for a seaman to steal anything," Keir told Raine. "We can't allow thievery on board. It sows discord amongst the men, which can be disastrous in battle when they must work as a cohesive unit—especially a gun crew. So you must tell me if anything of yours is missing."

Her jet eyes enormous in her heart-shaped face, Raine gazed at him solemnly. "Nothing of mine has disappeared."

"You'd tell me if it did?' he persisted. "You wouldn't try to hide a theft out of a mistaken sense of protecting someone from punishment?"

Raine looked away, avoiding The MacNeil's shrewd gaze. What would he say if he knew she'd been gambling with his men in an attempt to acquire enough coins to leave the ship?

"I will tell you if that happens," she promised, then asked in curiosity, "What would you do if you found someone had stolen from me?"

"I'd have the hide flogged off him," Keir stated with complete dispassion.

Raine tried to ignore the jab of fear that lanced through her. If it came to that, she'd have to tell the truth. Keir might want to flog the hide off *her*, but he wouldn't. Being an old family friend had its privileges.

THE MINUTE KEIR disappeared down the companionway, Raine hurried to find one of the ship's young gentlemen. Robbie Gibson sat on the main deck at the larboard bow, practicing his knotting and splicing. Fortunately, Barrows had guided Ethan up into the rigging, too far above them to hear.

Raine crouched down on the scrubbed planks beside Robbie. "I need you to find al-Rahman and tell him to meet me on the gun deck," she said, speaking barely above a whisper.

"The Moor?" Robbie asked in surprise, leaping to his feet. His eyes lit up, sensing the tension in her guarded tone. The sea breeze ruffled his unruly thatch of red hair. In the bright sunshine, the coppery freckles covering his round face made him look even younger than his ten years.

"Yes," she said. "Tell him to bring Simon Ramsay and Apollonius with him. But you have to hurry," she added, giving him a gentle push. "Don't waste a minute. And don't stop to talk to anyone but al-Rahman." Then Raine slipped away, hurrying to the gun deck before Barrows noticed she'd finished her conversation with the captain.

Grateful that no one was polishing the shiny brass cannon that afternoon, Raine waited impatiently belowdecks. The light streaming through the grating of the open hatchway above her head illuminated the darkness. The long guns were lashed securely in place against the ship's hull and their ports were closed and fastened tight.

She'd been there only a short time when al-Rahman appeared. The Moor touched his fingertips to his forehead as he bowed low. "You wanted to speak with me, *sultana*?" He smiled warmly, as though certain he knew the reason for their secret meeting "I do not have time for another game of dice now. Perhaps early tomorrow when the morning watch takes over."

At that moment, Apollonius and Ramsay arrived, walking toward them along the row of cannon.

Raine addressed the three men in a low, urgent tone. "I need to get my things back this very minute," she told them, fighting a sense of panic.

Al-Rahman's hand went to the lavender ribbon hanging from his neck, and he immediately began to lift it over his hairless head, making the gold hoops on both earlobes swing gently.

But Ramsay stared at her in mystification, thinking, no doubt, that she was attempting to renege on her former wagers. "That's nay the way it usually works, milady," he said, confusion written on his long, solemn features.

"I'll pay you for the ribbons," she added quickly, meeting their baffled gazes. "But I must get back everything I lost yesterday." She drew a deep, steadying breath and then continued in a rush. "Laird MacNeil suspects that you've stolen the items from me. He's noticed the hairbands and has leapt to the wrong conclusion. He's threatened to have the three of you flogged for theft."

"We would never steal from you, *domina*," Apollonius said with mild censure. His scarred, bearded features puckered in a scowl, enhancing the piratical aura that always surrounded him. "Surely, you would never tell him we did?"

Shaking her head, Raine paced up and down the gundeck. "I would never do that," she assured them. "I would never accuse any of you of stealing." She pressed her hand to her temple, trying to think. "But I also don't want your captain to know that I've been wagering. That's especially important to keep secret because if he suspects I've won money from you, he'll be very angry at me."

The three officers exchanged worried looks, which didn't surprise her. On land the sport of gaming was enjoyed by all levels of society. Wellborn ladies were known to be especially devoted to playing for high stakes. But if MacNeil was dead-set against her wagering, they could be in serious trouble.

"What can we do to help you, Lady Raine?" Ramsay asked, his eyes filled with kindness. His normally stern features softened in concern.

"Please allow me to buy back my things," she pleaded. She opened a small canvas bag tied with string. "I won thirty farthings. You can share the money between you."

Shaking his head, al-Rahman held out Raine's lavender hairband. "Keep your coins, *sultana*," the tall, broadshouldered Moor said. "Our glorious captain rescued me from slavery on a Turkish galley. He pays us well, and we share in his profits as a privateer. I am honored and most grateful to be a member of his crew."

Ramsay waved his large hand back and forth, indicating that he, too, refused to take her winnings. He untied the blue ribbon from his dark brown pigtail, reached over and pulled his friend's green tie loose as well.

"*Certe, domina,*" Apollonius agreed with a wide toothy smile. "Keep your coins in your purse."

"But I must warn you, milady," Simon Ramsay said, his blue-eyed gaze sober. "If Captain MacNeil questions us about this, we must tell him the truth. We can't lie to his face. He'll ken our deception in an instant, and we'll receive double the lashes as punishment for lying."

"The captain rarely has a man flogged," al-Rahman explained. "But if he thought we had stolen from you, the cat would come out of its bag."

Raine's vision blurred, her eyes overflowing with tears at their kindness. That three battle-hardened men could be so understanding and generous-hearted touched her deeply. "Yes, of course," she agreed, her voice trembling. "I will go up to my cabin and change into a gown at once. Then I'll appear on the main deck, wearing one of the ribbons. And I'll make sure MacNeil sees me. Now I must hurry before Barrows comes looking for me and finds us in collusion."

Chapter 10

"YOU WISH TO SEE ME, Laird MacNeil?"

Raine waited in the doorway of his quarters, ready to turn and flee if he started to upbraid her. She left the door wide open just to be safe.

Keir rose from his place at a small game table near one of the high inward-sloping windows at the very back of his cabin. She could see the sunset through the glass behind him, the drifting, wispy clouds rose colored. He gestured to the oak chair across from him.

"Please," he said in a voice conveying total authority.

She really had no choice.

Raine walked reluctantly across the thick rug and perched on the edge of the hard wooden seat. Dressed in the pale blue gown she'd worn to dinner earlier that evening, she'd tied her long braid, twisted into a figure eight at the nape of her neck, with the bright blue ribbon she'd retrieved from Simon Ramsay.

As Keir sat back down, Raine glanced about his luxurious quarters.

Lanterns had been lit in several places around the cabin in preparation for the darkness to come. Their flickering yellow light spread a lambent glow over the tapestries, carpets, and paintings gathered from all over Europe and the Ottoman Empire. She watched him cautiously, waiting for an explanation of his imperious summons.

Scarcely looking at the objects in his hands, Keir shuffled a deck of tarots, the cards flying through his agile fingers. "I'm told you like to gamble," he said quietly. His emerald gaze gave nothing away. But his softly spoken words sent a chill down Raine's back.

He knew.

Simon Ramsay had warned her they couldn't lie to him and get away with it.

And now Keir knew that she'd been wagering with members of his crew.

She stiffened, staring at him in silence, determined to give nothing away. He continued to shuffle the cards and the ominous sound of their clicking seemed to foretell that her punishment would be swift and unforgiving.

If his intention was to frighten her into a confession, he was going to be disappointed. Until she spoke with the seamen, she couldn't be certain if Keir was merely guessing or someone had disclosed the gambling and the extent of her winnings.

"Perhaps you'd like to play cards instead of dice," he suggested. "Are you familiar with the game of tarot?"

She caught glimpses of the trump cards—the riders

and the fool—flashing by, as he handled the tarot deck with astonishing skill.

Raine lowered her gaze to her hands folded tightly in her lap. "Somewhat," she hedged. Gideon had taught her card games starting from the age of seven. They'd played with tarot cards often—sometimes just the two of them, sometimes as a team against her mother and aunt. "I believe I can remember the rules," she added, trying to sound as innocent as an unsuspecting lamb being led to the shearer's barn. "But of course, never for coins."

"Why don't we strike a small wager, just to keep it interesting?" he suggested as he dealt the tarots.

"Is that allowed on board ship?" she asked, trying to hide her increased interest as she picked up her hand and scanned her cards.

Keir nodded. "Do you have anything to wager other than your pretty hairbands?" he continued, in the smooth patter of a light-fingered cutpurse just before he steals your money.

She looked up to meet his unreadable gaze. How much did he really know? "I have a few farthings that weren't in my purse when you took it," she said truthfully. "Not many," she hurriedly added, afraid he might insist on taking those from her as well.

He smiled and the sea-weathered corners of his eyes crinkled engagingly. His deep green gaze seemed to glow with friendliness. "Then let's start with two farthings a game," he suggested. "Later if you're feeling brave, we can raise the stakes."

Raine bit her lower lip as she debated the wisdom of betting against Keir.

It might not be such a wise idea.

They had played chess together when she was a youngster, but she'd always lost. At seventeen, however, she had defeated him for the first and only time. She'd been so thrilled she'd jumped up from her chair and executed an impromptu little victory dance. His reaction to losing the chess game had seemed incomprehensible.

Keir had departed Archnacarry Manor immediately, leaving Lachlan to make his younger brother's excuses to Lady Nina. From that day on, Keir MacNeil had kept his distance from Raine, treating her as someone he barely knew.

All because he'd lost a chess game to a young woman.

What unmitigated male vanity.

Now commonsense told her to back away from the contest and keep the few coins she'd already won in the dice game. She might spark his ire once again, if she bested him at cards.

Still the lure of gaining more funds for her escape proved too much to ignore in the end. Should he start to get angry, she'd think of an excuse, give back his money and beg to return to her cabin.

"Two farthings a game," she finally agreed and pulled open the silk purse that hung from her girdle.

Her worries proved unfounded. Keir cheerfully met defeat after defeat, until Raine had amassed a gratifying pile of coins. She knew her success wasn't necessarily all due to skill. She had a run of amazing good fortune that evening, and Keir's luck had run foul.

As they played, darkness had overtaken the last vestiges of sunset. In the lantern light the two card players were reflected in the pane of the tall window behind them. An intent young woman still perched on the edge of her seat and leaning forward in concentration. A powerfully built man in white shirt and black breeches slouched back in his chair, seemingly paying little attention to the card play.

Satisfied at her winnings, Raine decided to end the contest while she was ahead. "I think I'd best retire before I fall asleep at the table," she said, feigning a yawn. She started to gather up the coins in front of her.

"Let's play one last game," Keir suggested, reshuffling the tarots. "How would you like a chance to double your winnings?"

"Oh, I don't think so," Raine replied, about to push back her chair and stand up.

Keir reached into the sporran he'd placed close by. He threw two gold unicorns on the tabletop. "I'll wager these against your stack of farthings."

Raine sat up even straighter and stared mesmerized at the golden blur of the coins spinning on their edges before coming to rest with two soft clinks.

" 'Tisn't a fair bet," she protested. "I've not nearly that much money."

He flashed a cajoling smile, showing his even white teeth. "Indulge me, lass. Give me one last chance to win back the evening's losses."

Raine hesitated. The thought of passing up the opportunity to leave the table—and ultimately the ship—with two gold unicorns tucked into her canvas bag overpowered her fear of failure.

She gave a quick nod. "One last game then."

But her streak of luck disappeared in a trice. She watched in dismay as Keir took one trick after another with incredible speed, barely waiting for her to make her next play before tossing his trump card down.

As he counted his points for her at the end of the game, she rose, determined not to show her devastation. Her overriding need for the wherewithal to steal away from the ship had been her undoing. When she looked up from her few, paltry trump cards to meet his gaze, there was no trace of triumph in his eyes.

His features devoid of expression, he stood as well.

"Congratulations on your fine card play," she said, sounding stilted and hoarse to her own ears. Raine willed herself to remain calm till she could reach the sanctuary of her quarters. How could she have been so foolish and greedy?

"I could not allow you to leave the *Raven*," he said softly.

At his words, Raine realized he'd planned her debacle all along. Keir had enticed her into wagering everything she'd won from his crewmen with the full intention of taking it all. Right down to the last farthing.

In that moment she detested him for his crass exploitation of her need. Had he simply wrested the coins from her as he'd done before, she might have forgiven him. But not this coldhearted manipulation—giving her hope, till nearly the very end, and then snatching it all away at the last moment.

"Good evening," she said, the words coming out in a

pitiful croak. She hurried out of his quarters, paying no attention to his soft-spoken reply.

Keir watched Raine leave the cabin, her head high and her back straight in a futile attempt to hide the desolation she felt at her losses—and her unvarnished contempt for him. "Good night, my darling lass."

He'd really had no choice.

Keir had to make it clear to Raine that on his ship, his commands were to be obeyed. Completely and absolutely.

She had to realize he'd never allow her to run off again.

THE *BLACK RAVEN* caught a fair wind through the Sound of Harris, where colorful puffins with their bright orange beaks could be seen nesting along the banks. Gannets and cormorants circled overhead, scanning the waves for fish, while seals lay sunbathing on the rocks.

The sleek galleon entered the Little Minch close-hauled, the rigging humming. She arrived at the Isle of Skye two days after her sister ships, the *Sea Dragon* and the *Sea Hawk*. Entering the wide harbor of Loch Dùn Bheagain, the *Raven* fired a salute to the fortress, which promptly returned her salvo.

Dating back to the fourteenth century, mighty Dùn Bheagain Castle had been built on the site of an ancient Norse fort and had been the stronghold of the chiefs of Clan MacLeod for two hundred years.

By the time the *Raven* hove to and anchored alongside the *Dragon* and the *Hawk*, Keir had elicited an agreement of sorts from Raine on how to explain her presence on board his galleon.

"We'll say that your mother asked me to convey you to a kinswoman on Lewis who was nearing a possibly dangerous childbirth," Keir instructed. "By the time we'd arrived in Tolm, the infant had already been born, safe and sound. Since your help was no longer needed, it was decided that you remain on board the *Raven* until we find a suitable ship for passage to Appin, where your family can meet you."

She raised her arched brows in a manner calculated to irritate him and made no reply.

"Is that story clear?" he demanded, trying not to react to her blatant provocation.

She glanced at him from the corner of her eye. "I'm not an idiot," she replied with all the icy disdain of a princess.

Hell, she looked like royalty in the scarlet gown she'd chosen that morning, with her thick black braid crowning the top of her head. She wore her pearl earrings, and her shawl, made of the black-and-red Cameron tartan, was draped over one shoulder and pinned with a pearl-studded broach.

All the Scots on the *Black Raven* were attired in their colorful clan tartans, fully expecting a celebration of their safe arrival at Dùn Bheagain in the midst of a rebellion.

Descending the ladder first, Keir assisted Raine down in silence. Al-Rahman, clad in his fanciest caftan embroidered with multi-colored threads, guided her into the gently rocking longboat.

"Sit forward, *sultana*," the Moor suggested as he touched his hand to his forehead and bowed in a deep salaam. The *Raven*'s master navigator waited for his captain to be seated, then signaled the men to lift oars.

Keir was well aware that his entire crew was fascinated—nay, spellbound—by the elegant creature who walked among them with such unconscious grace. Most of the seamen had never been near a high-born lady, let alone talked to one so entrancing. And she visited with them daily, showing a sincere interest in their lives, both on land and on sea. He suspected she knew more about their lives ashore than he did.

So when Raine seemed unusually reserved that morning, the men were nearly desperate to cheer her. They acted like a goddamned bunch of Barbary apes, grinning and chattering and pointing to the enormous castle rising majestically against the pale morning sky and reflected with startling clarity in the cobalt blue loch.

"Silence!" al-Rahman called out.

The seamen grew instantly quiet, till all that could be heard was the splash of the oar blades cutting through the flat water.

Macraith, who'd come ashore earlier that morning with Hector, Ethan, and Robbie, waited as the sailors jumped out and pulled the craft onto the shore. He swung Raine out of the longboat and placed her on dry land, then turned to Keir.

"Alasdair MacLeod is here," Macraith said. "He's sworn his loyalty to the king. Howsomever, The MacLeod's nay certain where MacMurchaidh and Donald Dubh could have fled. We're welcome to take on fresh stores of water and victuals," he continued, "before we push on to Cairn na Burgh Mòr. A hunt has been planned for this afternoon, and we've been invited to a feast this evening."

"Aye," Keir replied with a quick nod. He placed a guiding hand at the small of Raine's back and accompanied her to the waiting horses. He tossed her up into the saddle on a dainty mare and then mounted a large black gelding.

Macraith drew his bay up beside hers. "You've some friends at the castle, milady, hoping to dance with you this evening after the banquet." His warm brown eyes twinkled with a teasing good humor.

"I'm looking forward to it," she replied with her first smile of the morning.

"Forbye, Colin and Tam are liable to trip over each other's big feet hurrying to ask you for the first galliard," he told her, his wide grin splitting his thick mustache and the full beard decorated with glass beads. "Especially considering the opportunity for a kiss at the end of the dance."

The fact that a galliard always ended in the bestowing of a chaste kiss on the lady's cheek by her gallant partner had never irritated Keir before. This morning, however, he fairly seethed at the idea of either Colin or Tam placing their greedy lips on Raine's flawless skin.

"MacRath and MacLean had best be getting their ships supplied," Keir interjected with a scowl. "We're in the middle of a bloody rebellion. We've no time to waste on foolishness."

"Bless us, now," Macraith said, breaking into laughter. "Only a petty-souled slug would consider kissing a bonny lassie a waste of time."

Resisting the temptation to glance at Raine—certain she was smiling in happy expectation of the dancing and the kissing—Keir kicked his heels against the black's flanks and galloped toward the castle.

"THINGS ARE GOING badly at Cairn na Burgh Mòr," confided Hugh Munro. "The choppy seas and the churning currents around the Treshnish Isles make it difficult for our guns to bombard the fortress with any degree of accuracy. And the bad weather doesn't help a damn bit. The ships keep lurching about in the rain and wind, nearly ramming into each other. It'll be God's own luck if the royal fleet doesn't founder at the mouth of Loch Tuath."

Upon his arrival just before sunset, the skinny, pockmarked messenger sent by the earl of Huntly met with the men who'd gathered in Dùn Bheagain's donjon to learn the latest news of the siege.

Keir and his two captains, Fearchar and Colin, along with Macraith and the other lieutenants, were seated at the huge trestle table across from Alasdair MacLeod and his elderly advisors. The chief of Clan MacLeod, somewhere in his mid-fifties, was commonly known as Alasdair Crotach, meaning "humpbacked," for he'd been crippled by battle wounds while a young man. Now his godson led their men into battle.

"Aye," Fearchar replied, his one pale eye filled with disgust. "Huntly's nay a sailor. The earl does fine leading an army on land, but the man has nay idea of battle formation at sea. He's probably never ordered a broadside drill in his life."

Keir nodded in unhappy agreement. "Any news from Edinburgh?" he asked Munro.

Hugh's crooked smile was more of a grimace. "Aye, sir. The king is sending his kinsman, the earl of Arran, with his master gunner. And Admiral Wood is to follow soon after. However, there's nay telling when the ships will reach the Treshnish Isles, for they'll be sailing from the Firth of Forth."

"And is Donald Dubh in the fortress on Cairn na Burg Mòr?" Colin asked, "along with MacMurchaidh?"

"No one knows for sure," Munro replied, running a thin finger thoughtfully along the side of his prominent hooked nose. "There's a rumor that one of Macdonald's allies has amassed a fleet of ten galleys filled with rebels gathered from across the Outer Hebrides. And that he took both the bastard pretender and MacMurchaidh off the island mere days before the ships under Huntly arrived. No one will know for certain until the castle falls—if it ever does."

"God rot their souls!" Alasdair MacLeod thundered. "You mean to tell me those bloody traitors could sail into my harbor any day with no one to stop them?" He slammed his fist on the table and met Keir's gaze. "I sent my godson with the bulk of my fighting men in our own galleys to search up and down the Hebrides, from Barra to North Uist. I can't afford to send any of my clansmen with you now, MacNeil. We dare not take the chance that Donald Dubh and MacMurchaidh are headed our way with a large fighting force gathered throughout the Isles."

"I understand," Keir said. "We must make sail as soon as possible." He turned to his captains and officers seated beside him. "We leave tonight for the Treshnish Isles."

"You're welcome to the stores of water and victuals you've already stowed," Alasdair added. "But we need to conserve our powder and shot on the chance there's a siege of Dùn Bheagain."

"Of course." Keir moved to his feet. He'd considered

asking MacLeod to shelter Raine in his castle until after the rebellion was quelled. Now it looked as though she might be safer with him on the *Raven*.

His men rose to stand alongside him. Keir looked at Fearchar and Colin, knowing they'd spent the day seeing that the supplies were quickly and properly stowed in the holds. "How long before you can sail?"

"The *Sea Dragon*'s ready now," Fearchar replied.

Colin jerked his chin in agreement. "As is the *Hawk*. We can leave at once."

"Very well," Keir replied. He grinned at Colin and Tam. "If you want to dance with the ladies, gentlemen, you have exactly twenty minutes to enjoy their charms before we return to our ships. We sail with the evening tide."

"I'VE BEEN TOLD that you're learning the constellations, my lady," Laird MacLeod's young nephew said. He guided Raine onto the floor of the great hall, which had been cleared of its tables and benches. The gangly adolescent seemed ill at ease, as though unused to the responsibility of entertaining a high-ranking female visitor.

Shaking her head, Raine laughed softly. "The extent of my learning has been greatly exaggerated, I'm sure," she replied. "I've practiced using a quadrant, but I haven't yet held an astrolabe in my hands. Mr. Barrows, the ship's sea-daddy, includes me in his lessons in navigation with the *Raven*'s two youngest midshipmen. Ethan and Robbie Gibson are destined to be captains in the king's navy, while I'm merely trying to pass my time on board ship in a meaningful way."

They both glanced at the pair of sturdy lads attired in their best shirts and kilts. The two brothers stood at the edge of the dance floor, eyeing the giggling lassies clustered together across the length of the room.

Raine's partner leaned closer than the steps of the stately pavane required. His hazel eyes glowed with appreciation as he bowed in a courtly *révérance*. "Still, I think 'tis admirable for a maid to have a curious mind," he continued, leading her in the promenade around the great hall. "The females in my family content themselves learning to embroider and make lace."

Raine smiled, wondering what the young man would think if he knew the unorthodox subjects she'd studied under her aunt's tutelage. "We each must follow our own interests," she replied sedately. "And 'tis quite usual for young ladies to wish to embellish their wedding linens."

Restless, Raine glanced around the cavernous hall. Once the meal was over, the men of fighting age had sequestered themselves in another part of the castle to discuss their plans to quash the rebellion. That left the young lads to entertain the ladies.

'Twas Alasdair MacLeod's nephew who'd led the hunting party that afternoon. Aside from the young man, only the ladies of the castle with their grooms and huntsmen had accompanied Raine on the hunt. The crews of the *Raven*, *Hawk*, and *Dragon* had been engaged the entire day in stowing fresh supplies in their ships' holds.

As the evening progressed Raine began to wonder if

the men would return from their battle plans in time to dance. At last she spotted Keir entering the great hall with Fearchar and Colin on either side. After them came their seconds in command, Macraith, Tam, and Walter. The men's grim faces betrayed the bad news.

Resplendent in his green-and-black tartan, Keir wore a white linen shirt with lace at the collar and cuffs beneath a green velvet jacket. A jeweled bodkin fastened the corner of his plaid on his broad shoulder. Shiny buckled brogues with checkered short hose had replaced his knee-high boots. Although he'd left his claymore on the *Raven*, he wore his broadsword and dirk, even in the crowded room.

Though Raine could hardly keep her eyes off him, Keir didn't so much as glance her way. He seemed so engrossed in his ongoing discussion with his captains, he was barely aware of the music.

At that moment, Raine was dancing with a jolly, carrot-haired lad, who was leading her in a sprightly galliard. From across the room, she saw Lady Flora Sutherland join the group of privateers. The shameless female boldly elbowed her way past Colin and Tam to place her hand possessively on Keir's sleeve.

Raine felt unaccountably breathless.

Not Flora Sutherland!

That past summer, Flora had made certain that all the ladies gathered in Edinburgh for the royal wedding knew she'd seduced The MacNeil. She had crowed with delight, telling them how she'd enticed the most ferocious warrior in Scotland into her arms. And her bed.

Chapter 11

"LA, MACNEIL, YOU'VE not said a word to me this entire day! I'm about to cause a scene if you don't ask me to dance this very minute."

Keir met Flora's inviting gaze and returned her insipid, self-satisfied smile with a scowl. He'd been unpleasantly surprised when he'd spotted her at the banquet table, thankfully too far away for conversation—for he'd been seated next to Raine. He'd hoped to avoid the infernal woman. Ideally for the rest of his life.

"I hadn't planned to dance this evening, Lady Sutherland," he told her with frosty politeness. "We've been deep in battle plans most of the day and since we intend to sail tonight, we'll continue our discussions well into the evening."

Her lower lip jutted out in a blatant attempt to entice him. "Surely you have time for one little dance," she protested. She batted her pale lashes and squeezed his forearm. Simpering coquettishly, the imposing blonde leaned closer, offering an unfettered view of her astoundingly ample bosom. "Or perhaps," she whispered *sotto voce*, "you'd like to join me in my room, where we can sip wine and reminisce about last summer."

Fearchar and Macraith grinned at the female's obvious invitation and waited with open hilarity for Keir's reply. Both men knew Keir had been intimate with the lady—if one could call her a lady.

"How is it you're visiting here at the castle?" he hedged, not wanting to incite the scene Flora was quite capable of making.

He'd committed the gross error of bedding the married woman once, realizing belatedly that her voluptuous figure had distracted him from the fact that she possessed the brains of an oyster.

"Laird Sutherland is with the earl of Huntly at the moment," she replied with a dramatic shrug, "attempting to put down this unfortunate rebellion. I came to Dùn Bheagain to visit Lady MacLeod, whom I met at the royal wedding. You can imagine how thrilled I was to learn you were expected once your brothers' ships sailed into the harbor. I rejoiced in telling all the ladies of the castle that I was intimately acquainted with one of the notorious Hellhounds of Scotland."

At that moment Raine came to join their group, her beautiful eyes grave. "Excuse me, Laird MacNeil," she said with stilted solemnity, "but I need to speak with you."

"Oh, not now, dear," Lady Sutherland protested with an over-bright smile. She clutched Keir's arm tighter as though afraid Raine might attempt to pry her fingers loose. "Laird MacNeil and I were just about to join the dancers for the galliard."

Keir could have gladly strangled the woman.

"We can talk later, Lady Raine," he said quietly. Determined to separate the two females as quickly as possible, he clasped Flora's plump elbow and turned to lead her toward the dance floor.

"I really need to speak with you now, Keir," Raine insisted, her worried tone conveying a sense of urgency. " 'Tis about something of great importance. Perhaps you can accompany me to the *Raven*, where we can talk in private."

"Fie, child!" Lady Sutherland exclaimed. She glared at Raine with unconcealed annoyance. "You are really too persistent! You should attempt a little coyness in your pursuit, my dear. The MacNeil will think you a strumpet!"

"Flora, be quiet," Keir growled. He peeled her dimpled hand off his green sleeve and transferred it to Colin's red one. "Captain MacRath," he ordered in a voice that brooked no refusal, "dance with Lady Sutherland. Now."

Colin's blue eyes widened in terror. His prominent Adam's apple bobbed up and down as he swallowed back his protest. "Of—of course. Hap-happy to, my—my lady."

Leaving Colin to fend for himself, Keir turned back to Raine. Placing his hand at the small of her back, he guided her toward the doorway. " 'Tis time for you to return to the *Raven*," he told her. "Al-Rahman is waiting nearby. He'll see that you get safely back to the ship."

"But I need to tell you something first," she insisted.

"Later," he said. "I'll be returning to the ship before very long. We can talk then."

By that time they'd reached the tall Moor, who stood in majestic silence with his arms crossed and his head high, ignoring the glances of all the intrigued females clustered nearby.

"Escort Lady Raine to the ship," Keir ordered al-Rahman, who made a deep salaam to her.

"No, no, wait!" she cried.

Ignoring Raine's plaintive call, Keir left her with the *Raven's* chief navigator and rejoined Macraith, Fearchar, and Walter, who'd been watching the scenario with unconcealed fascination. Tam, however, hadn't wasted a moment asking a bonny, dark-haired lassie for a dance. He was presently executing the intricate steps of the galliard with surprising skill.

The four men turned their attention to the unfortunate captain of the *Sea Hawk*. On the stone floor of the great hall, Colin held Lady Sutherland's hand by the tips of his fingers. He seemed to be trying to keep as much distance from her as possible. From his beet-red face, Colin appeared to be choking and sputtering on his words, all the while attempting to keep his gaze off her abundant cleavage.

Walter chuckled. "My son better hurry off to the safety of the *Hawk* before that she-devil drags him into her bed and has her pagan way with him," he said, his gravelly baritone rumbling around in his barrel chest.

"God, how I wish Colin *would* bed her," Keir answered, delighted at the prospect. "If he's half the man

Diana Pembroke claimed last summer, Lady Sutherland would soon have a new target in her sight."

"Nay, Colin's got too much sense to be caught in that man-trap," Fearchar said, readjusting the band of his eye patch and flashing a wide grin.

Keir met the giant's twinkling blue eye and laughed. "I certainly didn't use the brains God gave me last summer, did I?"

Clapping Keir on the shoulder, Macraith joined in the burst of masculine laughter. "Nay, ye hell-tarnished *bow-dykite*, ye certainly did not."

Determined to speak to Keir the moment he returned to the ship, Raine ignored Barrows' warning not to invade the captain's private quarters without permission.

"I'll give myself permission to wait in here," she told her sea-daddy. "You may wait for Laird MacNeil wherever you please."

Shaking his grizzled head, Barrows lit a lantern for her and left the cabin, closing the door behind him.

Raine sat at the small game table for a while, going over in her mind what had just happened at Dùn Bhe-again. Until that evening she'd been certain that she and Keir had been enchanted during their visit to the standing stones. Certain they'd been bound together by the Tuatha De Danann. Given their previous animosity toward each other, nothing else could explain the way they'd kissed so passionately. Now she wasn't quite so convinced.

She waited impatiently to learn the truth. If MacNeil

stayed at the castle and bedded Flora Sutherland tonight, what Raine thought she'd felt at Calanais had been a mistake.

'Twas why she'd tried so hard to talk to Keir earlier that evening before he succumbed to Flora's ample charms—just as he had in Edinburgh last summer. But last summer Raine had told herself she didn't care whom MacNeil had lain with. Now the thought of Flora in Keir's arms tied Raine's stomach into a painful knot.

As time passed slowly by, Raine's eyelids grew heavier. The cabin, lit only by the single lantern, grew darker as the stars came out, visible through the tall stern windows. Rather than place her head on the hard tabletop, she moved to the bed and sat on the edge of the mattress. As she fought against the sleepiness that threatened to engulf her, she glanced at the window and saw the reflection of a young woman, head bowed in sleepy contemplation.

KEIR AND HIS uncle returned to the *Raven* shortly after midnight. Leaving Macraith on deck to give orders to weigh anchor, Keir hurried to Raine's cabin to see if she was awake and still needing to talk to him. He tapped lightly on the closed door, not wanting to disturb her if she'd already fallen asleep.

At the sound of Keir's knocking, Barrows came hurriedly down the passageway from amidships. He'd obviously been waiting up for Keir's return.

"The lassie is nay in her cabin, sir," the bosun's mate said quietly. "Lady Raine insisted on waiting in your quarters. She would nay listen to me. Said she had to talk to you before retiring."

"You can go to sleep now, Barrows," Keir told him with a nod of understanding. Raine was nothing if she wasn't single-minded. He didn't expect anyone but himself to exert the least measure of control over her. "I won't need you until morning," he added in dismissal.

Entering his own cabin, Keir found Raine lying crosswise on his bed sound asleep. Still clothed in the scarlet gown she'd worn to the castle, she hadn't pulled a blanket over herself nor placed a pillow under her head. She must have fallen asleep while sitting there waiting for him.

He moved to stand beside the bed. She slept peacefully, her lips curved in a slight smile as though she were having a pleasant dream. Bending, he placed one hand beside her on the coverlet and took advantage of the opportunity to study her delicate features, bathed now in the soft lantern glow streaming over his shoulder.

Her lush black lashes cast shadows on her smooth cheeks. Ebony wisps had come free from the braid still fastened atop her head, feathering her heart-shaped face. He resisted the temptation to trace the tip of his finger along her fragile cheekbone, recognizing her vulnerability here in his quarters. He wouldn't take advantage of her unconscious state, though the thought made his heart thunder against his chest.

What was so damned important she was willing to fall asleep alone in his quarters, waiting until he returned?

"Raine," he called softly.

When she didn't stir, he knelt down on the rug and

deftly slipped off her shoes. He'd cover her with a blanket and leave her sleep. Since he was returning on deck immediately for their departure, she might as well be comfortable.

Keir reached beneath her shift to find her silk garters, fastened just above her knees, and slipped them over her ankles. He rolled down her stockings and removed them. His fingertips grazed her inner thigh, and he fought against the shock of sexual need that exploded inside him. A need so raw and vibrant, it threatened to overcome his resolve.

'Twould be easy to push her gown and smock up to her slender hips and feast on the sight of her long, tapering legs. To cup her female mound in his hand. To gently caress her delicate pink folds with his skilled fingers, till she awoke to a hot, pulsing arousal, nearly as intense and demanding as his own.

Instead he rose and gently swung her legs up onto the mattress and lifted her head to place a pillow beneath her. He instinctively bent closer, drawn by an overwhelming hunger simply to mingle his breath with hers. To inhale her pure, unsullied spirit as a balm to his cynical, battle-hardened soul.

Her lids opened slowly to reveal her slumberous eyes. Blinking, she smiled softly in welcome, and Keir's heart turned over in his chest.

My God, how he wanted her.

"Keir," she whispered. "I've been waiting for you."

"Aye, lass," he answered. "I see that. What's so important you need to tell me tonight?"

"Mm," she murmured sleepily, "only this." She raised

her hand to his face and ran her thumb along his jaw, then lifted her head to kiss him chastely on the mouth.

With a groan of frustration, Keir stretched out beside Raine and leaned over her. Inhaling the scent of lilacs and roses, he kissed her temple, her cheek, her chin. He placed kisses along the graceful column of her neck and dipped his tongue in the hollow of her collarbone.

"This is what you wanted to tell me?" he murmured. "Had I known, I would have returned to the ship much, much earlier."

She laughed softly, a delightful gurgle deep in her throat, and he smiled in pleasure at the singularly feminine sound.

Keir smoothed his hand over her supple waist and up to cup one small breast. He lowered his head to press kisses along the white frilled edge of the undergarment peeking above her stiffened outer bodice. The feel of her silken skin beneath his lips and tongue sent spurs of lust surging through every inch of his taut body. Hearing her sudden gasp, he realized he'd startled her with the unexpected intimacy.

Keir knew he should halt, even as his fingers found the satin ribbons that laced the front of her velvet gown. He loosened the ties fastening the outer bodice and pushed it aside. Her round areolas peeked through her sheer undergarment, tempting him beyond all endurance. He covered a rosy nipple with his open mouth and suckled her through the transparent fabric. Feeling her arch her back to allow him greater access, he moved to the other breast. She clutched his side-braids, pulling him closer.

"I was going to ask you something back at the castle," she whispered. "But now I know the answer to my question."

He smiled tenderly as he brushed his lips across the firm globes of her breasts. "What answer is that, lass?"

"I know you didn't lie with Lady Sutherland tonight."

"I didn't," he assured her. He pulled back slightly to look into her dark eyes, shining in the lantern light. "I was conferring with the other captains on the siege at Cairn na Burg."

"Mmm-hmm." She sighed. "I can tell from the way you kissed me that you didn't succumb to her obvious invitation," she said. "When I saw you with Lady Flora this evening, I thought perhaps I'd been mistaken about what happened at the standing stones. That I'd only imagined the passion that took hold of us that night. But nothing has changed between us."

He frowned. "What do you mean, Raine?"

"I told you that next morning, remember? We were enchanted—like Tristram and Isolde."

"You really believe that we were bound together by faeries?" Keir asked in disbelief. How could she be so foolish?

"Of course."

Keir moved back and studied her. "But you would never, of your own free will, have chosen me, would you?" he asked, his words thick and raspy. " 'Twould have to be an enchantment to bind you to me."

Clearly hesitant to give an honest reply, she gazed up at him with huge, solemn eyes.

"Tell me the truth, Raine Cameron," he insisted. "You never showed the least tender feelings for me in all the years you've known me."

"But neither would you have chosen me, Keir," she protested. "We seem so ill suited, even now. How else can we explain these feelings except by the intervention of the Tuatha De Danann?"

"These feelings, Raine," he said, more sharply than he'd intended, "are nothing more than carnal desire. A desire we can't allow ourselves to indulge in, for I am honor bound to return you to your family, untouched and unharmed."

Recognizing that it would be illogical to blame Raine for her naiveté or her unquestioning belief in magic, he rose from the bed. "Sleep here, if you'd like. I'll be on deck most of the night. We sail to Cairn na Burg Mòr with all due speed."

AFTER KEIR HAD left, Raine retied the ribbons of her bodice, gathered up her shoes, stockings, and garters, and moved to her own quarters. Barrows had lit a lantern for her earlier, and its welcoming glow showed a cabin no longer Spartan in its furnishings as it had been upon her arrival. Bit by bit—since the day Keir had entered her quarters to scold her—sumptuous pillows, coverlets, tapestries and a rug had appeared without explanation.

From the deck above, Raine heard orders being called, along with the bosun's shrill piping.

"All hands to make sail."

"Away aloft."

Wide awake now, she sat on the edge of her cot and listened to the now-familiar sounds of the ship getting under way.

Above deck the night watch weighed anchor. The topmen scurried up the ratlines in the moonlight and out onto the yards. In the glow of the *Raven*'s night lanterns, the sails were being unfurled and sheeted home. The feel of the ship gliding across the harbor's still water, the sound of the creaking blocks overhead and the muffled calls from the quarterdeck had grown so familiar it seemed like a mother's lullaby.

But lullaby or not, Raine couldn't sleep.

Keir had clearly been upset at the very idea they'd been bound together at Calanais. The fact that he hadn't been enticed by Lady Sutherland's obvious invitation this evening had nothing to do with any tender feelings for Raine. The chief of Clan MacNeil had simply been too busy making plans to quell the rebellion to take time to bed Flora. Perhaps when the war was over, he and Flora would resume their tawdry alliance.

Thankfully, Raine hadn't given in to the nigh overpowering yearning she'd felt for Keir when she awoke to find him bending over her. She needed to focus all of her attention on discovering a way to leave the ship and search for Torcall MacMurchaidh. After the fortress at Cairn na Burg Mòr fell, she might be able to convince Tam MacLean to help her. Perhaps he or Colin would loan her the coins needed to search for her natural father. In the meantime, she'd be careful not to bring up the subject of the Tuatha De Danann, for the mere mention of a faery enchantment only seemed to upset Keir.

Well, he could rebel against it all he liked. If they had truly been bound together as Raine suspected, there was nothing either of them could do to change it.

The memory of Keir fresh from his bath intruded on her pragmatic musings. The perfection of sinew and bone, of bulging muscles and flat planes, of tight buttocks and broad back, of the inked image of the *Black Raven* soaring across his shoulder blades and the battle scars etched across his chest hadn't been—couldn't be—forgotten. Bless her and save her, what woman in her right mind would want to forget such a magnificent sight?

But until she found her natural father, she couldn't allow her feelings for Keir to distract her from her self-avowed quest.

KEIR SPENT THE remainder of the night on the quarter-deck attempting to coax as much speed as possible from the weatherly galleon. The *Black Raven*, close-hauled and running before the wind, was making eight knots, her stern lanterns turning her wake into a phosphorescent path behind her. The *Hawk* and the *Dragon* followed in line-ahead formation. They'd left the Loch of Dùn Bheagain and the Little Minch behind and were passing Point Neist, on the Isle of Skye. The three warships were cutting south-south-east through the Sea of the Hebrides. The weather was clear, and the constellations stood out like brilliant diamonds in the black velvet sky.

" 'Tis safe to return to your quarters now," Macraith

told Keir cheerily as he came to join him by the starboard rail. "According to young Mr. MacFarlane, Lady Raine moved to her own cabin shortly after midnight."

Keir had just taken another reading on his astrolabe. He barely glanced at his uncle. "Nothing happened between us, if that's what you're thinking. The lady remains as virginal as a postulant in a nunnery."

"Aye, I've nay doubt," Macraith replied. "Else you would nay be up here on deck in the middle of the night like a heartsick fool instead of snuggling with a bonny lassie in your soft warm bed."

"Damn your eyes," Keir snapped. "Keep your voice down and your opinions to yourself." He glanced up into the shrouds to make sure no lookout was directly overhead, listening to their every word.

Aware of the officer of the watch at the mainmast, they moved closer to the railing before continuing their muted conversation.

"She's nineteen, ye glaikit gomerel, not a child," Macraith pointed out. "If it hadn't been for Gideon Cameron's untimely death, he'd have arranged a marriage when she turned seventeen. By now she'd be snug in some earl's castle, bouncing a wee bairn on her knee, instead of traipsing about the Isles for God knows what purpose."

"What I feel about Raine is irrelevant," Keir replied in a low growl. "She deserves a man with a sterling pedigree. A laird born into a household of unblemished lineage." Keir fisted his hands in frustration. "And you're goddamn right—Raine would already be married to an earl, if Cameron hadn't been murdered."

"Hell, if you think you must be an earl before you can marry the lass, ask King Jamie for the title. I'm quite certain he'd be happy to oblige, if he hasn't already made up his mind to it. Why, he'd joyfully attend your wedding and dance with the sonsy bride."

"You forget," Keir replied with biting self-derision, "I'm descended from a long line of murderous pirates. And by now—if Duncan Stewart has been successful in his negotiations—I'm already formally contracted to the maid of Strathfillan. Whoever does marry Lady Raine Cameron, it won't be me."

"Well, as to that," Macraith said, "who's to say your uncle entered into those negotiations with a full heart. The earl of Appin may have higher hopes for you than a loveless marriage with the timid daughter of Fillan MacNab.

Chapter 12

THREE DAYS LATER, the *Black Raven* and her consorts arrived at Calgarraidh, on the Isle of Mull. That morning the wide, welcoming bay with its white, sandy beaches lay smothered in a dense fog, blocking the sight of the nearby Treshnish Isles and the fortress of Cairn na Burgh. But the sound of cannon fire floated across the water like distant thunder.

At six bells, Macraith came to stand beside Keir, just as the faintest beams of light broke through the fog on the eastern horizon. The ship came alive with activity to the sound of the bosun's piping.

"Beat to quarters, Mr. MacFarlane," Keir said to the tall midshipman standing nearby.

At the roll of the drum, the waking seamen poured out of the hatches and hurried across the deck to their stations, so well trained they could meet any emergency at sea in minutes. Keir had handpicked his crew for strength, agility, and courage under fire. He'd drilled the men with their guns daily, using empty barrels for targets. They'd frequently match one team against the other, seeing which gun crew could sink the barrels first. But there'd be no time for a drill today.

At the stern, Stark Buchanan, the ship's best helmsman, used his brawn to control the tiller. Simon Ramsay stood on the forecastle deck as the *Raven* luffed into the harbor and hove to, followed by her sister ships.

"Mr. Ramsay," Keir told his quartermaster, "signal the *Hawk* and the *Dragon* to inspect guns and crews. After breakfast we'll proceed to Cairn na Burgh Mòr in line-ahead formation."

Keir didn't believe in sending his men into battle on empty stomachs. And there'd be no way to tell how long it would take to subdue Cairn na Burgh—not until he reached the fortress and could assess the damage already inflicted by the royal fleet. Soon the tantalizing smell of bacon floated up from the galleys.

"Aye, sir," Ramsay replied. He turned, repeating the orders to the quartermaster's mate responsible for the signal flags.

"Mr. Wyllie, prepare your gun crews for inspection," Keir told the bosun.

With Macraith on one side and the ship's Greek master gunner on the other, Keir walked through the gun deck, stopping at each long-range eighteen-pounder. At the moment the brass muzzle-loading cannon were lashed securely against the bulwarks, resting in place on their carriages.

"We'll encounter choppy seas very shortly as we approach the mouth of the sea loch," Keir told Apollonius. "The gun ports are to remain closed until we have the castle in sight and are ready to commence firing." He turned to his uncle. "Has our chief navigator finished his morning prayers yet?"

Macraith nodded, pointing to the tall Moor coming toward them. "Here he is now, sir. Praying rug stowed away and ready to go to work. And I hope to God, he said a prayer for all of us."

Attired in a caftan and loose trousers, Abid al-Rahman made a salaam, one hand touching his forehead, the other on the handle of his huge curved scimitar. "If it please you, sir, I'll consult my charts once again and then direct the steersman to the mouth of Loch Tuath and the Treshnish Isles." At Keir's nod of assent, al-Rahman turned and left.

When they'd finished the inspection of the cannons on the gun deck, they proceeded to the main deck and the fore and aft guns, long-rage nine-pounders.

"You may pipe all hands to breakfast, Mr. Wyllie," Keir said, pleased with what he'd seen.

At the bosun's whistle, the sound of feet thundered across the scrubbed planking as the watches hurried to their mess.

Keir glanced at his uncle. "We'll have breakfast now as well. God willing, by this afternoon all hell will break loose," he said with a grin of anticipation.

Keir loved a battle—nearly as much as making love to a beautiful woman.

"DURING OUR BOMBARDMENT of the castle, you're to remain belowdecks," Keir told Raine. "I don't expect we'll receive much damage from their cannon, but I want you in a safe place, all the same."

They were seated at the table in Keir's cabin, sharing breakfast with his uncle and the other officers, Buchanan, Ramsay, al-Rahman, and the galleon's three midshipmen—Hector MacFarlane and the two Gibson brothers.

Taking a deep, calming breath, Raine looked around the table at the ferocious privateers—for the moment, officers in the king's navy. From the tension visible on their faces, battle was imminent, though they appeared more excited than worried.

Raine felt her muscles tighten, till she worried her stiff, jerky movements would betray her own misgivings. If MacMurchaidh was in the fortress, he could very well be killed before she had the chance to speak with him. And if anything happened to Keir, Raine thought her heart might break—although she'd never admit it to him. Not for all the gold unicorns in Scotland.

"I brought my healing remedies from Archnacarry," Raine said, keeping her hands folded tightly in her lap and out of sight under the table, so no one would notice her shaking fingers. "If anyone needs assistance with an injury, I'll be able to help."

Keir scowled at the suggestion, clearly unhappy at her offer. "These are not the simple cuts and burns you've been used to attending with your mother and aunt at the manor," he said in a dismissive tone. "Barrows acts as our surgeon when need be. It can be quite a bloody mess in the cockpit."

"I'm not squeamish at the sight of blood," Raine assured him. "If I can be of any help at all, please allow me to do so."

"Very well," Keir agreed in a halfhearted manner. "But stay with Barrows at all times. We'll bring any wounded belowdecks. If we do take a hit, flying shards of wood can cause amazing damage. Once the bombardment begins, I don't want you sticking your head out of a hatch." He paused and studied her through narrowed eyes, then added, "And I'd like your word on that, Lady Raine."

Raine felt the heated flush of mortification creep up her neck and cheeks. Keir was apparently remembering the last time the *Raven* had sailed into a harbor intent on a siege. He'd believed her safe in the fishing village where he'd sent her. Every listener at the table knew the nearly disastrous consequences of her failure to follow their captain's orders.

"You have my word," she answered in a strangled voice. "During the bombardment of the castle, I will remain belowdecks. Where, by the way, is the cockpit?"

Ethan looked up from his plate and smiled knowingly, happy to give the answer. "That's where my brother and I have our quarters," the twelve-year-old lad informed her. "It's on the after-part of the lowest deck."

His blue eyes shining with pride, Robbie nodded. "During a battle, 'tis used as a station for the wounded. Then we have to scrub up the blood and gore before we can ready our cots for sleeping."

"Barrows will take you there," Keir told her. He seemed about to say more, then merely shook his head.

KEIR STOOD ON the *Raven*'s quarterdeck, watching the royal fleet under the command of the earl of Huntly. The

small ships lurched about in the churning sea with no sign
of planned maneuvers or the least familiarity with naval
warfare.

Some of the caravels had sustained direct hits, with
masts and sails showing damage. A few were taking water
in their bilges, for the pumps were sending gushers over the
side, a sign they'd been struck below the waterline. Their
gunners had tried unsuccessfully to bring the ships' cannon
to bear on the forbidding MacGillean stronghold perched
on solid rock and protected by the surrounding cliffs.

The rough water and Huntly's lack of expertise at gunnery had failed to produce any sign of significant damage
to the fortress. 'Twas apparent neither the king's kinsman,
the earl of Arran, nor his principal gunner had arrived yet
with extra gunpowder and greater experience at sighting
cannon on a moving deck.

Macraith, standing next to Keir, shaded his eyes with
his hand and squinted against the sun. "How likely is it
that Donald Dubh and Torcall MacMurchaidh are guests
of MacGillean of Duart, do you think?"

"Nothing is certain," Keir replied. "As we both know,
the clan chiefs shift their allegiance from the lord of the
Isles to King James and back again, depending on which
way the wind is blowing. Other than the ships under my
command, I trust no one. Not even the king's royal lieutenant, Archibald Campbell, wherever the hell he is."

"Aye," Macraith agreed, "somewhere safe, no doubt."
He spat over the side in disgust. "That damn pawky Argyll
is a close kinsman to both MacMurchaidh and MacGillean. And Donald Dubh is Campbell's bastard grandson,

not that it's likely to help the lad any. 'Twould be like having Satan himself as your grandsire. Argyll enjoys playing both sides against the middle, if 'twill line his pockets with gold or increase the size of his lands."

The two MacNeils, nephew and uncle, turned their gazes away from the king's floundering ships and studied their target.

The fortifications of Cairn na Burgh Castle straddled two islands guarding the entrance of Loch Tuath along the western side of Mull. The larger island of Cairn na Burgh Mòr, a solid block of granite rising sheer from the sea and protected by strong, treacherous currents, was almost impregnable. On it stood the main part of the fortress—including the barrack block, chapel, courtyard, and guardhouse. On Cairn na Burgh Beag, there was a second guardhouse and a well.

Although the castle was protected by the surrounding high cliffs, over the centuries it had changed hands more than once, for its position was of strategic importance to the southern Hebrides.

Earlier, as the *Raven* approached the scene of battle, Keir had signaled the commander of the royal fleet to withdraw to a safe distance. Now the three full-rigged galleons, *Raven*, *Hawk*, and *Dragon*, maneuvered into battle-line formation and the gun ports were opened.

Great puffs of smoke followed by the sound of artillery came from Cairn na Burgh's iron cannon mounted on their stationary emplacements along the parapets, as the defenders sighted the newly arrived ships.

A cannonball whizzed through the *Raven*'s rigging,

blowing a hole in her main-topsail. Another crashed onto the deck, smashing one of the boats and sending splinters in every direction. Ethan Gibson, who'd been carrying a cask of gunpowder from below to the bow guns, grabbed his left thigh with a grunt of pain and dropped to his knees. Robbie raced across the deck to his brother's side.

"Take him below," Keir shouted. "Barrows will see to him."

Davie Swinton, the ship's stocky barrel maker, scooped the lad up in his brawny arms and carried him down an open hatchway, while Robbie picked up the fallen cask of powder and hurried toward the forecastle guns.

Keir could see Colin on the *Hawk*'s quarterdeck and Fearchar standing at the *Dragon*'s starboard railing beyond. Both captains were waiting calmly for Keir's signal to begin the shelling. Their decks had been cleared for action as they'd cruised closer to the fortress in line-ahead formation under main and foretopsails.

"Silence, fore and aft," Macraith shouted.

"Signal the *Hawk* and the *Dragon* to commence firing at will, Mr. Ramsay," Keir said. The quartermaster's mate hurried to raise the signal flags.

Below, on the *Raven*'s gun deck, the crews waited impatiently for the order to fire.

"On the top of the roll," Keir told his master gunner. "Fire as they bear."

Apollonius shouted the order, to be repeated through the hatches covered by screens to the gun crews, who'd already sighted their cannon and now brought their slow-matches to the touchholes. With mighty explosions, the great guns lurched and recoiled one after another, as the crews jumped aside just in time to avoid being crushed. With the rolling broadside from the *Black Raven*, followed by her sister ships, the final bombardment of Cairn na Burgh had begun.

The three galleons' long-range brass cannon pounded the thick stone walls of the fortress, striking the parapets along the bartizan with the intent of dismantling their immovable guns. The gatehouse with its iron portcullis caved and fell inward. Great gaping holes appeared in the curtain walls and the round tower above the guardhouse slowly tilted to one side before crashing into the bailey below. Huge clouds of smoke obscured most of the destruction, but the sound of carnage carried over the water to mingle with the cheers of the gun crews after making a direct hit.

"Cease fire," Keir ordered. "Lower the boats."

"Landing parties away," his uncle shouted to the armed seamen waiting on deck for the order.

Leading his men, Keir scrambled over the gunwale with Macraith alongside. Al-Rahman, his curved scimitar jammed in his wide blue sash, followed right behind them. The *Raven*'s crewmen clambered down the rope ladders and into the longboats, armed with boarding axes, broadswords, and cutlasses.

Cutting through the roiling waves surging onto the shore, the landing boats from the *Black Raven*, the *Sea Dragon*, and the *Sea Hawk* headed toward Cairn na Burg Castle and the doomed rebels.

RAINE HAD CHANGED from her gown into her shirt and trousers before going to the lower deck to assist Barrows. After Swinton carried Ethan into the cockpit and hurried back to the main deck, Barrows carefully extracted the wood splinters from the lad's thigh.

Working by the dim light of a lantern hung from a beam overhead, Raine helped her sea-daddy inspect the raw wound, making certain they'd removed all the slivers and shredded pieces of cloth. Then Raine applied a salve her aunt had packed in her satchel, and Barrows gave Ethan a small tumbler of wine to ease the pain. Together Barrows and Raine bandaged the lacerated leg and waited for more injured to arrive in the cramped space.

After the sound of shelling ceased, Raine hurried up to the forecastle railing and gazed across the choppy water to the castle. Although small fires still blazed in parts of the fortress and some of the walls had crumbled under the artillery barrage, the thick walls of the keep remained intact. During the fighting, the women and children would have withdrawn to the safety of the donjon tower, much as she'd been shielded from harm deep inside the ship's lower deck.

Barrows and Robbie came to join her at the rail, where they stood side by side watching the scene in horrified fascination. Smoke from the cannon drifted in the air, carrying the stench of sulphur.

"Don't worry, Lady Raine," Robbie said, his voice ringing with youthful optimism. "None can best our captain. He's stronger than any five men put together."

Raine smiled as she wiped away the tears caused by the

soot and ash coming from the burning castle—and the terror she felt for Keir. "I—I know, lad."

Through the drifting smoke, they could see the long-boats carrying the landing parties. Oars were stowed and the craft dragged onto the steep, rocky shore. The seamen from the three galleons, led by their officers, charged over the broken ramparts and into the castle. Screams and shouts carried over the water, and Raine clutched the railing, her insides twisted into painful knots at the faint but unmistakable sounds of hand-to-hand combat.

Suddenly, the fortress grew eerily quiet.

"Look, my lady," Barrows said, pointing to the top of Cairn na Bugh's highest rampart.

Raine followed the direction of his finger and saw the pennant of the MacGillean clan being lowered. The royal flag of Scotland rose to the top of the pole. They could hear the cheering clearly over the water.

Her heart in her throat, she watched the *Raven* crewmen return in their longboats, as boats from the other ships of the royal fleet pulled toward the shore. Raine had learned earlier that the earl of Huntly would be in charge of taking all prisoners to Edinburgh for trial.

Several seamen were lifted up, unconscious, from the boats and over the gunwale. Then Keir came over the side, his shirt and breeches soaked with blood.

Fighting the nausea that churned in her stomach, Raine raced across the deck to meet him. His face was smudged with the grime of battle and his clothing reeked of gunpowder.

"Dammit, I told you to remain below," he snapped before she could say a word.

"I—I did," she replied, breathless from the fright that gripped her. "I—I waited below with Mr. Barrows until the shelling from the castle stopped." She clutched his wrist. "You're covered with blood. Are you hurt?"

He shook his head and gestured impatiently. " 'Tisn't my blood. Not much of it, anyway."

"Thank God," she said, barely above a whisper as relief washed through her.

"A few of the men have severe wounds to be tended," Keir continued, watching his crew return to the *Raven*.

"Did you take any prisoners?" Raine asked, hurrying along beside him as he moved toward the hatchway.

Keir nodded absently. "Aye."

"Was Torcall MacMurchaidh one of them?"

He shook his head, barely listening to her. His attention was focused on the four injured sailors being placed on boards and carried to an open hatch.

"Then he was killed?" she asked, her words hushed and breathless.

"Who was killed?"

"Laird MacMurchaidh."

Keir stopped and studied her intently. "Why would you care about him, Raine?"

Tears welled in her eyes, blurring her sight. "I—I don't care," she lied, dashing them away with the back of her hands. "I'm—I'm merely curious."

"Nay, that damn traitor wasn't there," he said, continuing across the main deck. "And more to the point, Donald Dubh wasn't there either, confound it."

Raine brought her hands to her mouth, covering her

cry of gratitude. "Oh, that's unfortunate," she mumbled through her fingers. But Keir appeared not to notice anything strange, for he turned to descend the hatchway before she'd even spoken.

Raine followed Keir down to sickbay, where the injured seamen had been carried. Barrows at his side, he moved to each man, quickly assessing the severity of his wounds. When he reached Ethan, he crouched on his haunches in front of the boy.

"How are you doing, lad?" he asked with a bracing smile.

"Fine, sir," the young gentleman piped. "Lady Raine wrapped my leg and told me tomorrow I'd be good as new."

"Never doubt it," Keir told him, giving him an encouraging pat on the head. He rose to his feet and met Raine's gaze. "Thank you," he silently mouthed.

Macraith came into the cockpit. "Let's see that arm," he said to Keir.

" 'Tis nothing," Keir told him. "A scratch, no more." But he perched on a sea trunk and rolled up his sleeve, revealing a deep gash on his forearm. "Perhaps a few stitches."

"I can help," Raine offered, "while your uncle assists Mr. Barrows with some of the others."

For a moment, Keir gazed at her in silence, then tipped his head in assent.

"I'm going to apply a solution first," she told him. "It may sting a little."

Reaching for her satchel, Raine pulled out a bottle, uncorked it, and dabbed a small cloth with its contents. She patted the soaked pad gently on the open wound.

"Jesus," Keir muttered with a ferocious scowl.

She smiled up at him. "I warned you."

"What the hell is that?"

"Something Aunt Isabel concocted to wash away the grime and debris of a battle wound. That way we can see where to put the stitches and do a neater job. You'll have a finer scar, that way. My aunt insisted on packing it in my satchel, along with my red velvet gown."

"I might have known 'twas Isabel's bitter creation."

Raine laughed and shook her head. "Oh,'tisn't Aunt Isabel's creation, at all. 'Tis a faery remedy she learned when she was young."

Keir's forehead creased in disbelief. "Where the hell would your spinster aunt learn anything from the faeries?" he scoffed.

"From her grandmother," Raine said, "whose grandmother before her lived with the Shining Ones when she was a young maid."

"God Almighty," Keir said with a soft laugh. "But I'm damn grateful to Isabel for packing that bonny red gown."

Raine looked up to meet his gaze. In spite of the pain of his wound and the sting of the cleansing solution, his emerald eyes sparkled. His words had evoked the memory of his loosening the satin ribbons on her velvet bodice and suckling her nipples through the sheer material of her shift. He looked at her with such tenderness, she suspected he was remembering too.

A warmth spread through Raine, spiraling deep inside. Flustered by the unfamiliar feeling, she bent over the cut to hide her confusion as she sewed tiny stitches to close the wound.

Keir looked down at the top of Raine's head. Her ebony hair parted in the middle, a single, long braid fell down her back, tied with a blue ribbon. He longed to place his lips on that severe part and then slowly loosen the interwoven strands.

He longed to spread her silken hair across her bare shoulders, then brush the strands aside to suckle her perfect breasts. He knew her small breasts were perfection, for he'd glimpsed the round ivory globes beneath her gauzy shift. Sexual hunger pulsed through him at the memory.

When she finished stitching his wound, Raine bent to snip the black thread with her teeth, revealing the elegant curve of her nape. 'Twas all Keir could do not to reach out and smooth his fingertips across her ivory skin.

"There," she said, rising to her feet. "I doubt you'll have much of a scar."

He grinned. "Another scar more or less would scarce make a difference."

"I'd better help Mr. Barrows now," she said, turning away.

Keir caught her hand and brought it to his lips. "Thank you, my lady."

She smiled in surprise at his chivalry. "You're welcome," she whispered.

Keir watched the lass move away to help Barrows bandage another man's shoulder. What could possibly be Lady Raine Cameron's interest in the traitor, Torcall MacMurchaidh?

Chapter 13

FOUR DAYS AFTER the fall of the fortress on Cairn na Burgh Mòr, the *Raven*, the *Dragon*, and the *Hawk* returned to Calgarraidh Bay, where the captains and their officers conferred. After quickly replenishing their stores of fresh water and making any needed repairs, the three warships would sail south, skirting the islands of Tiree and Coll and then turn north-northwest into the Sea of the Hebrides once again—their objective to search for Donald Dubh, the self-proclaimed Lord of the Isles, and any Macdonald allies willing to fight under his banner.

The third morning after they'd arrived at Calgarraidh, Keir stood on the starboard quarterdeck, watching the crew prepare the ship to leave the calm waters of its natural harbor. The top-men scurried aloft into the rigging and moved out onto the yards, ready to unfurl the sails at Macraith's command. Men from the morning watch waited at the capstan, about to lift anchor under the bosun's supervision. Al-Rahman stood nearby with his rolled charts under his arm, while Stark Buchanan waited at the tiller, ready to steer the galleon out of the bay and past the Isle of Coll.

Keir watched Raine come up the companionway and hurry to join him in spite of Barrows repeated warnings that absolutely no one was allowed to disturb the ship's captain while he was on the quarterdeck—unless he called for them.

Unperturbed by her inability to follow protocol at sea, Keir smiled a welcome. Some things weren't worth the fight.

"Good morning, my lady," he said, and then immediately became aware of her worried look. Raine's expressive eyes were shadowed, as though she hadn't slept during the night. Her ivory complexion lacked the glow of rosy cheeks. Her hair, usually braided tightly, streamed loose over her shoulders and blew about her face in the breeze. She looked as though she'd just got out of bed.

"You mustn't leave Calgarraidh Bay this morning," Raine stated in a breathless tone. "A fleet of ships is lying in stealth, waiting for you."

"Don't worry, lass," Keir replied, reaching out to push aside the strands of ebony caught in her luxuriant lashes. "There's no force on the sea that can defeat our ships. We're going to find the rebels, no matter how strong their forces. And at the present moment, there's no sign of a sail on the horizon. Not for as far as a man can see from the topmost yard." He smiled and added, "I know that for a fact. I've already been up there."

"But there are enemy warships lying in wait for you," Raine insisted, scowling at him. "I saw it in a vision."

Keir propped his hands on his hips and shook his head.

"A vision? What kind of a vision?" he demanded, trying to tamp down his irritation. When would Raine finally give up this improbable belief that she was a seer?

All around them flourished the activity of a ship about to leave harbor as the anchor was weighed and secured.

"Make sail," Macraith called.

Simon Ramsay, the lantern-jawed quartermaster, repeated the order. "Make sail!" he shouted.

The men in the shrouds let fall the topsails which were immediately sheeted home. The *Raven* caught the wind and surged forward like a great white bird freed of its cage.

"My vision came in a dream," Raine persisted, "as they often do. During the night, I dreamt that the *Raven* was attacked by armed carracks."

Unaware of their conversation, Macraith continued giving orders. "Pipe the morning watch to breakfast, Mr. Wyllie."

The bosun's shrill piping barely began before a stampede of feet hurried toward their watch's mess.

"I don't believe in visions, Raine," Keir told her, listening in satisfaction to the familiar sounds of his ship getting under way. "Nor am I afraid of a surprise attack. The Macdonalds and the other rebellious clans sail in oared galleys, not carracks. Your dream can't possibly come true. Our squadron will stay together. Both Colin and Fearchar are veteran seamen. We can outmaneuver and outfight anything on the sea."

The *Raven* gathered the wind in her sails and burst ahead, soon moving at six knots or better.

"You know that I have the second sight, Keir," Raine insisted, grabbing his shirtsleeve as though afraid he'd walk away. "You were there at Archnacarry when I described the fortress of Dhòmhuill, where Rory's wife was being held captive."

"Your description of gargoyles along the parapets could have described a half dozen castles in the Isles," Keir said, trying to rein in his mounting annoyance. " 'Twas mere luck that Lady Joanna was in the first Macdonald fortress we stormed."

"Not just any gargoyles," she insisted. "Eagles screaming into the wind with arrows clasped in their talons. Dhòmhuill is the only castle with those particular gargoyles on the parapets. You have to admit that."

"I admit to nothing," he told her with a cynical grin. "Magic, faeries, the second sight—they're all foolish beliefs held by our ignorant forebears, who claimed the Tuatha De Danann inhabited Scotland before the coming of mankind."

"You're the one who's foolish!" she cried, her dark eyes enormous in her pale face. "If you don't heed my warning and remain here at Calgarriadh, we'll—"

"Raine, look around you," Keir interrupted, his patience wearing thin. "We're already leaving the bay. If there's an enemy fleet somewhere out there, we'll find it and we'll be victorious." He took her elbow and turned her toward the companionway. "Now let's get some breakfast, shall we?"

A WEEK LATER, despite Raine's vision foretelling the approach of hostile ships, the look-outs in the tops of the *Black Raven* and her consorts hadn't spotted a single sail on the horizon. In the waters west of Mull the three men-of-war had nosed past the islands of Coll and Tiree and sailed out into the Atlantic Ocean, searching for any sign of the Macdonald traitor and his allies. Now they'd come about and were heading north toward the Sea of the Hebrides.

Shortly after the midday meal, Raine gathered her small box of sewing tools and tapped on the door of Keir's quarters. He opened it at once, for she'd explained at the noon sighting that it was time to remove the stitches on his forearm.

He made no attempt to refuse her entrance—as she feared he might—but stepped aside with a welcoming gesture and ushered her in. "Barrows can do this," he told her for the third time that day. "There's no need for you to continue nursing my wound."

"I know," she replied with an impatient shake of her head. "But the stitches I made are quite fine, and I have the small hands and tiny scissors to remove the thread without removing your skin with it." Trying to hide a smile that threatened to spoil her serious mien, she added with intentional provocation, "Unless you're afraid of me, Captain MacNeil. In which case, I promise to be as gentle as possible."

The sea-weathered corners of his eyes crinkled as he tipped his head back and burst out laughing. His long black hair, the side-braids fastened with strips of leather, along with the gold hoop swinging from an earlobe, gave him the aura of an insolent pirate. "The day I'm afraid of a wee lassie like you, Raine," he chortled, "will be the day I'm laid in my grave." He started to roll up the sleeve of his ruffled white shirt. "Come do your worst," he added, still chuckling. "I'll try not to beg for mercy."

"You've made your point," she snapped, frowning in exasperation. He'd always had a raucous sense of humor. "There's no need to keep laughing at your own idiotic jest."

That sent him into another bout of guffaws. Apparently, the sight of her acting like a petulant shrew tickled him down to his bones.

But mercy to heavens!

The sound of his rich, deep baritone seemed to wrap around her lungs, squeeze the air right out of her chest, and push it up into her head—where it whirled around her brain and buzzed in her ears.

When she spoke, her voice sounded high pitched and ill-tempered. "We both know very well I couldn't hurt you if I tried," she scolded. "I'm anxious to see how the wound has healed, and it's certainly time for the stitches to come out." She pointed to the game table in front of the tall stern windows—where he'd fleeced her out of the few coins she had left—and her next words came sharper than she'd intended. "Sit over there in the light."

Although he continued to grin at her obvious discomfort, Keir submitted to her directions and placed his bandaged forearm on the tabletop for her inspection. Raine pulled up a chair and scooted closer till they were sitting knee to knee. He was dressed in doeskin breeches and shiny leather boots. She wore her borrowed outfit of worn striped shirt, loose fitting trousers, and scuffed shoes.

Raine unwound the cloth covering his injury and ran her fingertips lightly over the stitches. No sign of oozing

puss nor the red puffiness that would indicate something
was wrong.

"Ah," she said with a sigh, smiling in satisfaction. " 'Tis
healed beautifully."

Raine had insisted on inspecting Keir's wound several
times after the battle at Cairn na Burg and had always
been pleased with its progress. Since the age of twelve,
Raine had been Aunt Isabel's ardent student in the potions
and ointments known to healers. 'Twas gratifying to learn
her studies hadn't been in vain.

Bending her head over Keir's muscular arm, Raine
began to carefully snip the precise row of stitches. She
tried to focus all her attention on the delicate task, but
his masculine presence proved overwhelming. Keir wasn't
simply larger than most men. He had the commanding
air of a natural-born leader combined with the physical
stature and strength of a Celtic demi-god. He was Cúchulainn and Fionn MacCumhaill and Manannán mac Lir,
all combined into one magnificent warrior.

"The crew is very impressed with your ability to tend
their wounds," Keir said quietly.

Without raising her head from her task, she shrugged.
"Most women have some knowledge of the healing arts.
Indeed we must, as long as our menfolk continue to wage
war."

"My sailors believe you have more than the ordinary share
of skill in mending wounds," he continued. "Mine wasn't the
only gash you sewed, and all their injuries have healed without a trace of diseased flesh nor scarcely even a scar."

At his words, Raine felt a warm glow spread through

her. " 'Tis gratifying to know they're regaining their strength."

"Barrows told me how you helped him set Will MacElvie's broken arm. And how the salve you put on Davidson's burn from an overheated cannon barrel healed the injury almost miraculously."

"To be honest, I've never set a broken limb before," she said. "Barrows told me what to do. I simply followed his directions."

"Most young lassies would have fainted at the sight of so much blood and gore," Keir added, his voice warm with admiration.

"In case you haven't noticed, I'm not a young lassie anymore," she stated.

"I've noticed."

Suddenly aware that he'd been studying her as she worked, Raine looked up to meet Keir's intent gaze and came to a startling realization. 'Twould be difficult to say exactly what was the most beautiful thing about him, but his emerald eyes outlined by thick black lashes would have to be at the top of anyone's inventory. Strange, she'd never before thought of the chief of Clan MacNeil as beautiful. 'Twas his handsome brother Lachlan whom Raine had admired since childhood.

As an adolescent, she'd always considered Keir too rough and outspoken when he came with his family for a visit at Archnacarry Manor. Later, when she was old enough to join the ladies at the Scottish court, she learned all about his profligate ways. He'd seduced and then discarded a string of bonny mistresses as easily as other men bought and sold prized horses. At the royal wedding that past summer, two married ladies had attempted to pull each other's hair out by the roots, only to learn the chief of Clan MacNeil had moved on to a third woman—before dusting his hands of them all and returning to sea.

Raine finished her task, replaced her scissors in her sewing box, and rose to her feet. Remembering the way the two jealous females had screamed at each other like fishwives in a market square, she scowled at him.

The faeries at Calanais must have been very irritated when Raine and Keir interrupted their frolicking in the moonlight. For there was no doubt the Shining Ones had been up to their usual tricks when they'd wrapped a bond of enchantment around her and Keir MacNeil, otherwise known as the Black Raven.

"There," she said, winding the bandage into a tight roll. " 'Tis finished and the scar is barely visible. You're just as you were before."

Unexpectedly, Keir reached out and pulled her onto his lap. "Am I, lass?" he asked, his deep voice husky. "Will I ever be the same, now that you've touched me?"

Raine knew he was alluding to the night he'd found her asleep in his bed. Of how she'd reached up and touched his face. "Neither of us will ever be the same," she admitted in all honesty. She lifted her face, expecting a kiss, and to her surprise, he brushed his lips across her forehead.

"Why did you ask about MacMurchaidh after Cairn na Burgh fell?" he questioned, his mouth pressed lightly against her skin. "Why would you be interested in that fugitive?"

"Oh, I'm not," she denied, gazing over his shoulder at the tapestry on the far wall. Twining one of Keir's side-braids between her fingers, she accidently bumped his earring and set the gold hoop swinging. "I've no special interest in Torcall MacMurchaidh whatsoever. I simply wanted to know if you'd caught the traitors. For when you do, the rebellion and the killing will be over."

"And when that happens," he said in a hushed tone, "I'll take you safely home to your family."

"Won't they be surprised?" Raine tried to imagine how her mother would react when she confided that Keir was her lover—and would be forever.

He lifted her chin with the tip of his finger and gazed thoughtfully into her eyes. "You left no message for Lady Nina as to where you were going?"

"Oh, as to that, yes. I wrote my mother a letter from Inverness telling her that I was with you and that I wanted to visit the standing stones at Calanais."

"And your aunt knew you were going and never said a word to your mother or uncle?"

"I'm certain Aunt Isabel reassured my family of my safety. She knew I would travel to Inverness with the Poor Clares, where I would place myself under your protection."

"When you were tending to my injury, you said that she'd packed the healing remedies in your satchel. How is it you knew just what to do for each injury? Had Isabel taught you how to use medicine in the past?"

Raine bit her lip and stared down at her lap. At the time she'd been too frightened and worried about Keir and the other wounded seamen to guard her words. "I didn't mean to imply that I was particularly skilled in the art of healing. Or that Aunt Isabel taught me anything that isn't commonly known."

"I understand," he said.

Keir understood that Raine was lying once again. The lass made a terrible liar—as bad at evading the truth as she was at playing cards. She always gave herself away by averting her gaze. He'd known since she was a tall, gangly filly—all long arms and legs—that when she looked him straight in the eye, she was telling the truth. He wasn't about to let Raine in on his discovery.

Keir tipped the slender beauty against the crook of his arm and gazed in admiration at her fine-boned features, her dainty nose, her full lips, her soft, milky skin, enhanced by sparkling jet eyes and ebony hair. She wore her usual long braid down her back and wispy tendrils framed her heart-shaped face.

He'd known other ladies at court who might be considered lovelier, certainly more buxom, but they lacked Raine's spontaneous energy and unbounded curiosity. Holding her in his arms was like gathering sunshine into a ball and trying not to let it slip through his fingers.

Keir bussed the tip of her nose, then nuzzled the curve of her throat. He could feel her confusion as she stiffened and attempted to sit up straight. He held her effortlessly in place and whispered in her ear. "My guess is that you are extremely skilled in the healing arts, Raine Cameron, though I can't think why you'd want to deny it."

She wriggled in his lap, making a fruitless attempt to push away and stand up, and Keir smiled in sensual pleasure. Her round little rump rocked over his thickened shaft, and his senses responded like the explosion of a cannonade. He pressed one hand against her abdomen. "Stay still," he ordered gruffly.

"Why?" she questioned. She glanced at the door as though listening for a knock. "Are you afraid someone will find us like this?"

Keir shook his head. "Because I can't bear any more temptation at the moment, lass, or I'll nay be responsible for what happens next."

She froze in his arms, clearly wondering what exactly might happen next if she continued to wiggle about. Her words carried an undercurrent of doubt. "My sitting in your lap gives you that much pleasure?"

"Aye," he answered, sliding his hand across the flat plane of her stomach to hold her in place.

"Pleasure to your body or to your mind?" she demanded to know.

"To both," he answered with a soft laugh. "Do you always approach an unfamiliar situation by attempting to dissect it with dispassionate reason?"

Her eyes flashed with indignation. " 'Tis what Gideon taught me to do."

"Sometimes passion overrides reason," he said huskily.

Keir cupped Raine's chin in his hand and gently lifted her face to his. He kissed her, brushing the tip of his tongue across the seam of her closed lips. When she immediately opened her mouth, he entered, caressing the soft edge of her tongue, coaxing her to return his caress. She timidly touched her tongue to his lips. He gently drew her warm, moist tongue inside, glorying in the sweet, seductive taste of her. The intimate penetration brought a jolt of desire and with it the graphic image of their coupling.

Raine caught the holy medal hanging around Keir's strong neck and pulled him closer as she explored his moist, welcoming mouth. Their breaths mingled, and she could feel her heart thudding as he slipped his hand beneath her shirt and camisole. The feel of his roughened palm covering her breast, his fingers tugging softly on her nipple sent a shock of carnal need through her. Her breasts, now lushly sensitive, grew heavy and firm beneath his caresses.

"Oh my God, Keir," she whispered in his ear. She arched up, giving him implicit permission to explore her body.

He deftly unfastened the buttons on her shirt and lifted the sheer camisole beneath to reveal her breasts to his sight. He bent his head and suckled her, licking her with his tongue, moving from one erect bud to the other. Ripples of exquisite pleasure coursed through her body.

They were interrupted by a soft knock on the door. Keir lifted Raine off his lap and crossed the cabin to stand in front of the closed door. "What is it?" he asked as he placed his hand against the wooden panel to prevent its being opened.

"If it please you, sir," Hector called from the passageway, "the lookout has spotted a strange sail."

"Inform my uncle at once," Keir told the midshipman. "I'll be there shortly."

Keir returned to find Raine trying unsuccessfully to button her shirt. Her fingers shaking, she'd fastened three of the buttons in the wrong holes.

Keir sank to his haunches in front of her. "Here, lass,"

he said softly, "let me do it." Gently pushing her hands away, he unfastened the shirt, pulled down the camisole underneath and tucked it into the drawstring waistband of her pants. Then he fastened the shirt.

Keir bracketed her slender hips in his hands and gazed into her passion-dazed eyes. "Rainey, love," he said quietly, "we must back away from this and never let it happen again. I can't take advantage of your present dependence upon me. Nay, nor your innocence and trust in an old family friend. Should I seduce you, I'd be the beast my enemies have labeled me. And everyone I love and respect would be shocked and disappointed in my self-serving behavior."

Keir knew he was like a wolf caught in a trap, who must chew off his paw to be free. When he took Raine home to Archnacarry Manor, he would have to tear out his heart and leave it there at her feet. 'Twould be the only way he could ever go on with the rest of his life.

"You mustn't blame yourself, Keir," she said with complete serenity. "We have no control over what's happening between us. Our feelings will overpower us, no matter how hard we try to stay away from each other. We are bound together by an enchantment that will last our lifetimes and beyond."

Keir rose to his feet and offered his hand, fighting the wave of tenderness he felt toward her sweet innocence. Drawing her up, he bussed her forehead. "I don't think Lady Nina and Laird Alex will agree with your unquestioning belief in the power of faeries. We'll talk about this later," he said, moving toward the door. "I must go now."

Chapter 14

KEIR SWUNG HIMSELF up into the rigging and joined the lookout at the top of the mainmast.

"There, sir," the seaman said, pointing north.

Keir searched the northern horizon and caught a faint glimpse of a far-off sail against the brilliant sky. It was too soon to identify the ship, but his instinct told him they'd spotted the lateen sail of a Macdonald galley hurrying toward the Little Minch and the safety of the countless islands of North Uist.

He slid down to the deck and told the quartermaster's mate, "Signal the *Hawk* and the *Dragon*: *Giving chase to strange sail. Remain line-ahead. Proceed all due speed north.*"

Macraith waited nearby for further orders, along with al-Rahman and Apollonius, who'd both hurried to the main deck at the first call of, "Ahoy the deck. Strange sail sighted."

"There's no need to clear for action right away," Keir said. "We'll have plenty of time to prepare. I doubt we'll catch her before nightfall." He glanced at Apollonius. "Check our powder and shot," he said. "Put the gun crews to work on it."

The *Black Raven* followed the patch of white sail all afternoon, never drawing close enough to identify the ship. Keir became convinced that no galley could move away from him quite so fast. The crew was piped to dinner, but the possibility of imminent battle had spread through the ship and voices were low and speculative. The seamen would share in any prize money or reward for capturing the rebel leaders.

By sunset Keir grew certain the stranger was deliberately staying just ahead of the *Raven*, not trying to slip away, but attempting to lure him onward.

But why? The Macdonalds would hardly engage three warships while armed with only longbows and crossbows. Not even if there were ten oared galleys ahead carrying a fighting force of a thousand men. The mighty guns of the Hellhounds of Scotland were legendary throughout the northern seas.

Raine came to join Keir on the quarterdeck at twilight. "You are sailing into a trap," she told him with calm self-assurance, though she kept her voice low so others wouldn't hear. "The ship you follow is not a galley, although there are certainly armed Macdonalds aboard."

Keir frowned into the gathering dusk. "Whether we chase a galley or a carrack, we came to the Isles to hunt down the traitorous clan chiefs. I intend to bring Donald Dubh and MacMurchaidh back to Edinburgh for hanging."

Wrapped in that damn serene aura that sometimes surrounded her, Raine turned and looked up at Polaris overhead.

Keir knew she could easily identify Ursa Major and Minor and point out Saturn glowing steadily in the darkening sky.

"Would you like another lesson in stargazing?" Keir asked with a smile, happy to have an excuse to stand close behind her.

She shook her head. "We'll soon be engulfed in fog. I believe I'll retire to my cabin and get some rest, in case I'm needed later."

Keir caught her elbow. "If we should come under fire, Raine," he told her in a hoarse whisper, "you are to stay belowdecks with Barrows. For God's sake, never attempt to come up on the main deck during a bombardment."

She smiled at the intensity of his words, her eyes sparkling with understanding. He was terrified for her safety. She reached up to touch his face, and he grabbed her hand to stop her. He didn't need the entire night watch witnessing his complete captivation with his female passenger.

"Believe me, Keir," she whispered, "I have no intention of grabbing a sword and dirk and joining the fray. When the time comes, I'll be needed below to nurse the wounded."

Keir watched her disappear down the hatchway. When he looked back up at the sails, the sky had changed.

Dense gray clouds now obscured the constellations.

They were forced to reef topsails and gallants, for the choppy currents of the Hebrides combined with the total blackness of the night made it necessary to back away from the chase. The bow lanterns were doused. Only the stern lanterns remained to guide the *Dragon* and *Hawk*, sailing close in the *Raven*'s wake.

Keir slept for four hours in the middle of the night and

was back on deck before the morning watch. He glanced up to see that Macraith had ordered more sails reefed, till they were moving under the mainsail and foresail only. As the last grains of sand slid through the ship's glass, Robbie heaved the log.

"Two knots, sir," Simon Ramsay called softly.

"Very well," Keir answered. "Steady as she goes."

They were shrouded in fog, just as Raine had predicted. He could barely make out the bow lights of the *Dragon* behind them. But he could feel the loom of the land on the larboard side. The treacherous currents of the Sound of Harris sweeping into the Little Minch could dash a ship against the rocks all along the small islands that made up the North Uist.

Where were the strange sails?

Keir had given strict orders to Barrows that Raine stay belowdecks with him. Perhaps he was being overcautious, but he couldn't shake the feeling of uneasiness that had haunted him through the dark, starless night. The Scottish clansmen, carrying longbows and crossbows, traveled throughout the Isles in oared galleys. It made no sense that the Macdonalds would be sailing in carracks armed with cannon, but Raine's premonition ran through his mind.

Staring out into the fog-cloaked morning, Keir saw a sudden flash of light directly on their larboard side, followed immediately by the boom of cannon.

"Everyone down!" he shouted, dropping to the boards at his feet.

The crew threw themselves flat on the deck. A ball whizzed over their heads and smashed against the mainmast. Splinters of oak flew through the air, but the mast held.

"Beat to quarters, Mr. MacFarlane," Keir shouted as he jumped back up.

Hector regained his feet, snatched up the drum and pounded out the call to battle stations. Seamen streamed through the hatchways and over the decks to take up their positions. Top-men scrambled up the ratlines and out onto the yards, ready to unfurl the sails on command. In the tops, the crossbowmen readied their weapons. On the gun deck below, the crews unleashed their cannon, dropped the gun ports and waited for Apollonius to give the signal to fire.

"Full and by, Mr. Ramsay," Keir shouted to his quartermaster.

Thank God, the fog was lifting and the wind was with them, giving the *Raven* the advantage of the weather gage. As the sails dropped from the yardarms and were sheeted home, the galleon leapt forward like a deerhound scenting the hind.

Keir turned to find Ethan at his side.

"The master gunner sent me for orders, if you please, sir," the young midshipman said.

"Run and tell Apollonius to fire as they bear."

The *Black Raven*'s crew were veterans of battles at sea. And the daily practice in gunnery enabled them to load and sight their cannon with automatic precision, unmoved by the boom and crash of broadsides from enemy ships.

Through the lifting fog, Keir saw an armed carrack moving swiftly with the current from the Sound of Harris on the larboard side, heading directly for the choppy water separating the *Raven* from her consorts. With a feeling of disbelief, he recognized the *Yellow Wasp* immediately.

An English privateer in the Hebrides.

He turned toward the bow to find the unidentified ship they'd been following all the previous day now lying directly across their path. Another English-built carrack—*the Osprey*—fully armed and waiting, ready to unleash a broadside against the *Raven*'s vulnerable bow.

Keir knew both ships and their captains from previous skirmishes in the North Sea and the Atlantic. They preyed on Scottish merchantmen along the trade routes to Europe. In the past, King James had awarded Keir and his brothers royal letters of marque and reprisal to hunt down the English pirates and destroy them.

The *Osprey*'s sixteen-pounders boomed, sending shot along the full length of the *Raven*'s deck, from bow to stern, tearing into boats and the rigging above.

Keir's crewmen, inured to the carnage of battle, refused to panic. They followed a routine practiced daily, each man at his station. From the tops, the crossbowmen readied their deadly arrows, waiting for the enemy ships to come into range.

Looking back over the taffrail, Keir could see the *Yellow Wasp* ready to rake his stern. The *Raven*'s seamen calmly sighted the two smaller guns mounted on the stern, unmoved by the sight of the twelve cannon ready to deliver a broadside.

Macraith was right beside them on the stern deck, shouting directions for sighting the long-range nine-pounders. By God's own luck, their shot struck a powder cask on the deck of the *Wasp*. The loose gunpowder blew up in a bellow of black smoke. The fire spread quickly down an open hatchway to the carrack's magazine below. The entire ship shook with the ensuing explosion.

The deadly shrapnel from the *Yellow Wasp* flew in every direction, some cutting up the sails on the *Raven*, other pieces hitting the deck of the *Sea Dragon*, behind the carrack.

Beyond the *Sea Dragon*, Keir now sighted a third privateer, the *Yorkshire*, attempting to cut between it and the *Hawk*. The English carracks had sailed from the western coast of the Outer Hebrides through the Sound of Harris. The *Raven* and her consorts had been caught in a well-planned ambush off Waternish Point at the narrowest part of the Little Minch. Clearly the Sassenach captains had hoped to drive the Scottish squadron up against the coast of Skye.

"Carry on," Keir shouted to his master gunner and raced to the *Raven*'s bow. Under al-Rahman's direction, the gun crews were firing the two nine-pounders mounted on the forecastle as fast as they could be reloaded.

Shouting men were milling about on the main deck of the *Osprey*, getting in the way of the English crew. They'd loaded so many Macdonald clansmen onto the carrack that the Islesmen swarmed over the main deck, making it impossible for the sailors to hear the orders of their own officers.

The choppy, treacherous currents of the Hebrides were playing havoc with the *Osprey*'s practiced gunners. Instead of firing unremitting broadsides, their poorly sighted cannon fired sporadically into the sea.

Keir couldn't risk boarding the *Osprey*. Nor allowing the *Raven* to be boarded. They were far outnumbered. He turned to Hector, waiting close by. "Tell Mr. Buchanan to continue straight ahead, until I give orders to turn sharply starboard. We're going to clip the *Osprey* on her stern. We'll try to dismantle her steering. Then warn the cockpit of the coming collision."

Keir looked up to the tops and shouted, "Bowmen, prepare to fire!"

He hoped to God, given the element of surprise, his maneuver would work. The English captain would never expect to be rammed.

WELL BELOW THE main deck, Raine and Barrows worked side by side in the cockpit. She'd laid out her medicinal remedies, while her sea-daddy placed his saws and splints on top of a sea chest nearby. They worked by the light of a lantern swinging to and fro from a beam above them. Fortunately, they were short enough that neither had to remain stooped over to keep from whacking their head on the ceiling.

Ethan and Robbie served as guides and messengers from the upper decks. The middies kept Raine and Barrows apprised of the battle taking place above them, and the nature of the injuries that would soon require their care.

The thunderous booms of the guns shook the galleon. Members of the crew started to bring down the wounded, and Raine and Barrows sorted the injured by severity.

Three seaman had suffered shrapnel wounds. Raine and Barrows carefully plucked the pieces of jagged wood out of their bodies, working together—one staunching the blood, while the other searched through the raw, lacerated flesh for splinters and pieces of cloth.

Raine had learned by now that burns from red-hot cannon barrels were a frequent injury. Several burned men were carried to sickbay, where she treated them with her herbal ointments.

As she worked, Raine could hear Isabel's voice in her ear. "Don't panic if there's been a severe injury, dearest niece. Someone's life could depend upon your calm, clear thinking."

Just when it seemed every injured sailor had been treated, Hector stuck his head into their small compartment amidships. "Captain says to hang on tight!" he shouted. "We're going to crash!"

The ship shuddered and groaned. The grinding shriek of wood against wood followed the terrible collision.

KEIR WATCHED FROM the starboard quarterdeck as the *Black Raven*'s long, pointed bowsprit struck the *Osprey*'s stern, emitting a horrendous screech. The crossbowmen in the galleon's tops unleashed their arrows, raining death down on the carrack's overcrowded main deck.

With the experienced Mr. Buchanan at the helm and the wind filling her sails, the *Raven* continued her starboard turn, glancing off the English carrack's rudder. There was a huge, satisfying crack, and the *Osprey* began to drift away as her tiller splintered apart.

Keir turned toward the *Raven*'s stern to see the *Dragon*

under Fearchar MacLean's expert command safely bypass the wreckage of the burning *Wasp* on her larboard side.

Meanwhile, the *Yorkshire* had pounded the *Sea Hawk* with broadside after broadside against her vulnerable prow. Under the brutal fire, the *Hawk*'s mizzenmast toppled and fell into the sea, still attached to the ship by ropes and creating a drag on the galleon's forward movement. Somehow Colin MacRath managed to maneuver his crippled ship alongside the English carrack. The two warships drew so close, they nearly collided.

Keir could do nothing but watch and pray that Colin didn't attempt a boarding. If the *Yorkshire* carried as many Macdonalds as the *Osprey*, that decision might prove fatal. The *Hawk*'s crew would be hopelessly outnumbered.

From high in the *Sea Hawk*'s rigging, her top mainmast suddenly dropped, with all its immense weight, straight as a caber to the deck of the *Yorkshire*. The massive projectile punched a hole through the carrack's main deck and—with luck—went right on down through the hull. 'Twas an old tactic in sea warfare which could still work if the enemy was caught unaware.

Before the crew of the English ship could throw their grappling hooks and lash securely onto the *Sea Hawk*'s gunwales, Walter MacRath raced to her stern and hacked through the ropes tied to the fallen mizzen with a boarding axe. Freed from the drag of the heavy mast, the *Hawk* leapt forward, leaving behind the *Yorkshire*, slowly sinking into the sea.

Chapter 15

FOR THE SECOND time that summer, the three Scottish galleons entered the wide harbor of Dùn Bheagain. But this time the *Raven* and the *Dragon* were shepherding the battered and limping *Sea Hawk* into the safety of the loch.

From his quarterdeck Keir looked across the waves to the *Hawk*. In the clear morning air, he could see the redheaded Colin standing on the ship's forecastle with his father, Walter MacRath. They had repaired the top mainmast and replaced the lost mizzenmast at sea with extra spars. Their ripped and shredded sails had been patched or new ones sewn. But the crew had suffered a brutal beating under the *Yorkshire*'s repeated close-range broadsides.

Raine and Barrows had transferred over to Colin's ship when the extent of the injuries had been ascertained, leaving Macraith to finish binding up the few injured seamen on the *Raven*. Unsure of how long she'd be needed on the *Hawk*, Raine had taken her leather satchel containing her medicinal remedies and her canvas bag with the few pieces of clothing she possessed. For the past six days she'd been on the *Hawk*, out of sight and out of reach.

The ships had signaled to one another at regular intervals, so Keir knew the lass was well and safe from harm. What he didn't know was if she was safe from the snares of Colin MacRath. Still 'twas better than having her on the *Sea Dragon* with that gilded-haired Tam MacLean, a known womanizer. At least Colin had been faithful to his married mistress—as far as anyone knew.

Being a realist, Keir had to chuckle inwardly at the rancor of his thoughts. His own reputation for seducing the ladies was probably unsurpassed. Raine must be well aware of his rakehell life. In the past, he'd wanted her to know about his unsavory repute, certain it would keep her at a distance.

Hell, he'd proposed marriage to Lachlan's pregnant mistress in front of the entire Scottish court, knowing Raine was there and would be shocked and disgusted by his behavior. She'd called him an idiot at the time, and she'd been right. He'd been a damn fool idiot to think he could ever stop wanting her. What he hadn't been prepared for was the raging jealousy that erupted inside him at the very possibility of another man touching her.

Keir knew that Alex Cameron had received at least four proposals for his niece's hand from wealthy noble families across the Highlands. At the royal wedding Raine had been surrounded by young men vying for her favor. Later Lachlan had told Keir that her uncle and guardian had turned down every offer, saying the lass was needed by her widowed mother. Keir knew that meant Raine hadn't become enamored of any of them.

God Almighty, if Lady Raine Cameron had stayed at Archnacarry Manor where she belonged, he wouldn't be going through the hammers of hell now.

As the *Black Raven* luffed into the harbor alongside her sister ships, Macraith came to join Keir on the quarterdeck, providing a welcome interruption to his unhappy thoughts.

"Och, I'll be glad to see the backsides of our sour-mouthed prisoners," his uncle stated gruffly. A scowl deepened the lines on his craggy features. "Those wretched pirates are worse than the Macdonald traitors. And we still didn't catch the fish we were after."

Keir nodded absently. "I'd hoped Donald Dubh would be among them," he agreed. "Along with MacMurchaidh. But the English sailors have no reason to protect treasonous Scots."

"God's bones! Not one of the filthy maggots could even tell us who paid their drowned captains to sail into Scottish waters. And under al-Rahman's questioning, the bastards would have sold their grannies to Beelzebub in exchange for an easy death."

Keir smiled. "The Moor has a way with words, doesn't he?"

Macraith chuckled mirthlessly. "Words backed up with that bloody scimitar he carries. Abid's blade can cut a fine slice on a man's bollocks. The mere mention of it and a captive's jaw clacks like a shopkeeper's on market day."

"How are our injured crewmen doing?" Keir asked.

His uncle propped his big hands on his hips, looked up

to the brilliant sky and shook his head. "To tell the truth and shame the devil, I've never seen wounds heal so completely and in such a short time."

Keir glanced at his forearm where Raine had sewn the deep gash with her needle and thread. There wasn't a sign he'd ever been hurt. Not even a faint white line where her tiny stitches had pulled the torn skin together. "Aye, the lass has a talent for healing," he said, half to himself.

"A'course, you recognize there's something special about Lady Raine, don't you?" Macraith prodded. His serious brown eyes revealed the intensity of his question. "Something that goes far beyond mere skill as a healer?"

With a frown of irritation, Keir stared at his uncle. "What exactly are you trying to say?"

"Raine told me at the time that she warned you about the English ships. And you refused to listen. She wanted me to reason with—"

"What was I supposed to do," Keir asked sardonically, "hide out in Calgarraidh Bay like a sniveling coward?"

"Nay, that's not what I'm saying and well you ken it!" Macraith retorted, his gravelly voice rising in aggravation. "We had no choice but to continue our search for Donald Dubh. What I'm saying is that she's *special*."

"Dammit," Keir exploded, "you think I don't ken how special Raine is?"

They both became aware, at the same moment, that they were the center of attention on the deck and in the yards. Heads turned at the sound of their raised voices. Though the hardheaded captain and his equally stubborn uncle had openly clashed in the past, they'd never before argued about a woman. And the sound of Raine's name had carried clearly in the harbor's calm air.

"Nay, I don't think you do understand," Macraith answered in a much lower tone. He leaned closer and continued. "Lady Raine Cameron has the second sight. She had a vision of the armed Sassenach carracks overflowing with Macdonald soldiers. That's the point I'm trying to make, if you'll let me get a damn word in edgewise."

Keir gave a snort of derision, but lowered his voice as well. "I don't believe in such nonsense. Her daft aunt filled Raine's head with foolishness from the time she was naught but a wee lassie."

Macraith ran his large hand down his dark braided beard in complete exasperation. "You don't ken what you're saying, lad. I, for one, have great respect for the myths of our Celtic tribes. Aye, and a firm belief in magic, too. And by the by, she's nay a wee lassie anymore. She's a woman grown and able to make a woman's choice about which man she fancies. And for all your fretting about Colin MacRath and Tam MacLean, you're too blind to see that she's already chosen."

Furious, Keir leaned in to make his own point. His words came low and terse and filled with an irrefutable finality. "Raine is too goddamn young and naïve to make that choice. I refuse to allow it."

For whatever reason, Macraith suddenly saw the humor in their disagreement. He gave a whoop of laughter. "Dod, man," he said, his sea-weathered face creased by a wide grin, "have it your way. You always do." Still chuckling, he turned and shaking his head, he left the quarterdeck and moved to the forecastle.

A WEEK EARLIER, Alasdair MacLeod's godson had returned to Dùn Bheagain with the laird's clansmen and his ten galleys—empty-handed, but ready to fete the arrival of the three warships nonetheless. It seemed as though everyone in the castle was in a celebratory mood.

Everyone except Keir MacNeil.

Keir had sent the *Sea Dragon*'s flirtatious lieutenant, Tam MacLean, out into the countryside to purchase enough cattle to feed the three ships' crews as they continued their search for the traitors. Colin was busy overseeing the repairs on the *Hawk*. Both young men would be kept occupied for days to come.

In the center of Dùn Bheagain Castle's great hall, however, a circle of MacLeod admirers wearing their colorful dress tartans surrounded Raine after the midday meal. This time there'd be more than smooth-cheeked lads to entertain their lovely guest on the dance floor after the evening's banquet.

"Why so glum?" Fearchar asked as he joined Keir and Macraith. They were standing near the wide entrance to the large hall watching the people mingle.

Before Keir could say a word, Macraith answered for him. "Och, man, there isn't a MacLeod here worthy enough to court Lady Raine Cameron, but that's nay keeping a single one from trying."

Fearchar grinned. The giant's blue eye sparkled mischievously. "The devil, you say!" he boomed in his deep baritone. He readjusted his black patch, making the flaxen braids at his temple swing gently.

"Aye," Macraith continued. "The cheeky knaves ken all too well that good manners demand we share the bonny lass at the dancing tonight."

"Hah! Balladmongers and chattering baboons and none worth a docken!" Fearchar agreed. "By morning we'll likely be celebrating a MacLeod wedding and us all the poorer for it."

Ignoring their raillery, Keir left his chortling kinsmen and shoved his way through the ring of aspiring beaus surrounding Raine. "If you'll pardon us, gentlemen," he said, "I believe Lady Raine deserves a bit of peaceful solitude after the noise and confusion of warfare at sea." He met her sparkling jet eyes and forced a smile, trying to make his next words sound like an invitation and not a command. Though of course it was a command, since he wasn't prepared to accept a refusal. "I suggest we take a ride."

"We'll be pleased to accompany you." MacLeod's godson had a toothy smile and not a mark on his handsome face.

Several other kinsmen immediately affirmed the good-natured proposal.

"Not necessary," Keir answered as he offered his arm to Raine.

Though she fairly glowed with health and vitality, Raine didn't dispute the need for peace and solitude. She placed her hand on his sleeve and smiled in approval. " 'Tis such a beautiful day," she said, "I'd enjoy going for a ride with you, Laird MacNeil."

THE WARM AFTERNOON offered perfect weather for a gallop. Raine and Keir raced their borrowed mounts along the mossy edge of Loch Dùn Bheagain.

Raine had accepted the loan of a dress suitable for riding from the castle's good-hearted young chatelaine, Lady MacLeod. The outfit came complete with a rust-colored archer's hat adorned with a long pheasant's feather. Her riding partner had changed from his green-and-black MacNeil tartan to breeches and high leather boots. Even on a lighthearted outing, Keir wore his broadsword at his side, his dirk in his belt and his huge claymore slung across his back.

As they raced along the bank, Raine glanced at him from the corner of her eye, admiring the way he controlled his restive mount with easy grace. The stableman had brought the magnificent hunter out for Keir to look over, saying the chestnut gelding had come from Ireland two summers ago and would have the stamina needed to carry the large laird. Then Keir had chosen a spirited black cob for Raine. The mare had a white blaze on her pretty face and a short arched neck, which she tossed in happy expectation of the coming jaunt.

Slowing the horses to a walk, they rode side by side, content to enjoy the stillness of the afternoon and the entrancing view of the loch's azure-blue water against the verdant summer grass of the countryside.

"When we sailed into the bay," Raine said, "I spotted a small island in the loch not far from here. There looked to be a ruin among the trees."

"Aye, 'tis the remains of Saint Finian's Abbey," Keir replied. "Would you like to explore it?"

"I would!" she exclaimed.

He chuckled at her enthusiasm, and she belatedly realized he'd planned their route for that very purpose. "Let's go, then," he said with a wicked grin. "We'll see if those old monastery walls are enchanted."

She laughed at his teasing tone and shook her head. "I hardly think a ruined abbey a few hundred years old can compare to the ancient stones of Calanais."

They continued along the loch until they came to a shallow crossing. The horses splashed across the sandy bottom and then bounded up the sloping bank. Through the leafy woods, Raine spied the remains of a bell tower ahead.

When they came to the ruins, they found a stone monument, broken and half tumbled to the ground. But the writing carved on the base must have been etched deeply by a master stonemason's chisel and hammer. The cloister dedicated to Saint Finian had been established in the early tenth century by the monks of Saint Columba, who'd sailed from Ireland to spread the Christian faith throughout the Hebrides.

The abandoned setting proved to be stunning. A dappled light shone through the canopy of trees that had grown up around the wrecked buildings. Moss half concealed the stones scattered throughout the open area once used for quiet contemplation.

Keir and Raine left their horses tied to a bush and walked together beneath an arch that led to the destroyed chapel. Broken walls covered in ivy rose up to the open sky above.

Keir watched his lovely companion studying the ruins with her innate sense of curiosity and wonder. He'd seen that same look as she'd turned her face up to the night sky, learning to identify the constellations. Raine was unlike any other woman he'd ever known: courageous, perceptive, and keenly intelligent. She was also willful and stubborn to a fault. Had she been born a man—with her education and noble birth—she could have become a powerful councilor in King James's court.

She pulled off her gloves and tucked them into the purse on her girdle, then looked up to catch him watching her. She tipped her head quizzically. "You look so serious, Laird MacNeil. What are you thinking of?"

"I was thinking I'm glad you weren't born a man."

She burst out laughing, believing, no doubt, that he'd spoken in jest. "Well, I'm just as happy that you were," she replied, wrinkling her nose impishly. "Born male, that is."

Keir held himself in check, fighting the near over-whelming urge to pull her into his arms. Her wide-set eyes sparkled with a winsome humor. Her borrowed dress, the brilliant orange of marigolds, set off her rich ebony hair—for once, unbraided. She'd piled the thick tresses loosely on top of her head and secured them under her hat. A single curl had come loose and it fell over her shoulder.

"I couldn't agree with you more, lass," he quipped with a mocking grin.

They resumed their explorations, wandering through the arched stone walls and what appeared to be the remains of the main kitchen with parts of its enormous stone fireplace still intact.

"How do you suppose the monastery came into such disrepair?" she asked. "It looks as though it's been abandoned for hundreds of years."

Keir tipped his head back and looked up at the tall bell tower. "Long ago Viking ships sailed into the loch of Dùn Bheagain. Their raiders were looking for monasteries to vandalize, knowing there'd be gold chalices and candlesticks possibly adorned with precious jewels. When they reached the Abbey of Saint Finian, they found the monks had taken refuge in the chapel. After pillaging everything of worth, they lit fires around the buildings. Most of the place burned to the ground and its inhabitants with it."

What Keir didn't mention was that the blood of those pagan marauders ran through his veins. The Black Beast of Barra had proudly claimed descent from a Norse king.

"We certainly do have a bloody history," Raine replied, a frown creasing her smooth forehead. "One of raiders and fugitives and traitors taken to Edinburgh for hanging."

"Not much different than now, is it?" Keir said. He removed his riding gloves and shoved them into his sword belt. Placing his hand at the small of her back, he guided her through a maze of stones to the tower.

They climbed the narrow stairs that led to the top. An enormous bronze bell, engraved with Gaelic inscriptions and covered with dust, lay on the floor, cracked and missing its clapper. Along the curved inside wall, wide stone benches now covered with moss had once offered the bell-ringers a place to sit and pray while waiting to chime the angelus and matins.

Keir removed the claymore slung across his back and placed it on one of the stone benches as Raine stepped around the broken bell and moved to one of the narrow arched windows opening to the sky. Going to stand directly behind her, Keir placed one hand on the window's edge and looked over the top of Raine's feathered hat at the scene below. Above the canopy of trees, Castle Dùn Bheagain rose on the high bank across the loch.

"Keir," Raine said softly, her head bent, "do you remember your father?"

He stiffened, his muscles tensing at the unexpected and volatile question. "Nay," he said abruptly and offered nothing more. He hoped she would take the hint and choose another topic.

She failed to notice the undertone of warning in his answer, but continued in a faint, whispery voice. " 'Tis said you look very like him."

"So I've been told." Keir waited for her to go on. He steeled himself, certain she'd speak of his father's notorious reputation. Did she know that Keir had been called the Black Beast's Spawn from his earliest years? Not that anyone had ever dared to use the epithet in front of him or his family.

Her next words came so soft and hesitant he could barely hear them, yet they struck him with the force of an eighteen-pounder fired at point-blank range. "Did you ever note how little I resemble Gideon Cameron—or anyone else in my family?"

"Nay, never," Keir lied.

Every fiber in Keir's body tightened with the need to protect her. He hoped to God that Raine hadn't learned that her father had been killed in an argument with a Macdonald clansman who'd insulted Lady Nina's honor. The violent and lethal disagreement had been based on those obvious familial differences. At the time of Gideon's murder, all the adults at Archnacarry Manor had rallied together, determined to keep the reason behind his death from the thirteen-year-old Raine.

"Don't be a hypocrite," she scoffed in an attempt at bravado. "At least show me the respect of telling me the simple truth."

"Such differences happen in life," Keir replied, his words thick and choked with the dread of causing her any more pain. "Not everyone so closely resembles the family they're born into as I."

She turned and looked up at him, her huge expressive eyes filled with confusion. "And yet," she said in a near whisper, "though you inherited the formidable build and dark hair of your father, you have the unmistakable green eyes of your maternal side. No one could dispute that Lady Emma is your mother, or Rory and Lachlan are your brothers. But who do I belong to, Laird MacNeil? Who am I, really?"

At a loss for words—for Keir had no answer to her gut-wrenching question—he pulled Raine to him. Wrapping his arms around her willowy form, he pressed a chaste kiss to her forehead. Though his hardened sex responded to her nearness with feverish anticipation, Keir had himself well under control.

He would comfort Raine and show her how desirable she was.

Nothing more.

"Don't fash yourself so, lass. You belong to the family who loves you," he said, his words husky and filled with the tenderness welling up inside him. Nothing in his past carnal pleasures had prepared him for this overwhelming need to protect and to cherish. Her floral scent drifted up to entice him. Inhaling the sweet cloud, he bent his head and touched the tip of his tongue to the delicate pink shell of her ear.

Raine scrunched up her shoulder and gave a gasp of surprise. "What are you doing, Keir?" she demanded on a ripple of laughter.

"I'm breathing in paradise," he murmured. He removed the snug archer's cap now sitting askew on her head and tossed it onto one of the benches. Her hair, previously held in place by the feathered headpiece, tumbled around her shoulders in a magnificent wealth of shiny curls. Keir slid his fingers into the tumbled locks, mesmerized by the feel of silk swirling in the hollow at the nape of her neck. "You are a Celtic princess stepping out of a man's dream," he whispered hoarsely. "You belong to the ancient race of shanachies and warrior-kings and royal households."

She immediately responded by sliding her arms around Keir's neck and raising her face to his. Tears welled in her expressive eyes and her lower lip trembled. Like a healing balm, the trust reflected on her fine-boned features filled the deepest recesses of his parched soul. He would sacrifice anything, anything to keep her from suffering.

Keir bent his head and covered her lips with his open mouth. Without a moment's hesitation, she met his questing tongue with her own. At the feel of her moist, welcoming softness, the image of Raine's lithe naked body pinned beneath his hard strength lit a fire of lust inside him. Keir's conscience shouted and carped in vain against the raging inferno that threatened to consume him.

He couldn't take her.

By God, he knew that.

But he could teach Raine the ecstasy of female climax.

And his imprint on her sexual memory would last long after the moment and the passion had fled.

Keir swung Raine up in his arms and carried her to a moss-covered bench. He sank down on its soft green carpet and cradled her in his lap. Readjusting the handle of his broadsword, he pushed it back out of his way. The tangy smell of crushed lichen mingled with her intoxicating scent. Her firm buttocks pressed against his taut, rigid flesh, and the exquisite torment seemed equal parts heaven and hell. Pleasure and pain mixed together in a delicious torture.

Keir eased Raine against the crook of his arm till her head tipped back, exposing the delicate curve of her throat. He paused for a breathless moment as he took in her ethereal beauty. There had always been an indefinable quality about her, even as a youngster. The fragile loveliness of a butterfly mingled with the deadly grace of a falcon. Her power over him was indisputable. She'd proven that from the first day she'd stepped aboard the *Black Raven*.

Looking up at him, Raine's dark eyes glowed with an unspoken invitation. He bent over her, kissing her forehead, her fluttering lids, the tip of her nose, and her delectable mouth. His practiced fingers found the lacing that fastened the outer bodice of her dress. Pulling on the gold cords, he freed her breasts from the stiffened fabric and bent to kiss the rosy aureoles visible through the gauzy shift.

"Trust me, Raine," he urged. "I'd never hurt you."

"I know," she answered on a breathy sigh.

The rays of the afternoon sun streaming through the bell tower's high arched windows played across her heart-shaped face, revealing her flawless ivory complexion, her smooth cheeks blooming with desire. Her mass of raven curls fell in wild disarray around her shoulders. Framed by dark eyebrows and luxuriant lashes, her sloe eyes shone with an innocent curiosity and an undeniable invitation.

Keir loosened the tiny blue ribbon at the top of her smock and pulled the flimsy material down beneath her high, firm breasts. His heart thundered with the knowledge that he could take her at will, should he choose—but he held himself on a taut rein.

He brushed his open mouth over the perfect round globes. He suckled her velvety nipples till he felt the buds harden against his tongue, assuring him of her burgeoning arousal. Her entire body responded with a marvelously uninhibited eroticism. Giving a soft whimper of need, Raine arched her back, allowing him greater access.

Listening to her muted sighs of pleasure, Keir smoothed his hand down the orange-gold skirt and under the hem of her voluminous white smock. Following the curve of her calf up the stocking, his searching fingertips found the garter just above her knee and the smooth bare skin beyond.

Keir drew the front of her dress and undergarment up to her hips, exposing her long slender legs clad in white stockings and blue garters. The open space at the juncture of her satin thighs revealed her dainty female mound. His heart slammed against his ribs. White-hot lust surged through his veins, nearly overcoming his tightly leashed control. Sexual hunger pounded through every inch of his large body, threatening to destroy all his chivalrous intentions to protect Raine, even from himself.

My God, she was so delicate and feminine. His hand shook as he reached down to touch her. He brushed his fingertips through the cluster of soft curls and stroked her fragile pink folds lightly and slowly. Placing a finger on either side of her inner petals, he rocked them gently till she grew moist and swollen beneath his practiced touch.

Keir whispered to her as he eased his finger inside her. "Don't be afraid, darling lass. I'm just going to give you a wee bit of pleasure."

She gasped in convulsive response to his unexpected invasion, then gave a low sigh of submission. She was unbelievably small and tight, too tight for more than one finger. A lump formed in his throat when her gaze locked with his as he continued to stroke her, careful not to bump too strongly against her maidenhead.

Her complete trust rocked him, for she'd certainly never experienced anything like this before—let alone with a man renowned for his violent nature and his love of battle. Did she realize he'd give his life for her without a second's hesitation?

Raine felt a pulsating sensation unfolding inside her as Keir slid his finger in and out of her secret place. He gently played with her throbbing flesh with the pad of his thumb.

"Keir," she whispered, " it feels so . . ."

He smiled down at her, his eyes shining with tenderness. "I ken, lass," he assured her. "Don't fight it. Just allow the pleasure to happen."

Her heart racing wildly, Raine drew in quick drafts of air. For an instant, she thought he was going to pull his hand away, and she reached down to grasp his forearm. "Don't stop," she begged. "Oh, please, not yet."

"Nay, not yet," he agreed, smiling down at her. "We're in no hurry, whatsoever. We can do this as long as you want."

At his words an overwhelming excitement shimmered through Raine, taking complete control of her body. Her heart pounded as though it might burst. With each penetrating stroke, the feeling of fullness inside—and the friction he built—sent wave after wave of unadulterated pleasure through the very core of her femininity. An exquisite pressure spiraled upward inside her, while an irresistible need for something unknown thrummed incessantly.

Keir seemed to know the moment when every rhythmic stroke brought mindless shafts of pleasure. "Let it happen, Rainey, love," he crooned. "Let the feelings go deep, deep within and spread through your sweet female body. I'm only here to pleasure you, lass. Think of my touch and forget everything else."

"Oh, Keir," she sobbed in confusion.

Raine could feel her own wetness slicken her folds as he slid his finger in and out, playing with her engorged tissues all the while. Time seemed to stand still. Suddenly her body stiffened against his hand. Tremor after tremor of pure ecstasy pulsated through her. Catapulted into convulsions of bliss, her sobs became one long, drawn out sigh of female fulfillment.

Languid and dreamy in the afterglow of her release, Raine's heartbeat and breathing gradually slowed to their normal pace. She curled against Keir's broad chest, barely aware of her surroundings, content to be held in his strong arms. As he smoothed down her shift and skirt, Raine looked up at him with a feeling of wonder. How could this ferocious sea raider be so caring and gentle? Never in the past would she have believed The MacNeil was capable of showing such tenderness.

Their gazes met, and she reached up to touch his battle-scarred face. She followed the line of his straight black brows with her fingertip, drawing it down the bridge of his broken nose to the seam of his lips. When he opened them slightly, she brushed across the edge of his teeth and touched the tip of his tongue. He sucked gently on her finger, much as he'd suckled her nipples.

Raine caught one black side-braid in her hand and laced it through her fingers, holding him captive with the tenuous strength of a spider's web. Searching his holly-green eyes, she smiled tremulously.

"Surely you must know by now that we are spellbound, Laird MacNeil?" she asked in a breathy whisper. She tugged him closer.

Keir bent toward her, an amused smile curving his lips. Then just as quickly he raised his head, listening. The sound of voices, male and female, carried up to the bell tower. He set Raine on her feet and rose to stand beside her. "We have company," he said.

Raine watched Keir quickly and expertly refasten the gold cords on her bodice, drawing the stiffened material tight. Reaching down, he grabbed his claymore's scabbard and strode to one of the tower windows.

"We need to go back down," he said. "They've found our horses." He slung the belt holding the great sword across his back.

"Who is it?" she asked, thinking they might be rebels using the ruin for shelter.

"Don't worry," he assured her. " 'Tis only a hunting party from the castle. They probably noticed our horses and stopped."

"Oh, thank God," Raine said in relief, grateful they were in no danger.

As she started for the doorway, Keir pointed to the bench. "Don't forget your hat, lass."

Raine struggled to shove her disheveled hair up under the archer's cap, but loose curls kept slipping out and falling down past her shoulders.

"Here," he said, "let me help." A smile skipped about the corners of his mouth. He scooped her long hair up and held the unruly mass on top of her head with one hand, while he placed the snug hat over her curls with the other.

"You're rather adept with women's clothing," she observed with a frown. "Though why it should surprise me, I can't tell. If you're practiced in taking a lady's garments off, it only stands to reason you must be skilled in putting them back on."

He had the effrontery to laugh. His white teeth flashed and the sun-weathered corners of his eyes crinkled as if she'd said something uncommonly clever. Raine hadn't meant her remark to be humorous, but evidently Laird MacNeil didn't suffer from an overly sensitive conscience, for he offered no excuse for his expertise with female clothing—undergarments included.

Raine quickly pulled on her gloves, then placed her hands on her hips and leaned toward him. "Dressing and undressing ladies is something you'll have to give up, now that we're bound together by the faeries' enchantment," she declared.

Not waiting for his reply, she hurried down the stairs and out of the bell tower. She could hear his footsteps coming right behind her.

The hunting party remained on their mounts near Keir and Raine's horses. The MacLeod kinsmen and their guests watched in quizzical silence as the two approached. Raine recognized several, including the laird's godson— and Lady Flora Sutherland.

"I wanted to see the view of the castle from the top of the tower," Raine explained as she hurried across the grass to untie her horse. "Laird MacNeil was kind enough to indulge my curiosity." She realized belatedly that the pheasant's plume on her hat had broken and now hung listlessly by the side of her face. She brushed it away, praying there wasn't any other part of her clothing that revealed exactly where her curiosity had led her that day.

Keir attempted no explanation whatsoever as he pulled on his riding gloves. He tossed her up into the saddle, then mounted his chestnut hunter.

"Let's go," he said to no one in particular. He reached over and slapped the black cob's rump, and the two horses took off together. The rest of the hunting party hurried to catch up.

Chapter 16

KEIR HAD TO admit that Macraith and Fearchar had been right.

Good manners demanded that the MacLeods be permitted to dance with their lovely, dark-eyed guest from Archnacarry Manor. It also meant the officers from the three warships anchored in the loch were expected to join the ladies of the castle in the evening's festivities. All the men wore their clan tartans, the kilts showing off their muscular calves.

After the banquet, with its jongleurs and shanachies to entertain them, the servants pulled aside the long tables and benches. Alasdair Crotach's bagpipers, admired throughout the Highlands and Isles—along with musicians skilled in lutes, drums, bells, and harps—played dances familiar to all.

Macraith, Walter, Tam, and Colin—whose shyness around the ladies impaired his speech, but not his feet—certainly did their part.

At first few females had the courage to dance with Fearchar MacLean, splendid in his Highland attire. His enormous frame and piratical looks, with a black patch over one eye, were admittedly daunting. But The MacLeod's tall niece, Evelyn, bravely joined Fearchar in a rousing galliard.

Everyone stopped to watch the couple. Fearchar, despite his size, proved amazingly light on his feet, and Evelyn, with her long legs and lithe grace, made an excellent partner. After that, females of all ages lined up to dance with the flaxen-haired giant, who—they were disappointed to learn—was a happily married man.

To his credit, Keir led the castle's pretty chatelaine, Lady Jeanne MacLeod, around the large hall in a stately pavane. And danced with her two married good-sisters, who were staying at Dùn Bheagain until the rebellion was crushed. He managed to avoid Lady Flora Sutherland for the better part of the evening.

His luck finally ran out.

"Oh, there you are, Laird MacNeil," Flora exclaimed, hurrying up to him. "I swear, I haven't had a chance to talk with you since we saw you at the abbey ruins with your little charge."

Gritting his teeth, Keir tipped his head politely. "Lady Sutherland," he replied and pointedly looked in another direction.

She wasn't about to be fended off quite so easily. Slipping her dimpled hand under his elbow, she clutched his sleeve and smiled ingratiatingly. "Do come dance with me," she chirped. "I've some juicy gossip to share."

Keir debated prying her plump fingers loose and striding away. But he knew from bitter experience the scope of her histrionics. She and another lady had attempted to pull each other's hair out by the roots in front of the entire Scottish court. At the time he'd assumed that no one else knew they were fighting over his attentions. Or rather, lack of them. But he hadn't been so fortunate. At the first opportunity his two brothers had roasted him on the spits of their sharp, wicked tongues. If Rory and Lachlan could see him now—with Lady Sutherland clutching his arm and dragging him toward the dance floor—they'd be shaking with laughter in their shiny black brogues.

Reluctantly he allowed Flora to pull him toward the spacious stone floor. Her purple gown had been tightened until her ample breasts nearly spilled over the stiffened bodice. Her large bosom rose and fell as she panted in agitation. "I must tell you the latest rumors," she insisted.

Keir partnered the blonde around the hall in a sprightly farandole, trying to pay as little attention to her prattle as possible. As they circled the room in the round dance, he caught Raine watching him with huge, worried eyes from across the hall.

Her sable locks fell over her slender shoulders in a riot of loose curls. She wore her red velvet gown, and a gold girdle encircled her narrow hips. She'd pinned the red-and-black plaid of Clan Cameron to her shoulder with a pearl brooch, and the shawl swirled around her graceful figure as she moved.

At that moment an unhappy thought struck him.

Raine must have been in the titillated crowd at Holyroodhouse last summer, when the two screaming females indulged in their catfight.

Damn.

" . . . so kind of Lady Jeanne to provide the pathetic lassie a suitable dress for riding," Flora was saying. "But when I learned the child asked her hostess for a loan, I couldn't help wondering why the poor thing didn't simply get the coins she needed from you. After all, I've been told she's your responsibility, whether wanted or not."

Flora now had Keir's complete and undivided attention.

He spoke through clenched teeth. "*Who* was asking Lady MacLeod for money?"

Flora's blue eyes lit up, obviously happy the news had not only surprised but upset him as well. "Oh dear, oh dear, I thought you already knew," she declared, batting her lashes and simpering. "I wouldn't want to get your unfortunate charge into trouble."

"And did Lady Jeanne offer her the money?"

"Only a few farthings, I believe." Flora raised her pale brows and lifted one shoulder dismissively. "I don't usually poke my nose into other people's affairs," she added with a sly smile. "La, I was half certain you already knew."

With the refrains of the lively dance still soaring though the room, Keir turned abruptly and hurried the exasperating tattle off the floor. He deposited her beside a group of chattering women and bent his head in brief dismissal. "If you'll excuse me, Lady Sutherland, there's someone I need to speak with. I'm sure you'll quickly have another invitation to finish the dance."

"Well, well," she huffed, lifting her chin. Spreading

her fingers wide, she placed her hands over the top of her large breasts. "I've certainly never wanted for male attention," she said proudly, "if that's what you mean."

Refraining from the pithy remark on the tip of his tongue, Keir turned and stalked away.

His gaze flew over the large room crowded with people.

Where the *hell* was his poor, pathetic, unfortunate charge, anyway?

RAINE STOOD IN the farthest corner of Dùn Bheagain's great hall, surrounded by six brawny MacLeods. Attired in their colorful tartans, the clansmen were cheerfully vying with one another for the next dance, when Keir suddenly appeared.

Not saying a word, he shoved his way into their midst. With his square jaw clenched, he looked ready to fight anyone who crossed his path. Raine felt the sharp ping of warning zigzag up and down her spine. Thankfully, Keir had left his enormous claymore on the ship. But his lethal broadsword hung at his side. From the look on his scowling face, he longed for any excuse to draw the weapon from its scabbard.

The chief of Clan MacNeil stood a good head and shoulders above the others—and none were small men. His prodigious frame bespoke solid muscle. An engraved black bodkin in the shape of a raven fastened the edge of his green-and-black plaid to the shoulder of his jacket. The raptor's emerald eyes glittered malevolently. Keir's own green eyes fairly crackled with anger, leaving Raine in no doubt—someone had told him about the money.

He reached out to take her hand.

She snatched it away before he could touch her.

"Laird MacNeil," she said with an air of disbelief, "have you finished the round dance with Lady Sutherland already?" She cupped her hand to her ear, inviting everyone around her to listen. "Why, I believe the music for the farandole is still playing." She glanced from one MacLeod to another and smiled encouragingly. "Still I must hurry and choose a partner before the next dance begins." With a flutter of her fingers, she gestured toward their eager faces. "Which you can see won't be an easy choice to make."

Keir clasped Raine by both elbows and pulled her to him with ease, despite the fact that she tried to dig in her heels. Red-hot sparks seemed to radiate from his tense body, right down to the steely fingers grasping her arms.

"Sorry, lads," he grated, his gaze locked with hers. " 'Tis my turn now."

Before Raine or her suitors could utter a single word of protest, Keir half dragged, half carried her along beside him to the first available spot on the crowded floor. A few moments later, the musicians began the lively introduction to the lavolta.

Cocking her head to one side, Raine listened to the refrain played in triple time. She feigned surprise and disappointment. "Oh dear, is that the new dance from Milan? I'm afraid I haven't yet learned it."

His straight black brows met in a murderous scowl. "You danced the lavolta at the king's wedding," he said tersely. "I watched you. You were quite adept."

She glared right back at him, refusing to cower. "Sorry to say, I've since forgotten the steps."

"I'll remind you," he said, showing a glimpse of his even white teeth. The smile never quite reached his flashing eyes. As the music swirled around them, Keir made the required *révérance* and took her hand firmly in his.

Raine dipped in the briefest of curtsies. "I'm a very poor learner, MacNeil," she warned.

"I'm an excellent teacher, Lady Raine," he replied. "You'll do fine."

Not waiting for her consent, he slid one muscular arm around her waist. Placing his other hand just below the stiffened bodice of her scarlet gown, he lifted her off her feet and spun her in a three-quarter turn.

Raine braced her arm along his powerful shoulders to keep her balance. "Did you enjoy the farandole with Lady Sutherland?" she asked sweetly, her mouth close to his ear. The barbaric gold hoop brushed across her cheek. She pushed the earring aside with her nose, only to feel his side-braid with its soft leather thong tickling her chin. Other than the two narrow braids, he'd left the rest of his straight blue-black hair to fall loose down his back.

He ignored her question and went straight for the throat. "I understand you've been begging for money."

Not to be waylaid by his accusation, Raine continued steadily on her own course. *He wasn't the only one angry, for God's sake.*

"I know for a fact," Raine said amiably, "Flora's a very *dear* friend of yours. She quite went out of her way to tell me so. Several times."

Keir lifted Raine up and twirled her again as easily as a newborn kitten. She held her petticoat and dress in place with one hand, lest the entire ballroom be treated to a view of her garters.

He pretended not to have heard. "Who else handed you money, Raine?" he demanded. "Besides Lady MacLeod?"

How could he flirt with Flora Sutherland after what had happened in the bell tower only that afternoon?

Raine refused to be bullied.

"In fact," she added with a toss of her head as she regained her feet, "I think she's quite fond of you."

He paused for the space of a beat, then whirled her again. "Lady MacLeod is fond of me?"

Knowing he'd phrased the remark in a question, Raine purposely chose to misunderstand. "You and Lady Jeanne!" she cried in a shocked half whisper. "Why, she's expecting a child. Don't you have any principles whatsoever, Laird MacNeil?"

Raine's partner stopped in the middle of the floor. Clearly irate, he clasped her upper arms in his strong hands, holding her in place in front of him. "Dammit! Tell me the truth, Raine. How much money do you have now?"

Determined to give as good as she got, Raine glared back at him. "Since you already stole all the money I brought from home," she stated, her voice shaking with anger, "I'd hardly tell you the truth, would I?"

"I swear to God, if you try to run away again, Raine Cameron," he bellowed, "I'll hunt you down and place you in shackles—providing I don't wring your obstinate wee neck first!"

Well, Dear Lord! He wasn't the only one who could raise his voice.

Raine propped her hands on her hips and leaned forward, squawking like a village scold. "I thought I'd made it clear to you, Laird MacNeil, that you're not to bed any other woman but me!"

At that exact moment they both realized the music had stopped. Everyone in the room stood perfectly still, listening—some in shock, some in outright glee—to their loud disagreement. Without another word, Keir grabbed Raine's hand and hurried her off the dance floor.

Macraith stood waiting for them near the wide entrance to the inner bailey. "Have a lover's quarrel, did we, now?" he asked his nephew, sporting a delighted grin. "Sorry to be the one to tell you, lad, but we're all on her side. We think you should lie with none but our own bonny lassie."

Keir glared at his garrulous uncle. "See that Lady Raine is taken to the ship at once," he ordered, the command low and curt. "Then ready the *Black Raven* to set sail in the morning. The *Hawk* and the *Dragon* can catch up with us as soon as they're repaired and provisioned."

He turned to Raine, standing beside him with her arms crossed and scowling like a stubborn donkey. "You may have a few minutes to say a quick good-bye to Lady MacLeod. Then Macraith will see you safely to the *Raven*. I need to speak with Colin and Fearchar before I leave the castle. But I'll be right behind you. We can finish this conversation on board. In private."

"I have nothing more to say to you," Raine replied with a rebellious lift of her chin. She scarcely deigned to look at him. "But I do want to thank Lady Jeanne for her kindness."

The moment she hurried away in search of their hostess,

Macraith turned to Keir, the wide smile still planted on his weather-seamed face. "Well, now, laddie," he said, stroking his braided beard with an air of satisfaction. " 'Tis fortunate your future bride will nay argue with her laird and master the way that cheeky lass just did. Rest assured, man, you'll never be subjected to such insolent behavior once you're properly married."

"What the hell are you talking about?" Keir demanded, baffled by his uncle's convoluted observation.

Macraith's brown eyes twinkled. "Why your future bride, Laird MacNeil," he said, his gravelly voice fairly bubbling with amusement. "I'm talking about your soon-to-be wife. The one Duncan Stewart is busily contracting for you to wed, no doubt as we speak. You ken, Lady Mariota would never be so bold as to lift her eyes to meet yours, let alone raise her voice to you in the middle of some other laird's crowded hall."

The image Macraith conjured up set Keir's teeth on edge. He placed his hand on his broadsword and moved closer to speak in his ear. "If you weren't my goddamn uncle, I'd run you through, right now."

The fact that Macraith spoke the truth made Keir even more furious than when he'd been arguing with Raine. 'Twas a wonder steam wasn't pouring out of his nostrils and flames weren't shooting up from the top of his head.

As Keir turned and stalked away, he could hear his meddlesome uncle whistling under his breath.

Goddammit to hell.

'Twas a tune of pure joy.

KEIR RETURNED TO the *Raven* later than he'd intended. He had spoken with the two other captains, going over their plans for joining him near Loch Baghasdail on the coast of South Uist within a week. Colin reported on the progress of his repairs to the *Hawk*, and Fearchar discussed Tam MacLean's forage into the countryside for fresh meat.

After their lengthy discussion, Keir met with Alasdair Crotach, who planned to send the ten MacLeod galleys to search the eastern coast of Skye for the Macdonald rebels.

The stars glimmered in the black canopy overhead as Keir strode across the gangway of his ship at last. Glancing up, he recalled the nights he'd stood on the quarterdeck with Raine, teaching her the constellations. Above him now Polaris beamed, constant and steady, marking true north for any wanderer lost on the trackless ocean. He could see al-Rahman at the taffrail, using his Persian astrolabe to sight the celestial pole. With only a slight correction, the North Star's altitude would equal their latitude, which would be duly noted in the ship's log.

Still up and awake, Macraith stood on the forecastle deck. He nodded to Keir, touching his fingers to his forehead in a brief salute, but made no attempt to converse. Keir exchanged a few quiet words with the bosun's mate in charge of the night watch, then moving to the stern, discussed their next destination with the *Raven*'s navigator. The Moor bowed in a salaam and hurried away to consult his charts and plot their course. In the rigging above, the seamen on duty moved about soundlessly, while the rest of the ship slept in the peace that only comes in a friendly harbor.

Keir hurried down the passageway. When he reached

Raine's cabin, he hesitated. Placing his hand on the bulkhead beside her door, he listened but didn't hear a sound. His temper had cooled a bit since their flare-up on the dance floor. It wouldn't make much sense to wake her now, only to continue their argument. Much better to wait until morning. Keir turned around and went to his own quarters.

A single lantern cast a warm glow throughout his cabin. He removed his sword belt, dropping his sheathed weapon on the floor next to his bed. He unpinned the bodkin holding the edge of his tartan, slipped off his jacket and threw it on a chair. Taking off his sporran, he laid it on the jacket, then unfastened the cuffs of his saffron shirt and pushed the full sleeves up on his forearms.

Keir poured wine from a silver flagon and tossed it off in one quick gulp. He poured another, walked over to the stern windows and studied the moon's reflection on the loch's calm water.

Hell, he had to admit it. He'd behaved like a jealous ass that evening. But when he'd learned Raine had been borrowing money from Lady MacLeod—and God only knew who else—Keir realized with stark clarity that Raine still intended to run away. Despite the intimacy they'd shared that afternoon, she hadn't given up her plan of leaving the ship. Aside from the crushing blow to his ego—and the fact that everyone in the castle now believed he'd mistreated his beautiful passenger—fear for her safety once again reared its ugly head.

Where on God's earth did she intend to flee?

And why was she so determined to go there in secret?

If he knew the answers, he'd have a better chance to

intervene before she left the ship—or to find her, should she succeed in sneaking off. That possibility made his blood run cold. Having Raine disappear with no clue to her whereabouts would be as close to hell as a man could get without burning alive in the flames.

Behind him the door to his cabin flew open with a bang. Keir whirled to find Raine standing in front of the portal, her dark eyes flashing with anger. Apparently Keir wasn't the only one still seething. Her temper hadn't completely cooled either.

She must have been listening for him and heard him pause outside her quarters before he continued on to his own. Clad in a voluminous white nightshift, she stood there with her hands fisted in front of her, her bare toes peeking out from under the gown's hem. Her loosened hair flowed freely about her shoulders and down to her waist, the tumbling curls glistening like rich sable in the lantern light. Her eyes glittered with the promise of retribution for the way he'd treated her at the castle earlier that evening. Save for a sword and shield, she resembled an avenging angel prepared to defeat Satan himself.

And Keir knew exactly whom she'd cast in the role of Satan.

He set his glass on a small table nearby, ready to finish the argument they'd started at Dùn Bheagain. Before he could say a word, Raine took three quick strides into the center of the room's thick rug.

"Here," she cried, her voice shaking with fury, "take my last penny, you selfish bastard!"

She pulled her arm back and hurled a fistful of coins directly at him. The farthings and half-farthings bounced off his chest and sprayed around the room. Not giving him a chance to reply, Raine pivoted and raced toward the open door.

Keir reached her before she could take a single step into the passageway. He caught her around the waist with one arm, pinning her against his much larger body, while he slammed the door shut with his other hand. Her alluring backside pressed against his hardened sex. Jesus. Whenever he was with her, he turned into a randy three-horned billy goat.

"You know damn well this isn't about the money, Raine," he grated in her ear.

Intending to lift her up and place her on a nearby chair where he could reason with her, he stepped on the hem of her nightwear. The garment split along its front seam with an audible sound.

"You big oaf," she cried. "Now, look what you've done to my only nightshift."

He hadn't intended to tear her clothes off, but her taunt lit the fire that had been smoldering all evening, fueled by carnal frustration, justified anger, and insane jealousy. "Let me see," he growled. "Maybe this clumsy oaf can fix it."

Keir swept Raine up in his arms, carried her to the bed, and dumped her on the coverlet. Taking the shift's torn edges in both hands, he ripped the fine material from neckline to hem. Seemingly speechless at his actions, Raine stared up at him in frozen silence.

Her exquisite body lay naked before him, the round pink-tipped breasts rising and falling in her anger and shock. A bolt of white-hot libidinal need speared Keir's groin as though shot from a crossbow.

Her fragile beauty took his breath away.

Raine lay supine across the satin coverlet as lissome and supple as a willow reed. The sight of her small waist, the gentle curve of her hips, the cluster of soft curls at the apex of her thighs, the long slender legs tapering down to her bare feet sent the rampaging lust he'd kept carefully banked spilling through his veins and pouring into his already thickened sex. Seeing her sprawled on her back, gloriously nude and utterly defenseless, Keir beheld a temptation no sane man could resist.

Not seeming to realize her own vulnerability, she gasped in outrage. "I know you've been with her," Raine insisted, her soprano voice rising shrilly in her agitation. "She told me she was going to seduce you tonight. She made a point of telling me so. That's why you're so late returning to the ship."

"Who the devil are you talking about?" he asked, his words clipped and demanding. "I've lain with no one this evening. Until now."

He bent over her, propping his palms on either side of her head. She hit him square on the nose with the flat of her hand. The harmless blow, coupled with her totally feminine display of wrath, came as a fascinating surprise.

Keir laughed softly, thoroughly delighted at Raine's courage. He'd never known a woman brave enough to physically defy him. Females had always proved far too eager to climb into his bed, not out of it. A thrill coursed through his battle-scarred frame as the need to conquer and subdue brought with it the anticipation of mastery and sexual triumph.

Aye, he wanted her.

He'd wanted Raine since that summer day when she was barely seventeen and his lustful body had reacted to her uninhibited joy in living and her unparalleled loveliness.

And now at last he was going to take what he wanted.

Keir slipped the two pieces of the rent garment down over Raine's bare shoulders, pinning her arms to her sides. He nudged her legs apart with one knee and braced his leg on the edge of the mattress. Placing his hands on the coverlet, he bent closer, his face only inches from hers. She squirmed and wriggled, furious that he'd locked her arms against her body, making it impossible to strike him again.

"Let me up," she insisted. "You're nothing but a cowardly womanizer."

"Why do you need the money, Raine?" he demanded. "Where is it you're so desperate to go?"

Realizing her struggles were fruitless, she gave up trying to free herself from the confines of the torn shift. Her sloe eyes glistened with a sudden wariness. She shook her head, refusing to accede to his greater strength. "I shan't tell you," she said between gritted teeth. "You can't make me."

"If you tell me, lass," he coaxed, "perhaps I can take you there."

She shook her head, refusing to answer.

Keir could read the mulish determination in the set of her jaw. She had no intention of revealing the truth. She was merely stalling for enough time to concoct the next lie. He fought the desire to turn her over his knee and paddle her bare bum. She was behaving like an obstinate halflin, pushing him to the very limit of his patience. Though she didn't know it, she held the winning hand, for he'd never purposely hurt her. Never, ever strike her in anger.

"My God, Raine," he growled in exasperation, "what am I supposed to do with you?"

She went suddenly still. Her eyes filled with tears and her lower lip trembled. "You're supposed to want *me*, Keir. Not . . . not . . . someone else."

"Want you? *Want you?*" he said, incredulous. "You think I don't want you? Dammit, my bollocks have turned permanently blue from the wanting."

"That's not my fault," she answered peevishly. She pressed her lips into a tight, flat line and scowled at him.

"Do you even ken what I'm talking about, Raine?" he asked with a gruff laugh.

"Nay, and that's not my fault either," she declared.

"Then let me show you just how much I want you," Keir whispered in her ear. Nearly insane with lust, his entire body throbbed with an erotic need that refused to be ignored.

He kissed her with his open mouth, his tongue playing with hers until he felt her begin to release her anger and respond to his practiced seduction. Lowering his head, he ran his parted lips down her neck, dipping his tongue into the hollow of her collarbone. He kissed her firm, up-tilted breasts, licking the pliant crests into sweet rosy buds.

Keir's heart hammered painfully against his ribs. His breath seared his suffocated lungs. His big body grew taut and tense with a raging sexual ardor. He was harder and hotter than he'd ever been in his life.

"How could I not want you, darling lass," he murmured, "when you are absolute perfection?"

Cupping the round ivory globes in his sword-hardened palms, he set them swaying gently as he flicked his thumbs across the velvety nipples. He pressed his lips against her flat abdomen and dipped the tip of his tongue into her belly button, breathing in the intoxicating scent of floral soap and female skin.

"Release me this instant, Keir," Raine demanded. "Pull this shift off my arms or I swear I'll kick you."

Keir burned with desire, his sex rigid and heavy. "Nay, not yet, ye wee, stubborn donkey," he told her, smiling at her feisty pluck. "Not before I taste you everywhere. Touch you everywhere."

He slid his hands down the curve of her hips to clasp the backs of her thighs and pull her closer to the edge of the mattress. Sitting back on his haunches, he cupped her bare bottom in his palms. Keir drew her toward him and lifted her long legs over his shoulders. He gently spread her, revealing the fragile pink folds hidden by her female mound.

Raine must have felt his breath on her sensitive tissues as he blew softly across the delicate petals to heighten her anticipation. She gasped in surprise and stiffened as though a flash of lightning raced through her.

"Oh, dear God above," she murmured, making a strangled sound deep in the back of her throat.

"Nay, 'tis me, the clumsy oaf at your feet," he chuckled, nipping the inside of her thigh and brushing the stubble of his day-old beard across her silken skin.

Her entire body quivered beneath Keir's deliberate sensual onslaught. Her breath came in short, quick pants as he prepared her for the access he sought.

"Keir?" she whispered, the single word a question of amazement and disbelief.

"Rainey, love," he answered.

Holding her hips in his hands, Keir touched her wee nub with the tip of his tongue and felt her sex grow erect and turgid. Using his lips and tongue, Keir laved and sucked her until Raine writhed and sobbed with pleasure. She moaned deep in her throat at the intimacy of his caresses as Keir introduced her to the voluptuous love play that would bind her to him. Forever. He was determined to capture more than Raine's sweet, beautiful body. He wanted her clever mind and her fearless spirit.

Marvelously responsive and uninhibited, she accepted his expert manipulations with an unreserved eroticism. As her swollen tissues began to convulse with the spasms of female climax, Keir continued, drawing out her sensual gratification, not satisfied until he heard her soft, ongoing cry of bliss.

Keir gently lifted Raine's legs off his shoulders. Standing above her, he eased the torn nightshift down her arms and over her hands, freeing her at last.

Chapter 17

RAINE WAS BARELY conscious of Keir's movements, basking in the pulsating afterglow of orgasm. She gradually realized that he stood above her, watching her with a gaze of undiluted tenderness. When he abruptly left the bedside, she thought he was going to go back on deck, leaving her alone in his bed. She scrambled to her knees on the soft mattress.

"Keir," she called breathlessly, "please, stay with me a while longer."

"I'm not going anywhere, sweetheart," he assured her with a deep laugh. Moving to his sea chest, he lifted the carved wooden lid, reached inside and pulled out a small, blue glass jar.

"What are you doing?" she asked with unabashed curiosity.

"You're nay the only one who has magical remedies," he told her, his even white teeth flashing in a grin. Returning to the bed, he placed the jar on the coverlet beside her.

"Tell me what it's for," Raine insisted. She picked it up, but didn't open it, too unsure of herself when it came to amorous games to hazard a guess. One thing she was certain of—she didn't want to be restrained again. She wanted her hands free to touch him, just as he'd touched her.

"In a minute," he answered, his deep baritone reassuring. His eyes sparkled with a wicked playfulness. He took the mysterious jar and replaced it on the bed. "Try for a wee more patience, lass," he chided, his words filled with amusement.

Still on her knees on the bed, Raine rested her hands on Keir's shoulders, silently urging him to come even closer. He immediately complied. She ran her fingers lightly across the saffron material that covered his chest and his powerful upper arms. Pulling the tail of his shirt out from under his belt, she slid her hands beneath to explore the feel of his marvelous male body. She brushed her palms across his scarred skin. He tensed reflexively when she buried her fingertips in his chest hair and caressed his flat nipples till they tightened and pebbled. Clasping the holy medal he wore on a silver chain around his strong neck, she tugged him nearer yet.

"Take your shirt off," she whispered. "I shouldn't be the only one without a stitch of clothing on."

Keir jerked the garment over his head and let it drop to the floor. "Aye, lass," he said, placing his hands on her waist. "Now that you're starting to pet me instead of threatening to kick me," he added with a chuckle, "I'll be happy to accommodate your every wish."

She giggled at the thought that she could tame this

invincible warrior. "I want to hear you purr, Laird Mac-Neil," she declared, wrinkling her nose impudently, "just like my pretty tabby at home."

"Oh, I'll purr for you," he said, a wicked grin lighting up his blunt, scarred features. "You just keep petting me, my wee sprite, and I'll rub my big hairy body against yours, begging for more."

Raine leaned forward and kissed the battle wounds running across his chest, pleased to hear his surprised intake of air. She grabbed both of his side-braids and gently pulled his lips close to hers. Their open mouths met, their tongues dueling in frantic possession.

Bracing her forehead against his chin, Raine reached down and fumbled at the belt that held his kilt. Her hands fumbled in her excitement, making her progress far too slow. Keir gently pushed her hands aside and released the buckle. Belt and tartan fell to the floor at his feet. He slipped off his brogues, rolled down his checkered short hose and kicked them away.

Raine sank back on the bed to look at the fearsome Highland chief, her pulse pounding erratically. Until the morning she'd interrupted him dressing, she had never seen an unclothed adult male. And she'd only caught sight of his muscular backside with the *Black Raven* inked across his shoulder blades before he'd pulled on his breeches and turned to face her. She stared now in mute captivation, caught up in the sheer, predatory beauty of the man standing before her.

Stark naked, Keir seemed even taller, larger and far more formidable. Here was lethal male aggression held in abeyance only by his wish to please her. Majestic in his strength, he was broad shouldered, all hard flesh and long limbs. The inverted triangle of hair on his deep chest, criss-crossed with the scars of past battles, trailed downward across an abdomen ridged with muscle. His engorged sex surged outward from the black mat covering his groin.

The sight of him sent an ache of desire spreading through Raine's belly and thighs to pool in her still swollen tissues. The thought that this fierce privateer had used his lips and tongue to gently fondle her most intimate parts sent a thrill of exhilaration spiraling through her.

Raine raised her admiring eyes to meet his, and the intensity of his gaze seemed to scorch her. Her breath stalled in her chest as she realized how much he enjoyed having her look at him—completely without shame, naked and magnificent in all his male glory—just as he'd studied her nude female body without a trace of compunction.

Keir lifted the jar and removed the lid, then handed it to her. "Put it on me, darling," he urged hoarsely.

At his words Raine's heart raced, pumping the blood through her veins and spreading the hunger of desire through every inch of her body. "What is it?" she asked breathlessly, taking the small blue container from him.

" 'Tis a balsam used in Turkish harems," he explained. A corner of his mouth turned up in a wry half smile. "But I believe the recipe originated in the Orient."

"Turkish harems?" She gaped at him in astonishment. "Have you been inside a harem?"

He shook his head, his deep laughter filling the room. "Nay, love. In my voyages to the Mediterranean, 'twas quite easy to find such an exotic treasure in one of the many bazaars."

Raine dipped two fingers in the oil scented with almond and mint. She rubbed her fingertips against the pad of her thumb. "What's it for?" she asked dubiously.

Raine had no knowledge of sexual interplay between a man and a woman. Being raised around horses and other livestock, she understood the basic physical act of procreation. But little more.

" 'Tis used to enhance our pleasure," he told her softly, "while making my entry easier for both of us. Do you remember when I put my finger inside you?"

Feeling the heat of a blush on her cheeks, Raine stared at him, curiosity overriding her shyness. A haze of sexual arousal seemed to engulf her. She nodded, afraid to trust her own voice.

"You felt so tight," he explained with unruffled calm, as though such conversations took place every day. "I could tell that I would need something to ease my penetration, should we couple. Do you understand what I'm saying, Raine?"

She gazed into his eyes, the intensity in their green depths rocking her to her core. "I do," she whispered.

His next words held the promise of unimaginable pleasures. "And do you wish to couple with me?"

"Oh, I do," Raine answered without a moment's hesitation. "We are meant for each other."

At her naïve, innocent words, Keir's battered moral compass struggled to regain control of his unbridled lust. He was taking advantage of Raine's foolish belief in magic and faery enchantments. She was certain the Tuatha De Danann had bound them together for all eternity at the standing stones of Calanais. In her mind there was no need for the reading of banns at Sunday Mass. Nor the marriage contract signed and witnessed before the priest. Nor the vows spoken to each other in front of their families and friends.

But he knew better.

Keir had no right to take Raine without the explicit permission of her guardian. If he continued in this seduction, he risked the condemnation of the few people who loved him—his mother and brothers and uncles.

Consumed with overpowering sexual desire, Keir wrestled his caustic, berating conscience to the ground. Every bone, every fiber, every drop of blood in his veins called out that Raine belonged to him.

That she'd always belonged to him.

That he should take her now.

Now, before she realized her belief in magical spells was nothing more than superstitious nonsense.

Now, before he was left a brooding, empty shell of a man.

"Aye, darling sprite," he agreed, his voice raw and hoarse in his aching throat, "we are meant for each other."

She tilted her head to one side and frowned thoughtfully. "Though we probably should wait till we return home and tell my mother and uncle."

"Our waiting is over, sweetheart," Keir said, deliberately stomping on the remaining shreds of his black, tortured soul. He'd rather burn in hell than give Raine up.

Nor would anyone expect more from the spawn of the Black Beast of Barra.

Looking down at the jar in her hand, Raine swirled two fingertips in its smooth, aromatic liquid, unsure what to do next. The thought of touching this predatory male so intimately sent a wild, nearly frantic thrill of excitement coursing through her. Seeing her hesitation, Keir took her hand and guided it to him, showing her how to smooth the oil along the hard length of his erection.

Raine glanced up to find him watching from under shuttered lids as she lightly spread the balsam around the warm, firm velvet of his manhood. "Am I doing this right?" she whispered.

His deep baritone seemed to reverberate with a rapacious sexual longing. "Aye, darling lass, this couldn't be more right."

Raine's fingers were shaking so badly, she was afraid she'd spill the oil. She sighed in relief when Keir gently pried the jar from her and set it safely on the floor. He caught her waist in his large hands, lifted her up with ease and laid her on the coverlet. Stretching out next to her, he moved Raine onto her side to face him. He cupped her breasts in his palms, lowered his head and suckled her nipples, already swollen and cherry-red from his previous kisses.

Raine responded to his touch, the longing building inside her once again. An unfamiliar energy raced through her veins, making every muscle tighten with a mysterious tension. She boldly met Keir's eyes as he lifted her thigh over his, opening her to him. His hand slipped between her legs to caress her, his fingertips lightly fondling her sensitive tissues.

"Keep looking at me, Rainey, love," he said gruffly. "I want to see the need for me reflected in your beautiful eyes."

Raine drew in a deep breath as Keir inserted his finger inside her. Slowly, surely, he built a throbbing rhythm till she grew moist and slick once more. Sexual desire swamped her, an all-consuming hunger to feel, once again, the marvelous convulsions deep in her female core.

She clutched his upper arms, brushing her sensitive nipples against his solid chest. A shiver of anticipation rippled through her as she breathed in his musky male scent. "Keir," she panted, "I want , , , I need . . ."

He seemed to understand exactly what she longed for. Easing her onto her back, he spread her legs and moved between them. He rose up on his knees and his massive physique loomed above her, the long, hard contours of his bones outlined beneath the firm unyielding flesh. Placing his hands on either side of her head, Keir positioned himself over her, his erection heavy and thick between their naked bodies. Strength, vitality, and sexual prowess emanated from him in waves of heat, and Raine felt overwhelmed by his primal masculinity.

"Touch me, darling," he whispered hoarsely. "Bring me to you."

Raine reached out to cup and stroke him, his thickened shaft slick and smooth with the scented balsam. He groaned with pleasure deep in his chest as she guided him to her entrance. She smiled at Keir's response to her caress.

He'd been right.

He purred beneath her touch.

Keir's heart felt ready to explode with the rush of blood surging through it. He eased his turgid sex inside Raine's soft, welcoming warmth, finding the tightness he'd already been prepared for. The almond oil provided the lubricant he needed, along with the tantalizing tingle of wintergreen. She was so incredibly tight. He'd never experienced such mind-numbing pleasure. He inched slowly inside her, the cooling balm easing his way.

Keir gathered her long gleaming locks in his hands and braced his forearms on either side of her head. Resting his weight on his arms, he bent over her nubile body. Bit by bit, he moved carefully inside her until the sensitive tip of his engorged sex bumped gently against her maidenhead. His entire frame tensed in the effort to slow down, to remain in control and wait for her slight female form to accommodate his large erection.

"Rainey, love," he said huskily, "I'm going to take you for my own now."

She met his gaze, complete trust shining in her luminous, thick-lashed eyes. "And I'm going to take you for my own, Keir," she whispered.

He smiled tenderly at her innocent words. With one quick thrust of his hips, he broke through the fragile barrier, taking her virginity and giving his entire being, body and soul, in return. She drew in a startled breath as his shaft touched her womb.

" 'Tis all right," he assured her. "I knew I couldn't bury myself to the hilt." He nuzzled her neck as he continued softly, "We'll wait for a moment to let our bodies get used to being joined together. Try to relax, sweetheart, and accept me inside you. I know I'm big, but I'm not too big, for I'm already there and the hardest part is behind us."

The moment Keir felt Raine begin to relax and her slender body accept his invasion, he started to move his hips in slow, steady, rhythmic strokes. With practiced expertise, he built the tension to a peak, then allowed it to diminish, only to rebuild it once again. Bracing his large body above her, he lifted his hard shaft up inside her, giving her all the pleasure possible.

Raine wrapped her legs around Keir's hips as the throbbing passion built within her once more. The overwhelming feeling of fullness seemed to ignite a fire inside, while the cool, tingling sensations of the wintergreen awakened every inch of her female core. She could feel the pressure of his powerful flanks between her thighs and the heavy maleness of him buried deep within her. The increasing rhythm as he thrust and withdrew brought her to an ever higher level of sexual fervor.

"Come with me, Raine," he murmured, his lips close to her ear. "Let's explore the constellations together. Give yourself over to me, darling sprite, and we'll sail among the stars."

Raine's mind and body responded to his softly spoken words of enticement. Her breath coming in quick, short pants, she arched upward, tensing, seeking release as her swollen inner tissues began to convulse around him.

Keir reached between their bodies to find Raine's sensitive nub and gently caress her. Her surrender came on a long, soft keen of joy and wonder. At the sound, his heart seemed to stall for a moment on his thundering ride to fulfillment. With an unbearable tension clutching his entire body, he poured his seed deep inside her. The intense pleasure of his climax surpassed anything he'd experienced before.

With a low groan of male satisfaction, Keir rolled over onto his back, taking Raine with him, his engorged sex still buried deep inside her. She sat astride his hips, her long legs bent on either side of his body, and rested her smooth cheek on his hairy chest. Her lustrous waist-length curls tumbled around her shoulders, tickling his neck and chin. A feeling of unfathomable happiness seeped into his beleaguered soul.

Keir could hear Raine taking in deep drafts of air and listened with contentment as she gradually returned to her normal breathing. When his thickened shaft moved reflexively inside her, she stirred and started to sit up.

Keir clasped her smooth round buttocks in both sword-hardened palms and held her easily in place. "Don't move, sweetheart," he said with a satisfied chuckle. "Our night's just begun."

THE STORM SEEMED to come from out of nowhere. The powerful wind shrieked through the rigging, tearing the sails loose from their moorings. Rain poured in torrents from the black clouds, which had suddenly appeared overhead as though blown from the mouth of Poseidon. In minutes, the sunny day became dark as night.

The waves grew ever higher, and the Black Raven pitched about wildly. The ship wallowed in the giant troughs, then rose up on the white crest of each huge new wave, only to sink down, down, down into the deep valley again. In the yards overhead, the seamen fought frantically to reef the topgallants and topsails. The roar of the wind and driving rain united with earsplitting booms of thunder.

Lightning flashed, casting an eerie light across the menacing ocean that surrounded them. Over the noise of the tempest came a mighty crack as one of the masts gave way beneath nature's merciless onslaught and crashed to the deck.

Coming up the hatchway, Raine watched in horror as two sailors were swept off a yardarm by the howling gusts and blown into the chaotic sea. Others hurried to the railing, but the men had disappeared in the roiling waves. Cries of "man overboard" sounded faintly, but no one knew where to attempt a rescue in the blinding rain.

Raine turned to see Keir standing on the quarterdeck, the savage gale whipping his side-braids about his streaming face. He shouted orders to the men above him in the shrouds, seemingly unaware of the enormous wave approaching the ship on the larboard bow. Raine screamed a warning, but nothing could be heard over the mounting crescendo of the storm. The gigantic wall of water crashed over the Raven's deck, and Keir vanished from sight. . .

RAINE AWOKE, HER heart pounding in terror at the vision she'd just seen in her sleep. Looking around in confusion, she realized she was alone in Keir's big bed. Sprawled on her stomach beneath the covers, she wore his saffron shirt from the night before. And nothing else.

Disoriented, she rolled onto her back and gazed at the wooden panels overhead. She covered her face with her hands, trying to dispel the feeling of impending doom that sat like a weight on her chest. The terrible dream was a portent of things to come. The thought of Keir being swept away in a violent storm turned the blood in her veins to rivulets of ice, and she started to shiver uncontrollably. She drew the blanket up to her chin, forcing herself to let go of her fear for the moment and concentrate on the very real complications of awakening in Keir's cabin, alone and practically nude.

Memories of the previous night flooded through her with all the impassioned emotions she'd felt. In spite of the frightening vision and all it might mean, a tiny smile curled her lips.

She had coupled with Keir MacNeil.

Then slept in his arms.

The king's fiercest warrior and most feared privateer had taken her not once, but three times during the night, crooning love words in her ear—sweet, tender words she'd never imagined the ferocious chief of Clan MacNeil would ever whisper to any woman, let alone to the tall, skinny, gangly lass he'd known from her childhood. And the sensual pleasure he'd given her was beyond anything Raine had ever dreamed. Nothing in her sheltered life had prepared her for the wild, unbridled explosion of passion between them.

Who could have foretold that coupling with Keir Mac-

Neil would bring mind-shattering, heart-stopping, soul-plumbing carnal bliss? During the long breathless hours of the night, Keir had encouraged Raine's uninhibited participation in every voluptuous act he'd suggested. And she'd joyously complied.

Clearly, clearly, they'd been enraptured by the Tuatha De Danann at the stones of Calanais. Nothing else could explain the sudden and inexplicable change in their feelings toward each other. But no matter what happened in the future, she'd never, ever regret the marvelous night in his arms.

On the deck above her the clank and rumble of an anchor being weighed, accompanied by the shrill piping of the bosun, caught her attention. The familiar sounds of the *Raven* leaving her mooring brought Raine up to a seated position on the mattress. With a start, she felt the movement of the ship beneath her.

Oh, dear God above! They couldn't leave Dùn Bheagain now! They would sail straight into the fatal storm she'd seen in her vision.

Raine found her discarded shift on the floor beside the bed. She pulled it on and held the torn edges tightly together. Racing to her own cabin, she quickly changed to her sailor's clothing. There was no time to braid her hair, so she tied it back with a ribbon, then hurried through the passageway and out into the light.

Above her, Keir stood on the quarterdeck, talking to Abid al-Rahman. They were studying a navigational chart which the Moor held open in front of them.

"Laird MacNeil," she called breathlessly as she raced

up the steps to join them. Her heart pounded in fright that she'd be too late. "I must speak with you at once. Please!"

From the forecastle deck at the prow of the ship, Macraith called out, "All hands to make sail."

The sailors raced up the shrouds and out onto the yards, where they waited for Adam Wyllie's shrill *tweet-tweet-tweet*, signaling them to let loose the reefed canvas and sheet the sails home.

As Raine reached the quarterdeck, Keir turned to watch her hurry toward him, the warmth in his eyes beckoning her. "Lady Raine," he said, "did you sleep well?"

Al-Rahman, attired in a long caftan and loose trousers, bent in a deep salaam, the twin hoops in his earlobes swinging gently. "*Sultana,*" he greeted in his precise diction, "may I wish you good morning." Folding up the chart, he beamed at her and smiled, his teeth gleaming against his close-trimmed black beard.

Raine smiled and nodded to the handsome Moor, then glanced quickly around the ship. The ordinary seamen were busy with their usual tasks—swabbing decks, checking lines, splicing and knotting ropes—and paying no particular attention to the party on the quarterdeck. Frightened at the activity that signaled a return to the open sea, Raine met Keir's gaze once again.

"Are you ready for breakfast?" he asked, clearly trying to maintain their previous manner in front of the others. "Cook's been holding it off until you woke." Nothing on his blunt, scarred features betrayed the fact that she'd awakened in his bed that morning. Or how she came to be there.

Raine shook her head impatiently. She touched his sleeve and then quickly jerked her fingers away when he frowned a warning. Did he think she was going to speak of last night in front of his crew? Surely he knew her better than that. "There's something I must tell you at once, Laird MacNeil," she pleaded.

The boom of the sails as the stretched canvas caught the steady breeze gusting across the loch interrupted all chance of conversation. The sound of creaking blocks, the rattle of lines, the groan of the ship's timbers filled the air as the *Raven* heeled over, dipped her bowsprit into the sea, and then surged ahead with the grace of a Scottish deerhound.

At that moment, Macraith came to join them on the quarterdeck. "Lady Raine," he said, his eyes twinkling with good humor, "I hope you've come to join us for breakfast."

Raine returned his smile, though she began to tremble in alarm. From the corner of her eye, she saw Dùn Bheagain slip by on the starboard side as the galleon headed out of the loch on her way to the Little Minch. "We mustn't leave," she told Keir, her voice high-pitched in her panic. "We mustn't leave yet. We need to wait here in the loch, where 'tis safe."

His strong jaw covered with a day-old stubble, Keir glanced at her, then looked up at the clear blue sky overhead. "Did you forget something at the castle?" he asked, maintaining his air of dispassionate concern.

Last evening he'd worn the tartan of a Highland chief. Attired once again in breeches and knee-high black boots with his sheathed broadsword at his side, he looked every inch a pirate.

For a second, Raine debated whether she should simply agree with his erroneous supposition. But odds were, he wouldn't turn back for such an inconsequential reason. He'd simply signal the *Hawk*, and Colin would fetch the forgotten item for her.

"Not that," she said. She took a deep breath in an effort to control her rising sense of terror. " 'Tis what I saw in my dream last night," she explained. "There's a terrible storm coming. We need to remain here in the safety of the loch."

In the breeze, Raine's hastily fastened ribbon came loose. Al-Rahman reached out to snatch the lavender band as it floated by and offered it to her. She tried to push the long strands tangling in her lashes out of the way, then gave up the attempt to tie back her hair.

"Don't worry, Lady Raine," Macraith assured her with an encouraging grin. He stroked his braided beard complacently. "The *Raven* has ridden out many a blow. She's weatherly enough to swim through the worst of the elements. Forbye, there's nay a gale out there that could sink her."

"Oh, no," Raine said, her soprano shrill with alarm. "Not the dreadful rainstorm that's coming, I promise you! I saw it all in a vision. We cannot put out to sea!"

"That's superstitious nonsense," Keir declared, loud enough to be heard all the way up to the topgallants. He folded his arms across his massive chest and scowled. "No one can predict what will happen in the future, least of all by something so commonplace as a bad dream."

What I see will come true," Raine insisted. At his continued intransience, she stepped closer and tried to adopt a calm, even tone, though a quaking feeling started to churn in her belly. In her fear and agitation, her breath came in short, strangled huffs of air. "The danger . . . is very real. You'll be swept . . . away by the tempest . . . unless we turn back for the safety . . . of the harbor."

"I'll hear no more about foul weather," he insisted, his full baritone carrying across the entire deck. "No one can foretell the future. Only ancient crones believe in the second sight. And empty-headed lassies."

"I am not empty-headed," she said, stressing each word as her breathing gradually returned to normal.

Macraith and al-Rahman listened politely, not venturing to interrupt the heated conversation between her and their captain. But all around them, the crew began to mutter among themselves, and the words *storm* and *second sight* could be heard repeated over and over across the length of the galleon.

"Silence, fore and aft!" Adam Wyllie shouted. His long mahogany braid tucked into his belt, the tall bosun in charge of the deck crew glowered at the ordinary seamen. "Get back to your work!"

Keir took Raine's arm and started to lead her toward the quarterdeck stairs. "Forget about this senseless folly," he said, "and let's go to breakfast."

She balked, her voice rising hysterically in her frustration. "You must learn to listen to what I say, Keir Mac-Neil," she cried. "I do have the second sight."

Clearly irritated at her single-mindedness, he dragged

Raine up next to him. Painfully aware of the latent power in his arms and hands, she was forced to tip her head back to meet his glittering eyes.

"Nay," Keir answered through clenched teeth. "*You* must learn to listen to *me*, Lady Raine." He jerked his head in dismissal to his uncle and al-Rahman. "Carry on, Mr. Wyllie," he called to the bosun on the main deck below. "You may send the morning watch down to breakfast once we're well under way."

Keir placed his hand firmly under Raine's elbow, holding her uncomfortably close. He hurried her toward his cabin and their waiting breakfast before she could say another word.

As he dragged her along, she could hear him muttering under his breath. "Damn it to hell. There's none more superstitious than a sailor."

Raine bit her lip, keeping her own scathing thoughts to herself. 'Twas fortunate she wasn't wearing a gown. She'd have tripped on the hem. Then her bullheaded captor would have been forced to catch her in his arms or let her fall flat on her face. At the moment, she wasn't certain which choice Laird MacNeil would make.

Raine glanced back over her shoulder.

On the main deck, every member of the crew stood watching them in brooding silence.

Chapter 18

Castle Calbhaigh
Loch Baghasdail
South Uist, Outer Hebrides

TORCALL MACMURCHAIDH EYED his brother-in-law, Archibald Campbell, earl of Argyll, with grave suspicion. They'd been circling each other like curs in a dogfight since the moment Argyll had entered the castle's great hall alongside their host, Laird Allan MacRanald. The chief of Clanranald had issued the invitation to Torcall for a parley at Argyll's behest.

Torcall had agreed to meet with his kinsman for one reason only. They both were dedicated to keeping young Donald Dubh Macdonald, high chief and lord of the Isles, out of the hands of Keir MacNeil and the king's retribution.

However, Torcall didn't trust Argyll enough to tell him that Donald Dubh was hiding on the MacMurchaidh galley moored in the harbor at that very moment.

"My friends, please, please, sit down," Laird Mac-Ranald said with an ingratiating smile to his guests. A short, stocky man, he had to look up at both of them.

As he talked, his bald head swung back and forth like a weathercock in a changing wind. "Sit down, I beg you," he insisted. "If we can set aside our past animosities and misunderstandings, I think we can come to an agreement which will profit us all."

"Very well," Torcall agreed as he took his place in a wooden armchair at the trestle table. Like the other two men, he wore his clan plaid with a broadsword buckled at his side.

Argyll gave a curt nod and sat down across from him, leaving the place at the head of the table for their host. From the wince of pain on Argyll's face as he took his seat, it appeared the wealthy earl was suffering from gout again.

Ostensibly loyal to James IV, as master of the king's household and ranking member of the Lords of Council in the Scottish Parliament, Argyll had been instrumental in stirring up the rebellion in the Isles.

Three years ago the councilors had abandoned the king's initial attempts at appeasement and had turned to a policy of coercion, instead. Whether it had been his goal or not, Argyll riled the clan chiefs throughout the Highlands and Isles with his heavy-handed attempts to undermine their authority and push them toward the acceptance of Crown control of the lordship. Argyll's machinations had resulted in the opposite effect. The Macdonalds and their allies rose up in rebellion.

Allan MacRanald clapped his pudgy hands and a servant hurried in with a tray of pewter goblets and a tall beaker of ale, which he poured and placed in front of the three lairds. Then the servant bowed and quietly left the hall.

Torcall had reluctantly accepted the bid to negotiate with

Argyll, in spite of the knowledge that his kinsman couldn't be trusted. "Well," he said abruptly, "why are we here, Archibald? If you've come to sue for peace on behalf of the king, you're wasting your time. I'll sign no accord with a tyrant."

"First of all," Argyll replied with a sneer, "I'd like to know if my grandson is with you, and if he's in good health."

"Donald Dubh is not here at Calbhaigh," Torcall lied without compunction. "The lad is with another clan chief for his own safety and for the cause of the rebellion. I can only say that your grandson is well and in the best of spirits. He's being treated according to his status as high chief and lord of the Isles." Tapping the tabletop with his forefinger, Torcall added emphatically, "You may be assured, my goodbrother, he's being given far more respect now than he received from your guards while imprisoned at Innischonaill."

Argyll leaned forward, a contentious look on his face. His umber eyes glittered malevolently. "I placed my daughter's illegitimate son in the fortress on Loch Awe for his own protection. I knew that if the Macdonalds or their allies ever got hold of the poor lad, he'd be used as a pawn by the rebellious clans. And in time he'd be captured, taken to Edinburgh and hanged as a traitor. So 'tis I, not you, Torcall, who has Donald's best interests at heart."

"My good friends, please try to calm yourselves," MacRanald intervened. He lifted his palms in a gesture of supplication. "This bickering will do us no good. None whatsoever. Going over our past disagreements will never bring us to a solution of the problem we all face—namely, the continued safety of Donald Dubh and victory for the lordship of the Isles."

"Indeed," Argyll said, a sneer on his thin lips. "I'd be pleased with an explanation as to what the devil happened to the three Sassenach privateers I supplied with my own coin. Their captains were sent with orders to destroy Mac-Neil's squadron. Had they succeeded, the blame for that bastard's death would have been placed squarely on the English Crown, for no one in Edinburgh would suspect otherwise. We'd have ended the treaty of peace once and for all."

"Aye, let's start there," Allan agreed and turned to look expectantly at Torcall.

Torcall glared at Archibald Campbell. "Hell and damnation," he exclaimed, "you ken as well as I do what happened. I met the English captains at Port nan Long just as you'd proposed in your letter, where I provided them with a sea chart of the Sound of Harris. That sonofabitch Mac-Neil sent all three of those armed carracks straight to the bottom of the Minch along with nine hundred men loyal to the Macdonald cause."

There followed a quiet lull, as the three collaborators remembered the personal friends and comrades-in-arms they'd lost in the tragedy at sea. Had the scheme been successful, not only would the treaty have been destroyed, but James IV would have declared war on England as well, seeking revenge for the loss of one of his favorite privateers. Namely, Keir MacNeil.

"There's no sense sitting here bemoaning what's already done," Argyll said, breaking the silence at last. He fastidiously brushed a piece of lint from the sleeve of his doublet and offered his peculiarly humorless smile. "I suggest we decide where we go from here. We must keep my grandson safe at all cost."

"The question is," Allan said, "how do we do that?"

Torcall drained his goblet and wiped his mouth with the back of his hand. "Gentlemen, I believe I have the answer. MacNeil has already searched for Donald Dubh at my castle at Steòrnabhagh and come up empty. 'Tis highly unlikely that he'd think of searching there again, at least not soon. I'll be sailing from here in a few days once my galley has the needed supplies. I'll take the young lord of the Isles under my wing once again, and we'll retreat to the safety of Lewis."

Picking up his black bonnet with the three plumes of a chief, Argyll pushed his chair back with a loud scraping sound. In his early fifties and gray-haired, he retained his solid warrior's build. "I will return to Edinburgh at once and report to the Council of Lords that I believe the young pretender is presently with MacIan of Glencoe. The king will order the ships under MacNeil's command to turn their cannon in that direction." Leaning on his walking stick, he started to limp to the door, then paused and looked back at them. "A word of warning, however. King James would surely unleash all his fury on any man who killed Keir Mac-Neil. So I suggest that you make certain the blame never falls on your head. I believe I've made myself clear."

"Oh, aye," Allan MacRanald said with a knowing grin. " 'Tis why you sent the Sassenach privateers to be rid of him."

"Should by any chance the Black Beast's Spawn come to Steòrnabhagh," Torcall replied, "I won't hesitate to kill the bloody bastard, and the king of Scotland be damned."

FOUR DAYS AFTER leaving Dùn Bheagain, Raine's prediction of bad weather had proven false—exactly as Keir had expected. The summer sun had continued to shine down on the *Black Raven* as she glided out of the loch and entered the Little Minch.

They'd explored the jagged coast of Benbecula with its many inlets and islands, peering into the harbor of Griomsaigh for any sign of a strange sail. They remained constantly on guard, for there was no way of knowing if more English-built carracks had been dispatched into the Hebrides and were now lying in wait. Every afternoon Midshipman Ethan Gibson beat to quarters on his drum, and the entire crew participated in gunnery practice and preparations for boarding an enemy vessel.

Who'd sent the ships remained a mystery as well. Someone with a fortune to spend, that much was certain. But the purpose behind it wasn't so clear, for neither the pretender, Donald Dubh, nor the traitorous chief of Clan MacMurchaidh had been on one of those damn privateers. 'Twould seem the Sassenach squadron's only goal had been to destroy the three galleons under Keir's command.

Although the weather had remained perfect, Keir had been unable to dispel the gloom of remorse that hung over his head since the morning they'd left MacLeod's castle. He'd certainly failed to live up to his own expectations or those of his family and friends. Had Rory and Lachlan known what he'd done, his brothers would have been the first to condemn Keir's self-serving behavior. For he'd taken advantage of a young, innocent lass, using her belief in magical enchantments as leverage to seduce her into his bed. He'd behaved like an ass. Worse, like Ruaidh Athaeuch MacNeil, the rapacious beast who'd sired him.

Keir had no right to touch Raine.

And goddammit, he sure as hell wouldn't let it happen again.

After their private discussion four days ago, when Raine had tried to convince Keir that the *Black Raven* was sailing into a horrendous storm—and he'd patiently explained that her wild speculations were frightening his crew, which he couldn't allow, and refused to hear another word about it—she'd refused to spend another moment in his company.

Keir was left free, however, to wallow in self-reproach, unable to forget the haunting memories of the night she'd spent in his arms. Or ignore the painful surety that Raine would never have lain with him had she not been convinced that they'd somehow been bound together by the faery folk.

To tell the truth and shame the devil, Keir had bedded Raine under false pretenses. Not only did he feel guilty as hell, he smarted under the wound to his male pride as well. For without her unwavering belief in such lunacy, she'd never have chosen him as her mate. She'd made that clear enough at the royal wedding that previous summer in Edinburgh, when she labeled him an idiot for proposing to Lachlan's pregnant mistress—not long after two of Keir's former paramours indulged their jealous animosities with a catfight in front of the whole damn Scottish court.

ON THAT FOURTH day out of Dùn Bheagain, Keir invited Ethan and Robbie Gibson to join him for the midday meal in his cabin—an event that must have given the two lads pause, for they usually ate amidships next to the ordinary seamen's galley. In addition he told them to remain after the dishes were cleared from the table. He wished to talk to them.

Macraith, Abid al-Rahman and Apollonius the Greek had also joined Keir for the meal. They discussed the possible places where the pretender, Donald Dubh, could be hiding as they enjoyed a hearty beef pie. During the lengthy conversation between the adults, the ten- and twelve-year-old middies had ample time to squirm while they examined their guilty consciences.

Raine had been included in the invitation as well, but sent word by way of Mr. MacFarlane that she preferred to eat alone in her cabin. Only Lady Raine Cameron would have the audacity to refuse a captain's summons to join him for a meal. At sea such a request served as a command.

The Gibson brothers' sea-daddy, Jasper Barrows, hurried into Keir's quarters just as the *Raven*'s navigator and master gunner were leaving. The gray-haired bosun's mate took his place behind Ethan and Robbie, who now stood in the center of the cabin directly in front of their captain. Onboard Barrows was responsible for teaching young midshipmen their duties. Macraith remained beside Keir, as well. As second-in-command, his uncle was ultimately responsible to the captain for the actions of every crewman on the galleon.

Like all the members of his close-knit family, Keir was fond of children. His wee nieces and nephews brought joy to everyone around them. But the charge laid against Ethan and Robbie by the *Raven*'s cook was a serious one. Keir stood in front of the two midshipmen giving them a cold, appraising look. A look reputed to leave able seamen shaking in their shoes.

"Cook has complained that food has been disappearing from his galley," Keir told the lads with a severe frown, "and he believes you two are the culprits. As I'm certain you know, stealing food is one of the worst crimes that can happen at sea," he reminded them. "Our supplies must be protected for the benefit of all. The punishment for a grown man is a flogging of fifty lashes. For a lad 'tis a whipping, which I'll personally administer. I owe no less to your parents who placed the two of you in my charge."

The youngsters stared up at him, wide-eyed and clearly frightened, but didn't offer a word in explanation. Beneath their unruly thatches of hair—one bright red, the other deep auburn—their immature faces turned pale. They moved closer together till their shoulders bumped, as though seeking moral support in each other's presence.

"If you don't speak up in your own defense, lads," Keir said, "I'll have to mete out punishment, whether you're guilty or nay."

Ethan and Robbie peeked at each other. They likely knew that a thrashing from the captain would be applied with the full force of his considerable strength.

"We—we—we took the pudding, sir," Ethan admitted, his voice quavering with fear, "but—but we didn't eat any. 'Twasn't for—for ourselves we took it."

Keir glowered at the two pint-sized middies. "Don't compound your crime with a lie," he warned them sternly

" 'Tis the truth, sir," Robbie piped up, showing admirable

spunk for a ten-year-old. "We didn't take the plum duff and the sugar buns for ourselves."

In his valiant effort to speak in his own defense, the color drained from Robbie's chubby face, making the orange freckles stand out plainly on his pug nose. With eyes the deep blue of a summer sky, he stared up at his captain in obvious terror.

"Well, then," Keir demanded, "just who were the sweets for if not for the two of you?"

"We—we took them for Lady Raine," Ethan answered with a noisy gulp. His brown eyes grew enormous in his tanned face. "We put them in her cabin secretly."

"Why in the hell would you do a damn thing like that?" Keir asked, though he suspected he already knew the answer.

Apparently he wasn't the only one thoroughly entranced by the *Black Raven*'s charming female passenger. When Raine first came on board, Keir had sent silk pillows, an embroidered down comforter, and gilded lanterns to brighten the Spartan quarters she'd inherited from Macraith.

"We knew the beautiful lady was fretting about the terrible storm that's coming," Robbie explained earnestly. He blinked, pausing to lick his lips before continuing. "We wanted to make Lady Raine happy again. We don't want her to go on looking so sad and worried."

Standing beside Keir, Macraith appeared to be trying his best not to grin. Rocking back on his heels, he folded his burly arms and pressed his lips flat in a failed attempt to conceal his mirth. "Och, a douce, admirable sentiment for a pair of untried weans," he offered in his gravelly baritone.

But the young midshipmen's innocent summation pricked Keir's already overburdened moral code. He was the cause of the beautiful lady's unhappiness. Everyone present knew it, though no one was rash enough to put it into words.

"There's no storm coming," Keir stated unequivocally. "The summer weather holds." He pointed to the stern windows at the rear of his cabin. "Look outside. Do you see a storm?"

They both shook their heads.

"Any black rainclouds out there?" he prodded.

They made no audible reply, not daring to contradict their captain but clearly not convinced either.

"And if we ask Lady Raine about the pilfered food, will she corroborate your story?" Keir demanded. At their puzzled expressions, he added, "Will she tell us someone's been leaving sweets in her cabin?"

They nodded their heads in tandem, looked at one another in obvious relief, then nodded vigorously again. "Aye, sir," they answered in perfect unison.

Keir glanced at Barrows and gave a quick jerk of his chin toward the door. Their gray-haired sea-daddy hurried out to fetch the beautiful lady in question.

In a matter of minutes Lady Raine swept into the cabin, Barrows at her heels. With her dark hair braided and wound into a coronet on the top of her head, the tall, willowy lass looked every inch a princess. She wore the bright rose-colored gown she'd acquired during their last visit to Dùn Bheagain.

When they'd first reached Laird MacLeod's castle

four weeks ago, Keir had given Lady Jeanne's seamstress a handful of farthings to sew new items of clothing for Raine. They'd been coins well spent.

Moving to the center of the rug, Raine folded her hands, smiled warmly at Macraith and the two lads, then turned a curious face to Keir and waited politely. He assumed Barrows had explained the reason she was needed in the captain's quarters, since she'd deigned to enter the previously scorned premises at all.

"Has anyone been leaving food in your cabin, Lady Raine?" Keir inquired.

"Oh, indeed," she replied. Tilting her head, she looked at Ethan and Robbie expectantly. "Were the sweets from you?" she asked. "How kind!"

"Then, for the record, I take it you've received their offerings," Keir stated.

Her sloe eyes sparkling with amusement, Raine nodded. "My favorites, too! Plum duff and sugar buns."

Keir addressed the brothers with the stern demeanor of an Edinburgh magistrate. "From now on, Mr. Ethan Gibson and Mr. Robert Gibson, there'll be no more taking food from the seamen's galley amidships," he pronounced. "Is that understood? If Lady Raine would like an extra portion of dessert in the evening, she merely has to tell Cook and he'll be happy to supply it. I'll see to that."

"Aye, sir," Ethan said, the relief on his youthful face almost comical.

Beside him, Robbie nodded. "Aye, sir," he agreed. "No more plum duff," he promised, shaking his head vigorously for emphasis. "And no more sugar buns."

"Very well," Keir stated, "you are all dismissed." He glanced at his uncle and Barrows to include them, then turned back to Raine. "If you'll be so kind, Lady Raine, please stay a few moments longer. I'd like to speak with you in private."

Her delicate features suddenly wary, Raine shrugged a reluctant assent. "As you wish, Laird MacNeil."

After the others had filed out and Macraith had shut the door behind them, Keir stepped closer to Raine. He started to reach for her hand, then thought better of it. She'd been avoiding him since they'd left Dùn Bheagain.

"If you'll permit me," he said quietly, "I'd like to beg your forgiveness for what happened."

She lifted her brow in puzzlement, her long, thick lashes framing her wide-set eyes. "I must apologize as well," she confessed. "I should have told you sooner that the lads have been leaving gifts of food in my cabin these past few evenings. To tell you the truth, I didn't realize 'twould be considered such a grave offense and nearly bring a whipping down upon them."

"I wasn't apologizing for that," he clarified, his low words thick with remorse. The ache of regret for what he'd done tortured him like a prisoner stretched on the rack. "I meant what happened between us, Raine. What I caused to happen through my abysmal lack of self-control."

She glanced to the large bed at the rear of his cabin, then met his gaze once again. Her ebony eyes grew solemn in her heart-shaped face. "If you are speaking of the night we spent together, Keir," she said, "there is no need to beg my forgiveness. I was a willing, even eager, participant."

The corners of her lips curved in a hesitant smile. "As I'm certain, you must be aware."

"Nay, lass," he insisted, fighting against the memory of her lithesome body pinned beneath his far greater strength. Of her wearing his shirt for a nightdress, her long shapely legs bare beneath its hem. "I took advantage of your youth and inexperience. And your naïve belief in faery enchantments."

Frowning, she stepped back, clearly dismayed at his choice of words. "Well, of course I'm inexperienced," Raine replied, her cheeks blooming. "But I'm not naïve nor particularly young either. Many become brides long before they turn nineteen."

"Dammit, I didn't mean to upset you, lass," he assured her. "I only hope you can set aside your anger, and we can go on as friends just as before."

"Set aside my anger?" she exclaimed, her face mirroring her apparent shock. "Keir, I'm not angry at you for seducing me. Our fate was sealed the evening we visited the stones of Calanais. Oh, no! I'm furious because you refused to heed my warnings about the coming storm."

"Jesus, Raine!" he said, his patience ebbing at her impossible stubbornness. "Are we back to that again?" He grabbed her elbow and dragged her over to the cabin's tall windows. "Where is that storm you saw in your dreams? Tell me that, will you, because I certainly can't see it."

She didn't even bother to look out on the calm sea or up at the clear sky overhead. Her dark eyes sparking with wrath, she glared at him. "The storm is coming, Laird Mac-Neil," she said, her jaw clenched, her words low and clipped.

"Eventually, aye, there will be bad weather," he agreed, trying to keep a tight rein on his own mounting ire. "It can't stay perfect forever, lass. But in the meanwhile, my crew is riddled with superstitious terror because of your ridiculous claim to be a seer."

"Why?" she cried, lifting her hands in exasperation and looking up at the ceiling. "Why did the Tuatha De Danannn bind me to such an impossible dolt?"

Jabbing her elbow into his belly, she tried to shove past him and run for the door. Keir caught her before she'd taken two strides. Finally reaching the end of his patience, he brought her up fast against him and caught her chin in his hand.

"You tell me, Raine, why I have to lust after a female so pig-headed and willful she'd turn any man into a raving lunatic."

Their faces mere inches apart, they gazed into each other's eyes and the vexation between them slowly melted away, to be replaced with an unspoken, nearly palpable hunger. The carping voice inside Keir's head reminded him that this was not to be allowed, while his entire body throbbed with an erotic need that refused to be ignored. 'Twas as though the outside world and all its restraints disappeared, leaving only the two of them and their insatiable longing to touch each other in the most primitive way possible.

The desire Keir had struggled to tamp down for the last four days flared like a slow-match held to the loaded cannon's breech. Hard and hot, more taut with sexual excitement than he'd ever been in his life, Keir knew, without a doubt, that this unquenchable thirst for Raine would never end. Not in his lifetime.

Inhaling the perfume of roses that drifted from her hair and skin, he bent over her. "God Almighty, Raine," he whispered as he grazed her soft lips with the calloused pad of his thumb. "How I want you."

Keir slid his fingers down to caress the fragile bones at the base of her throat. Intoxicated by the delicate feminine scent of her, he brushed his mouth across her smooth cheek and along the elegant column of her neck. Through the pulsing sexual need that enveloped him, he could feel Raine tugging on his side-braids, trying to draw his mouth closer to hers.

"Keir," she whispered impatiently, "kiss me."

He raised his head and touched his tongue to the seam of her closed lips. In response, she threw her arms about his neck and returned his kiss with her open mouth. Holding her rump in his palms, Keir lifted Raine higher and rocked her against the thickened bulge at his crotch.

A sharp, insistent knocking penetrated Keir's haze of lust. He allowed Raine's supple form to slide down the length of him. "Enter," he called, releasing her but keeping his hand at her waist.

Macraith opened the door just wide enough to stick his head inside. "Storm's here, Captain," he said and just as quickly closed the door.

Chapter 19

KEIR AND RAINE whirled to look out the high stern windows. The morning sunshine had disappeared and dark rainclouds scudded across the gray sky. Together they ran out onto the quarterdeck where Macraith and Adam Wyllie, the tall bosun, stood waiting for them. The wind was already gusting and raindrops pelted the oak planking at their feet.

"All hands, all hands," Keir shouted. "Clear the decks."

The bosun's shrill whistle rose above the mounting wind, bringing the entire crew up to the main deck. The seamen spilled out of the hatchways and raced to their stations as Wyllie supervised the removal of all unnecessary items from the decking.

"Looks like 'tis going to be a big one," Macraith cried over the rising crash of the waves. "She's blowing south-southwest. We're double-binding the boats to the booms now."

"Reef the topgallants, Macraith," Keir ordered. "We'll run straight before the wind with only the sails she'll bear."

Keir looked up at the spread of canvas above him. In the sudden violent force of the wind and rain, 'twas already too late to bring the topgallant masts down safely to the deck. He could only pray they'd hold against the storm's power.

Macraith hurried away, signaling Wyllie to send the men into the rigging. At the sound of the bosun's piercing whistle, the able seamen swarmed up into the shrouds, fighting against the blast of the gale to reach the highest yardarms where they would close-reef the topgallants, making the area of the uppermost sails as small as possible.

Al-Rahman and Apollonius, who'd been standing on the forecastle as the storm roared in, joined Keir on the quarterdeck.

Keir turned to the Moor first. "We'll point her toward the Atlantic and try to outrun the storm beneath all feasible sail. We must get away from these islands and inlets. If we can't reach open water, at least we'll be as far from land as possible."

Nodding his understanding, the ship's navigator raced across the main deck and down the companion ladder to fetch his charts. Other than a ship foundering in the high seas, nothing could be worse than running aground where the waves would dash the vessel to pieces on the rocks. The *Black Raven*'s helmsman, Simon Ramsay, would need all the guidance the brilliant Moor could give him to leave the Sea of the Hebrides safely in their wake.

Next Keir addressed Apollonius the Greek. "Take your men and double-breech the cannon, then lash them tightly against the side. Make certain all gun ports are securely shut." The swarthy master gunner touched his fingers to his forehead in a quick salute and went in search of his skilled gun crews amidst the crowd of men on deck.

Keir reached out and caught Raine's hand. "Go below," he told her. "You're already soaked."

She shook her head and her long braid which had torn loose from the coronet flew behind her in the powerful gusts. "I want to stay with you!" she cried over the sound of the rain pounding on the wooden deck at their feet. Her lovely rose gown was drenched and raindrops cascaded in rivulets down her nose and chin.

In an effort to shield her from the worst of the storm, Keir brought her tight against him and turned his back to the wind. She clung to his shirt, holding on as though she were afraid she'd be blown away.

"Go below, Raine," he ordered, speaking close to her ear, "or you'll be just one more problem I have to worry about. Right now, I need to attend to my ship and my crew."

She tightened her grip on his shirt, her fingers trembling. Her dark eyes looked huge in her pale, frightened face. "Keir, I can't leave you now. Not in this storm. I can't. I can't."

"Go below, sweetheart," he repeated insistently. He could feel her shivering in his arms. "The Raven has been in weather as rough as this before. She'll swim through it, never fear. And you'll be more help in sickbay than up here on deck." He looked over the top of her head and found Barrows hovering close by, ready to help with his female charge. "Escort Lady Raine below," Keir called to the gray-haired bosun's mate over the roar of the wind.

Raine must have recognized the determination in Keir's voice for she nodded halfheartedly and turned toward the hatchway. Her grizzled sea-daddy clasped her hand in his gnarled fingers and pulled her along the gangway to safety.

The sea around the *Black Raven* churned and roiled as the gigantic waves crashed over the main deck in mountains of foam. In order to keep moving in front of the storm, they had to maintain the galleon's forward speed even throughout the lulls inside the huge troughs. Flying before the wind, they needed to spread as much canvas as 'twas safe, which meant a constant changing of sails and ropes to control the ship's direction.

The sailors strung lifelines from fore to aft, crisscrossing the main deck, forecastle and quarterdeck. Other crewmen stretched tarpaulins across the open hatchways, battening them down to keep the sea from flooding the cabins, galley, and hold below.

Keir cursed under his breath. How could he have let the storm race up on the *Raven* so unprepared? Yet there hadn't been a glimpse of dark clouds on the horizon before he'd gone into his cabin for the midday meal. The thought of Raine's warning came to the fore, and he quickly brushed it aside.

BELOWDECKS IN THE cockpit, Raine worked alongside Jasper Barrows in the faint light of two lanterns swinging from beams overhead. One by one, injured seamen stumbled through or half-pitched themselves down the small opening in a canvas-covered hatchway, where Ethan met them. Showing amazing maturity for his twelve years, the young midshipman calmly helped the wounded men make their way through the darkened passages and into the *Raven*'s small surgery.

Meanwhile, Robbie had fetched Raine's sailor outfit and her leather satchel from her cabin. She slipped behind a bulkhead and changed from her sopping wet gown into the dry shirt and trousers. Then the red-haired middy helped her pull out bandages and salves and set them on a sea chest.

Whistling calmly under his breath, her sea-daddy laid out his few sharp instruments on another available chest. Raine said a quick prayer there'd be no need for his saw today. An amputation on a ship in the middle of a storm would be a gruesome matter.

Together Raine and Barrows treated a seaman with a broken arm, taped up another's cracked ribs, and applied a plaster to a third man's bruised skull. Robbie held a jar of salve for her while she smoothed it over an ugly abrasion on Cook MacMillan's forearm.

They worked in an ever-shifting, ever-moving space, doing their best under the cramped conditions and meager light. But the raging storm over their heads grew steadily worse, and the vessel bucked and rolled and shivered around them. Enormous booms of thunder rattled their already lacerated nerves.

During a break in their work, Barrows glanced up at

the beams overhead. He appeared to be listening to the timbers creaking and groaning. The look on his seasoned face confirmed what Raine already suspected. The violent turbulence that raged above them was growing worse.

"Don't worry, my lady," he told her, with a reassuring grin. "As long as our feet our dry, we've nay a care in the world."

Raine tried to hold her hands steady, for her trembling fingers threatened to interfere with her work. Her stomach churned with each roll of the ship, and she fought the sensation of smothering in the dim, confined space. The thought of the sea slowly rising up around them as the vessel sank to the bottom terrified her.

Like an invisible hand tearing at her throat, desperation took hold and—in spite of all her resolve to be brave—Raine felt the tears running down her cheeks.

The memory of her vision flashed before her.

Keir shouting orders to the men above in the shrouds, unaware of the enormous wave approaching . . . the gigantic wall of water crashing over the Raven's *deck and Keir vanishing from sight. . .*

Raine never doubted her visions. She remained convinced that Keir would be lost at sea. Dear Lord above, she had no wish to live without him. Her only thought was to be with Keir in their last moments on earth.

As she started to rush out of sickbay, Barrows reached for her sleeve. "Wait! Wait, my lady," he called. " 'Tisn't safe for you above deck!"

Torn between the responsibility to remain safely in the cockpit and help the injured or try to save Keir's life, Raine fought the confusion and fear that clouded her mind. Without a conscious decision, she found herself hurrying through the darkened passageways till she came to a small opening in a hatch and climbed up the ladder into the swirling chaos above.

IN THE MIDST of the gale, Keir felt his uncle's hand on his shoulder. Macraith was pointing toward a hatchway in the ship's waist. Keir squinted against the brutal wind, peering through the pouring rain and the dense white haze of spray. His heart slammed against his ribs at the sight of Raine clinging to a lifeline strung near the starboard rail.

Dressed in soaked shirt and loose sailor's trousers, she was trying to pull herself hand over hand along the rope toward him, but the deluge impeded her progress. The *Raven*'s prow plunged into the high seas and rose again, pouring water off her decks and pointing the carved wooden raven on her bowsprit upward to the heavens.

"Stop, Raine!" he roared, his throat torn raw from shouting orders over the incessant scream of the wind. "Stop! Go back, Raine, go back!" But she couldn't hear him over the roar of the crashing waves and the pounding rain.

Taking advantage of a temporary lull as the *Raven* slid to the bottom of an enormous trough, Keir started toward her. He'd discarded his boots and socks earlier so he could move about on the slippery, constantly moving deck. Tearing along the gangway, he reached Raine just as the ship started to ride the crest of another wave, up, up, up into the wild, screeching howl of the storm. Holding fast to the man-rope, Keir clutched Raine to him as a wave of foam and water six feet high washed over them.

Brilliant streaks of lightning flashed, followed by an explosion of thunder. The galleon labored beneath the turbulent elements, caught in a savage cross-sea that tossed her about like a rowboat. A change in the wind had caused the waves to smash together from different directions. Gigantic rollers broke over the *Raven*'s prow, covering the forecastle completely. Still, still, they were flying straight through the storm under close-reefed topsails and courses.

With an ear-splitting crack overhead, the fore-topgallant mast catapulted to the deck. As it fell two seamen were knocked from the mainmast's yardarm into the raging sea. Adam Wyllie's piercing whistle barely penetrated the fury of the gale, and five sailors raced to the starboard railing, trying vainly to see through the blinding rain.

"Man overboard," someone called again and again, the words coming faint and soon blown away.

With Raine clutched in his arms, Keir looked over the top of her head to see a monstrous wave coming toward the *Raven* on her larboard bow. Too late to reach the security of the hatch, he held Raine tight in his arms. As the wave broke over the galleon, the lifeline snapped off at both ends and the two of them sailed over the main deck's gunwale and into the wicked, raging sea.

PLUNGING UNDER THE roiling green water, Keir kept Raine locked fast in his arms, his hand covering her mouth and nostrils to keep the water out of her lungs. By brute strength alone he kicked his way to the top and took his hand away from her face. She sputtered and gasped but didn't struggle against his hold. And blessed of all—she didn't panic.

"Get ready to pinch your nose and cover your mouth," he croaked, his throat so inflamed from shouting he could hardly speak. "Keep your head pressed against me, tuck your elbows in tight and wedge your arms between our bodies. I won't let go of you, sweetheart. Watch out. Another one's coming."

The wave crashed over their heads and Keir, his lungs bursting, his muscular limbs straining, fought to bring them back to the surface and air once again.

Another wave came and at the bottom of the trough that followed an empty barrel floated beside them. Thankfully the safety line which had severed under their combined weight was still with them, caught between their bodies. With sheer determination, Keir caught the storm's refuse with one hand and pulled it toward them.

"Here," he gasped, "hold onto the barrel while I tie us together." She nodded and clung to the wooden staves, too short of breath to utter a word. "Brave lass," he said in encouragement.

He quickly wrapped the man-rope around Raine's waist and lashed her to him, then tied his left forearm to the buoyant flotsam just before the next wave rolled over them. This time, thanks to their improvised raft, they rode on top of the swell.

"Why did you come back on deck?" he shouted through the downpour. "Goddammit, I told you to stay below!"

"I . . . couldn't let . . . you . . . be washed . . . away," she said, coughing and spitting and struggling for air. "I . . . had . . . to save you!"

"You should never have risked your life like that!" Keir told her, not bothering to hide his wrath.

She rested her head on his shoulder, catching her breath, then lifted her face close to his. "Don't . . . be afraid," Raine reassured him, her words coming in quick, ragged pants. "We won't . . . die, Keir. Aunt Isabel promised . . . as long as I stayed with you, I'd be safe. That's when . . . she gave me the magic rune. I have it tucked . . . in the pouch . . . tied to my waist."

Unable to cling to his anger knowing they might be only moments from death, he shook his head in resignation at her foolish beliefs. "Well, then," he shouted, just before another roller washed over them, "we have nothing to fear, do we?"

"Raine. Raine, wake up, lass."

Raine could hear Keir's insistent words through the fog that surrounded her. She tried to ignore the command and slip peacefully back into oblivion.

"Raine," he called again, "Raine, get up!" This time, the urgency in his voice brought her to full, reluctant awareness.

Finding herself flat on her stomach in the sand, she crawled onto her hands and knees and bowed her head in thanksgiving.

The storm had passed.

They were alive.

Thanks be to God—and her faery rune.

Keir gently lifted Raine to her feet, holding her steady on her wobbly knees until she got her land-legs under her. The world swayed and rolled in a sickening motion. Exhaustion from their fight to stay afloat had left every muscle as weak as a newborn's. Her stomach churned from the salt water she'd swallowed. She fought the feeling of nausea as she lurched back into the world of sight and sound and complete awareness.

The morning sun shone through patches of fluffy clouds in an azure sky. Nearby on the beach, the barrel they'd clung to during the night now lay in pieces scattered about them. Somewhere in that great expanse of ocean her shoes and socks floated on the crest of a wave.

"We have company coming," Keir told her quietly. "Don't say a word, love. Keep your eyes down. With luck, they may think you're a lad."

Raine could understand his hope that she'd be mistaken for a young seaman. Encrusted with salt and sand from the top of her head to her bare toes, she was certain she'd hardly recognize herself.

Although Keir had brushed away some of the sand clinging to him, he also showed the effects of their harsh battle to survive. His shirt hung in tatters on his large frame. His long black hair had come loose from the braid that had hung down his back and now framed his scarred features in sand-covered strings.

The sound of hooves thudding along the water's edge carried clearly across the beach, and Raine turned to look in their direction. A large group of horsemen rode toward them, kicking up the sand and splashing through the edge of the water as they came. Forty riders, at the very least.

Raine could sense Keir's rage and frustration as he eased her behind him. He had no weapon. In the height of the gale on board the *Raven*, he must have removed them— claymore, broadsword, and dirk. Even the small dagger he kept in his boot was gone. In the storm, his weapons and boots would have weighed them down as they floundered helplessly in the huge waves. But now the two of them were defenseless should these men be enemies.

Raine shielded her eyes with one hand and studied the approaching Isles-men. Well-armed and well-mounted, some were attired in the red-and-blue plaid of Clanranald. At their head rode Allan MacRanald, chief of that line of Macdonalds. The paunchy, baldheaded laird had attended the royal wedding in Edinburgh the previous summer, where Raine had seen him at the Scottish court dancing with his sweet-natured wife.

Beside MacRanald rode a second laird sporting the three-plumed bonnet of a chief. He wore the distinctive yellow-and-black tartan of Clan MacMurchaidh and was accompanied by a contingent of his kinsmen.

When the large party of horsemen slowed and halted a short distance away, Raine's heart squeezed painfully. Beneath his chief's bonnet The MacMurchaidh had a full head of dark brown hair tinged with silver. His nut-brown eyes met her astonished gaze without a hint of recognition and then passed on to study Keir through narrowed lids.

Raine staggered backward, rocked to her core. She

was looking into the eyes of her natural father for the first time. In a cloud of fear and hope she barely felt Keir's hand at her elbow, holding her steady.

A thrill of excitement flooded through Raine, lifting her heart and spirit as she recalled the vision that had first sent her on this quest.

Her mother clutching Torcall's hand and telling him she loved him . . . the future chief of Clan MacMurchaidh begging Nina to go with him . . . the two lovers promising to flee together the next morning. . .

Dear Lord above!

She had found the man she'd been seeking since the day she'd left Archnacarry Manor.

"Laird MacMurchaidh," Raine called loudly. "I am your daughter!"

Keir tightened his grasp on her arm, his startled eyes revealing his shock as he looked down at her. "Be quiet, Raine," he ordered in a hushed tone. "Say no more."

MacMurchaidh urged his mount forward and regarded her with an expression of mild bemusement. "What did you say to me, lass?"

Trembling with shock, Raine studied the laird carefully. There was no doubt he was the young, dark-haired man of her vision. Older now, of course, with gray at his temples and lines in his cheeks. But the same intelligent dark eyes. The same handsome face that her mother had kissed so lovingly.

"I am your daughter, Torcall MacMurchaidh," she repeated, unable to keep the exhilaration from her creaky voice. A rush of conflicting emotions—joy, dread, expectation mixed with apprehension—sent shivers through her. She fought to stay upright while the sand beneath her seemed to move.

Torcall dismounted and stepped closer, scrutinizing Raine with open curiosity, as though wondering which woman in his past had produced a female offspring unbeknownst to him.

With a jolt of chagrin, Raine suddenly realized how dreadful she must look, covered with sand, dressed in sailor's garb, her damp hair matted to her head. The heat of mortification stung her salt-crusted cheeks. Never had she imagined her first meeting with her natural father would be so humiliating.

As MacMurchaidh came near, Keir placed himself squarely between the two of them. "Don't touch her," he warned in a low, threatening growl. He fisted his large hands, ready to defend her at the cost of his own life.

At the sound of Keir's voice, the chief of Clanranald climbed down from his horse and hastened to join them. "Laird MacNeil!" he cried in astonishment. "How the devil did you come to be here at Calbhaigh?" The pudgy man glanced up and down the empty beach, the whites of his eyes pronounced in his fear. "Where's your ship and your men?" he demanded, turning in a circle as though expecting them to appear by magic.

MacMurchaidh peered closely at Keir, then lifted his brow in surprise. "Well, well," he said with a sneer, "if it isn't the Black Beast's Spawn himself. The king's own Hellhound come to pay us a call. I didn't recognize you covered in filth, MacNeil." He propped a hand on his sword belt and smiled mirthlessly. "Aye, 'tis true then, what they say," he continued. "You're as ugly as your blighted father. But not quite so ferocious, I think."

Keir lifted his head higher, his strong chin jutting out, as he openly flexed his powerful arms. Raine realized that only the thought of her safety kept him from striking the older man down where he stood.

"If you try to harm her, you goddamn bloody traitor," Keir said with cold dispassion, "I'll break you in two before your lackeys can even reach you."

MacMurchaidh immediately stepped back out of arm's distance and lifted one hand to signal his kinsmen forward. Twenty soldiers dismounted and hurriedly gathered around Raine and Keir.

"Who is your mother, lass?" MacMurchaidh asked, returning his attention to Raine.

"My mother is Lady Nina, whom you loved in your youth," she said. Her voice cracked in her fear and agitation. She wrung her hands, suddenly overcome with dread that he might not accept her as his daughter.

"Nina Paterson," Torcall said speculatively, half to himself. Clearly astonished, he peered at Raine, looking her over from head to toe. His eyes narrowed in suspicion. "You don't favor Nina in the least," he said, his cutting words laced with sarcasm and disbelief. "Clearly you haven't her golden hair and blue eyes."

"I believe I take after my father," Raine stated boldly, refusing to be crushed by his obvious rejection.

"Pay the lassie no attention," Keir interjected. "She's crazed from our night spent in the storm and the sea. 'Twould addle any man's wits, let alone a weak female's.

Lady Raine is the daughter of Gideon Cameron. Leave her to me, for I am responsible for her safekeeping."

MacMurchaidh stiffened and his face grew pale. "I know of Laird Cameron," he said through clenched teeth. A muscle twitched in his cheek. "I heard the bastard was murdered by a Macdonald over five years ago, and I rejoiced at the news."

Raine stepped back in dismay at the callous words. "How can you speak so ill of the dead?" she asked, choking back a sob. "No man could have been more devoted to his family."

"Gideon Cameron took the woman I loved," MacMurchaidh gritted. He reached out to grab Raine's arm.

The instant his fingertips grazed her hand, Keir smashed his fist into Torcall's belly. As the older laird doubled over in pain and shock, Keir caught the man's chin with his other fist. A half dozen soldiers piled onto Keir's shoulders, and he staggered to his knees under their weight.

Raine watched in horror as five men struggled to pin Keir to the ground, while a sixth struck him a vicious blow on the head with a sword handle.

"Stop! Stop!" Raine cried. She tried to reach Keir, lying unconscious at the men's feet, but they held her back.

"Bring the lass," Torcall ordered and turned to go.

"What about MacNeil?" asked one of the soldiers standing over the still form.

Torcall never looked back. "Kill him."

"You can't kill him!" Raine cried, frantically clutching at her father's sleeve. "Laird MacNeil is my betrothed."

Not bothering to answer her, MacMurchaidh continued walking across the sand to his horse.

"Wait!" Allan MacRanald cried in a high-pitched shriek. Elbowing his way into the circle of MacMurchaidh kinsmen, he frantically waved his chubby hands in their faces. "Wait! Stop! Wait, I say! MacNeil's worth a bloody king's ransom alive! He's worthless dead! Worse than worthless! Those cursed Hellhound brothers will come and raze my castle to the ground."

"As you wish," Torcall agreed in a bored tone as he mounted his horse. He looked down from the saddle in seeming detachment at their prisoner sprawled unconscious on the sand. "He's your hostage, Laird MacRanald. Do what you wish with the bastard."

Chapter 20

THREE DAYS LATER Keir stood on a rough-hewn bench looking out the narrow window at the galley that had been repaired in the loch below. Amongst the many islands of the Hebrides, clansmen armed with longbows and crossbows had used similar vessels to get about under the combined power of both oars and sails since the time of the Vikings. Too light for cannon, they provided quick and easy transportation into the countless lochs and inlets.

MacMurchaidh's galley had been caught in the tail-end of the storm and suffered little real damage. His men had finished setting its two new masts the previous afternoon.

Prior to the gale Allan MacRanald's smaller, lighter, single-masted galley had been pulled onto the sand, laid on its side and secured with heavy ropes to ride out the weather unharmed. It now waited in the loch's gentle swell beside the larger galley.

Each day Keir had studied the horizon, hoping for a glimpse of the top-gallants that would foretell the coming of the *Black Raven* and her two sister galleons. He knew without doubt that Macraith, Fearchar, and Colin were searching up and down the eastern coast of South Uist. They wouldn't rest until they'd found him and Raine alive—or were convinced they'd both been lost to the sea.

Fettered by a three-foot chain manacled to one wrist and bolted to the stone wall beneath the barred slit, Keir stared morosely out the window of his prison cell high in one of Castle Calbhaigh's towers. His gut twisted inside each time he thought of Raine—and he thought of her constantly. He had no knowledge of her whereabouts or how she was being treated. He'd failed to protect her, and his abysmal failure festered like a wound that wouldn't heal.

In impotent rage, he kicked the morning's wooden bowl of sodden oat porridge off the bench and watched it fly across the straw-covered floor to crash against the opposite wall.

The creaking of iron hinges pulled his attention to the door, and Keir jumped lightly down from his perch. As he waited, hoping for the opportunity to catch his jailers unprepared, the door opened just enough for a solitary person to pass through. Strange, since his two guards had always swung it wide and entered together. One would stand cautiously out of reach with a loaded crossbow aimed at Keir's chest, while another, his tall, thin form shaking visibly, brought in water and food.

This time instead of his jailors, Raine stepped into the

cell and the heavy door slammed shut behind her. "Keir," she whispered, her thick-lashed eyes brimming with tears. "Thank God, you're alive."

Relief surged through him at the sight of her cherished face, her clear skin unmarked by bruises, no visible injury to her limbs. Keir's heart leapt up to lodge in his throat. He tried to speak. Nothing came out but a harsh, unintelligible groan.

With a tremulous smile, Raine started across the dirty stone floor toward him.

"Wait!" he croaked, motioning her to stay back. "Don't come close. I stink of the prison."

"Why would I care?" she asked, laughing in delight. The bell-like sound seemed to wrap around his lungs, squeezing the breath out of him.

"But I care," he said with a rueful smile. "I smell like a pig."

"I need to touch you, Keir," she insisted, moving quickly to him. "I need to feel your heart beating beneath my hand and know that you are truly alive."

In spite of his wretched condition, Keir opened his arms and she fell into his embrace. "Darling, darling lass," he murmured huskily, bringing her soft female form against his hard, aching body.

Raine raised her head, offering her lips, as she clutched his holy medal in her fingers. Keir kissed her with all the love he felt in his heart. Their tongues met in silent communion, telling each other without words the depth of their joy and heart's ease. They were safe in each other's arms, the physical and emotional longing between them pushing everything else aside.

Too soon Keir broke the kiss to take Raine's hands in his. He held her at arm's length, checking her from head to toe for any sign of ill treatment.

The soiled seaman's outfit she'd been wearing had been replaced with a fine green satin gown, its wide sleeves trimmed with fur. Her freshly washed hair, adorned with a green ribbon and falling in loose ebony curls around her shoulders, smelled of perfumed soap and pampered femininity.

"You've nay been hurt?" he asked, needing her spoken reassurance.

In the past three days he'd told himself over and over that it would make no sense for Raine's captors to harm her. Not when her family would willingly pay a fortune to rescue her. Yet he'd been haunted with the fear that she'd suffered abuse at their hands.

"I've been well treated," she assured him. "But I've been so worried about you! They refused to let me see you, no matter how many times I begged."

Her confirmation acted as a balm to his tormented soul. "Thank God, you're unharmed," he said. "That's the only thing that matters."

"Oh, but look at you, my darling," she cried softly. With heart-stopping tenderness, Raine cupped his battered face in her palms, the tears spilling over and sliding down her cheeks. "What did they do to you, Keir?" she asked with a strangled sob. Shaking her head, she touched the tip of her finger to his mouth with the weightless pressure of a butterfly. "I should never have kissed you."

"You should always kiss me, love, he said with a slow half grin, ignoring the sting of his split lip. "They gave me a thumping, nothing more," he affirmed, as she gently explored the lump on his forehead. Wherever she touched him, the pain disappeared. "I take it I look like the very devil, but I wouldn't have missed this visit for all the gold in the kingdom."

Raine smoothed her hands down his arms and chest, exploring his body for injuries, just as he'd done to her only moments before. "No broken bones," she said with a sigh of relief. "Although they could have given you decent clothes and some shoes."

"I've suffered far worse in battle," he asserted with a dismissive shake of his head. His ragged shirt and torn breeches were the least of his concerns. "MacRanald needed me strong enough to write a letter to my family asking them to pay my ransom."

She nodded and smiled, hopefulness lighting up her delicate features. "I thought so, though they'd never tell me what they had planned."

"I was happy to write the ransom demand," he told her. "I just didn't want them to know how pleased I really felt about it. Once Rory and Lachlan receive my letter, they'll come, never fear. My brothers will reduce this castle to a pile of smoking rubble."

Keir led Raine to the bench and motioned for her to sit down. Kissing her lightly on the forehead, he sank to his haunches in front of her, trying to ignore the humiliating rattle and clank of his chain. Placing his hands on either side of her hips, he buried his face in her lap, inhaling the intoxicating scent of her, then looked up into her astonished eyes.

"I can do no more than breathe in your essence, love," he said softly, fighting the passion stirring in his blood. "The guards could interrupt us at any moment."

She nodded in understanding. "Keir," she whispered, "I've come to say good-bye. I'm leaving this morning with Laird MacMurchaidh."

"Nay," he answered gruffly. Shocked at her words, he leaned forward and placed his hands on the wall behind her, imprisoning her within his arms. "I forbid you to go with that traitor, Raine. You must stay here at Calbhaigh with me."

She frowned and leaned back against the stones, widening the distance between them. "You cannot forbid me to do anything, Keir," she said, clearly annoyed. She pressed her hands against his shoulders in a useless attempt to shove him away. "I'm free to make my own decisions."

"You are not allowed to make decisions that will endanger you," he explained, making a futile attempt to conceal his anger. "When you placed yourself in my keeping on the *Black Raven*, I became responsible for you. Therefore, I will decide what is best." He rose to his feet and strode to the end of his chain in growing frustration, then turned and glared at her. "This is where my brothers will come for us—if Macraith, Fearchar, and Colin don't find us first. Right now, they're scouring the coastline up and down South Uist searching for us. You need to be here when they come for us."

"Oh, I'm certain they'll rescue you," she said with a placating smile. "Otherwise, I would never choose to leave."

"If you remember," Keir stated coldly, no longer trying to hide his fury, "I told them to meet the *Black Raven* here at Loch Baghasdail. I planned to secure Laird MacRanald's fealty to the Crown. Believe me, lass, they will never quit looking for us until they are convinced we're no longer alive."

"Still, Laird MacMurchaidh insists that I go with him," Raine said, moving to her feet and standing in front of him. "I really have no choice in the matter." Folding her hands together, she looked down at the tips of her borrowed shoes, then up to meet his eyes. "Dearest, I'm sorry, but I must leave you here in this prison cell."

"What in God's name are you thinking?" Keir clasped her wrist and brought her closer, searching her gaze. "You can't go with that bastard rebel."

Raine reached up and touched her finger to his lips as though silencing an obstreperous child. "I have a very good reason, Keir." She inhaled deeply and released a long, drawn-out sigh, as though her patience was quickly unraveling. "I saw Laird MacMurchaidh in a vision the summer after Gideon died," she explained. "He was with my mother, and they were pledging their love. I believe MacMurchaidh is my father."

"Stop!" he said, holding up a hand in warning. His lungs compressed, squeezing the life's breath out of him. "Don't tell me you dreamt about someone who looked like that sniveling traitor and now you think he's your father. I refuse to listen to this rubbish."

"That's the reason I left Archnacarry Manor," she continued, as though she was unaware of the raw pain in his voice, "and traveled to Inverness with the Poor Clares. And why I pleaded with you to be taken onboard the *Raven*. I wanted to reach Steòrnabhagh and speak with Torcall MacMurchaidh before he was brought to Edinburgh to be tried as a traitor."

"Raine, you had a dream, nothing more," he insisted, desperate to make her see reason. "He's using you as a pawn. My God, lass! Can you not tell his intentions?"

Shaking her head in denial of the obvious truth, she placed her hands on his chest. He covered her fingers with his own. A smile of certainty curved her lips. "Keir," she said softly, "do you remember when I told your brother, Rory, where he could find Joanna when she'd been abducted by her kinsmen?"

"That 'twas only by chance," he protested. "We all knew Joanna would be kept in a Macdonald stronghold somewhere in the Isles. You made a lucky guess when you suggested Dhomhuill Castle."

She lifted her arched brows, as though he were the foolish one. "And what about the royal wedding, when I told your brother, Lachlan, that he'd be triply blessed in love? Francine gave birth to triplets. Was that mere chance as well?"

"Saying someone's marriage will be blessed is as common as attending the wedding feast," Keir pointed out, certain he was on solid ground with that one.

Raine laughed, the musical notes filling the cell with the marvelous sound he'd come to adore. "And the storm?"

she asked. "Did I not warn you that you'd be swept overboard?"

"Now there I have you," he told her earnestly. "We would never have washed over the side, if you'd stayed below in sickbay. If you'd followed my orders, Raine, none of this would have happened."

"Oh, you're so very wrong," she said in a tone of absolute conviction. "If I hadn't been with you, Keir, the magic rune could never have saved you."

In that moment, Keir realized the depth of her conviction about the power of magic. Raine obstinately clung to the belief that if she hadn't come above decks to rescue him with her ancient carved stone, he would have drowned. Any emotions she had felt toward him were based on her nonsensical belief in faery enchantments. Yet 'twas only by the grace of God they'd both survived their harrowing ordeal.

Trying to ignore the rattle of his chain, he clasped her shoulders and gave her a gentle shake in an attempt to bring her to her senses. "Rainey, love, you mustn't go with Torcall. You must stay here until we're rescued. 'Tis far too dangerous to go to Steòrnabhagh."

"I have told him I will go," she pointed out in her stubborn, hardheaded way.

"How can you be so blind?" Keir demanded, his heart sinking to his toes. "MacMurchaidh plans to use you as a hostage. That cunning bastard knows there'll be a siege and his castle will be taken. When it does fall, he won't hesitate to use you as a shield."

"I know that he's supporting a losing cause," she admitted. "Both he and Donald Dubh will eventually be caught by the king's forces."

"Taking you with him is merely a ruse to protect his own life," Keir told her bluntly. "No one, least of all Mac-Murchaidh, thinks you are a seer."

"But I did see him in a vision, whether you or anyone else believes it," she said with quiet certainty, as though there was no need to discuss it further.

Looking up at the ceiling, Keir rubbed the back of his neck, trying to get a rein on his exasperation. "Has Mac-Murchaidh actually told you that he believes you have the second sight? Or that he thinks you may be his daughter?"

Her eyes widened, and the pain in their luminous depths tore at Keir's heart. "Nay," she whispered. "Not yet, but I'm sure he will, once we reach Murchaidh Castle and safety."

Keir drew Raine into his arms. "Rainey love," he murmured, "I'm not trying to hurt you. Stay with me, darling lass." He kissed her passionately, attempting to convince her that she must remain at Calbhaigh with him. If reasoning wouldn't work, perhaps sexual desire could.

"We'll spend the rest of our lives together, Keir" she pleaded, her voice shaking with emotion. "But I'll have only a short time with my father. Once you are ransomed you will bring your ships and your men to storm his castle. MacMurchaidh will soon be killed or captured and transported to Edinburgh for trial and hanging. Please, I beg you, dearest, give me this one chance to become acquainted with the man who sired me."

The screech of the iron hinges interrupted them. "Time

to go, my lady," a guard said with a respectful bow. The burly man retreated, leaving the door partly open.

"Keir, I want you to keep this," Raine said. She held out her hand, the rune in her palm. " 'Twill keep you safe until you are rescued or ransomed. Please promise you'll keep it on your person at all times."

"I don't need that idiotic trinket," he growled. "That damn thing won't protect me from a gnat."

Pressing her lips together in stubborn determination, she reached out, took his hand and placed the carved heart into his palm. He fisted his hand around it, knowing reason wouldn't sway her. "I'm telling you not to go, Raine," he gritted through clenched teeth. "If you betray me now, I'll never forget it."

The door swung wide and this time the guard stood waiting. "Laird MacMurchaidh has sent word, my lady," he said, bowing so deep his long narrow frame nearly bent in two. " 'Tis time to go aboard."

"Goddammit," Keir said through clenched teeth. "When I find you, Raine, I'll thrash you within an inch of your life." The rage inside him made every muscle tighten and clench as though preparing for battle. "And I will find you," he promised.

"Good-bye, Keir," Raine said, her words thick and mournful. "Please try to understand and forgive me." She offered a tremulous smile of apology, then turned and started to walk to the doorway.

"Wait, Raine!" Keir called. Foreboding chomped at his gut—and an almost paralyzing fear that he might never see her again. He moved to grab her arm, only to be jerked up short by the chain that bound him to the wall. "Don't go with that bastard!" he shouted. "Don't betray me like this, Raine! Goddammit! Come back here!"

The iron hinges creaked noisily as the solid wooden door slammed shut behind her.

Hurling the rune with all his strength against the closed portal, Keir turned and clambered up onto the bench. Cursing, he grasped the bars on the window. Looking down at the loch below, he watched until he saw Raine walking beside the conniving rebel who'd pretended to believe in her visions.

Keir's heart thudded painfully as he gripped the iron bars with whitened knuckles. "I'll come for you, MacMurchaidh!" he roared, his voice hoarse with fury and disillusionment. "I swear by God I'll come for you! And when I do I'll kill you!"

The pair turned in tandem and looked up at Keir. Tears streamed down Raine's face, but her resolve remained apparent in her stiffened posture. Then they continued across the gangplank and onto the ship. The galley slipped its moorings and sailed north toward the Isle of Lewis and Steòrnabhagh, its white sails filling in the steady breeze.

Shortly afterward, the MacRanald galley also set sail, heading eastward toward Castle Stalcaire, in the Highlands, carrying Keir's letter to his family along with his captor's request for a payment of ransom.

Keir slid down onto the bench. Crouched over in bitterness, he clenched his fists on his knees. How could Raine have ignored his commands and gone with his sworn enemy?

Doubt seared Keir's heart like a corrosive acid.

Maybe she'd only pretended to care.

Like every other female he'd ever bedded, 'twas possible Raine had merely wanted the thrill of lying with the infamous Black Beast's Spawn.

FOUR LONG, TEDIOUS days passed before Keir caught a glimpse of the topgallant sails he'd been hoping to see on the eastern horizon. By the following dawn, the *Raven*, the *Dragon*, and the *Hawk* had sailed in line formation across the mouth of the loch, their gun ports open, their eighteen-pounders aimed directly at Castle Calbhaigh. When the ships' cutters were lowered and rowed toward the sandy shore by three landing parties without a shot being fired, Keir knew the Clanranald banner had been struck from the battlements the moment the warships came into view.

Less than ten minutes later, the heavy door to Keir's cell swung open. Allan MacRanald rushed in waving his hands excitedly. The two guards followed behind him, not a crossbow in sight.

"Laird MacNeil," the stocky man cried, his eyes enormous in his fright, "I hope you understand that I harbor no ill will toward you, sir. I always meant to free you whether a ransom came or not." MacRanald's round, pink countenance faded to a pasty white. He turned to the two guards behind him. "Quick! Quick! Unfasten his chain, you fools!"

Keir waited impatiently while a guard fumbled clumsily, trying to get the key inside the manacle's lock. The sound of boots pounding up the tower's stone stairs seemed to turn the jailor's thin fingers into pieces of wet straw.

With a ferocious glower on his bearded face, Macraith—resembling Woden, himself—appeared in the open doorway holding a two-headed boarding axe poised to strike. The moment he spied Keir being released from his chain, he lowered the weapon and grinned like a halflin with his first pony.

"Laddie!" he boomed, his deep gravelly voice echoing against the stones. "What in the hell are you doing here trussed up like a boar for the oven? Forbye, the last we saw, you and the lassie were swimming toward Ireland."

The lock snapped open and the terrified jailor jumped back, hurrying to stand with his partner near the farthest wall. They kept their worried gazes fixed on the deadly axe in Macraith's large hand, clearly aware he could take off one man's head with his forward stroke and the other's on his back swing.

Without a word, Keir rubbed his bruised wrist, bringing the blood back into his numb hand as he moved toward the door. His uncle tossed him his sheathed broadsword and belt, and Keir quickly fastened his weapon to his side. He took his dirk and jammed it into the leather belt.

"Your boots are on the *Raven* along with your dagger," Macraith said with a chuckle, unperturbed by his nephew's cold, enraged silence. "So you'll have to come aboard in your bare feet. But boots or nay, Adam Wyllie will pipe you over the side like you're the king's own brother."

Allan MacRanald's pudgy knees visibly knocked under the hem of his red-and-blue kilt. He folded his hands together as though in prayer. "Surely you understand, Laird MacNeil," he said, his jowls wobbling in his fright, "that I never wished you ill. 'Twas Laird MacMurchaidh who wanted you dead. Not I! Never I! I never entertained the idea for a second."

With an annoyed grunt, Keir shoved the cowardly traitor out of his way, as he exited the prison and started down the tower steps.

"What should I do with the wee, fat laird here?" Macraith hollered from the top of the stairs, casually bracing the large wooden axe handle on his wide shoulder.

"Leave him for now," Keir said. "MacRanald can swear his oath of fealty to the king or we'll take him along as a prisoner." He paused and looked back up at his uncle. "How did you find me so soon?"

"We were stopping every ship we came across in the hopes they'd rescued you and Lady Raine during the storm. 'Tis how we intercepted MacRanald's galley carrying the ransom letter addressed to Lady Emma MacNeil."

At that moment, Fearchar appeared at the bottom of the stairwell. With a black patch covering one eye and the good blue eye twinkling benignly, the seven-foot giant smiled at Keir and touched the back of his fingers to his battle-scarred forehead in a pirate's salute.

"We've secured the castle," he reported with unruffled serenity. "The women and children have been herded into the keep. If you listen closely, lad, you can hear their caterwauling all the way to the top of the tower."

His sword at the ready, Colin came to stand beside Fearchar. "We've nay found Lady Raine," he said, his freckled brow creased with worry. "We've searched everywhere. The ladies swore to me that Raine was here but she's been gone for several days."

"They're right," Keir said, his words clipped and short as he joined them at the bottom of the stairs. "Lady Raine isn't here any longer." He was livid with himself for his failure to safeguard Raine and humiliated to have to admit it to Colin.

"Not here?" Colin stared at Keir, clearly appalled. "My God, what happened to her?"

"She's nay been harmed," Keir answered tersely.

Shocked, the tall redhead met Keir's gaze and belatedly had the sense to stop asking ill-considered questions.

After Fearchar and Colin left to oversee the crews' return to their ships, Macraith came to walk beside Keir on his way to the captain's cutter. "Where's Lady Raine?" his uncle asked in a worried tone.

"She went with MacMurchaidh," Keir gritted, the rage still boiling inside. "Raine thinks that traitorous bastard is her father."

"Is he?"

"How the hell should I know?"

Chapter 21

On first coming aboard the *Raven* at Castle Calbhaigh, Keir studied the navigational charts with Abid al-
Rahman, who immediately set their course for the Isle of
Lewis. Next Keir inspected the cannon with Apollonius
and ordered the eighteen-pounders unleashed from their
double frappings so the gun crews could resume their daily
afternoon drills. Then he'd gone over the needed repairs
with Macraith and the ship's burly carpenter. The galleon
had weathered the violent storm passably well, not considering the two seamen lost and the cracked top mainmast
that had to be replaced.

Initially a pall had fallen over the ship once the seamen
realized that Lady Raine hadn't come aboard with Keir.
Their cheers of welcome had tapered into disheartened
silence. Gloomy faces stared at their captain in disbelief,
unwilling to even consider that the precious lassie might
have been lost at sea. Upon learning she'd survived but

remained in the custody of the villainous chief of Clan MacMurchaidh, the entire crew worked furiously to slip the moorings and get under way as quickly as possible.

Keir felt the full impact of their justified censure. Even Ethan and Robbie looked at him with grave disappointment on their young faces. Yet no one felt Keir's failure to protect Raine more keenly than he did.

On the afternoon of the second day, the three galleons passed the Sound of Harris on the larboard side without spying so much as an inch of Sassenach sail. They were now flying before the wind, northward through the Little Minch.

That second dark night lit by only a sliver of moon, Keir stood on the quarterdeck gazing up at Ursa Major and remembering how enthusiastic Raine had been, learning the constellations. Her vivacity and intelligence made all other women seem dull and ignorant in comparison. He'd spent the previous night on deck. Sleeping alone in his large bed proved impossible. The memories of lying with Raine, her slender body cuddled against his, brought a knot to his throat, making it painful to swallow.

He refused to dwell on her betrayal.

Like a clumsy idiot, he'd opened himself up for that inevitable kick in the teeth. Christ almighty, he had no one to blame but himself. He'd actually begun to hope that Raine cared about him—not loved him, nay, not that—but certainly desired him physically and wanted to stay with him. But even her fanciful belief in the faery enchantment at Calanais hadn't kept her beside him for long.

Ignoring the ache in his gut, Keir told himself 'twas all for the best.

How could a man trust a female who refused to follow his advice, let alone obey his commands? Tenacious, willful and fearless, with her head stuffed with faeries dancing around standing stones and the magical power of ancient runes, Raine Cameron would always be traipsing off, following some illogical whim in the belief she'd seen it all in a dream. Leaving her distraught husband standing all alone with his teeth kicked in.

THREE DAYS OUT of Loch Baghasdail, the *Black Raven* and her sister ships raced along under a full press of canvas, making twelve knots with easy grace. On the quarterdeck Keir looked up into the yards, satisfied that every square sail had been hauled tight as the cover on a drum. The fair wind made scarcely a sigh in the taut rigging. Putting his hand on a line to gauge its tension, he glanced back toward the stern railing. The *Sea Dragon* and *Sea Hawk* followed in close line formation.

For the past three days Keir had barely spoken to anyone, leaving Macraith to issue orders, al-Rahman to chart their course, and Apollonius to lead the gunnery practice. The entire crew crept about making as little noise as possible whenever their captain came on deck. His wretched inner pain must have shown on his usually stoic face, for even the ship's exuberant boys tiptoed quietly around him.

Late that third afternoon, Macraith joined Keir as he came down the steps of the quarterdeck. They walked along the gangway to his cabin for the evening meal in companionable silence.

Deep in his own thoughts, Keir barely heard Macraith speaking as they sat down at the table, until he caught the words *Lady Raine*.

Frowning, Keir looked across the board at his uncle and tried to ignore the acute sensation that his heart had just been sliced up like mincemeat for a pie at the mere sound of her name. "Sorry," Keir apologized, "I didn't quite catch what you were saying."

"I'm saying that you need nay blame yourself, laddie," Macraith replied as he leaned back to let Hector place a steaming lamb pastry in front of him. "The good Lord alone kens what you could have done to keep MacMurchaidh from taking the lassie with him, seeing as how you were pegged to the stones of that damn prison cell."

Keir waited for his own plate to be set in front of him, then nodded to Hector. "That'll be all," he said, and watched the young man leave the cabin.

Since his initial outburst at Castle Calbhaigh, Keir had refrained from mentioning Raine's treachery again—not even to his uncle. "Aye," he agreed, his jaw tight with anger, "had I not been chained to the wall, I would have killed that wretched traitor on the spot. But what rankles most is that Raine may have left with my enemies of her own free will."

"Are you certain of that?" Macraith asked. His scarred brow furrowed in disbelief.

"Raine believes that she's seen MacMurchaidh in her dreams," Keir replied. He tried to ignore the painful feel of his heart banging against his ribs like broken main chains in a storm. "She insists that Torcall is her real father, not Gideon Cameron."

Stunned, Macraith slumped back in his chair. "I can scarcely believe it," he said softly. "I thought . . . well, never mind what I thought. When we reach Steòrnabhagh, what is it exactly you intend to do?"

Keir spoke through clenched teeth, his voice ragged with hatred. "Either MacMurchaidh and Donald Dubh surrender unconditionally or I'll kill them both on the spot."

"I was speaking of Lady Raine."

The softly uttered words came like a blow to his gut. Briefly Keir covered his eyes with his hand, then looked up to meet his uncle's concerned gaze. "Do I have a choice? I'll take her home to her family, where she belongs."

"Dod, man, we always have a choice. What if Raine refused to go willingly with MacMurchaidh? The scoundrel may have coerced the lass into leaving with him in order to keep you alive. 'Tis not such a farfetched notion. Other men have been known to abduct defenseless females against their will."

Keir gave a harsh laugh. "Are you referring to MacMurchaidh or the Black Beast of Barra?"

Macraith leaned forward and rested his folded arms on the table. His dark brown eyes grew serious. "My older brother was merciless in battle," he said, his words somber, "but Ruaidh was no more a beast than you or I, laddie. His enemies hung that goddamn title on him, not his friends. And most certainly not his family."

"That's nay what I'd been told," Keir said. Pushing his chair back, he rose and strode restlessly to the rear of his quarters. He leaned his hand on the window frame and gazed out at the darkening sky with unseeing eyes.

Macraith followed to stand beside him. He placed his large hand on Keir's shoulder. "And is that why you think you're nay worthy to be Raine Cameron's bridegroom?" he asked, his gruff voice creaky with compassion. "Because you've been labeled the spawn of a beast?"

Keir looked up absently at Polaris twinkling above them. "Since I was no more than a halflin, I've been told I'm the spirit and image of my father. What does that make me but a beast?" Keir met his uncle's concerned gaze and shrugged. "In my own defense, I've never abducted and raped a woman. Nor forced her to marry me and give birth to my unwanted child."

Macraith stared at him, clearly appalled. "What makes you think that Ruaidh did any such thing?"

Racked with humiliation, Keir recalled the painful childhood memories. "I learned the truth about my father when I was eight years old."

Macraith's sea-weathered features revealed his shock. "Surely," he gasped, "Lady Emma never told you any such thing!"

Keir shook his head. "My mother never said one unkind word about Ruaidh Athaeuch MacNeil. 'Twas a kinsman who took great delight in telling me the whole sordid tale." He leaned his shoulder against the window frame and crossed his arms, gazing across the cabin with unseeing eyes. "Shortly after Ruaidh died in battle, my father's cousin offered to train me in the use of the sword. While parrying with me, he proceeded to speak disparagingly of my parents. I became so enraged that I disarmed and nearly killed him." Keir lifted one shoulder dismissively. "I was always big for my age."

"Ah," Macraith said, nodding in understanding. "It runs in the family. And was your inept tutor Silas MacNeil?"

Keir met his uncle's steady gaze, surprised that he could guess so quickly. "Aye," he concurred, "Silas predicted I'd grow to be as cruel and callous as Ruaidh."

"What else did that miserable poltroon tell you?"

Keir fought the same sickening feeling he'd felt as a lad suffering from the recent death of his father. "That my mother had been brought to Barra against her will. That my father had forced her into marriage. That she detested him but stayed at Kisimuth Castle to protect her baby son. That my birth caused her unimaginable pain."

Incredulous, Macraith's deep voice roughened in anger. "And you never questioned Lady Emma about all this?"

"How could I?" Keir asked. "I believed any mention of my father's mistreatment would cause her needless anguish. I wondered how she could love me, when I was the source of such unhappiness. I'd assumed that I was the reason she stayed at Barra until Ruaidh died on the battlefield."

"Did you never speak of it to your brothers?"

"At the time, Rory was sixteen and Lachlan, thirteen. They were both fostered and lived elsewhere. Later, when we were adults, I felt too ashamed to confide that I was the product of our mother's brutal rape."

"Blood and bones!" Macraith exclaimed. "What else did that lying whelp tell you?"

"Silas predicted that I'd grow up to be exactly like Ruaidh—a crude, rough sea pirate who'd have to abduct a wife, for no gently born lady would ever willingly marry a beast like me."

Macraith dropped into the chair by the game table in front of the stern windows. "Sit down, lad," he said, pointing to the chair across from him. Once Keir was seated, he continued.

"As to the abduction," Macraith said, "it may or may not be true. I'd heard the rumors when Lady Emma appeared so suddenly at Kisimuth Castle. Ruaidh was prone to act on the spur of the moment and then rue his impetuous behavior in leisure. But I never once, by word or gesture, saw him behave unkindly toward Lady Emma." He shrugged. "Only your lovely mother could say what happened in the privacy of their rooms, but I sincerely doubt that your father forced himself on her. Forbye, 'twas clear to everyone that Ruaidh fairly doted upon his sonsy bride. Had she claimed 'up was down,' he'd have agreed with a smile."

Stunned, Keir stared at his uncle. "All this time I believed that Silas had told me the truth. Even when I looked back as an adult, there seemed to be no reason for my father's cousin to lie to a grieving child about his dead parent."

"My guess would be jealousy," Macraith said. He stroked his long beaded beard thoughtfully. "Silas always resented that your father was chief of Clan MacNeil. And who knows, maybe he wanted your mother for himself after Ruaidh's death and she spurned him."

Keir grinned at the possibility. "Soon after my father's burial, Mother took me to Stalcaire Castle to live with her brother."

"Aye, your Uncle Duncan Stewart! A fine man!" Macraith said, his wide grin splitting his moustache and beard. "Perchance by now, he's succeeded in finalizing your contract of marriage with the maid of Strathfillan."

At the unexpected remark, Keir jumped to his feet. "Jesu!" he cried, wondering how he'd ever thought 'twould be a wise decision to wed Mariota MacNab. He met his uncle's twinkling eyes and grinned back at him. "Let's finish our supper," he said, gesturing to their abandoned meal on the table. "After which I need to write a letter to Duncan explaining there's been a change of plans."

Macraith's good-natured laughter boomed out, filling the cabin and bouncing off the walls. "Hell and thunder, laddie! 'Twill cost you a pretty farthing to get out of that contract and nay be skinned alive!"

Castle Murchaidh
Steòrnabhagh Harbor
Isle of Lewis, Outer Hebrides

HIGH ON THE battlement walk, Raine could see across the harbor to the town of Steòrnabhagh. Guarding the entrance to the bay, Arnish Point was clearly visible in the afternoon sun and far beyond lay the tiny fishing village of Sanndabhaig with its few small stone crofts. She smiled to herself, remembering the kindness of the fisher wife and her husband who'd so gallantly taken her aboard his yellow sailboat.

Laird MacMurchaidh's galley lay moored not far from the road leading up the green sloping bank to the ancient castle. The great oared ship wouldn't be there for long, however. Donald Dubh Macdonald and a few loyal men would sail in the morning for the safety of Ireland. News had reached the castle of the capitulation of the other rebellious chiefs, leaving Torcall as the last supporter of the self-proclaimed lord of the Isles.

Since arriving at the castle a week ago, Raine had made a habit of wandering along the battlements. She wanted to get away from the solar and its bevy of unfamiliar women who engaged her with distant politeness.

Raine suspected that Torcall had warned the ladies of the castle to treat his female guest kindly or they'd be punished. Certainly, no one had mistreated her during her stay. Yet her attempts to speak to Torcall had been spurned repeatedly. She'd had the sickening realization that her father may have taken her with him solely to use her as a hostage.

"Oh, there you are, Lady Raine," Amie MacMurchaidh called out. "I thought I'd see if you'd like some company."

The young daughter of Laird Torcall and Lady Catriona, Amie possessed a bubbly disposition. Only thirteen, she laughed and chattered easily with anyone who'd listen.

"Thank you," Raine replied and gave the lass a welcoming smile. "Indeed, I'd be pleased if you'd join me."

Amie slipped her arm through Raine's, and they walked together along the battlement, passing guards who bowed their heads in deference. "Father says you're our special guest, since you're the daughter of a dear friend from his youth. Were they very good friends, do you think?"

"Oh, I think so," Raine told her. "My mother knew your father quite well, I believe."

Amie's wide brown eyes sparkled. "Then that makes us almost kin," she said with a happy gurgle. "I have lots of cousins, but no one nearly as pretty as you. I've never seen anyone with black eyes before nor such beautiful long black curls."

Raine tried to ignore the uneasiness inside, a disquiet that had increased with each passing day. "Do none of your brothers or sisters have black hair like mine?"

"Oh, nay," Amie answered, giggling at the thought. "I have two half-brothers, for my father was married twice before, and both their mothers died. But I'm the only one with dark brown hair and eyes exactly like our father."

At the sound of footsteps on the stone battlement, they turned in unison. "There's Father now!" Amie exclaimed.

Laird Torcall drew closer, and the lass hurried toward him. With a welcoming smile, he put his arm around her shoulders, bent his head and kissed her brow. "Are you entertaining our guest?" he asked her fondly.

"I was telling Lady Raine how pretty she is," Amie told him with a happy little laugh. "Don't you think so, Father?"

Torcall met Raine's gaze and smiled. "I do, indeed," he said. "I can see the similarity to her mother's nose and mouth and her flawless skin."

Seeing them standing side by side, Raine could discern the startling resemblance between father and daughter. Amie's youthful features were much softer and clearer, but the facial structure was the same, the wide brow and high cheekbones along with the strong chin.

Raine felt a ghost of doubt pass through her. She grew painfully aware that Torcall's dark brown hair and eyes certainly weren't jet-black like hers. Nor did she have his identical features like Amie. For the first time since leaving Archnacarry Manor, Raine began to question the meaning of her vision. Her heart beat a rapid drum roll, calling forth a rush of uncertainty.

Could it be the Tuatha De Danann had sent her on a fool's errand?

His arm wrapped loosely around Amie's tiny waist, Laird Torcall came to stand in front of Raine. "I trust you've been made welcome," he said warmly. "As you must know, I've been very busy with my other guest."

"Everyone has been most kind," Raine answered, her mind racing in her confusion.

Torcall and Raine had exchanged no more than mere pleasantries since leaving Calbhaigh. Each time Raine tried to approach him, he told her sharply that her questions would have to wait. The success of the rebellion outweighed all other considerations. While onboard the galley, he and Donald Dubh had spent most of the voyage in quiet, seemingly desperate conversations. Upon reaching the castle, the two men had been closeted together all week long.

Never once had Torcall given Raine an opportunity to ask about his relationship with her mother. In fact, this was the first time Torcall had mentioned Raine's mother, even obliquely, since the day he'd found Raine on the beach after the storm. 'Twas as though he'd purposely avoided the mention of Lady Nina or his love for her since expressing his hatred for Gideon Cameron.

Torcall turned to look out over the sheltering harbor, his gaze roaming across the calm waters to Arnish Point, where a cannon emplacement protected the narrow entrance.

"This is a good vantage place to watch for intruders," he said, his quiet voice sounding unconcerned by the inevitable siege to come. "My sentries stand on the battlements day and night." He looked back at Raine and smiled once more. "But no strange sails today."

"They will come," she told him bluntly. "Once Laird MacNeil is ransomed by his family, he'll bring his ships here, and my visit will come to an end. If there is anything you wish to tell me, Laird Torcall, 'twould be better spoken sooner rather than later."

"There's no need to speak of what is better left unsaid," he told her, his firm voice warning her not to question his decision in front of his youngest child.

Raine's hopes for an open acknowledgement that she was his daughter were crushed. Torcall had no intention of upsetting his family by the intrusion of an illegitimate offspring into their midst. She could understand his reservations, but that didn't ease the heartrending ache of complete and utter rejection.

She'd found her father but her quest had been in vain.

What she'd really sought was her father's love.

Fighting back tears, she lifted her chin and met his gaze. "At least we've had the chance to get to know each other," she said.

"Aye," he answered softly. His gaze conveyed his sympathy but nothing more. "Meeting Lady Nina's lovely daughter has touched me deeply. I was very fond of your sweet mother in my green years, and her memory has remained in my heart." He looked down at his brown-eyed daughter and gave her a paternal squeeze. "Now, lassies, shall we proceed to the hall? I believe the midday meal will soon be set on the tables."

Raine's inner pain nearly brought her to her knees. 'Twas as though her heart was sobbing for the loss of a dream. A dream of meeting her natural father one day. A father who'd joyously welcome her into his arms and into his life.

Glancing over her shoulder at the fishing boats sailing across the calm harbor, Raine joined Laird Torcall and Amie to walk down the tower steps to the great hall.

THAT EVENING RAINE returned to the battlements. Looking up at the starry summer sky, she located Ursa Major—the Great Bear. She smiled at the memory of Keir teaching her how to recognize the constellations. Along with the Gibson brothers' high-spirited attempts to help, Keir had told her the story of Hera, the wife of Zeus, who—in a jealous fit—turned her husband's ladylove, Callisto, into a bear.

Raine smiled to herself at her own similar folly. She'd felt the same blind jealousy toward Lady Flora Sutherland at Dùn Bheagain Castle.

On the night Keir and Raine had visited the standing stones of Calanais, he'd taught her the story of the Seven Sisters, whom Jupiter had changed into doves.

Now, Raine searched the myriad of stars spread across the black velvet sky, until she found Orion chasing the Pleiades across the heavens.

That same night, Keir had kissed her for the first time.

And the faeries had wrapped an enchantment around them to form a bond of love that would last forever—or so she'd believed at the time.

Dear Lord above, how things had changed.

Keir had been so enraged when Raine left with Laird Torcall and Donald Dubh, he'd roared death threats from the barred cell window. She wondered if Keir still desired her, or if his anger had poisoned his feelings toward her.

Raine had been so certain that Torcall MacMurchaidh was her father. She'd never imagined that he'd refuse to acknowledge his natural daughter in order to protect the harmony within his legitimate family.

Somewhere in the Outer Hebrides, Keir was studying the stars tonight. Hopefully he'd been freed from the prison cell and was even now sailing toward Steòrnabhagh. Raine had no doubt he'd take the castle and when he did, he'd kill Torcall—unless she could intervene to save his life.

It didn't matter that Raine's father had refused to recognize her as his child. Or that he might be planning to use her as a hostage should the need arise. She couldn't willingly stand by and let him be killed. Which meant, of course, that Keir would never forgive her for defending his sworn enemy, the traitorous chief of Clan MacMurchaidh.

Raine's eyes filled with tears. The bright twinkling stars overhead seemed to blur into the soft glow of a ship's lantern, the lantern that had hung in Keir's quarters on the night he'd taken her into his bed. As the tears ran down her cheeks, Raine's heart seemed to shrivel inside with the bitter ache of disillusionment.

How had everything gone so wrong?

Chapter 22

KEIR MET WITH his captains and their lieutenants in the
starboard watch's mess. The *Raven*, the *Hawk*, and the
Dragon had hove to in a sheltering inlet along the eastern coast of the Isle of Lewis. A map of Steòrnabhagh's
harbor lay spread across the long rectangular table in front
of them.

Keir looked at his three most seasoned veterans. Macraith MacNeil sat beside him. Directly across, Fearchar
MacLean and Walter MacRath waited intently. The trio
of hardened warriors were experienced not just in sea battles, but also at infiltrating the enemy's land defenses in
stealth and with lethal skill.

Keir knew he could count on Tam MacLean and Colin
MacRath, seated on either side of their ferocious kinsmen,
to make up in strength and courage what they lacked in
experience.

Standing behind Keir, Abid al-Rahman, Adam Wyllie,

Apollonius the Greek, and Hector MacFarlane listened to their captain's plans with unwavering concentration. Wyllie had been the *Raven*'s bosun since the day the ship was launched. At seventeen, Hector was young, but 'twas time for the midshipman to get a taste of leading men into battle. One day he'd be captain of his own merchantman and would have to fight off pirate attacks on the open sea. Meeting their earnest gazes, Keir knew he could count on each and every man present.

"We risk the safety of Lady Raine if we immediately attempt to bombard the castle into submission," Keir told them. "I have no knowledge of how MacMurchaidh has treated her—whether as a guest or a prisoner. Or if the bastard intends to use the lass as a hostage, should we begin a siege. We must therefore assume the worst and make our plans accordingly."

"Which means we'll have to penetrate the keep at the same time we start our bombardment," Macraith said.

"Aye," Fearchar agreed. "The castle is surrounded by a dense woods. If we come through the trees, we can scale the rear walls unnoticed. That's depending we have a big enough diversion in the harbor. We'll need the ships' initial volleys to draw every MacMurchaidh soldier to the front battlements."

Bending over the map, Macraith pointed to the outcrop that guarded the entrance to the bay. "A small party can spike the guns on Arnish Point first," he said, his beaded side-braids swinging gently as he leaned over the charts. "That way we can silence the lookouts before they give a warning shot."

"It worked before," Colin agreed. Excitement at the prospect of hand-to-hand combat rang in his voice. His blue eyes shone with anticipation as he glanced at his father.

"First we need to send the infiltrating party well ahead of our ships," Walter cautioned. He rubbed a gnarled forefinger alongside his big broken nose as he looked at Keir in speculation. "How do you propose to get close enough to the castle without being seen? Travel overland from here?"

" 'Tis a good twenty miles," Macraith added, "but we could do it easily enough."

Keir shook his head at the suggestion they tramp across the countryside. "Going overland would take too much of our precious time," he said, "and some nosey crofter could give a hue and cry and warn the fortress."

"What then?" Walter asked, curiosity written on his broad, blunt features.

"We're going to approach the castle grounds in a fishing boat," Keir told them with a grin. " 'Tis the only way we can get across the open harbor without being noticed. We'll sail just before dawn when the fishermen usually start out to sea for their day's catch. Only instead of sailing out of the harbor, we'll be sailing past Arnish Point in the direction of the town docks."

"It could work, laddie," Fearchar said. He readjusted his black eye patch and studied the map thoughtfully. "Right before sunrise the harbor is usually bustling with fishing craft."

Keir's oldest brother, Rory, had sailed the *Sea Dragon* with both Fearchar and Tam aboard into Steòrnabhagh's harbor before the current rebellion. They were well acquainted with the lay of the land surrounding the fortress.

"How do we steal a fisherman's boat without causing an uproar in the town?" Tam asked.

"I don't think we're going to steal one, are we?" Colin interjected. His intelligent eyes alight in his freckled face, the redhead smiled knowingly.

"We're not," Keir agreed. He tapped his fingertip on the tiny dot that marked the village of Sanndabhaig. "We're going to hire a certain fisherman's sailboat. I don't doubt that he'll be willing to take us across the bay to the castle grounds for the right price."

"Aye," Walter said, his wide grin revealing his chipped front tooth. "If any man has the stones to sail his wee boat right up to the castle's grassy bank, 'tis the pawky fisherman who took Lady Raine's gold in return for a ride across the harbor right under our noses—and us with our gun ports open."

The men chuckled as they recalled the incredible sight of the yellow fishing boat sailing past the three warships bristling with guns.

"After we've had enough time to scale the walls and get inside," Keir continued, "I want our galleons to sail in battle formation into the harbor and begin bombardment." He met each man's gaze, including Apollonius. "Make certain your best gunners measure the range with exact precision. Set your sights for the outer walls and the main gate and portcullis. Castle Murchaidh is one of the oldest fortresses in the Hebrides. Its outdated ordnance can't match our advanced artillery. Nor will it withstand much pummeling. Once you've knocked a hole through the mortar and stones, send the landing parties to take the outer bailey."

"Who's going with you in the sailboat?" Tam queried. He pushed his long golden hair back away from his handsome MacLean face, clearly hoping he'd be one of the lucky fellows chosen for the daring assignment.

"I'm taking Macraith, Fearchar, Walter and al-Rahman," Keir replied, knowing the younger men would be disappointed. It couldn't be helped. When it came to rescuing Raine unharmed, he refused to take any more chances than necessary.

"That's all the men you're taking?" Colin asked with a frown. He ran his long, thin fingers through his coppery hair in apparent frustration.

"Just the five of us," Keir reiterated. "We've done this before. We can move swiftly and silently into the castle. I want to locate Lady Raine first. Then we'll hunt down MacMurchaidh and Donald Dubh, while the rest of you storm through the curtain walls and into the bailey. Their soldiers will put up a stiff resistance, so you'll all get a taste of battle, never fear."

KEIR STOOD IN the woods looking up at Castle Murchaidh's ancient walls. Armed with his claymore and spiked targe slung across his back, broadsword sheathed at his side, dirk in his belt, and dagger hidden in his short hose, he carried a long rope with a grappling hook over his shoulder.

The fact that the trees had been allowed to grow so close to the fortress gave silent testimony to just how remote and inaccessible the chief of Clan MacMurchaidh believed his lair remained. And that in spite of the fact that Cairn na Burgh—protected by the choppy seas of the Treshnish Isles and once deemed secure from the king's wrath—had fallen beneath the guns of the royal fleet earlier that summer.

Similarly armed, Macraith, Fearchar, Walter, and al-Rahman stood beside Keir and waited for the signal to leave the cover of the woods and scale the high stone walls.

They didn't have long to wait.

In the quiet of early morning, startled cries of alarm carried across the length of the parapets above them. The three warships had been sighted sailing past Arnish Point and into the wide bay.

Just as Keir had foreseen, the guards raced along the battlement walks toward the main gate of the castle, which faced the wide natural harbor. The town of Steòrnabhagh lay to the left along the coastline, close to where Keir's small party had landed in the bright yellow fishing boat just before daybreak.

The thundering booms of the galleons' first salvos carried on the harbor's breeze to the five waiting men hidden in the woods.

"Let's go," Keir said. He led them out of the trees and up to the base of the curtain wall.

Using his great height and immense strength, Fearchar tossed the grappling hook to the edge of the parapet far above their heads. After testing the hook's stability, first

Keir and then Fearchar pulled himself up, hand over hand, feet braced against the stones, to the top of the battlement wall and over the parapet's edge. One by one Macraith, Walter and al-Rahman followed them in a feat of power and endurance worthy of much younger men.

Moving in silence, Keir motioned for them to spread out along the stone walkway in both directions, searching for any guards who'd lingered behind their comrades.

In startled surprise Fearchar came upon a large brute of a fellow rushing toward the sound of artillery fire coming from the bay. The seven-foot giant and the distracted guard crashed into each other. Before the confused soldier emitted a sound, Fearchar caught the man's chin in his left hand, completely covering the open mouth, and jerked the helmeted head back—then neatly slit the exposed throat with the dagger held in his right hand. In a matter of seconds the wide-eyed corpse dropped to the stone walkway at the pirate's feet.

The five intruders proceeded quickly to the tower's archway. Keir cautiously pulled a heavy wooden door open, and they moved soundlessly along a narrow, winding passage. At its end a sentry stood with his back to them.

Before the unsuspecting sentinel realized his danger, Keir picked the man up, brought him lengthwise across his bent knee and neatly popped his backbone. Despite the guard's steel breastplate, his spine snapped like a piece of dry kindling.

Three more soldiers had the unfortunate luck of standing in their path and were left with their throats slashed, their life's blood draining out onto the stones in puddles.

Working their way upward in stealthy silence till they were high in the keep's tower, the intruders, liberally splashed with blood, entered the ladies' solar—four with their broadswords drawn, the fifth holding his huge scimitar. The already frightened females, who'd been clustered together in a tight bunch, shrieked and tore about the room like hens in a coop invaded by a weasel.

"Silence!" Fearchar roared. "Blood and bones, women. Be quiet! You've nay been hurt. Yet."

Two ladies fainted on the spot—whether at the sight and sound of the massive pirate with his black eye patch and battle-scarred features or the exotic Moor dressed in an embroidered caftan and loose trousers and brandishing an enormous curved sword over his bald head, Keir couldn't tell.

But he grinned at the ludicrous scene. At least there were two men alive more frightening to look at than he was himself.

RAINE STOOD IN front of the solarium's round stained-glass window watching her rescuer enter with his ferocious privateers. The chief of Clan MacNeil, magnificent in his green-and-black kilt, held his lethal broadsword in his large hand. His blue-black hair fell loose to his powerful shoulders, the two side-braids tied with leather thongs. His blunt-cut features, sliced and broken in battle, concealed his tenderness as a lover. A tenderness she'd come to know so well.

Raine's heart leapt with a thrill of admiration as he

scanned the panicked, screaming females, searching for her. Across the chaotic room she met Keir's gaze, praying to God he'd forgive her for running off with his enemies.

The moment he saw Raine, he sheathed his weapon and hurried to her. "You've nay been hurt?" Keir asked, his familiar baritone tight and strained. The concern in his eyes revealed what she'd longed to know—that he still cared in spite of her treachery.

"Aye," she whispered, swallowing the lump in her throat. "I've been well treated."

"Thank God." With a smile of heart-stopping gentleness, Keir enfolded her in his embrace.

The relief of being in his protective arms made her suddenly breathless. "Oh, my darling," Raine said, gasping for air as she lifted her face to his. "I'm so sorry."

He held her tight against his solid frame for a few brief moments, then released her. "We'll speak of this later," Keir said, so quietly only she could hear. He kissed the top of her head. "Stay in the solar with the other women. I'll leave al-Rahman to guard you."

"There's no need for that," Raine assured him. "I'll be quite safe with the other ladies. They've been very kind to me."

He looked around the room. Most of the women had sought a chair or a bench and now sat quietly waiting, convinced for the moment they were in no imminent danger. A few had even resumed their abandoned needlework, possibly in an attempt to calm themselves. "Then remain here until I come for you," Keir ordered, his gruff words conveying absolute authority.

Raine knew better than to argue.

Her heart stuttered in dread as she waited for Keir and his men to leave and continue their search for Donald Dubh Macdonald and Torcall MacMurchaidh.

She couldn't remain safely in the solarium, as Keir had ordered.

Not now.

Raine had to find her father before Keir found him.

OUTSIDE THE SOLAR, the men split up. Fearchar, Walter, and al-Rahman started down the stairway to search for Donald Dubh in the castle's private apartments. The usurper's life was far too valuable to the rebellion's cause to risk his death in the siege.

Keir and his uncle raced to the top of the inner battlements and looked out over the fortress and the harbor beyond. As he'd predicted, the castle's ponderous culverins, locked in position in their keyhole gun ports, proved no match for the ships' eighteen-pounders on their pivoting mounts. The punishing broadsides from the three galleons had come to a halt and thick yellow-gray smoke drifted across the water, bringing the acrid stink of sulphur. The sound of battle cries rang out as the landing parties poured through the holes that had been punched in the ancient castle's curtain walls.

The MacNeil battle cry carried above the clang and smash of weapons.

Buaidh na Bàs! Victory or Death!

The heavy wooden gate and iron portcullis, along with

half the watchtower, had been blown away. The outer bailey quickly filled with a melee of fighting clansmen. The yellow-and-black kilts of Clan MacMurchaidh were clearly visible as the castle's vanguard raced to push back the intruders.

Keir searched for their chief among the fighting men but not one of them resembled his prey. He realized with grim dispassion there wasn't a single Macdonald plaid amongst the defenders. Hell and damnation. He wouldn't have the pleasure of arresting Donald Dubh today. The scoundrel must have made his escape in MacMurchaidh's galley before the three galleons sailed into the harbor.

The clash of steel rang out as MacNeils fought along-side MacLeans in their green-and-black tartans and Mac-Raths in red-and-black plaid. The fighting flooded into the inner bailey directly below Keir. He caught sight of Colin, tall, lean, and easily recognizable with his shock of coppery hair. The young man swung a double-bladed boarding axe with whipcord strength and neatly decapitated a large, burly soldier, sending the head soaring above the other fighters. Rich, red blood spattered over them like a summer shower. On the back stroke, Colin sliced across another man's torso, opening his chest all the way to the beating heart.

With Macraith right behind him, Keir raced down the winding outer steps to join the fray. Screaming and shouting, clansmen fought with swords, dirks, and long-handled pikes.

Keir met a castle soldier swinging a Lochaber axe. Dodging the deadly forward swing, he parried the blow with his solid wooden targe and skewered his opponent with his broadsword.

Keir looked over just in time to see Tam run his sword through a beefy guardsman, then stand on the man's chest to jerk his blade free from between the ribs. The yellow-haired MacLean grinned at Keir, lifted his bloody sword in a brief salute, and turned to find another opponent.

In the chaos, Abid al-Rahman worked his way methodically through the crush of fighters, swinging his scimitar with deadly accuracy, lopping off MacMurchaidh heads, arms, and legs with indiscriminate precision.

Keir spotted Fearchar coming down the outer stairs from the ramparts above. "Have you seen MacMurchaidh?" he shouted.

Fearchar pointed toward the wide stone steps leading to the donjon. "Look over there, laddie," he said with a chuckle. "Someone's waiting for you."

At that moment a guard with a pike attacked the colossus, swinging wildly. Light-footed and resilient, Fearchar evaded the oncoming blade and hacked downward with his two-handed claymore, splitting the pikeman from head to crotch before he could begin his back swing.

Amongst the carnage the landing parties relentlessly pushed the castle's defenders into tight groups fighting for their lives in close-quarter combat. Facing certain death, the soldiers began to throw down their weapons and surrender.

Keir moved in the direction Fearchar had indicated. Torcall stood waiting in front of the donjon's open doorway, his huge claymore held in his two hands.

Keir handed his broadsword and wooden targe to Macraith. Reaching behind his head, Keir withdrew his own claymore from its sheath on his back.

"Laird MacMurchaidh," Keir shouted across the wide bailey scattered with corpses, the injured, and dying. "I arrest you in the name of the king!"

Beneath his dark brown hair, Torcall's face turned white, but he came down the steps and approached Keir with a look of deadly determination. "I owe no allegiance to the king of Scotland," he answered, his voice sharp with scorn. "I've sworn on my life to defend the true lord of the Isles, Donald Dubh MacDonald.

Without warning, Raine Cameron bolted through the donjon's doorway and raced down the steps. "Stop, Keir, stop!" she cried. She didn't halt until she was standing between the two men armed with claymores, their four-foot long-blades catching the morning sunlight and reflecting it back to the fascinated onlookers.

Raine held out her arms to keep them apart. "Don't kill him, Keir! I'm begging you not to kill him! Laird Mac-Murchaidh is my father."

By unspoken, mutual consent, Keir and Torcall stepped back from the distraught lass, neither willing to take a chance on injuring her.

Keir glanced over to his uncle, who stood watching beside Fearchar and al-Rahman. Macraith came over and gently lifted Raine off her feet. He carried her like a child's doll to where the others stood well out of danger. Setting her down, he kept his large hand firmly on her shoulder and held her in place beside him.

The two combatants turned to each other and gave a quick salute with their swords. Keir immediately closed in on his enemy, circling lightly on his feet as he sought an opening. Their blades crashed together in an explosion of sound. Torcall grunted under the strength of Keir's brutal blows but managed to keep his blade up and recover his balance.

In his mid-forties, MacMurchaidh clearly excelled at swordplay. He had the strong arms and deep chest of a practiced swordsman. And his years had provided him with a wily ability to predict his opponent's next move. He advanced in a crouch and then lunged. Keir pivoted and blocked the slicing blow.

Again and again their claymores clanged together as each opponent tried to beat down the other's blade. Wrenching and parrying, the two enemies moved across the open bailey, stepping over bodies sprawled across their makeshift arena. The mighty steel blades gleamed in the summer sunshine as the two experienced swordsmen moved back and forth, causing the bystanders to leap out of their way, only inches from the deadly points.

For Keir there was never a doubt who would emerge the victor.

The older man began to slow, nearly tripping on a dead kinsman lying in the way. His face grew red. Sweat poured down his neck and soaked his shirt.

Keir used his greater strength and longer reach to drive the traitor backward relentlessly. MacMurchaidh staggered under the merciless offensive and his arms began to shake beneath his breath-stealing exertion.

Their eyes met. In that instant both men recognized that neither wanted to deliver a death blow to his opponent. Not in front of the heartbroken lassie cradled in Macraith's brawny arms.

Fatigued and gasping for breath, Torcall began to grow clumsy. His blade wavered, the weight of the enormous sword dragging his wrists downward.

With the tip of his claymore, Keir deftly snagged the large cross-guard on the handle of his opponent's sword and sent the weapon flying.

Shouts of warning rang out through the crowd as the sharp blade soared through the air over their heads. The mighty battle-sword finally skidded across the stones to rest harmlessly at Colin's feet.

Weaponless, MacMurchaidh stood in front of Keir with his head high, waiting with the indomitable courage of a Scotsman for the death blow to come.

"Please, Keir, I beg you," Raine screamed, her anguished plea carrying across the bailey in the sudden, breathless quiet that had descended around the two swordsmen. Frantic, she tried to pull away from Macraith, who refused to let her go. "Please, don't kill my father!"

Keir heard the raw pain in her voice and remained absolutely still.

Against his sense of duty, honor, and loyalty to his family and clan, against all he believed as a warrior and faithful defender of Scotland and his king, he lowered his sword and spared the traitor's life.

Keir's love for Raine trumped everything else.

The moment Keir took a step back, his uncle released

Raine. She ran over to the two enemies, tears streaming down her face.

The chief of Clan MacMurchaidh gently clasped Raine's shoulders and met her gaze. His face looked suddenly haggard and lined with defeat. His head bowed, Torcall spoke softly, so only she and Keir could hear. "Lady Raine Cameron, I am not your father. You should have been my daughter, and I wish to God you were, but 'tisn't so.

"I should have told you the truth at Calbhaigh, but I wanted you to accompany me willingly. I hoped that your mother would come to my castle when she learned that you were my hostage.

"Nina Paterson and I were once deeply in love. We planned to run away together, for I was even then a hunted man. I waited in the woods for Nina for three long days, but she never came. As God is my witness, I swear to you, lass, when I fled the Highlands, your exquisite mother and I had never lain together as man and woman."

Raine's face turned white. Her wide-set black eyes seemed to lose their glow, as if a light had been extinguished inside her. Stepping back from Torcall, she started to stumble.

Keir put his arms around Raine, his heart aching for her bitter disappointment. She turned into his embrace and buried her face against his chest, sobbing inconsolably.

Macraith, Fearchar, and Colin, holding the claymore, slowly approached, their sympathy for the distraught lass written on their dirty, battle-weary faces.

"What shall we do about the castle?" Macraith asked quietly.

Keir turned to look at MacMurchaidh, head bowed, standing in defeat before his partly ruined fortress.

"Leave it," Keir told them. "Leave it all just as it is. If King James wants the place destroyed, he can send someone else. I'm taking Lady Raine back to her mother in Archnacarry Manor."

His teeth flashing in his bearded face, Macraith grinned at his companions. "Come on, lads," he said joyfully. "We're going home to the Highlands."

Chapter 23

Raine stood in front of the stern windows in Keir's cabin, watching the Isle of Lewis grow smaller in the distance. The *Black Raven*, the *Sea Dragon*, and the *Sea Hawk* had left the harbor of Steòrnabhagh that morning and were now spread out across the Minch in a homeward race. Whichever crew reached Loch Linne first would be handsomely rewarded by their captain.

Three members of the *Raven*'s crew had been killed in the fighting, and their bodies solemnly consigned to the sea. Raine had spent the rest of the day in the ship's cockpit working alongside Jasper Barrows. At first Keir had tried to dissuade her from helping with the wounded, saying she'd gone through enough upheaval since leaving Castle Calbhaigh. But Raine had been adamant. The need to be of assistance to those suffering overrode any sorrow that weighed on her mind and heart.

Raine and her sea-daddy had patched and bandaged

the men who'd sustained injuries during the siege and ensuing battle. Iain Davidson, the ship's carpenter, had suffered a deep cut across his upper arm. 'Twas fortunate no major vein or bone had been severed, but the bleeding had been profuse. Their first step required staunching the blood using a long scarf tightened above the wound. In order to see the ragged edges of torn skin clearly and match them together, Raine washed the cut with the special concoction of herbs she'd brought from home. Then she and Barrows carefully stitched up the ugly laceration.

Assisted by Ethan and Robbie, Raine and Barrows set and splinted several broken bones. Davie Swinton, the *Raven*'s cooper, had sustained a bad burn from a red-hot cannon barrel, which required Raine's special salve.

After all the patients had been treated and given a ration of rum to ease the pain, Barrows grinned at Raine in triumph. "Nay a single amputation today," he said, pleasure lighting his weather-lined face. "It warms my heart, lassie, to have you bring your magical medicine into my sickbay."

She smiled at his choice of words and shook her head. "Nay, not magical," she told him, "but healing recipes I learned from my Aunt Isabel."

At the sound of her aunt's name, Raine felt the acute stab of homesickness—so sharp and poignant she thought her broken heart might shatter into pieces.

Dear Lord, how she yearned to be home again with her family at Archnacarry Manor.

IN THE EVENING twilight Raine watched the stars come out through the four tall stern windows. She slowly unbraided her hair, letting it fall in waves about her shoulders as she absently picked out the familiar constellations. Ursa Major. Ursa Minor. The Pleiades and Orion. By now she could also find Pegasus, Hercules, and Aquarius, as well as the planets Mars, Jupiter, and Saturn. And of course Venus, the Evening Star, hung low in the western sky.

But in spite of the brilliance of the summer night, Raine felt numb, drained of all the violent emotions that had tossed her about like the storm she'd survived, until she was too exhausted to think.

The ordinary sounds of the galleon moving before the wind comforted her. The deep male voices calling out to one another as the sails were being hauled and trimmed to catch the most wind possible. The shrill *tweet-tweet-tweet* of the bosun's pipe marking the change of the watch. The calling out of the ship's speed in knots as the log was being thrown. In the midst of all these muffled noises, she heard Keir enter his quarters and turned to greet him.

The chief of Clan MacNeil wore only his belted green-and-black kilt and leather sporran. His chest and feet were bare and his damp hair fell loose to his shoulders. "I cleaned up with the crew on the main deck earlier," he explained. "After a battle we strip off our soiled clothing, suds ourselves down, and pour buckets of water over our heads to wash away the blood and grime and the stink of gunpowder."

"Barrows explained the ritual," Raine replied, "and warned me to stay below with him amidships."

Keir's marvelous green eyes conveyed the depth of his compassion. Without words Raine knew he felt her pain as though it were his own. He glanced at the dishes on the table and back to her with a worried frown. "Did you eat?"

"I ate a little," she said, forcing a tiny smile in the hopes of easing his concern.

"I can request something more," he suggested. "Something sweet—perhaps pudding like the lads used to steal from the cook and secrete away in your cabin."

"Thank you but nay," Raine answered as she recalled their smiling faces. "Ethan and Robbie were so happy when I came back on board this morning," she added. "Everyone was wonderful."

After the battle Raine and Keir had been rowed out to the *Raven* in the ship's cutter, along with Macraith and other members of the landing party. The entire crew had cheered when Keir assisted Raine up the ladder, while Barrows helped her over the side and onto the gangway.

"If you hadn't come back with me," Keir said with a lopsided grin, "there would have been a mutiny on the *Raven*."

Raine tried to smile. Instead she had to bite her lower lip to keep it from trembling. She looked down absently at her bloodstained shirt and trousers. She'd changed out of her borrowed gown and into the sailor's garb before going belowdecks to sickbay. Her fingers shaking, she tried to brush away a dark spot and gave up, realizing 'twas a hopeless task.

"I've ordered a bath for you," Keir said, the timbre of his deep baritone as gentle and reassuring as if he spoke to a child.

"A bath would be nice," she agreed.

Raine looked away, not wanting him to see the tears that suddenly welled up in her eyes. Feelings of loss and confusion continued to wash over her in waves. For the last two years she'd been positive that she understood her vision. She had believed without a doubt that the chief of Clan MacMurchaidh was her father.

They heard a polite knock and turned toward the source.

"There's your tub now," Keir said and went over to open the door wide.

Hector rolled in a large wine vat that had been cut in half. Ethan and Robbie followed, carrying two buckets of warm water each and poured them into the wooden tub. The lads smiled at her shyly, then ducked their heads, no doubt embarrassed at the thought of filling her bath, and hurried out of the cabin.

"Will that be all, sir?" Hector asked after adding two more large pails of hot water and then lighting a lantern. He glanced over at Raine, his eyes filled with sympathy. By now the entire crew had been apprised of all that had happened at Castle Murchaidh.

"Aye," Keir told him. "That'll be all, Mr. MacFarlane. You may retire for the evening. I won't need you again tonight."

With a brief bow to Raine, the pale-haired young man left, closing the door quietly behind him.

Taking a deep breath, Raine sank down in a chair beside the game table in front of the stern windows. She met Keir's gaze and blurted out the thought that'd been running through her mind all afternoon. "Do you think Laird MacMurchaidh was telling the truth?"

Keir didn't seem the least surprised at her question. He crossed the cabin and dropped to his knees in front of her. "Aye, I do," he said as he began to remove her shoes. "I believe the man spoke the truth, love. There'd hardly be a reason for him to lie."

Leaning forward, Raine braced her hands on Keir's bare shoulders. She recalled the way he'd held her secure in his arms when they'd been swept overboard. And his undaunted courage as he'd fought the enormous waves and the violent storm to keep her alive. She doubted any other man could have done the same.

She bent her head close to his and continued in a near whisper. "I know he's very fond of his daughter, Amie. She's such a sweet lass and clearly loves her father. Maybe Torcall didn't want to upset his family by recognizing me as his natural daughter."

" 'Tis possible," Keir agreed, rolling down her stockings and gently massaging her calves and feet. "But I don't think MacMurchaidh would do that. Not after he acknowledged how desperately he once loved your beautiful mother." As Keir lightly rubbed Raine's toes, he looked up and gave her a bracing smile. "If you recall, the laird swore to God he wished you were his daughter."

Raine nodded, releasing a long, drawn-out sigh, unable to put her bereft feelings into words. 'Twas as though someone she loved had just died, and she was trying to come to grips with her loss.

"I used to hate my father," Keir said, his quiet words

filled with understanding. He unbuttoned Raine's blue striped shirt and slipped her arms out of the long sleeves. "I thought the evil things said about Ruaidh Athaeuch were true. Now I'm nay so certain." He pulled her soiled shirt away and tossed it on the rug, then bracketed her hips with his palms. "Since I was eight years old, I believed a lie told out of envy and spite. I thought my father had abducted and raped my mother, and I was the result of his despicable act. When people called me the Black Beast's Spawn, I thought 'twas justified."

Shocked at his admission, Raine touched Keir's jaw, covered with a thick stubble of beard. "Oh, my darling!" she said, her fingers trembling, "I never once suspected how you felt."

"Nor did anyone else," he said with a shrug, "for I hid my shame well."

Her thumbs resting at the corners of his mouth, Raine shook her head in amazement. "Whenever you came to visit us at Archnacarry, you always seemed so arrogant and brash, so cocksure of yourself."

Kissing her fingertips, Keir grinned at her honesty. "Hell, I acted like an arrogant, brash pup. 'Twas a wonder my brothers didn't thrash the daylights out of me just to teach me some humility." He brought Raine to her feet and unbuckled the belt that held her loose trousers. Bending on one knee before her, he pulled the rough material down to her ankles.

"Sometimes," Raine confessed as she lifted one foot and then the other, allowing him to remove the sailor's trousers and drawers, "I feel guilty about wanting to know my natural father. Gideon was so loving and kind to me. Mayhap, I shouldn't try to replace him."

Keir lifted the hem of her shortened chemise and rising to his feet, pulled it over her head. "Mayhap, that'd be for the best."

"Keir," she said on a sigh, barely cognizant that she stood unclothed before him, "do you think that Gideon was my father?"

Raine met Keir's gaze and read the honest answer in his compassionate eyes. "Rainey, love," he said softly, "it doesn't matter who your father was. You are not your father, no more than I am mine. I swear to you, lass, that as long as I am alive, no man will ever dare to question your heritage."

Keir's heart hammered against his ribcage at the sight of Raine's slender, naked form. Beneath his kilt, his groin tightened with primal anticipation. Recognizing her feelings of loss and confusion, he deliberately tried to gain a measure of control over his licentious body. His head and his heart were schooled on a short, tight leash. Under his blue-and-green tartan, however, his erect manhood refused to be tamed.

God above, how he wanted her.

His rapacious gaze moved over her supple figure, the firm ivory globes and velvet nipples, the small waist, the gentle curve of her hips, the puff of ebony curls at the juncture of her thighs hiding her fragile petals. Like a starving man, he feasted on the sight of her perfect female body. 'Twas all he could do to keep from reaching out and palming her exposed breasts or flicking the pad of his thumbs over their delicate, rosy tips.

Keir wanted Raine more than he'd ever wanted anyone or anything in his life. But even more than his own sexual fulfillment, he wanted to ease her heartache and bring her a measure of comfort throughout the night.

Trying to ignore the carnal desire pounding through his heart and flooding every vein, Keir opened his leather sporran and withdrew the heart-shaped stone inscribed in an ancient, unknown language.

"I'm returning your magic rock," he said with a teasing grin. He placed the heart-shaped stone beside the chessboard on the table nearby.

"You kept my rune!" she exclaimed, her midnight eyes alight with pleasure. "I was certain you'd thrown it away in your anger." She smiled at last. 'Twas like the sun peeking from behind storm clouds.

" 'Tis more important for you to feel safe," he told her, making no attempt to hide his skepticism.

"If we stay close together," she whispered softly, as though revealing the secret solution to a faery riddle, "its magic will work for both of us."

Keir bent down and brushed his mouth over her soft lips. "Oh, aye, lass," he murmured, "from now on 'tis my intention that we stay very close together."

When he scooped her up, Raine slipped her arms around his neck and bussed him lightly on the mouth. He returned the kiss, telling her with his lips and tongue how intensely he longed to ease her sorrow. Carrying her to the large vat, he set her down on her round little rump in the steaming water.

"Wait a moment," he told her as he walked across the

cabin. "I've something for your bath." He opened the lid of his sea chest and returned with a soft cloth and soap scented with exotic spices from the Indies, which he dropped into the clear water in front of her.

"Oh, my," Raine said in delight, "perfumed soap." She lifted it to her nose and inhaled deeply, then raised her arched brows in surprise. "How is it you have this—" she started to ask, then shook her head. "Never mind."

Keir quirked an eyebrow at her unfinished question. "I'm a lad who likes to be prepared," he informed her with a lascivious grin.

Raine's laughter burst out, and the musical notes seemed to wrap themselves around his heart. "I refuse to ask what you're prepared for," she declared.

Keir bent and kissed the top of her head. " 'Tis just as well, for I don't intend to say." He knelt down beside the wooden tub. "Lean back and wet your hair," he instructed, "and I'll wash it for you."

He waited as Raine obediently slipped all the way under the warm water, then sat up and wiped the drops from her eyes. She allowed him to wash and rinse her long black tresses. As he cupped his hands and poured water over her bent head, it splashed across the front of his sporran and kilt.

"Damn," he muttered in mock disgust, hoping to hear her laugh again. "I just dried off."

Her eyes alight with mischief, Raine shook her sopping-wet locks, spraying water all around them. As the drops ran in rivulets down his face and bare chest, she broke into giggles. "I thought a canny lad like you would be prepared for a dousing," she teased. "Mayhap you should have worn a carpenter's apron. Or a serving maid's."

Keir awarded Raine with his best diabolical grin. "Since I'm already soaked," he said with a smirk, "I might as well get into the bath."

As he rose to his feet, she shrieked with laughter. "You can't get in here with me! You're far too big! You'll never fit!"

Keir unbuckled his belt and let it fall to the floor, along with his kilt and sporran. "If you don't mind, lass, I'll be joining you in the tub now."

Her startled gaze flew to his engorged sex, then slowly moved up his scarred abdomen and chest to meet his eyes. "I'm . . . I'm not certain there's room for the two of us," she said, her choked words soft and husky.

"Let's find out," Keir suggested. He sat down in the large wooden vat across from her, his bent knees sticking out of the water, his feet on either side of her hips. Then he clasped her ankles and tugged her closer, till her heels rested on his thighs.

Raine smiled at him shyly. Her wide sloe eyes grew luminous in the rising steam of the bath. "We fit," she conceded, "but just barely."

Keir's breath stalled in his chest at her innocent words. His heart slammed against his breastbone at his lustful thoughts. His words came thick and suffocated. "Barely is all we need, darling lass."

Using the soft cloth, Keir lathered the scented bar and proceeded to bathe her supple body. He lingered as he washed her up-tilted breasts, brushing lightly across the rosy aureoles and bud-tight nipples. He reached around and swabbed Raine's back, then lifted her feet and scrubbed her toes.

"Mm," she murmured with an appreciative sigh. " 'Tis wonderful, what you're doing, Laird MacNeil."

"I can make it more wonderful than this," he promised, his deep voice hoarse with longing. He caught Raine about her waist and drew her toward him, the water sloshing across their bodies in gentle, lapping waves. Steam from the bath rose up around them, wafting an exotic, spicy perfume.

Every muscle in Keir's massive frame tensed in erotic anticipation. He guided Raine's long legs around him, showing her how to straddle his hips. Then he played with her gently, letting the water swirl around her delicate pink folds as his practiced fingers built the sexual yearning within her.

Beneath his touch, Raine's lids drooped slowly. An expression of sensuous elation swept over her bonny features. Her thick, black lashes, clumped into wet spikes, shadowed her ivory skin. Her mouth opened slightly as her breath came faster.

"I'm going to lift you on top of me, Rainey, love," he whispered.

Her eyes flew open and a tiny smile curved her lips. "While we're still in the bath?"

Consumed with desire, Keir nodded. "Let me show you," he murmured. He bracketed Raine's slender hips with his hands, lifted her up, then guided her slowly downward, till the sensitive tip of his thickened sex pressed against her tight female sheath. "Let yourself open up to me, darling," he urged. " I'll come into your sweet body slowly and carefully."

Raine buried her fingers in his damp hair. She met his gaze and a burgeoning excitation shone in her wide sloe eyes. "Keir," she sighed on a long, drawn-out breath as she followed his directions.

"That's the way, love," Keir encouraged. He kissed Raine deeply, his tongue moving in and out of her mouth, showing her what he planned to do, pouring all the longing he felt into his kiss.

Raine looked down to watch their bodies join together beneath the moving water, and her heart seemed to skip beats in her frantic excitement. Bit by bit she sank down on top of him, until his turgid manhood filled her completely. Keir moved up slightly, pushing deeper inside, and gently bumped against her womb. An unbelievable pleasure spread through Raine's secret parts. She moaned in delight, unable to resist the waves of exquisite sensations surging through her.

Nudging the gold hoop in his ear aside with her nose, Raine pressed her face into the curve of Keir's strong neck. Her fingers clasped the silver chain that held his holy medal. Then she lifted her head and traced her tongue lightly over the scars on his face and showered kisses on his lids, his broken nose, his cheeks, his lips—just as he'd once done to her—and felt him smile beneath her kisses.

Raine slowly became aware that she was rocking the sensitive layers of her female tissues against Keir's firm male flesh. She felt his strong hands beneath her buttocks, helping her move, sustaining the rhythm she'd set without thinking. "Am I doing this right?" she asked, suddenly unsure of herself and painfully embarrassed.

"You're doing it perfectly, darling," he whispered in her ear. "You're taking me straight to heaven."

Raine shook her head and nipped him on the shoulder. "I'm not certain such an earthly pleasure should be described in heavenly terms."

"If this isn't bliss," Keir answered huskily, "I can't imagine anything else that would come even close."

Raine splayed her hands on his muscled chest and traced the battle scars with her fingertips. Brushing her palms across his flat nipples, she could feel the *thump-thump* of his heart steadily increase beneath her touch. Their breaths mingled as their tongues met, and she sighed against his mouth in pure exhilaration. Each slight movement she made brought ripples of intoxicating pleasure through her body. She hummed beneath her breath, telling him without words how much she delighted in his every touch.

Keir thrust his hardened sex inside Raine's soft female tissues while he explored her sugared mouth with his tongue. Aware of her mounting excitement, he sought to prolong their voluptuous lovemaking.

"Slip your arms around my neck and keep your legs locked around my hips," Keir urged softly. "Now hold on tight, sweetheart. We're going to stay joined together while I move us to the bed."

He could hear Raine's gasp of surprise as he grasped the edges of the wooden barrel and pushed himself upright in the water, his manhood still snugly embedded up to her womb. Then he cupped her buttocks in his palms, adjusted her comfortably against him, and stepped out of the tub.

"Look at us, Rainey, love," Keir whispered, moving so she could see their bodies reflected in the tall stern windows.

Dazed with passion, Raine turned her head. In the glass's hazy reflection, she saw Keir's powerful torso, his long, muscled limbs, his strong hands holding her up with ease as she wrapped her arms and legs tightly around him.

Male and female, they stood naked and joined together in a dance as old as time, their wet, heated bodies glistening from the warm, soapy bath. The lantern light cast a golden glow around them as they kissed again and again, lost to the world outside.

Time and space shrank to just the two of them—there in Keir's quarters, on the *Black Raven*, sailing before the wind.

Sailing homeward.

"My God, lass, you're bonny," he told her, his words hoarse with sexual need. "Do you have any idea how beautiful you are?"

Raine brushed her nipples back and forth across his hard chest in a ploy of instinctive feminine seduction. " 'Tis you who are beautiful," she answered with a teasing smile, "my braw Highland warrior. 'Tis no wonder you're so arrogant and brash."

Keir moved to his large bed where he laid Raine down on the soft mattress and then carefully eased his throbbing sex out of her tight sheath.

"Oh, Keir," she whispered, and he could hear the disappointment in her sigh.

"We have all night, lass," he assured her, "and I intend to take my time. I'm going to spend the midnight hours worshiping you with my body."

Keir came over Raine, his hands braced on either side of her head, careful not to catch her long, wet curls beneath his palms. He kissed her brow, her fluttering lids, the tip of her nose, her soft lips. Dipping the tip of his tongue into the hollow of her throat, he moved lower to suckle each perfect breast.

Raine gazed up at the superb male leaning over her, deeply aware of his all-consuming sensuality and her open capitulation to his every wish.

"Don't be afraid to touch me, love," he murmured in her ear, "just as I am touching you."

Battered by waves of physical pleasure, Raine responded to his hushed words without hesitation. She moved her hands across his massive frame, admiring the strength of his chest, his arms and thighs. She felt his corded muscles tense beneath her lightest touch.

Through a haze of sexual arousal, Keir listened to Raine telling him how much she admired his male body. He moved over Raine's moist, perfumed figure, kissing and caressing every silken inch.

Sliding to his knees on the floor, Keir placed Raine's long, slender legs over his shoulders. He gently spread the delicate folds of her sex and touched his tongue to her sensitive petals, licking and suckling until Raine writhed and moaned in ecstasy. As she grew moist and slick beneath his hedonistic onslaught, Keir's aching bollocks tightened, his hard shaft throbbed for release.

"Keir," she whispered, "I want you inside me."

To his delight, Raine reached toward him as he moved over her once again.

Her fingers curling around his engorged sex, she stroked and cupped him. The sweetness of her gentle touch seemed to suck the breath out of his lungs. He gasped with pleasure.

"Aye, love," Keir answered hoarsely. "I want it too."

Surrendering to what they both craved, Keir positioned himself between Raine's silken thighs. He moved inside her, withdrawing and re-entering, inching into her honeyed warmth until he'd sheathed himself deep in her vulnerable flesh. The pressure of her female tissues clutching and pulling on his tumescent manhood brought jolt after jolt of undiluted pleasure.

Taking her with him, Keir rolled onto his back so that Raine straddled his hips, her bent knees beside his flanks. Firmly embedded inside her, he lifted up, increasing her enjoyment. She gasped, her eyes widening in surprise. When she instinctively started to move her soft folds against him, Keir grasped her smooth buttocks and held her fast in place.

"Raine," he said, making no attempt to hide his easy male dominance, "we're going to be married."

"Of course, we will," she said in an absent tone, still trying to rock against him.

"At once," he informed her, holding her immobile. "I won't be satisfied until I hear you vow in church before both our families to be meek and mild in bed and at board. I won't have you running off against my will the way you did at Castle Calbhaigh."

Immersed in carnal gratification, she failed to recognize his lingering wrath over her willful disobedience nor even remember his threat of punishment as he raged against his chains.

Instead Raine gave him a brilliant smile. "I told you at the stones of Calanais that we were bound together for life, but you refused to believe me. All in all I think I'd rather have my vows written by the faeries, who—as everyone knows—are anything but meek and mild."

"Goddammit," he grated, his temper rising, "this isn't about any idiotic faery enchantment. I love you, and you love me. Now repeat that loud and strong."

Her brilliant eyes sparkled with naughtiness. Raine bent down, her long hair falling over them like a damp satin curtain, and nibbled on his lips, then thrust her tongue in his mouth in blatant provocation.

Keir rolled over on top of her. "Don't you have something to say to me?" he demanded.

She gave a deep throaty laugh, one of sultry female seduction. "Would you truly believe me, if I did? Or would you blame my feelings on a silly belief in the faery folk?"

"Say it, Raine," he commanded, bending over her and nipping her earlobe. He moved deeper inside her, then started to pull back as if he planned to withdraw completely.

She threw her arms around him, attempting to hold him in place. "I love you, you brash, arrogant warrior,"

Raine answered, then sighed happily. "Though I never thought I would ever say that."

"Neither did I." Joy flooded Keir's big arrogant body. "Tell me again," he insisted as he moved in and out rhythmically, building their carnal excitement to a higher and higher pitch. "I want to hear you say it every day of my life," he told her, his breath coming in deep drafts, "till I'm an old man and you need to shout in my ear just to be heard."

Leaning on his forearms, he moved within her, plunging and retreating in steady, rhythmic strokes.

Raine responded to the cadence Keir set, her body moving of its own volition. She matched his increasing tempo, as sparks of white-hot excitement ignited within her. Pulsating with a need fueled by each thrust and withdrawal, she found herself chanting to the rhythm he set. "I love you, Keir MacNeil. I love you, I love you, I love you."

Every fiber in Raine's quivering body reached for Keir. She took in deep drafts of air, breathing in his musky scent, rubbing her face across his muscled shoulder, touching the inked Celtic images on the bulging muscles of his upper arm with her tongue. His powerful thrusts rocked her as each jolt brought her nearer to the whirling sensations that threaten to push her across the brink of ecstasy.

"Keir," she gasped in breathless wonder. Waves of exquisite pleasure spiraled through her body, as she called his name again and again in a cry of total female surrender.

Keir reached between their bodies to play with Raine's engorged tissues as he continued to drive into her, increasing and extending her rapture. His entire body tightened and jerked in the breath-stealing convulsions of release. "Rainey, darling," he uttered as he poured his seed into her soft, nurturing warmth. "I love you."

Gasping for air, Keir stretched out beside Raine on the satin coverlet. He slipped an arm beneath her shoulders and brought her limp, satiated body tight against his. She gazed at him in astonishment, her eyes shining in the afterglow of sexual fulfillment. He understood her look of dazed quiescence, for he was filled with an unalloyed happiness such as he'd never kenned before. He smiled at the ceiling above them.

Keir had desired Raine for two long, self-recriminating years.

And in the end he'd been awarded his heart's delight.

Perchance 'twas magic after all.

He didn't care.

Chapter 24

September 1504
Archnacarry Manor
Western Highlands

Once the *Raven* and her sister ships passed the Isle of
Mull and entered the Firth of Lorne, word quickly spread
that their topgallants had been sighted. Upon reaching
port, the crews of the three galleons were given permission to go ashore, save for a watch left to guard the ships
under Abid al-Rahman's supervision. Ethan and Robbie
Gibson's parents met them at the gangplank to take the
lads home until shore leave was over.

Colin and his father, Walter, planned to travel to Kin-
rath Castle to visit Lachlan MacRath and his wife, Lady
Francine. Fearchar and Tam would ride to Kinlochleven
Castle to stay with their cousin, Rory MacLean, and his
wife, Lady Joanna, as well as Fearchar's wife, Maude.
After time spent in the port town arranging for supplies,
Macraith assured Keir he'd join him at Kinlochleven for
the wedding.

Riding from the *Raven*'s anchorage in Loch Linnhe,

Keir brought Raine home to her mother. He could sense Raine's excitement the moment Archnacarry Manor came into view through the surrounding trees. The gray stone building with its four flanking towers had once been a primitive square keep.

Under Gideon Cameron's capable stewardship, the upper part of the manor house had blossomed into a castellated skyline of gables, turrets, and dormers.

Keir felt his own tension rising as his time to face Raine's uncle and guardian, Laird Alex Cameron, approached.

With his arm placed protectively around Raine's shoulders, Keir entered the manor's great hall, where Raine's mother, Lady Nina, and Uncle Alex would most likely be waiting.

Word had traveled even faster than Keir expected.

To his surprise his own mother, Lady Emma MacNeil, and his uncle, Duncan Stewart, earl of Appin, stood next to the Camerons, along with Raine's dotty Aunt Isabel. In honor of the voyagers' safe return, the men wore their clan dress kilts. The ladies had tartan shawls pinned across the shoulders of their pretty gowns.

Lady Nina smiled the moment her daughter appeared in the open doorway. She stepped toward them, holding her hands out in welcome. "Raine, my dearest! And Keir!" she called across the wide expanse of the large room. "How wonderful that you've both returned to us safely."

As always Nina Cameron resembled a compassionate angel, with her red-gold hair and creamy complexion. But Keir could imagine the lady's keen disappointment once she learned that he'd taken advantage of her naïve young daughter.

That he had in fact taken her innocent daughter into his bed.

Keir refused to dissemble.

Nor try to make excuses for his inexcusable behavior.

Standing just inside the doorway, he held Raine close beside him, his arm about her slender waist. He could feel her lithe body trembling with the exhilaration of homecoming. He hoped she'd remain true to the promise he'd elicited before they'd disembarked. Raine had agreed—reluctantly—to let him do all the explaining, so everyone's disapproval would fall on his guilty head.

With an upward jut of his chin, Keir met their curious eyes. Lady Emma watched him with her usual composure. A loving smile curved her lips and her holly-green eyes glowed in welcome. He feared she wouldn't be smiling long.

"Raine and I are going to be married," Keir announced in the voice of authority generally reserved for his crew. He wanted to make clear to everyone present that the subject wasn't open for discussion. Nor did he intend to haggle with Raine's guardian over the particulars of the marriage settlement.

Alex Cameron could insist that a large sum be paid to the bride's widowed mother to compensate for the sudden, unexpected loss of her only child. And the title to a large tract of land in Barra might be demanded from her guardian in retaliation for Keir's failure to follow accepted protocol. Keir didn't care what the marriage contract would cost him. After all he *had* seduced their bonny, intelligent lass and by sheer good fortune won her heart in the process.

Keir intended to marry Raine no matter who objected. Not even his own lovely mother, who'd surely be appalled at his unchivalrous conduct.

Keeping Raine at his side, he stopped partway up the long hall and waited, expecting to hear an angry chorus raised in dissent and condemnation. Instead, each and every person standing in front of the room's enormous fireplace beamed their approval and offered their joyous felicitations on the impending wedding. To Keir's astonishment, the cavernous hall echoed with deep male laughter and feminine cries of delight.

Lady Nina opened her arms and Raine ran to her mother. " 'Tis wonderful news, dearest child," Nina said, hugging her daughter close. "I'm so happy for the two of you."

Keir watched in relief as Raine returned her mother's kisses, her musical laughter spilling over at last. "I promised Keir I'd be quiet long enough for him to announce our intentions. But he failed to tell you the most important news of all." Raine paused and looked around the room at her loved ones, who appeared to be holding their breath as they waited for her glad tidings. "Keir and I are deeply and truly in love!"

Her eyes flashing with a droll humor, Aunt Isabel embraced Raine. "Didn't I tell you, child, to stay close to Laird MacNeil and you'd be safe?" she asked with knowing smile. "I was certain how things would turn out in the end."

Wisps of gray hair stuck out from under Isabel's old-fashioned horned headdress. As always, the short, plump spinster had bits of oatmeal sprinkled on her shoulders in the idiotic belief that it would ward off faeries. And the small pair of scissors hanging around her neck was thought by the foolish and ignorant to be a great protection from the entire elfin race.

Isabel turned to Keir and gave him a warm hug. "On the day of Raine's birth," she told him with a happy laugh, "I didn't know whether to be relieved or disappointed she wasn't born with a pair of wings."

'Twas clear Raine loved her aunt, so Keir intended to keep his skeptical thoughts to himself for the moment. He'd wait until they were in private to explain to Raine once again that the Celtic people's near-universal belief in the fairy faith had been based on ancient wonder tales created out of sheer nonsense by their Druidic ancestors.

With a sincere smile, Laird Alex offered his hand to Keir. "Congratulations, Laird MacNeil, and welcome to our family."

Stunned at his obvious pleasure, Keir shook his hand, then turned to his own mother. "I have your blessing as well?" he asked, still prepared for her disapproval.

No one needed to tell Keir that he wasn't worthy of marriage to Raine. As her protector on their dangerous voyage, he should have kept his hands off her—and he damn well knew it.

"Certainly you have my blessing," Lady Emma told him, her wide smile crinkling the corners of her eyes. Taking Keir's hands, she stood on tiptoe and kissed his cheek. "The two of you were made for each other, my dear. But I sometimes wondered how long it would take for you both to realize it."

Uncle Duncan grinned and thumped Keir on the shoulder. "Good for you, lad! Good for you!" The earl of Appin's astute eyes twinkled with merriment. "I'd begun to lose hope that you and Raine would stop bickering long enough to perceive what those around you could see so clearly—the pair of you were already half in love, but too stubborn to admit it." Duncan leaned closer and whispered in Keir's ear. "Of course that fiasco with two women fighting over you in Edinburgh didn't help your cause any."

Keir returned his uncle's good-natured grin. "Never again," he promised with a rueful laugh. "I can assure you, sir, that travesty will never happen again."

Everyone began to talk at once. Servants carried trays of wine among the happy family members. Toasts were made to the fortunate couple.

In the midst of the din, Keir drew his uncle aside and spoke in a quiet tone. "Did you receive my message to cease negotiations with Laird MacNab?"

A dapper man in his early fifties, the earl of Appin was perceptive and shrewd. Keir had total confidence in his uncle's ability to unravel any promises that might have been made.

"Your letter came too late, I'm afraid," Duncan replied.

Keir frowned in disappointment. "You mean I'm officially contracted to Mariota?"

His hazel eyes twinkling with merriment, Duncan shook his head. "Nay, lad," he answered, "but brace yourself for a shock." Amusement flitted across his aristocratic face, but his tone was solemn. "I'm obliged to inform you that your offer of marriage has been turned down by Mariota's apologetic and rather mortified father."

Keir grinned in relief. "Fillan MacNab disapproved of me then?"

"I'm sorry to say 'twas the maid herself who disapproved. When Mariota learned that her parents intended to hand her over to one of the Hellhounds of Scotland, she ran away with a mild-mannered lad she'd known since childhood. So I'm afraid you've been rejected by your first choice for a wife."

Keir held up his glass of wine. "Here's to being rejected."

Duncan touched his glass to Keir's. "And a toast to both the happy couples. May they prosper and be blessed with many children."

At that moment Raine came up. Slipping her arm through Keir's, she leaned her head against his shoulder and sighed in obvious contentment. "What two happy couples?"

"It seems, sweetheart," Keir said, "we're not the only ones soon to be married. The maid of Strathfillan has eloped with a secret admirer."

Her sloe eyes wide with disbelief, Raine looked at Keir in astonishment. "Mariota MacNab refused your offer?" She turned to Duncan, utter bewilderment on her lovely features. "How could this possibly be?"

Speechless, Duncan gazed at Raine, clearly mystified that she knew about Keir's offer of marriage to another woman. Most ladies would have a far different reaction, given the female penchant for jealousy.

Keir chuckled as he brought Raine closer and bussed her forehead. "Not every lass is brave enough to marry a notorious privateer, darling."

LATER THAT MORNING Raine peeked into the music room, pleased to find it just the same. The heavy damask curtains on the tall windows were pulled back to allow the autumn sunshine to fill the room. A harp and virginal stood near an inside wall where three different-sized lutes hung, ready to be lifted down and played at a moment's notice. Bookshelves and paintings graced the walls. Armchairs and small tables were scattered about the room, which had always been her favorite place in the manor. 'Twas here that the family had often gathered, playing and singing, and entertaining guests.

Taking a deep breath, Raine walked across the rug to stand in front of the fireplace. She looked up solemnly at the portrait of Laird Gideon Cameron. As always her father smiled down at her.

Memories of his kindness filled her heart. When she was tiny, he'd lift her up in front of him on his mount. He'd shown Raine how to ride her first pony and when the time came, taught her how to jump a hunter over a stone wall. Her childhood had been filled with his loving presence, always there to guide her with a gentle word.

During his lifetime Papa had earned the respect and admiration of all who knew him. He'd taught Raine to strive for high ideals. To be courageous, true to herself, and considerate of others.

Gideon had been a scholar of history and geography. Rather than leave her schooling to a hired tutor, he'd instructed Raine in all her lessons, He'd only begun to teach her about astronomy when he'd been murdered defending his wife's honor—and ultimately, his daughter's unblemished birthright as the maid of Archnacarry.

There was no doubt in Raine's mind that Papa had loved her. She'd sailed through the Hebrides in the midst of a rebellion, foolishly searching for a man she'd believed was her father. She'd been wrong. Gideon Cameron had been her father in every sense of the word and she couldn't have asked for a better one.

Lost in reverie, Raine sank down on the high-backed settle that faced the fireplace. She understood now why her mother had always admonished her for questioning her own heritage. It hadn't mattered to Papa that his daughter was a black-eyed, black-haired child in a family of pale-eyed blonds. It no longer mattered to Raine.

The rustle of satin brought Raine's attention back to the present. Her mother stepped through the doorway. "There you are, dear," she said and came to sit with Raine on the high-backed settle.

She put her arm around Raine's waist and drew her close. Together they looked up at the portrait of Gideon.

"I was just thinking what a wonderful father I had," Raine said quietly.

"We were the center of Papa's world," Mama agreed,

tears glistening in her eyes. "No one could have loved us more."

HE'S A BEAUTY, Mother. Thank you." Keir looked at the black colt in admiration, then back to Lady Emma standing beside him.

Slightly taller than most women, Emma MacNeil exuded a vivacious loveliness combined with unruffled serenity. 'Twas a quality few possessed.

"I thought you deserved a gift to celebrate your safe return," she told him. Her green eyes glowed with pleasure. "I purchased a pregnant mare when Duncan and I were visiting the king and queen at Stirling Castle this past spring. I was thinking especially of you, dear, when I chose her. The foal was born in June just as you were leaving to fight the rebellion. Duncan and I decided to bring them from Stalcaire to surprise you."

The spirited colt raced about the Archnacarry paddock with several yearlings, giving a spectacular display of beauty and grace, while the mare watched her offspring's antics placidly. The black colt had a well-shaped head on a muscular neck, a blaze of white on the forehead. Two long white stockings stretched up his hind legs from the fetlocks nearly to the hocks.

Keir put his arm around his mother's shoulders and gave her an affectionate squeeze, then looked back to admire the lively youngster again. Putting two fingers to his lips, Keir gave a piercing whistle. The colt stopped still and looked in their direction. He whinnied and tossed his mane, bold eyes flashing. Keir held out an apple, and the colt came trotting over, apparently used to receiving treats. The chestnut mare followed right behind, wanting to make certain her foal was in safe company.

When the young horse reached Keir and Lady Emma standing by the fence railing, he whickered in curiosity. He nuzzled Keir's hand and sniffed the shiny red fruit with his velvet nose, then accepted the offering while Emma fed the mare an apple as well.

Smiling with approval, Keir patted the colt's head fondly. "Have you named him?"

Lady Emma nodded. "I've named him Ruaidh," she answered, then peeked up at Keir from the corner of her eye. "I hope you like it, son."

Keir stiffened at the mention of his father's name. "Since you've chosen it, I like it well enough," he said with measured restraint. He wouldn't spurn his mother's gift or cause her unhappiness for the world.

The breeze from the woods nearby drifted around them. The foal turned and raced back across the paddock. Kicking his heels and frisking in glee, he rejoined the yearlings, while the mare moved to stand in the stable's shade.

"Mother," Keir asked in a low tone, "did you love my father?"

Emma placed her hand on Keir's forearm and squeezed compassionately. "I take it you've heard the stories that surrounded our unlikely courtship."

"Were you abducted?"

Emma laughed softly. "That particular rumor was true.

Ruaidh swooped me up and took me to his castle in Barra. He claimed that I was surrounded by so many suitors at Stalcaire, he didn't have a chance to catch my attention." She patted Keir's hand affectionately. "Perhaps your father was right, dear, for I don't remember speaking with him once until I found myself on his galley sailing to the Outer Hebrides. As you know, Ruaidh's line descended from Celtic and Norse kings," she reminded her son with a tender smile, "and sometimes he acted in a most impulsive and high-handed manner—like someone else I know."

"What happened at Barra?" Keir asked, his voice gruff in his constricted throat. "Tell me the truth, Mother. Please don't lie in a mistaken attempt to protect me."

His mother slipped her arm through his. "Oh, Keir, I hope you never believed that Ruaidh harmed me in any way. Your father behaved with great chivalry. He promised that I could leave Kisimuth Castle at the end of a month if he could not convince me of his devotion. He wooed me like a knight from the ancient sagas. And by the close of the thirty days, I had fallen deeply in love with him."

"Then you didn't marry my father to provide me with legitimacy?" Keir asked, the bitter words torn from deep inside. "To insure that I would be the next chief of Clan MacNeil?"

"Keir!" Emma cried in astonishment, "how could you think such a thing? My dear son, you were conceived in love on our wedding night. I had no idea you held such a dreadful misconception. Why did you never ask me about this before?"

His words came low and filled with a wretched sorrow. "I feared my questions would bring you too much pain."

Keir felt once again the terrible shock of being told—at the age of eight—that his father had raped his mother and he was the tragic result. Knowing now that he'd been lied to, Keir had the sickening realization that if his father hadn't been killed he might have loved the man he'd hated for so long.

"Your father loved us both very much, Keir," Emma said. "Ruaidh was so proud the day you were born. When you were a toddler, he'd lift you up on his shoulders and carry you about—just as I've seen you carry your nephew with the same love in your eyes. Have you no memory of your father whatsoever?"

Keir shook his head. "Nothing but vague glimpses of a black-haired giant with no meaning behind them. Ruaidh had been gone for a long time in the wars of rebellion, and I was only seven when he was killed in battle."

Emma nodded sadly. "And the next year I took you to Stalcaire to live with my brother. I couldn't bear to stay at Kisimuth with the memories of my beloved husband lingering in every room. A few years later, Duncan used his influence at court to have you fostered to the king's admiral, Sir Anthony Wood, until it was time for you to attend the university in Paris."

" 'Twas a wise choice all the way around," Keir assured her. "As Uncle Macraith insists to this day, the MacNeils are born with salt water in their veins." He enfolded his mother in his arms and kissed her on the forehead. "You can't imagine the joy I feel, Mother, knowing you loved my father and mourned his passing. And that when you look at me, you feel no sorrow or regret."

Emma reached up and framed Keir's face in her hands. "My darling son," she said, tears welling up in her eyes, "I am so proud that you are the spirit and image of your father."

LATE THE NEXT morning, Raine and Keir reached Rannoch Mill on horseback. She'd asked to go for a ride after breakfast, suggesting they might enjoy a bit of privacy. She hadn't disclosed that she wanted to talk with him alone without the chance of being interrupted. He'd agreed at once. Raine suspected her future husband had an entirely different reason for seeking seclusion.

The abandoned millhouse stood on the confluence of the River Leven and Loch Leven beneath the shadow of Garbh Bheinn's rocky peak. 'Twas a perfect autumn morning with a cool breeze in the shade of the tall pines.

Raine looked about her with pleasure. The reflection of the clouds scudding across the deep blue sky, the snow-capped mountain peaks and the dark green forest shimmered in the loch's turquoise water.

They dismounted and while Keir tended to the horses, Raine spread a red-and-black Cameron tartan on the grassy bank. She placed the wicker basket Cook had packed for them on a corner of the wool plaid.

Raine peeked at Keir in admiration as he removed the saddles and laid them on the grass nearby. He wore the MacNeil green-and-black kilt, and his bonnet sported the three plumes of a clan chief. Long-limbed and muscular, he moved with a lithe grace that belied his immense strength.

From their shady bower beside the broken waterwheel, they could see the walls of Kinlochleven Castle sitting high on the rugged cliffs above. They could hear the rushing waterfall that plummeted down to the cold waters of the deep loch. The castle was the home of Keir's oldest brother, Laird Rory MacLean, and his wife, Lady Joanna. Gideon Cameron had fostered Rory as a young lad and the families had a deep and abiding friendship.

A large party from Archnacarry planned to ride to Kinlochleven the next day to visit the MacLeans and their children. Soon Fearchar would also be at the castle, reunited with his loving wife, Maude.

"This is one of my favorite places," Raine said.

"Aye, 'tis lovely," Keir agreed, removing his sword belt and bonnet and dropping them on the blanket. He sat down and leaned against a tree trunk, his long legs stretched out in front of him. "I remember riding here on a hunt from Archnacarry stables. Though you were only fourteen, you managed to keep up with the rest of the hunters." He flashed her a teasing smile. "You were always a fearless rider, even at a young age."

Raine nodded absently as she set out the cheese and meat along with a loaf of bread, freshly baked that morning. "Keir, there's something I need to talk to you about," she announced, her soprano sounding more high-pitched than usual. "Something important, which could affect our future together."

She had his instant and undivided attention.

"And what would that be?" Keir asked gruffly, as though he suspected he might not be pleased with what she had to say. He must have sensed her anxiety during their long ride. Or her shrill, worried voice had just given her away. "We're to be married as soon as the banns are read in Kinlochleven's chapel," he added in a voice of unquestioned authority. Before she had a chance to reply, he reached out to catch her hand and bring her closer.

Settling down beside him, Raine offered a tentative smile. "Before those announcements are made at Mass, I've something to ask you which might change your mind."

"Change my mind about what?" Keir growled. His eyes glittered like emerald shards, making it clear he wasn't going to even consider that he might not want to wed her. No matter what she said.

"About your wish to marry me," she blurted out.

"Go on." He waited, his stubborn jaw set, his brow furrowed.

"Do . . . do you remember what Aunt Isabel said when we announced we were going to be married?"

Keir grinned, clearly diverted by her question and unaware of course that what he found so amusing was at the very crux of her dilemma.

"Aye," he answered with a short laugh. "Isabel said she always knew we were meant for each other." He slipped his arm about her waist to bring Raine even closer. "Have you changed your mind about the faeries at Calanais, love?"

Raine tried to wriggle out of his hold, only to discover he held her clamped against his side with maddening ease.

She met his gaze, glowing now with outright amusement at the turn in their conversation. "Never mind about the faeries at the standing stones," she said. "Don't you remember what else my aunt said?"

"Certainly." Keir lifted Raine onto his lap and nuzzled the curve of her neck. His hand slid from her waist to cup her breast, and he moved his thumb across its crest provocatively. "Isabel said she didn't know whether to be relieved or disappointed when you were born without a pair of wings."

Determined to continue, Raine pushed against his wide chest with the palms of both hands till she was able to look into his eyes once again. "And that doesn't worry you?"

"Not a bit." Keir tipped her back so she was resting in the crook of his arm. He bent his head and brushed his lips against hers in a light, teasing kiss.

Impatient Raine pressed two fingers against his mouth. "I'm not through," she insisted. "There's more I need to say."

"Go on, love," he murmured as he kissed her fingertips. "You have my complete attention."

Raine drew a deep, steadying breath and her words tumbled out in a rush. "If Aunt Isabel were right—if I *were* part faery—would you still want to wed me?"

He took her earlobe between his teeth and gave her a playful nip before he whispered in her ear. "I'd marry you, Raine, if you were half witch."

"Well . . . well," she sputtered, indignant at the very suggestion. She struggled to sit up, to no avail. "I'm most definitely *not* a witch," she stated unequivocally.

Laughter rumbled deep in his chest. Keir appeared

vastly entertained at her annoyed reaction. "I'm nay so certain you're not a witch," he told her in a teasing tone. "Let's find out."

Before Raine realized his intention, Keir lifted her off his lap and onto the blanket. Rising to his feet he first kicked off his brogues and then removed her half-boots. Without a word of explanation, he bent down and scooped her up in his arms. He marched down the grassy bank to the river's edge and continued straight into the moving water.

"What are you doing?" Raine squealed. "You'll get us both wet."

"That's the idea," he said with a wicked grin. "If you're a witch, you'll float."

She shrieked as the cold water sloshed over her skirts. "You already know I can't swim!" Raine grabbed his side-braids and gave a warning tug. "I won't let go, no matter what!' she declared. "I'm warning you, Keir! If I go under I'll take you with me!"

Her threats seemed to go unnoticed. "What else do you need to ask me, Lady Raine?" he demanded, making it clear he'd allow her one more question and only one.

Raine met his gaze, determined to face the truth no matter how painful. "Would you still want to marry me, Laird MacNeil, if 'twas I who cast a spell over you at Calanais?"

She could feel his laughter rumbling deep in his chest. "Rainey, love," he said, his deep baritone filled with happiness, "you wrapped me in your spell long before we visited the Isle of Lewis."

"I did?"

"You did."

"I find that hard to believe," Raine protested. She scowled at him. "You've wanted nothing to do with me for the last two years. Not since the day I bested you in chess when I was seventeen."

He grinned as he walked farther into the water. "You think that's why I stayed away from you, sweetheart? Because I was angry that you'd bested me in a chess game?"

"Well, of course," she replied. "You left Archnacarry immediately, not even saying farewell to my mother."

He chuckled as he placed a kiss on her brow. "That wasn't why I left. Or why I stayed away."

"Why did you then? For you all but avoided me after that."

He carried her even deeper into the river, till the water was nearly up to his waist. "Lady Raine Cameron—soon to be Lady MacNeil—I avoided you because I've lusted for you from the moment you did that victory dance celebrating my defeat. I stayed away because I was convinced I could never have you."

"Oh, what nonsense," she said with a laugh. "Women were pulling each other's hair out fighting over you."

"While you were calling me an idiot."

"Is that why you're carrying me into the river, Laird MacNeil? You're getting us both soaked to our skin because I called you an idiot?"

Keir's eyes smoldered with erotic intention. "Now that we're soaked to our skin, Rainey, love," he replied in a husky tone, "we'll need to strip off our wet clothes and spread them out on the grass to dry in the sunshine."

"Mm," Raine said, batting her lashes seductively, "whatever shall we do while we're waiting for them to dry?"

"First," he said, "I'm going to teach you how to swim."

"And after that?"

"I'll think of something."

Epilogue

May 1505
Kisimuth Castle
Isle of Barra, Outer Hebrides

THE *BLACK RAVEN*, the *Sea Hawk*, and the *Sea Dragon* rode at anchor in the protected harbor of Castle Bay. The MacLeans and the MacRaths had gathered for the imminent birth of Laird and Lady MacNeil's first offspring.

Lady Nina and Lady Emma, accompanied by her brother, Duncan Stewart, earl of Appin, had arrived a month before. Keir had sent Macraith to bring them in the *Raven*, wanting to be certain the ladies were at the castle in ample time should the bairn arrive early. Laird Alex Cameron and his sister, Isabel, had also sailed with them.

Three weeks after that, Laird Rory MacLean, Lady Joanna, and their two children reached Kisimuth in the *Dragon*, along with Fearchar and Maude.

Then two weeks ago, Laird Lachlan MacRath, earl of Kinrath, and his wife, Lady Francine, arrived with their four children. They'd brought their nursemaid, Signora Grazioli, to help with the young triplets, who'd been born the previous spring. Lachlan's cousin, Colin, and his uncle, Walter, had sailed the *Hawk* into the wide bay, hove to and dropped anchor.

The crews of the three galleons were fed daily in the castle's enormous great hall. The seamen spent the daytime hunting, fishing, and enjoying games such as lawn bowls and archery contests on the extensive castle grounds, for the entire island belonged to the chief of Clan MacNeil. The sailors spent their night hours on the ships.

For the past few weeks, Kisimuth Castle had rung with children's voices in play, high-pitched feminine chatter, and the deep, resounding laughter of men bonded by the ties of kinship and brotherhood.

That very morning a galley sailing all the way from the Solway Firth, which lay between Scotland and England, had arrived in Castle Bay, carrying bags of grain, bolts of cloth, fresh fruits and vegetables—and a special guest few were aware of, save Francine and her husband, Lachlan.

After the midday meal in the great hall had been cleared away, some of the crewmen left for a hunting foray. Others went on a fishing expedition in the ships' longboats. While the nursemaids put the little ones down for a nap, the castle's womenfolk went upstairs to attend the mother-to-be and prepare the clothing for the newborn babe.

The gentlemen of the three families stood before the huge fireplace as a servant carried around a beaker of port and wineglasses on a tray. Once Rory MacLean saw that every kinsman had been served, he turned to his Uncle

Duncan. "What's the latest news from Edinburgh?" he asked.

"I was with the king," Duncan replied, "when the earl of Argyll defended himself from accusations of treason. The wily old fox pleaded that he knew nothing of the release of his grandson from Innischonaill until it was an accomplished fact. He adamantly denied any contact with his brother-in-law, Torcall MacMurchaidh. Nor did he know anything about the English-built carracks that had invaded Scottish waters."

Incredulous, Macraith stroked his long brown beard with its glass beads. "And did King James believe Argyll in spite of Allan MacRanald's testimony to the contrary?"

Duncan Stewart, a counselor and kinsman to the king, shook his gray head. His astute hazel eyes revealed his perplexity. "Whether James Stewart believed Argyll or MacRanald, 'twas impossible to tell," he confessed. " 'Twas one man's word against the other. For no one except Laird MacRanald actually claimed to have seen Argyll with MacMurchaidh. And Archibald Campbell is by far the more powerful laird."

Rory's handsome, auburn-haired brother nodded. "Aye," Lachlan agreed. "The king needs Argyll to keep the clans of the Western Highlands in check. Without the earl's far-reaching influence throughout the Isles, the rebellion will never be completely quelled, and Scotland will never be strong enough to defeat its foreign enemies."

"And what about MacMurchaidh?" Rory asked Laird Alex Cameron. "I understand that Parliament summoned him to answer the charge of treason."

Alex was the surviving brother of Rory's foster father. A deep bond had been forged between them when Gideon Cameron was murdered. Rory and his two brothers had pledged to find the killer and bring him to justice.

"Laird Torcall is still entrenched in his fortress at Steòrnabhagh," Alex replied. "The rumor is that Donald Dubh has returned from Ireland now that winter is over."

Colin MacRath stood next to his cousin, Lachlan, listening attentively. The tall, lean redhead stuttered nervously around the beautiful ladies. But with the men, he easily joined in the conversation. Rory had always admired the lad's sincere commonsense.

"I've heard the king will send the earl of Huntly to capture MacMurchaidh and his traitorous guest," Colin said. "The royal fleet will sail to the Isle of Lewis to lay siege to his castle sometime this year. I'm thinking of sailing with them."

The gathering of men grew quiet as they paused to recall the events of last summer. Keir had chosen to leave Castle Murchaidh standing and its laird unharmed solely because of his devotion to Raine. King James, being a romantic himself, hadn't punished The MacNeil. Neither had the title of earl been forthcoming as most had expected at the onset of the campaign.

At that moment Francine and Joanna bustled into the hall.

"Is it the baby?" Rory asked his wife, who'd come to stand beside him.

Small-boned and vivacious, Joanna wrinkled her nose and shook her head. "Not yet," she answered with a happy laugh. "But my good-sister has something to announce."

Lady Francine's brown-eyed gaze flew around the group to light on her husband, who responded with a knowing grin. "Lachlan and I have invited a guest from England," she explained to the curious gentlemen. "The lady is a dear friend of mine, who's recently become a widow." Francine turned to the hall's wide entryway expectantly.

Intrigued, Rory waited to see who the mysterious guest could be.

But for several minutes, no one appeared.

Then a lovely brunette, somewhere in her late twenties, peeked around the edge of the entryway. Her gray eyes, framed with dark, luxuriant lashes, betrayed her hesitation, as though she were uncertain of her welcome.

Rory recognized the Sassenach lady immediately. He'd met her at the royal wedding two summers ago. Colin had engaged in a passionate affair with the married lady, whom he'd met on the journey from England to Edinburgh. The lad had been heartbroken when she'd been forced by protocol and custom to return home with her elderly husband.

"Come in, Lady Diana," Lachlan encouraged with a wave of his hand. He gave her a wide, welcoming smile to reassure her. "I believe there's someone here who'll be especially glad to see you."

Everyone turned to look at Colin, whose freckled face grew beet red. For the space of a long minute, he didn't say a word, just stood staring at the bonny young widow in dumbfounded surprise.

Standing in the entryway, Lady Diana Pembroke ducked her head and gazed at him through lowered lashes, as though afraid he might not even remember her.

Without a sound Colin left the group of men at the fireplace, walked across the great hall and took Diana in his arms. Their impassioned kiss, filled with love and longing, seemed to go on and on. Still without saying a word to anyone, Colin took Diana's hand and led her through the doorway and out of sight.

Walter shook his head and grinned unabashedly. "My son always did have a way with the ladies."

Laughter broke out among the men, but the appearance of Fearchar's wife at that same moment interrupted their hilarity.

"Is it the baby?" Fearchar boomed, his full-throated baritone echoing through the cavernous hall.

Sturdy and solid like her husband, Maude smiled and nodded. "The birth contractions are coming strong and fast now. We thought the husband would like to know." Then she bobbed a curtsy and left. Francine and Joanna immediately hurried after Maude to join the other women upstairs.

The men looked around for the new father-to-be, only to realize that Keir was nowhere in sight.

"Come to think of it," Macraith said with a frown, "I've nay seen my nephew since early this morning. He looked a little green at the time."

"Where could Keir be?" Duncan remarked. "I can't remember when I spoke with him last."

Lachlan looked at Rory with a worried frown. "Where the hell is our little brother?"

"Let's try the chapel," Rory suggested. "That's where I spent the night at Kinlochleven when Jamie was born."

RORY AND LACHLAN stepped through the vestibule's arched portal and into the central nave, where Keir Mac-Neil had been baptized as a newborn babe. There at the front of the chapel, surrounded by a brilliant shimmer of light, he knelt at the altar railing, his dark head bowed in prayer.

Every vigil candle in the place had been lit.

The poor box had probably been stuffed with gold unicorns as well.

The two Highland warriors, known by their enemies as the Hellhounds of Scotland, moved quietly up the center aisle, knelt down on either side of their youngest brother, and made the sign of the cross.

Keir's face was buried in his folded hands. His deep voice sounded muffled and forlorn. "I've made a vow," he told them in a strangled whisper. "If God will let Raine and the baby survive, I'll never lay a hand on my wife again. Not for as long as I live."

Over the top of Keir's bent head, Rory met Lachlan's amused gaze.

This was their ferocious younger brother, whom they'd watched take down eight men in as many seconds, dispatching two at a time, one with his broadsword and the other with his dirk, in a merciless display of close-quarter fighting that would make most men's blood run cold. 'Twas no wonder his enemies had labeled him the Black Beast's Spawn after his equally ferocious father.

Rory placed his hand on Keir's shoulder in a gesture of comfort and understanding. "I made the very same vow the night that Jamie was born," he said, trying hard not to smile. "But Joanna would have nothing to do with it. She reminded me that I'd made another vow first in front of God and the priest at the altar. I had promised on our wedding day to worship Joanna with my body for the rest of my life. And as my wee, red-haired wife summed the matter up, that was that."

Lachlan grinned. "I can just hear Joanna saying it in her own inimitable way."

Keir shook his head, but managed a weak smile. "Since both of you lived through this same intolerable waiting, I'm surprised every hair on your heads isn't white."

At that moment Lady Emma came into the chapel by a side door. "I thought the three of you might be here," their mother said with a loving smile. "I came to fetch Keir. The baby has arrived."

His swarthy complexion drained of color, Keir jumped to his feet. His words came thick and choked with fear. "And Raine?"

"Mother and child are fine," Lady Emma assured him. She stood on tiptoe and kissed her youngest son's cheek. "Congratulations, Keir. You're a father."

"A boy or a girl?" Lachlan asked.

"I'll let Keir find out for himself," their mother replied. She slipped her arm through Keir's and together they left the chapel to go upstairs.

Lachlan and Rory returned to the great hall to share the happy news with the other gentlemen and pass around a bottle of whisky in celebration. In the harbor of Castle Bay, cannon boomed in a salute to the newest MacNeil.

LADY EMMA KNOCKED softly on the bedchamber door, and Raine's mother opened it at once. With an angelic smile, Lady Nina reached up to kiss Keir on the cheek. "Come in, my dear," she said, her blue eyes shining. "Someone's waiting to meet you."

The large bed was surrounded by a bevy of females. Aunt Isabel, Francine, Joanna, Maude, and Signora Grazioli quickly moved away to let Keir approach his wife and child. Carrying soiled linens and basins of water, the women hurried out the door and closed it softly behind them, leaving the new family alone.

Propped up on pillows and dressed in a fresh white nightgown, Raine smiled at Keir. Her ebony eyes sparkled with happiness as she motioned for her worried husband to approach the bed. "Come see your new daughter," she whispered.

His heart lodged in his throat, Keir slowly walked to the bed and looked down at the tiny bundle cradled in the crook of Raine's arm.

"Don't be afraid, dearest," Raine said. "Take her in your arms."

Keir lifted the baby girl wrapped in swaddling clothes, trying to see the wee face through his tears. "She's beautiful," he croaked, though all he could discern was a tiny red blur. A wave of immeasurable love washed over him.

He placed the fragile, helpless newborn carefully back in her mother's arms and sank to his knees beside the bed. He took his wife's hand and lovingly kissed her fingers. "Thank God, thank God," he murmured.

"Keir," Raine asked softly, "what shall we name her?"

"Titania," he answered at once. "Since my daughter might be part faery, I think she should have the name of a faery queen."

His wife's eyes widened in surprise, for they'd discussed naming a girl after his mother. Then Raine smiled and beamed with pleasure.

"Titania Emma MacNeil it will be."

About the Author

KATHLEEN HARRINGTON, winner of the Colorado Romance Writers' Award of Excellence, has touched the hearts of readers across the country with her sparkling tales of high adventure and unending love. Her historical romances have been finalists for Romance Writers of America's RITA® Award, the *Romantic Times* Reviewers' Choice, Virginia Romance Writers' HOLT Medallion, and the Phoenix Desert Rose Golden Quill. Her fabulous heroes have garnered the K.I.S.S. (Knight in Shining Silver) Award. She lives in Southern California.

www.kathleenharringtonbooks.com

Discover great authors, exclusive offers, and more at HC.com.